D0505218

www.hants.gov.uk/library

Hampshire
County Council

Love
YOUR LIBRARY

Tel: 0300 555 1387

Behind her, Charles stepped closer, but he didn't touch her as the cool flesh under her fingertips warmed. They all stood frozen in place. Anna knew that all she had to do to end this was to remove her hand, but she was strangely reluctant to do so.

The shock on Asil's face faded, and skin around his eyes and mouth softened into sorrow that grew and deepened before tucking itself away, where all private thoughts hid from too-keen observers. He reached out and touched her face lightly, ignoring Charles's warning growl.

WITHDRAWN

C016795270

## By Patricia Briggs

# Cry Wolf

## Patricia Briggs

www.orbitbooks.net

ORBIT

First published in the United States in 2008 by Ace,
an imprint of Penguin Group (USA) Inc.
First published in Great Britain in 2009 by Orbit
Reprinted 2009, 2011, 2012, 2014

Copyright © 2008 by Hurog, Inc.

The moral right of the author has been asserted.

*All characters and events in this publication, other than those
clearly in the public domain, are fictitious and any resemblance
to real persons, living or dead, is purely coincidental.*

All rights reserved.
No part of this publication may be reproduced, stored in a
retrieval system, or transmitted, in any form or by any means, without
the prior permission in writing of the publisher, nor be otherwise circulated
in any form of binding or cover other than that in which it is published
and without a similar condition including this condition being
imposed on the subsequent purchaser.

A CIP catalogue record for this book
is available from the British Library.

ISBN 978-1-84149-794-5

Typeset in Garamond by Palimpsest Book Production Limited,
Grangemouth, Stirlingshire
Printed and bound in Great Britain by
Clays Ltd, St Ives plc

Papers used by Orbit are from well-managed forests
and other responsible sources.

MIX
Paper from
responsible sources
FSC www.fsc.org FSC® C104740

Orbit
An imprint of
Little, Brown Book Group
100 Victoria Embankment
London EC4Y 0DY

An Hachette UK Company
www.hachette.co.uk

www.orbitbooks.net

*Amanda, fashionista, musician and hairstyle artist.*
*This one's for you.*

# ACKNOWLEDGMENTS

The usual bunch for editorial service above and beyond the call of duty: Michael Briggs, Katharine and Dave Carson, Michael Enzweiler, Anne Peters, and Kaye and Kyle Roberson. My patient and terrific editor, Anne Sowards. And my research sources: my good friend CthulhuBob Lovely (this time I hope I spelled it right); Shelley Rubenacker and her Latin Forum buddies; Bill Fansler, forest recreation staff officer, Kootenai National Forest – and especially my husband, Mike, who has aided and abetted my research attempts for years (he, unlike me, is not shy on the phone). As usual, if it's good, it's their fault – all mistakes are mine.

# PROLOGUE

Northwestern Montana, Cabinet Wilderness: October

No one knew better than Walter Rice that the only safe place was away from other people. Safe for them, that is. The only problem was that he still *needed* them, needed the sound of human voices and laughter. To his shame, he sometimes hovered on the edge of one of the campgrounds just to listen to the voices and pretend they were talking to him.

Which was a very small part of the reason that he was lying belly-down in the kinnikinnick and old tamarack needles in the shadow of a stand of trees, watching the young man who was writing with a pencil in a metal-bound notebook after taking a sample of the bear scat and storing the resultant partially filled plastic bag in his backpack.

Walter had no fear the boy would see him: Uncle Sam had ensured that Walter could hide and track, and decades of living alone in some of the most forbidding wilderness in the States had made him into a fair imitation of those miraculously invisible Indians who had populated the favorite books and movies of his childhood. If he didn't want to be seen, he wasn't – besides, the boy had all the woodcraft of a suburban housewife. They shouldn't have sent him into grizzly country on his own – feeding grad students to the bears wasn't a good idea, might give them ideas.

Not that the bears were out today. Like Walter, they knew how to read the signs: sometime in the next four or five hours there was a big storm coming. He could feel it in his bones, and the stranger didn't have a big enough pack to be prepared for it. It was early for a winter storm, but this country was like that. He'd seen it snow in August.

That storm was the other reason he was following the boy. The storm and what to do about it – it wasn't often anymore that he was so torn by indecision.

He could let the kid go. The storm would come and steal away his life, but that was the way of the mountain, of the wilderness. It was a clean death. If only the grad student weren't so young. A lifetime ago he'd seen so many boys die – you'd think he'd have gotten used to it. Instead, one more seemed like one too many.

He could warn the boy. But everything in him rebelled at the thought. It had been too long since he'd spoken face-to-face with anyone . . . even the thought made his breath freeze up.

It was too dangerous. Might cause another flashback – he hadn't had one in a while – but they crept up unexpectedly. It would be too bad if he tried to warn the boy and ended up killing him instead.

No. He couldn't risk the little peace he had by warning the stranger – but he couldn't just let him die, either.

Frustrated, he'd been following for a few hours as the boy blundered, oblivious, farther and farther from the nearest road and safety. The bedroll on his backpack made it clear he was planning on staying the night – which ought to mean he thought he knew what he was doing in the woods. Unfortunately, it had become clearer and clearer it was a false confidence. It was like watching June Cleaver roughing it. Sad. Just sad.

Like watching the newbies coming into 'Nam all starched and ready to be men, when everyone knew that all they were was cannon fodder.

Damn boy was stirring up all sorts of things Walter liked to keep away. But the irritation wasn't strong enough to make a difference to Walter's conscience. Six miles, as near as he figured it, he'd trailed the boy, unable to make up his mind: his preoccupation kept him from sensing the danger until the boy student stopped dead in the middle of the trail.

The thick brush between them only allowed him to see the top of the boy's backpack, and whatever stopped the boy was shorter. The good part was that it wasn't a moose. You could reason with a black bear – even a grizzly if it wasn't hungry (which in his experience was seldom the case), but a moose was . . .

Walter drew his big knife, though he wasn't sure he'd try to help the boy. Even a black bear was a quicker death than the storm would be – if bloodier. And he knew the bear around here, which was more than he could say about the boy. He moved slowly through the brush, making no noise though fallen aspen leaves littered the ground. When he didn't want to make noise, he didn't make noise.

A low growl caused a shiver of fear to slice through him, sending his adrenaline into the ozone layer. It wasn't a sound he'd ever heard here, and he knew every predator that lived in his territory.

Four feet farther and he had nothing impairing his view.

There in the middle of the path stood a dog – or something doglike, anyway. At first he thought it was a German shepherd because of the coloring, but there was something wrong with the joints of its front end that made it look more like a bear than a dog. And it was bigger than any damned dog or wolf he'd ever seen. It had cold eyes, killer's eyes, and impossibly long teeth.

Walter might not know what to call it, but he knew what it was. In that beast's face lurked every nightmare image that haunted his life. It was the thing he fought through two tours of 'Nam and every night since: death. This was a battle for a blooded warrior, battered and tainted as he was, not an innocent.

He broke cover with a wild whoop designed to attract attention and sprinted, ignoring the protest of knees grown too old for battle. It had been a long time since his last fight, but he had never forgotten the feeling of the blood pounding through his veins.

'Run, kid,' he said as he blazed past the boy with a fierce grin, prepared to engage the enemy.

The animal might run. It had taken its time sizing up the boy, and sometimes, when a predator's meal charges it, the predator will leave. But somehow he didn't think that this beast was such an animal – there was an eerie intelligence in its blindingly gold eyes.

Whatever had kept it from attacking the boy immediately, it had no qualms about Walter. It launched itself at him as if he were unarmed. Maybe it wasn't as smart as he thought – or it had been deceived by his grizzled exterior and hadn't realized what an old veteran armed with a knife as long as his arm could do. Maybe it was aroused by the boy's flight – he'd taken Walter's advice at face value and was running like a track star – and just viewed Walter as an obstacle to its desire for fresh, tender meat.

But Walter wasn't a helpless boy. He'd gotten the knife from some enemy general he'd killed, murdered in the dark as he'd been taught. The knife was covered with magic charms etched into the blade, strange symbols that had long ago turned black instead of the bright silver they'd been. Despite the exotic fancy stuff, it was a good knife and it bit deep in the animal's shoulder.

The beast was faster than he, faster and stronger. But he'd gotten that first strike and crippled it, and that made all the difference.

He didn't win, but he triumphed. He kept the beast busy

and hurt it badly. It wouldn't be able to go after the kid tonight – and if that boy was smart, he'd be halfway to his car by now.

At last the monster left, dragging a front leg and bleeding from a dozen wounds – though there was no question as to who was worse wounded. He'd seen a lot of men die, and he knew from the smell of perforated bowel that his time had come.

But the young man was safe. Perhaps that would answer, in some small part, for all the young men who hadn't lived.

He let the muscles of his back relax and felt the dried grass and dirt give way beneath his weight. The ground was cool under his hot, sweaty body, and it comforted him. It seemed right to end his life here while saving a stranger, when another stranger's death had brought him here in the first place.

The wind picked up, and he thought the temperature dropped a few degrees – but that might just have been blood loss and shock. He closed his eyes and waited patiently for death, his old enemy, to claim him at long last. The knife was still in his right hand, just in case the pain was too much. Belly wounds weren't the easiest way to die.

But it wasn't death that came during the heart of the first blizzard of the season.

# 1

Chicago: November

Anna Latham tried to disappear into the passenger seat.

She hadn't realized how much of her confidence had been tied to having Charles beside her. She'd only known him a day and a half, and he'd changed her world . . . at least while he was still next to her.

Without him, all of her newly regained confidence had disappeared. Its mocking absence only pointed out what a coward she really was. As if she needed reminding.

She glanced over at the man who was driving Charles's rented SUV with casual ease through the light after-morning-rush-hour traffic on the slush-covered expressway as if he were a Chicago native instead of a visitor from the wilds of Montana.

Charles's father, Bran Cornick, looked for all the world like a college student, a computer geek or maybe an art major. Someone sensitive, gentle, and young – but she knew he was none of these things. He was the Marrok, the one all the Alphas answered to – and no one dominated an Alpha werewolf by being sensitive and gentle.

He wasn't young, either. She knew Charles was almost two hundred years old, and that would necessitate his father being older yet.

She looked hard, out of the corners of her eyes, but except for something in the shape of his hands and eyes, she couldn't see Charles in him at all. Charles looked pure Native American, as his mother had been, but still she thought she should have been able to see a little resemblance, something that would tell her that the Marrok was the kind of man his son was.

Her head was willing to believe Bran Cornick would not harm her, that he was different from the other wolves she knew. But her body had been taught to fear the males of her species. The more dominant the werewolves were, the more likely they were to hurt her. And there was no more dominant wolf anywhere than Bran Cornick, no matter how harmless he might seem.

'I won't let anything happen to you,' he said without looking at her.

She could smell her own fear – so of course he could smell it, too.

'I know,' she managed to say, hating herself for allowing them to turn her into a coward. She hoped that he thought it was fear at the idea of facing the other wolves from her pack after she'd precipitated their Alpha's death. She didn't want him to know she was scared of him, too. Or even mostly.

He smiled a little, but didn't say anything more.

All the parking places behind her four-story apartment building were filled with strange cars. There was a shiny gray truck towing a small, bright orange and white trailer with a giant manatee painted on the side just above lettering that let anyone within a block know that Florida was 'The Manatee State.'

Bran parked behind the trailer without worrying about blocking the alley. Well, she realized as they got out of the car, she wouldn't have to worry about what her landlord thought anymore. She was going to Montana. Was Montana 'The Werewolf State'?

Four wolves in their human forms waited for them at the security door, including Boyd, the new Alpha. His shadowed eyes took in every bit of her. She dropped her gaze to the ground after that first glance and kept Bran between her and them.

She was more afraid of them than the Marrok after all. How strange, because today there was none of the speculation, the avarice in their eyes that usually set off her fears. They looked controlled . . . and tired. Yesterday, the Alpha had been killed, and that hurt all of them. She'd felt it herself – and ignored it because she thought Charles was dying.

Their pain was her fault. They all knew that.

She reminded herself that Leo needed killing – he had killed so many himself and allowed the deaths of many others. She wouldn't look at any of them again. She'd try not to talk to them, and hope they'd ignore her.

Except – they'd come here to help her move. She'd tried to stop that, but she wasn't up to arguing with the Marrok for long. She dared another quick glance at Boyd, but she couldn't read his face any better this time.

She took her key and went to work on the lock with fear-clumsy fingers. None of the werewolves made any move that indicated they were impatient, but she tried to hurry, feeling their eyes on her back. What were they thinking? Were they remembering what some of them had done to her? She wasn't. She *wasn't*.

*Breathe*, she chided herself.

One of the men swayed on his feet and made an eager sound.

'George,' said Boyd, and the other wolf quieted.

It was her fear that was pushing the wolf, she knew. She had to get a handle on herself – and the sticky lock wasn't helping. If Charles were here, she could deal with everything, but he was recovering from several bullet wounds. His father had told her that he had a stronger reaction than most to silver.

'I didn't expect you to come,' said Bran – she presumed he wasn't talking to her since he'd manipulated and talked her into leaving Charles alone this morning.

It must have been Boyd he was talking to, because it was Boyd who answered him. 'I had the day off.'

Until last night Boyd had been third. But now he was the Alpha of the Western Suburb Chicago Pack. The pack she was leaving. 'I thought it might hurry matters a bit,' Boyd continued. 'Thomas here has agreed to drive the truck to Montana and back.'

She pulled open the door, but Bran didn't go in immediately so she stopped in the entryway just inside the door, holding it open.

'How stand your pack finances?' Bran asked. 'My son tells me that Leo claimed he needed money.'

She heard Boyd's typical humorless smile in his voice. 'He wasn't lying. His mate was expensive as all hell to keep. We won't lose the manor, but that's the only good news our accountant has for me. We'll get something from selling Isabella's jewelry, but not as much as Leo paid for it.'

She could look at Bran, and so she watched his eyes assess the wolves Boyd had brought like a general surveying his troops. His gaze settled on Thomas.

Anna looked, too, seeing what the Marrok saw: old jeans with a hole in one knee, tennis shoes that had seen better days. It was very much like what she was wearing, except that her hole was in her left knee, not the right.

'Will the time it takes to drive to Montana and back put your job at risk?' Bran asked.

Thomas kept his eyes on his toes and answered, soft-voiced, 'No, sir. I work construction, and this is the slow season. I okayed it with the boss; he says I have two weeks.'

Bran pulled a checkbook out of his pocket and, using one of the other wolves' shoulders to give him a solid surface to write on, made out a check. 'This is for your expenses on this trip. We'll figure out a pay rate and have money waiting for you when you get to Montana.'

Relief flashed in Thomas's eyes, but he didn't say anything.

Bran went through the door, passed by Anna, and started up the stairs. As soon as he wasn't watching them, the other wolves lifted their eyes to look at Anna.

She jutted her chin up and met their gazes, forgetting entirely her decision not to do just that until it was too late. Boyd's eyes were unfathomable, and Thomas was still looking at the ground . . . but the other two, George and Joshua, were easy to read. With Bran's back to them, the knowledge of what she'd been in their pack was fully visible in their eyes.

And they had been Leo's wolves by inclination as well as fact. She was nothing, and she had brought about their Alpha's death: they'd have killed her if they dared.

Just try, she told them without using words. She turned her back on them without dropping her eyes – as Charles's mate, she supposedly outranked all of them. But they weren't only wolves, and the human part of them would never forget what they had done to her, with Leo's encouragement.

Her stomach raw, and tension tightening the back of her neck, Anna tried to keep an even pace all the way up to her apartment on the fourth floor. Bran waited beside her while she unlocked the door. She stepped aside so he could go in first, showing the others that he, at least, had her respect.

He stopped in the doorway and looked around her studio

apartment with a frown. She knew what he saw: a card table with two battered folding chairs, her futon, and not much else.

'I told you I could get it packed this morning,' Anna told him. She knew it wasn't much, but she resented his silent judgment. 'Then they could have come just to carry out the boxes.'

'It won't take an hour to pack this and carry it down,' said Bran. 'Boyd, how many of your wolves are living like this?'

Summoned, Boyd slid past Anna and into the room and frowned. He'd never been to her apartment. He glanced at Anna and walked to her refrigerator and opened it, exposing the empty space inside. 'I didn't know it was this bad.' He glanced back. 'Thomas?'

Invited in, Thomas, too, stepped through the door.

He gave his new Alpha an apologetic smile. 'I'm not quite this bad, but my wife is working, too. The dues are pretty dear.' He was almost as far down the pack structure as Anna, and, married, had never been invited to 'play' with her. But he hadn't objected, either. She supposed that it was more than could be expected of a submissive wolf, but that didn't keep her from holding it against him.

'Probably five or six then,' Boyd said with a sigh. 'I'll see what can be done.'

Bran opened his wallet and handed the Alpha a card. 'Call Charles next week and set up a conference between him and your accountant. If necessary, we can arrange for a loan. It's not safe to have hungry, desperate werewolves on the streets.'

Boyd nodded.

The Marrok's business apparently concluded, the other

two wolves surged past Anna, George deliberately bumping against her. She pulled back from him and instinctively wrapped her arms protectively around herself. He gave her a sneer he hid quickly from the others.

'*Illegitimis nil carborundum*,' she murmured. It was stupid. She knew it even before George's fist struck out.

She ducked and dodged. Instead of a fist in her stomach, she took it in the shoulder and rolled with it. The small entryway didn't give her much room to get away from a second blow.

There wasn't one.

Boyd had George pinned on the ground with a knee in the middle of his back. George wasn't fighting him, just talking fast. 'She's not supposed to do that. Leo said no Latin. You remember.'

Because once Anna realized that no one else in the pack except Isabella, who she had thought was a friend, understood Latin, she'd used it for secret defiance. It had taken a while for Leo to figure it out.

'Leo is dead,' said Boyd very quietly, his mouth near George's ear. 'New rules. If you are smart enough to live, you won't hit Charles's mate in front of his father.'

'Don't let the bastards grind you down?' said Bran from her doorway. He was looking at her like a child who had been unexpectedly clever. 'That's horrible Latin, and your pronunciation needs some work.'

'It's my father's fault,' she told him, rubbing her shoulder. The bruise would be gone by tomorrow, but for now it hurt. 'He had a couple of years of Latin in college and used it to amuse himself. Everyone in my family picked it up. His favorite saying was, "*Interdum feror cupidine partium magnarum europe vincendarum.*"'

'"Sometimes I have the urge to conquer large parts of Europe"?' Boyd said, sounding a little incredulous. Isabella hadn't, apparently, been the only one who understood her defiance.

She nodded. 'Usually he only said it when my brother or I were being particularly horrible.'

'And it was his *favorite* saying?' Bran said, examining her as if she were a bug . . . but a bug he was growing pleased with.

She said, 'My brother was a brat.'

He smiled slowly and she recognized the smile as one of Charles's.

'What do you want me to do with this one?' asked Boyd, tilting his head toward George.

Bran's smile fled, and he looked at Anna. 'Do you want me to kill him?'

Silence descended as everyone waited for her answer. For the first time she realized that the fear that she'd been smelling wasn't hers alone. The Marrok scared them all.

'No,' she lied. She just wanted to get her apartment packed and get done with this, so she never had to see George and those like him again. 'No.' This time she meant it.

Bran tilted his head, and she saw his eyes shift, just a little, gleaming gold in the dimness of the outer hall. 'Let him up.'

She waited until everyone was in her apartment to leave the anonymity of the landing. Bran was stripping her futon down to the bare mattress when she entered her apartment. It was sort of like watching the president mowing the White House lawn or taking out the trash.

Boyd approached her and handed her the check she'd left on the fridge door, her last paycheck. 'You'll want this with you.'

She took it and stuffed it in her pants. 'Thanks.'

'We all owe you,' he told her. 'None of us could contact

the Marrok when things started getting bad. Leo forbade it. I can't tell you how many hours I spent staring at the phone trying to break his hold.'

She was startled into meeting his eyes.

'It took me a while to figure out what you were.' He gave her a bitter smile. 'I wasn't paying attention. I tried really hard not to pay attention or think. It made things easier.'

'Omegas are rare,' said Bran.

Boyd didn't look away from her. 'I almost missed what Leo was doing, why he chose you for such treatment when he had always been the "kill 'em quickly" kind. I've known him a long time, and he's never condoned abuse like that before. I could see that it sickened him – only Justin really enjoyed it.'

Anna controlled her flinch and reminded herself that Justin had died last night, too.

'When I realized why Leo couldn't rely on you following his orders, that you weren't just a very submissive wolf, that you were an Omega . . . it was almost too late.' He sighed. 'If I'd given you the Marrok's number two years ago, it wouldn't have taken you so long to call him. So I owe you both my thanks and my humblest apologies.' And he dropped his eyes, tilting his head to show her his throat.

'Will you . . .' She swallowed to moisten her suddenly dry throat. 'Will you make sure it doesn't happen again? Not to anyone? I'm not the only one who was hurt.' She didn't look at Thomas. Justin had taken great delight in tormenting Thomas.

Boyd bowed his head solemnly. 'I promise.'

She gave him a short nod, which seemed to satisfy him. He took an empty box out of Joshua's hands and strode to the kitchen. They'd brought boxes and tape and wrapping material, more than enough to pack everything she owned.

She didn't have any luggage, so she took one of the boxes and put together the basics to take with her. She was very careful to keep her eyes to herself. Too much had changed, and she didn't know how else to deal with it.

She was in the bathroom when someone's cell phone rang. Werewolf hearing meant she got both sides of the telephone conversation.

'*Boyd?*' It was one of the new wolves, Rashid the doctor, she thought. He sounded panicked.

'You've got me. What's wrong?'

'*That wolf in the holding room, he's—*'

Boyd and his cell phone were in the kitchen, and she still heard the crash through the speaker.

'*That's him,*' Rashid whispered desperately. '*That's him. He's trying to get out – and he's tearing the whole safe room apart. I don't think it'll hold him.*'

Charles.

He'd been groggy when she left, but had seemed happy enough to leave her in his father's hands while he slept off the effects of having a few silver bullets dug out of him last night. Apparently things had changed.

Anna grabbed her box and met Bran in the doorway of the bathroom.

He gave her a searching glance, but didn't seem upset. 'It seems that we are needed elsewhere,' he said, sounding calm and relaxed. 'I don't think he'll hurt anyone – but silver has a stronger and more unpredictable effect on him than on some wolves. Do you have what you need?'

'Yes.'

Bran looked around, then his eyes fell on Boyd. 'Tell your wolf we'll be there as soon as possible. I trust you to make certain that everything is packed and the apartment is clean when you leave.'

Boyd bowed his head submissively.

Bran took her box and tucked it under one arm and then held his other out in an old-fashioned gesture. She put her fingers lightly on the crook of his arm, and he escorted her all the way back to the SUV that way, slowing her down when she would have run.

He drove back to the Naperville mansion that the Western Suburb pack kept for its own without breaking any traffic laws, but he didn't waste any time, either.

'Most wolves wouldn't be able to break out of a holding room,' he said mildly. 'There's silver in the bars, and there are a lot of bars, but Charles is his mother's son, too. She'd never have allowed herself to be held by anything as mundane as a few bars and a reinforced door.'

Somehow, it didn't surprise Anna that Bran would know how the pack's safe room was built.

'Charles's mother was a witch?' Anna had never met a witch, but she'd heard stories. And since becoming a werewolf, she'd learned to believe in magic.

He shook his head. 'Nothing so well defined. I'm not even sure she worked magic – strictly speaking. The Salish didn't see the world that way: magic and not magic. Natural and unnatural. Whatever she was, though, her son is, too.'

'What will happen if he breaks out?'

'It would be good if we get there before that happens,' was all he said.

They left the expressway, and he slowed to the posted speed limit. The only sign of his impatience was the rhythmic beat of his fingers on the steering wheel. When he pulled up in front of the mansion, she jumped out of the SUV and ran to the front door. He didn't appear to hurry, but somehow he was there before her and opened the door.

She ran down the hall and took the cellar stairs three at a time, Bran at her shoulder. The lack of noise was not reassuring.

Usually the only way to tell the safe room from the basement guest rooms was the steel door and frame. But great plaster chunks had been torn off the wall on either side, revealing the silver-and-steel bars that had been embedded in the wall. The wallpaper from inside the room hung down in strips like a curtain, keeping Anna from seeing inside.

There were three of the pack in human form standing in front of the door, and she could feel their fear. They knew what they had in that room – at least one of them had watched as he killed Leo, even though Charles had been shot twice with silver bullets.

'Charles,' said Bran in a chiding tone.

The wolf roared in response, a hoarse howling sound that hurt Anna's ears and contained nothing but blind rage.

'The screws were coming out of the hinges, sir. On their own,' said one of the wolves nervously, and Anna realized the thing he was holding in his hands was a screwdriver.

'Yes,' Bran said calmly. 'I imagine they were. My son doesn't react at all well to silver and even less well to captivity. You might have been safer letting him out – or not. My apologies for leaving you here alone to face him. I thought he was in better shape. It seems I underestimated Anna's influence.'

He turned and held out his hand to Anna, who had stopped at the base of the stairs. She wasn't bothered nearly as much by the raging wolf as she was by the men who stood in the basement. The walls of the hallway were too narrow, and she didn't like having so many of them close to her.

'Come here, Anna,' said Bran. Though his voice was soft, it was a command.

She brushed past the other wolves, looking at feet rather than faces. When Bran took her elbow, Charles growled savagely – though how he had seen it through the hanging wallpaper was beyond Anna.

Bran smiled and removed his hand. 'Fine. But you're scaring her.'

Instantly, the growls softened.

'Talk to him a little,' Bran told her. 'I'll take the others upstairs for a bit. When you're comfortable, go ahead and open the door – but it might be a good idea to wait until he quits growling.'

And they left her alone. She must have been crazy because she immediately felt safer than she had all day. The relief of being without fear was almost heady. The wallpaper fluttered as Charles paced behind the barrier, and she caught a glimpse of his red fur.

'What happened to you?' she asked him. 'You were fine when we left this morning.'

In wolf form, he couldn't reply, but he did stop growling.

'I'm sorry,' she ventured. 'But they're packing up my apartment, and I had to be there. And I needed to get clothes to wear until the trailer makes it to Montana.'

He hit the door. Not hard enough to do damage, but in clear demand.

She hesitated, but he'd quit growling. With a mental shrug she threw the bolt and opened the door. He was bigger than she remembered – or maybe it was just that he looked that way when his fangs were so prominently displayed. Blood oozed out of the hole in his left hind leg and trickled down to his paw. The two holes in his ribs were trickling a little faster.

Behind him, the room, which had been pretty nicely furnished when she left, was in shambles. He'd pulled large chunks of plaster off all four of the walls as well as the ceiling. Shreds of the mattress carpeted the room, intermingled with pieces of the chest of drawers.

She whistled at the damage. 'Holy cow.'

He limped up to her and sniffed her carefully all over. A stair creaked, and he whirled with a growl, putting himself between her and the intruder.

Bran sat on the top stair. 'I'm not going to hurt her,' he commented. Then he looked at Anna. 'I don't know how much he's actually understanding right now. But I think he'll do better in his own home. I called our pilot, and he's ready to fly out.'

'I thought we'd have a couple of days yet.' She felt her stomach clinch. Chicago was her *home*. 'I have to call Scorci's and tell Mick I'm leaving, so he can find another waitress. And I haven't had a chance to talk to my neighbor and tell her what's going on.' Kara would worry.

'I have to get back to Montana today,' Bran said. 'Tomorrow morning we're holding a funeral for a friend of mine who just died. I was going to leave you here to follow me later, but I don't think it's a good idea now.' Bran nodded at Charles. 'He's obviously not healing as well as I thought. I need to get him home and have him checked out. I have a cell phone. Can you call your neighbor and your Mick and explain things to them?'

She looked down at the wolf who'd put himself between her and his father to keep her from harm. It wasn't the first time he'd done something like that.

Besides, what was her alternative? Stay in the Chicago pack? Boyd might be a vast improvement over Leo, but . . . she had no desire to stay with them.

She put her hand on Charles's back and feathered her hand through his fur. She didn't have to reach down to do it, either – Charles was a big werewolf. He altered his stance until he pressed against her though he never took his eyes off of Bran.

'Okay,' she said. 'Give me your phone.'

Bran smiled and held it out. Charles didn't move from between them, forcing Anna to stretch out and grab it while Charles stared coldly at his father. His attitude made her laugh – which made it much easier to convince Kara that Anna was going to Montana because she wanted to.

2

After the disaster this morning, Anna had dreaded the flight to Montana. She'd never been on a plane before in her life, and she'd have thought that it would be terrifying, especially in the little, six-passenger, twin-engine Lear Bran led them to.

Bran sat in the copilot's seat, which left all six of the passenger seats empty. Charles pushed her past the first set of forward-facing seats with a nudge of his nose and stared at the pair of backward seats until she sat down. When he settled in the space on the floor and put his head on her feet, she set her box on the seat next to her, buckled up, and waited for takeoff.

She didn't expect to have fun, especially when Charles so emphatically was not. He rode stiff and grumpy at her feet, growling softly when the plane bounced a little.

But riding in the small plane was like being on the world's tallest amusement-park ride. A gentle one, like the Ferris wheel, but with an edge of danger that just made it all the more fun. She didn't really think they'd plummet out of the sky any more than she believed that a carnival Ferris wheel might break free and go rolling down the arcade. And no Ferris wheel in the world had a view like this.

Not even swooping in to land on an itty-bitty strip that looked smaller than a Wal-Mart parking lot spoiled her mood. She buckled in and braced herself with a hand on her box so it wouldn't fall on Charles as the plane dropped, and her stomach tried to stay where it had been. She found herself grinning as they hit the tarmac and bumped twice before the wheels stayed on the ground.

The pilot taxied into a hangar big enough to hold two planes that size, but the other half of the building was empty. Anna gathered her box and followed Charles out of the plane. He was limping badly – staying still for so long clearly hadn't done him any good. He was still keeping himself between her and his father.

Once on the ground, she started shivering. Her jacket was a little thin for Chicago, but here it was barely adequate. The hangar wasn't heated, and it was cold enough to see her breath.

She hadn't realized how close Charles was, and when she turned to look at the plane, her knee hit his bandaged side. He didn't show any sign it bothered him, but it had to have hurt. It was his own fault, though. If he hadn't been crowding her, she wouldn't have bumped him.

'Ease up,' she told him, exasperated. 'Your father is hardly going to attack me.'

'I don't think he's worried about my *hurting* you,' Bran said, amused. 'Let's get you somewhere away from all the other males so he can relax a little.'

The pilot, who'd followed them out and had been engaged in some sort of maintenance, grinned at that. 'Never thought I'd see that old Indian so worked up.'

Charles gave him a look, and the pilot dropped his eyes, but not the grin. 'Hey, don't glare at me – and here I got you home, safe and sound. Nearly as well as you could have done it, eh, Charles?'

'Thank you, Hank.' Bran turned to Anna. 'Hank has to button down the plane, so we'll go warm up the truck.' He put his hand under her elbow as they stepped out of the protection of the hangar into ten inches of snow. Charles growled; Bran growled back in exasperation. 'Enough. *Enough.* I have no designs on your lady, and the ground is rough.'

Charles stopped making noise, but he walked so close to

Anna that she found herself bumping into Bran because she didn't want to hurt Charles. Bran steadied her and frowned at the werewolf beside her but didn't say anything more.

Other than the hangar, airstrip, and two ruts in the deep snow where someone had recently driven a car, there was virtually no sign of civilization. The mountains were impressive, taller, darker, and rougher than the soft Midwest hills she knew. She could smell woodsmoke though, so they couldn't be as isolated as it looked.

'I thought it would be quieter here.' She hadn't meant to say anything, but the noise startled her.

'The wind in the trees,' Bran said. 'And there are some birds that stay year-round. Sometimes when the wind is still and the cold is upon us, the quiet is so deep you can feel it in your bones.' It sounded creepy to her, but she could tell from his voice that he loved it.

Bran walked them around behind the hangar, where a snow-covered gray crew-cab truck waited for them. He reached into the truck bed, pulled out a broom, and banged it good and hard on the ground to dislodge snow.

'Go ahead and get in,' he said. 'Why don't you start the truck so it can warm up. The keys are in the ignition.' He brushed snow off the passenger door and held it open for her.

She put her box on the floor of the cab, and climbed in. The box made sliding across the leather seat to the driver's seat a little awkward. Charles hopped in after her and snagged the door with a paw so it shut. His fur was wet, but after her initial flinch, she found that he generated a lot of body heat. The truck purred to life, blowing cold air all over the cab. As soon as she was sure it would keep running, she slid to the middle seat.

When the truck was mostly cleared of snow, Bran tossed the broom back into the truck bed and hopped into the driver's seat. 'Hank shouldn't be much longer.' He took in her shivering form and frowned at her. 'We'll get you a warmer coat and some boots appropriate to the winter here. Chicago isn't exactly tropical – you should have better winter gear than that.'

While he was talking, Charles stepped over her, forcing her to move to the outside passenger seat. He settled between them, but in order to fit, half of him draped over her lap.

'Had to pay the electric, gas, water, and rent,' she said lightly. 'Oof, Charles, you weigh a ton. We waitresses don't earn enough for luxuries.'

The back door opened, and Hank climbed in and put on his seat belt before blowing on his hands. 'That old wind has quite a bite to it.'

'Time to get home,' Bran agreed, putting the truck into drive and starting out, though if he followed a road, it was buried under the snow. 'I'll drop off Charles and his mate first.'

'Mate?' She had her face forward, but it was impossible to miss the surprise in Hank's voice. 'No wonder the old man is so worked up. Man alive, Charles, that was some fast work. And she's pretty, too.'

And she didn't appreciate being spoken of as if she weren't there, either. Even if she was too intimidated to say so.

Charles turned his head toward Hank and lifted a lip to show some very sharp teeth.

The pilot laughed. 'All right, all right. But nice work, man.'

It was only then that her nose told her something she hadn't realized on the plane: Hank wasn't a werewolf. And he clearly knew that Charles was.

'I thought we weren't supposed to tell anyone,' she said.

'Tell them what?' Bran asked.

She glanced back at Hank. 'Tell them what we are.'

'Oh, this is Aspen Creek,' Hank answered her. 'Everyone knows about werewolves. If you haven't married one, you were fathered by one – or one of your parents was. This is the Marrok's territory, and we're one big, happy family.' Was there sarcasm in his voice? She didn't know him well enough to tell for certain.

The air blowing in her face had warmed up, finally. Between that and Charles, she was starting to feel less like an ice cube.

'I thought that werewolves have no family, only pack,' she ventured.

Bran glanced at her before looking back to the road. 'You and Charles need to have a long talk. How long have you been a werewolf?'

'Three years.'

He frowned. 'Do you have a family?'

'My father and brother. I haven't seen them since . . .' She shrugged. 'Leo told me I had to break all ties to them – or else he'd assume they were a risk to the pack.' *And kill them.*

Bran frowned. 'Outside of Aspen Creek, wolves can't tell anyone except their spouses what they are – we allow that for their spouses' safety. But you don't need to isolate yourself from your family.' Almost to himself, he said, 'I suppose Leo was afraid your family might interfere with what he was trying to do to you.'

She could call her family? She almost asked Bran about it, but decided to wait and talk to Charles instead.

Like the plane ride, Charles's house was different than she'd expected. Somehow, since it was in the backwoods of Montana, she'd thought he'd live in one of those big log houses, or something old, like the pack's mansion. But the house where Bran dropped them off was not huge or made of logs. Instead, it looked like a simple ranch-style house, painted a rather pleasing combination of gray and green. It was tucked up against the side of a hill and looked out over a series of fenced pastures occupied by a few horses.

She waved a thank-you at Bran as he drove off. Then she carried her box, which was looking a little bedraggled since it had gotten wet on the floor of the truck, up the steps, with Charles skulking at her heel. There was a light covering of snow over the steps, though it was obvious that usually it was kept shoveled off.

She had a bad moment when she realized that she'd forgotten to ask Bran to unlock the door – but the knob turned easily under her hand. She supposed that if everyone in Aspen Creek knew about werewolves, they'd know better than to steal something from one. Still, to her citybred self, it seemed odd for Charles to leave his house unlocked while he traveled halfway across the country.

She opened the door – and all thoughts of locks fled. The exterior of the house might be mundane, but the interior was anything but.

Like her apartment floor, the living-room floor was hardwood, but his had a parquet pattern of dark and light wood that edged the room in a pattern that struck her as Native American. Thick, soft-looking Persian rugs covered the central part of the living room and dining room. Against the far wall was a huge granite fireplace, both beautiful and well used.

Comfortable-looking couches and chairs were intermixed with handcrafted bird's-eye maple tables and bookcases. The oil painting of a waterfall surrounded by a pine forest could have hung in a museum and, she calculated, probably cost more than she'd earned in her entire life.

From the doorway she could see straight into the kitchen, where subtly glittering light gray granite countertops contrasted with dark Shaker-style oak cabinets that were just irregular enough to be handmade, like the furniture in the living room. Stainless-steel appliances trimmed in black should have looked too modern, but somehow it all blended together. It wasn't a huge kitchen, but there was nothing in it that would have looked out of place in a mansion.

She stood dripping melted snow on the highly polished floor and knew without a doubt that she and her box didn't belong here. If she'd had anyplace to go, she'd have turned around and left, but all that awaited her outside was cold and snow. Even if they had taxis out here, she had four dollars in her wallet, less than that in her bank account. The check still in her pocket might get her halfway to Chicago if she could find a bank to cash it at and a bus station.

Charles had brushed by her and padded on into the house but stopped when he realized she wasn't following him. He took a long look at her, and she tightened her arms around the wet cardboard. Maybe he was having second thoughts, too.

'I'm sorry,' she said, dropping her eyes from his yellow gaze. Sorry she was a bother, sorry she wasn't stronger, better, something.

Power flared over her skin and jerked her eyes back to him. He'd dropped to the ground and was starting to change back to human.

It was too soon, he was too badly injured. Hastily, she shut the outside door with her hip, dropped her box on the floor, and hurried to his side.

'What are you doing? Stop that.'

But he'd already begun, and she didn't dare touch him. Changing either way hurt – and even a gentle touch could leave him in agony.

'Damn it, Charles.'

Even after three years of being a werewolf, she didn't like

watching the change – her own or anyone else's. There was something horrible about seeing someone's arms and legs twist and bend – and there was that stomach-churning part in the middle where there was neither fur nor skin to cover the muscle and bone.

Charles had been different. He told her that either his mother's magic or being a werewolf born made his change quicker: it had also made it almost beautiful. The first time she'd seen him change, she'd been in awe.

This time wasn't like that. It was as slow and horrible as hers. He'd forgotten the bandages, and they weren't shaped right to change with him. She knew that the bandage would tear eventually, but she also knew it would hurt.

So she slid along the wall to avoid touching him, then ran to the kitchen. She pulled open drawers, searching frantically until she found the one where he kept his sharp and pointy things, including a pair of scissors. Deciding that she was less likely to stab him with scissors than a knife, she grabbed them and went back.

She cut as he changed, ignoring his rumbling growl as she forced the blade under too-tight cloth. The additional pressure would hurt, but it would be better than waiting until the stress on the fabric finally tore it to pieces.

The speed of his change slowed more and more as it continued, until she worried that he was going to be stuck halfway between: she'd had nightmares about being stuck in neither one form nor the other. At last he lay curled on his belly at her feet, fully human.

She thought he was through, but then clothing formed around his naked body, flowing over his skin as his skin had flowed over flesh as he changed. Nothing fancy, just jeans and a plain white T-shirt, but she'd never known a werewolf who could do that. This was real magic.

She didn't know how much real magic he could do.

She didn't know a lot about him other than he made her heart beat faster and nudged her usual state of half panic away.

She shivered, then realized it was cool in the house. He must have turned down the heat when he'd come to Chicago. She looked around and found a small quilted throw folded over the back of a rocking chair and snatched it up. Careful not to brush too hard on his oversensitized skin, she laid the blanket lightly over him.

He lay with one cheek against the floor, shuddering and breathless.

'Charles?' Her impulse was to touch him, but after a change, the last thing she wanted was touch. His skin would feel new and raw.

The blanket slid off his shoulder and when she lifted it to cover him again, she saw a dark stain growing rapidly on the back of his shirt. If his wounds had been of the usual sort, the change would have mended them more than this. Silver-inflicted wounds healed a lot slower.

'Do you have a first-aid kit?' she asked. Her pack's first-aid kit was equipped to cope with wounds dealt in the half-serious fights that broke out whenever the whole pack got together. Impossible to believe that Charles wasn't as well prepared as her . . . as the Chicago pack.

'Bathroom.' His voice was gravel-rough with pain.

The bathroom was behind the first door she opened, a big room with a claw-foot tub, a large shower stall, and a white porcelain pedestal sink. In one corner of the room was a linen closet. On the bottom shelf she found an industrial-sized first-aid kit and took it with her back to the living room.

Charles's usually warm brown skin was gray, his jaw was clenched against the pain, and his black eyes were fever-bright, glittering with hints of gold that matched the stud he wore in his ear. He'd sat upright, the quilt pooling on the floor around him.

'That was stupid. Changing doesn't help silver wounds,' she scolded him, her sudden anger fueled by the pain he'd caused himself. 'All you did was use up all the energy your body needs to heal. Let me get you bandaged up, and I'll find some food.' She was hungry, too.

He smiled at her – just a little smile. Then he closed his eyes. 'All right.' His voice was hoarse.

She would have to take off most of the clothes he'd put on. 'Where do your clothes come from?'

She'd have assumed they were what he'd been wearing when he'd changed from human to wolf, except she'd helped strip him so the Chicago doctor could examine him. He hadn't been wearing anything except bandages when he'd changed into his wolf.

He shook his head. 'Wherever. I don't know.'

The jeans were Levi's, worn at the knee, and the shirt had a Hanes label. She wondered if there was someone somewhere who was suddenly running around in his underwear. 'Sweet,' she said as she carefully peeled up his shirt so she could get a look at his chest wound. 'But this would be easier if you hadn't dressed.'

'Sorry,' he grunted. 'Habit.'

A bullet had pierced his chest just to the right of his sternum. The hole in the back was worse, bigger than the one in his front. If he'd been human, he'd still be in the emergency room, but werewolves were tough.

'If you put a telfa pad on the front,' he told her, 'I can hold it for you. You'll have to hold one on the back. Then wrap the whole thing with vet wrap.'

'Vet wrap?'

'The colored stuff that looks sort of like an Ace bandage. It'll stick to itself, so you don't need to fasten it. You'll probably have to use two pads to get enough coverage.'

She cut his T-shirt off with the scissors she'd found in the kitchen. Then she ripped open the telfa pads and set one against the little gaping mouth on his chest and tried not to think about the hole that ran inside him from his front to his back. He pressed the pad harder than she'd have dared to.

She sorted through the kit, looking for the vet wrap, and found a full dozen rolls on the bottom. Most of them were brown or black, but there were a few others. Because she was angry with him for hurting himself more when he could have just stayed in wolf form for a few days, she grabbed a pair of fluorescent pink rolls.

He laughed when she pulled them out, but it must have hurt – his mouth thinned, and he had to take shallow breaths for a while. 'My brother put those in there,' he said when the worst of it was over.

'Did you do something to annoy him, too?' she asked.

He grinned. 'He claimed that was all he had in the office when I restocked the kit.'

She was ready to ask a few more questions about his brother, but all desire to tease him died when she looked at his back. In the few minutes she'd spent organizing her bandaging efforts, the blood had pooled in the area between his skin and the top of his jeans. She should have left his shirt alone until she had everything ready.

'*Tarditas et procrastinatio odiosa est,*' she told herself and cut open a package of telfa pads.

'You speak Latin?' he asked.

'Nope, I just quote it a lot. That was supposed to be Cicero, but your father tells me my pronunciation is off. Do you want a translation?' The slice from the first bullet, the one he'd taken protecting her, burned a puffy red diagonal line above the more serious wound. It was going to hurt for a while, but it wasn't important.

'I don't speak Latin,' he said. 'But I know a little French and Spanish. Procrastination sucks?'

'That's what it's supposed to mean.' She had already made things worse; he ought to have a doctor for this.

'It's all right,' he said, answering the tension in her voice. 'Just get the leak plugged.'

Grimly, she set about doing just that. She gathered his waist-length, sweat-dampened hair and pushed it over his shoulder.

There weren't any telfa pads big enough for the wound in his back, so she got two of them and held them in place with judicious pressure from her knee while she reached around him with the roll of vet wrap. He took the end for her without her asking and held it to his ribs. She used that anchor to wind the rest of it around him the first time.

She was hurting him. He'd almost quit breathing except in small, shallow pants. Giving first aid to werewolves was fraught with danger. Pain could make a wolf lose control like he'd done this morning. But Charles just held himself very still as she pulled the bandage tight enough to hold the pads where they needed to be.

She used both rolls of the wrap and tried not to notice how good the bright pink looked against his dark skin. When a man is on the verge of passing out from pain, it seemed wrong to notice how beautiful he was. His smooth dark skin stretched over taut muscles and bone . . . maybe if he hadn't smelled so good under the blood and sweat, she could have maintained a distance.

*Hers. He was hers*, whispered that part of her that didn't worry about human concerns. Whatever fears Anna had about the rapid changes in her life, her wolf half was very happy with the events of the past few days.

She got a dishcloth from the kitchen, wetted it down, and cleaned the blood from his skin while he recovered from her clumsy efforts at first aid.

'There's blood on your pant leg, too,' she told him. 'The jeans have to come off. Can you just magic them off the way they came on?'

He shook his head. 'Not now. Not even to show off.'

She weighed the difficulties in getting a pair of jeans off and picked up the scissors she'd used on his T-shirt. They'd been nice and sharp – and they cut through the tough denim as easily as they'd cut through the shirt, leaving him in a pair of dark green boxers.

'I hope you've got a good surface on this floor,' she murmured to help distance herself from the wound. 'Be a shame to stain it.'

His blood had spread all over the fancy patterning on the floor. Fortunately, the Persian rugs were too far away to be in danger.

The second bullet had gone right through his calf. It looked worse than it had yesterday, puffier and sore.

'Blood won't bother it,' he answered as if he bled on his floor all the time. 'It's got four coats of polyurethane applied just last year. It'll be just fine.'

His kit was out of pink, so for his leg she chose the next-most-objectionable color, a chartreuse green. Like the pink, the brilliant shade suited him. She used the whole roll and another pair of telfa pads to keep the bandage from sticking – and he was done, leaving the quilt, his clothes, and the floor covered in blood. Her clothes hadn't fared too well, either.

'Do you want me to get you to bed before I deal with this mess, or would you rather have a few minutes to collect yourself?'

'I'll wait,' he said. His black eyes had changed to wolf yellow while she'd worked. Despite the temper tantrum he'd thrown this morning that had scared the Chicago wolves, his control was very, very good to allow him to hold still for her – but there was no reason to push him.

'Where's your laundry room?' she asked, grabbing a change of clothes from her box.

'Downstairs.'

Downstairs took her a minute to find. At last she opened a door in the short wall between the kitchen and dining room that she'd assumed was a closet and found a stairway. The laundry room she found in one corner of the half-finished basement – the rest of the basement was a weight room equipped with an impressive thoroughness.

She threw the rags of his bandages and clothes into the trash next to the washing machine. He had a sink in the laundry room, and she filled it with cold water and loaded it with everything salvageable. She let them soak a few minutes while she changed into clean clothes, dumping her bloodstained shirt and jeans into the sink, too. She found a five-gallon bucket filled with folded, clean rags sitting next to the dryer, and grabbed a few to clean the floor.

He didn't react when she came in; his eyes were closed and his face composed. He should have looked silly sitting in bloodstained underwear with stripes of pink and green bandage wound around him, but he just looked like Charles.

The blood on the floor cleaned up as easily as he'd promised. She gave it one last polishing swipe and stood to go back downstairs with her bloodstained rags, but Charles caught her ankle in one big hand and she froze, wondering if he'd lost control at last.

'Thank you,' he said, sounding civilized enough.

'I'd say anytime, but if you make me bandage you very often, I'd have to kill you,' she told him.

He grinned, his eyes still closed. 'I'll try not to bleed more often than necessary,' he promised, releasing her to her tasks.

Once the washer was churning away downstairs, she busied

herself nuking frozen burritos from his freezer. If she was hungry, he must be starving.

She didn't find any coffee, but there was instant hot chocolate and a variety of teas. Deciding sugar was what was needed, she boiled water for cocoa.

When everything was done, she took a plate and a cup of cocoa into the living room and set them on the floor in front of him. He didn't open his eyes or move, so she left him alone.

She looked through the house until she found his bedroom. It wasn't difficult. For all the luxuriousness of his furnishings and trimmings, it wasn't a huge house. There was only one room with a bed.

That gave her an unpleasant little pause.

She pulled back the blankets. At least she didn't have to deal with sex for a few days yet. He wasn't in any shape for gymnastics right now. Being a werewolf had taught her – among other things – to ignore the past, live in the present, and not think too much about the future. It worked, too, as long as the present was bearable.

She was tired, tired and completely out of place. She did what she'd learned to do over the past few years and drew on the strength of her wolf. Not enough that another wolf could sense it, and she knew that if she looked in a mirror, it would be her own brown eyes staring out at her. But under her skin she could feel that *Other*. She'd used the wolf to get through things her human half wouldn't have survived. For now, it gave her more strength and insulated her from her worries.

She smoothed her hand over the forest green sheets – Charles seemed to like green – and returned to the living room.

He was still sitting up, his eyes were open, and both the cocoa and the burritos she'd left him with were gone – all good signs. But his gaze was unfocused, and his face was still paler than it should be, with deep lines of strain on it.

'Let's get you to bed,' she told him from the safety of the hallway. Best not to startle a wounded werewolf, even one in human form who was having trouble sitting up on his own.

He nodded and accepted her help. Even in human form he was big, a foot or more taller than her five feet two. He was heavy, too.

She could have picked him up and carried him if she'd needed to, but it would have been awkward and she'd have hurt him. Instead, she put her shoulder under his arm and propped him up on the way to his bedroom.

So close to him, it was impossible not to respond to the scent of his skin. He smelled of male and mate. Aided by that scent, she let herself sink into her wolf's certainty of him, welcoming the beast's contentment.

He didn't make a sound the whole way to his bed, though she could feel the extent of his pain in the tension in his muscles. He felt hot and feverish, and that worried her. She'd never seen a werewolf feverish before.

He sat down on the mattress with a hiss. The blood left on the waistband of his boxers was going to stain the sheets, but she didn't feel comfortable pointing it out. He looked ready to collapse – he'd been in a lot better shape before he decided to change to human. As old as he was, he should have known better.

'Why didn't you just stay wolf?' she scolded.

Cool eyes met hers with more wolf than man in their yellow depths. 'You were going to leave. The wolf had no way to talk you out of it.'

He'd gone through that because he was worried she'd leave him? Romantic . . . and stupid.

She rolled her eyes in exasperation. 'And just where would

I have gone? And what would it have mattered to you if you'd managed to bleed to death?'

Deliberately, he dropped his gaze.

That this wolf, this man, so dominant that even humans skittered away when he walked by, would give her the advantage took her breath away.

'My father would take you wherever you wanted to go,' he told her softly. 'I was pretty sure I could talk you into staying, but I underestimated how badly hurt I was.'

'Stupid,' she said tartly.

He looked up at her, and whatever he saw in her face made him smile, though his voice was serious when he answered her charge. 'Yes. You throw my judgment off.'

He started to lie back in the bed, and she quickly put her arm around him, just above the bandage, and helped him ease back onto the mattress.

'Would you rather lie on your side?'

He shook his head and bit his lip. She knew from experience how much lying down could hurt when you were badly injured.

'Is there someone I could call for you?' she asked. 'A doctor? Your father?'

'No. I'll be fine after a little sleep.'

She gave him a skeptical look that he didn't see. '*Is* there a doctor? Or a medical person who knows more than I do around here somewhere? Like maybe a ten-year-old Boy Scout?'

He flashed a quick grin, and it warmed his austere beauty until it hurt her heart. 'My brother is a doctor, but he's probably still in Washington state.' He hesitated. 'Maybe not, though. He'll probably be back for the funeral.'

'Funeral?' Bran's friend's funeral, she remembered – the reason Bran hadn't been able to stay longer in Chicago.

'Tomorrow,' he answered, though that wasn't what she

meant. Since she wasn't sure she'd wanted to know more about who was dead and why, she didn't ask again. He fell silent, and she thought he was sleeping until he spoke again. 'Anna, don't trust too easily.'

'What?' She put her hand on his forehead, but it didn't feel any hotter.

'If you decide to take my da up on his offer to leave, remember he seldom does things for simple motives. He wouldn't be as old as he is, wouldn't hold as much as he does, if he were a simple man. He wants you for his own use.' He opened his gold eyes and held her in his gaze. 'He's a good man. But he has a firm grip on reality, and his reality tells him that an Omega might mean that he never has to kill another friend.'

'Like the one whose funeral is tomorrow?' she said. Yes, that was the undercurrent she'd been sensing.

He nodded once, fiercely. 'You couldn't have helped with this one, no one could have. But maybe the next one . . .'

'Your father won't *really* let me leave?' Was she a prisoner?

He caught her anxiety. 'I didn't mean that. He doesn't lie. He told you that he'd see to it that you could leave if you wanted to – and he will. He'll try to get you to agree to go where he needs you most, but he won't keep you against your will.'

Anna looked at him, and the wolf inside her relaxed. 'You wouldn't keep me here if I didn't want to be, either.'

His hands moved with breathtaking speed, clasping her wrists before she could react. His eyes lightened from burnished gold to bright wolf amber as he said hoarsely, 'Don't count on that, Anna. Don't count on that.'

She ought to have been afraid. He was bigger and stronger than she was, and the speed of his movement was calculated to scare her – though she wasn't sure why he felt he had to unless he wanted to make sure she understood. But with the wolf ascendant, she couldn't be afraid of him – he was hers and would no more hurt her than she would willingly hurt him.

She leaned forward, resting her forehead on his. 'I know you,' she told him. 'You can't fool me.' The conviction settled her. She might have known him only a short time – a very short time – but in some ways she knew him better than he knew himself.

Surprisingly, he laughed – a quiet huff that she hoped didn't hurt too much. 'How did Leo manage to fool you into behaving like a submissive wolf?'

All those beatings, the unwilling couplings with men she didn't want – she looked down at the scars on the wrists that Charles held. She'd used a silver knife, and if she hadn't gotten impatient, if she'd waited until she was home alone, she'd have died.

Leo had been trying to break her because she wasn't a submissive, she was something else entirely. He hadn't wanted her to know it. She was outside the pack structure, Charles had told her. Neither dominant nor submissive. Omega. Whatever that meant.

Charles's hand traveled rapidly from her wrists to the sides of her face. He pulled her away from him until he could see her face. 'Anna? Anna, I'm sorry. I didn't mean to—'

'It wasn't you,' she told him. 'I'm all right.' She focused and noticed that he looked even more tired than he had before. 'You need to sleep.'

He looked at her searchingly, then nodded and released her. 'There's a TV in the dining room. Or you can play on the internet on my computer in the study. There are—'

'I'm tired, too.' She might have been conditioned to walk around with her tail between her legs, but she wasn't stupid. Sleep was just what her exhausted mind needed to try to

cope with the abrupt changes in her life. Exchanging Chicago
for the wilds of Montana was the least of it: Omega and
valued, not submissive and worthless; a mate and whatever
that meant. Better than she'd had, that was for darn sure,
but it was still a bit traumatic.

'Do you mind if I sleep here?' She kept her tone diffi-
dent, not wanting to intrude where she wasn't wanted. This
was his territory – but her wolf was reluctant to leave him
alone and wounded.

It felt awkward, this needing. Awkward and dangerous,
as if what he was might reach out and swallow her whole –
or change her beyond recognition. But she was too tired to
fight it or even figure out if she wanted to fight it.

'Please,' he said, and it was enough.

She was right, he knew. He needed to sleep.

After she'd come back from the bathroom in a thread-
bare flannel shirt and faded pajama pants, she'd curled up
next to him and dropped right off. He was exhausted, too,
but he found he was unwilling to give up any of the time
he could spend with her in his arms, his unexpected gift.

He didn't know what she thought about him. Prior to
being shot, he'd been planning on taking more time courting
her. That way she'd be more sure of him before he dragged
her out of her territory.

The look on her face when she'd stepped into his home . . .
she made a noise, and he loosened his arms. He'd done some
more damage to himself with that change, and he'd heal
even slower in human form – but if he'd lost her, that would
be a wound he suspected would never heal.

She was tough to have survived Leo's treatment and still
come out whole in the end. No matter what she said about
her lack of options, he knew if he hadn't distracted her, she'd
have run from him. The weariness he felt now and the pain

of the change were well worth it. He'd waited a long time to find her, and he wasn't about to chance losing her.

It felt strange to have a woman in this bed – at the same time it seemed as if she'd always been there. His. She had her hand lying over the wound in his chest, but he ignored the ache for a fiercer, more joyous pain.

His.

The Marrok's voice floated into his head and out again, like a warm stream. *The funeral will be at nine in the morning. If you can't make it, let me know. Samuel will be there; he'll want to take a look at your wounds afterward.*

Bran wasn't a true telepath; he could send but not receive. Samuel had once told Charles that Bran hadn't always been able to do even that much, but sometime after becoming an Alpha for the first time, he had developed the talent for it.

*And there is something I need from you . . .*

His father's voice trailed off, and Charles knew he wasn't meant to hear that part. Or at least his father hadn't meant him to hear it.

He'd never questioned either his father's faith in God or his grandfather's faith in the spirits, because he knew them both. God seldom talked to him, though He sometimes warned or lent comfort or strength. But the spirits were more demanding, if often less beneficent, and Charles had learned to recognize when one of them was tugging at him.

'Sorry,' he whispered to Anna as he reached for the telephone, which was thankfully not too great a stretch from his side of the bed. But she didn't stir.

He dialed his father's cell phone.

'Can't make it to the funeral? Are you worse?' Even before caller ID, his father had always known who was calling. With Charles, he'd long since ceased to waste time on greetings and jumped straight into conversation.

'I'm fine, Da,' Charles said. Anna's muscles tightened

against him just a little as she woke up. 'But you had some-thing else to tell me.'

There was a pause. 'If I'd known your mother was a medicine man's daughter, I'd never have taken her to mate.' He'd said that ever since his son had begun showing signs of his mother's talents. Charles smiled: his father knew better than to believe even he could lie to another werewolf – or at least not to his sons. Not even over the phone.

'Fine,' Bran said, when Charles continued to wait. Frustration made his voice sharp. 'There's been a kill up in the Cabinet Wilderness. An elk hunter was torn to bits a couple of days ago, on the last day of the season. One of our contacts with the rangers told me. It'll be in the papers tomorrow. They're officially blaming it on a grizzly.'

'Rogue wolf?' asked Charles.

'Maybe. Or maybe someone trying to make sure that I know that making the wolves public would be a bad idea.' Anna had gone very still by his side. She was awake and listening.

Bran continued, 'The Cabinet Wilderness is right in our backyard, where I'd be sure to get the message. We haven't had a rogue in Montana for fifteen or twenty years.' Most of them were smart enough to stay away from the Marrok's personal territory. 'The rangers also had a report a month or so ago about some monster a grad student ran into – it was within a few miles of where they found the dead hunter.

'The student said this thing just came out of the woods. It roared at him and flashed fangs and claws – everyone assumed it was a cougar, though the student was pretty hot that they'd think he wouldn't recognize a cougar. He main-tained it was a monster until they wore him down into changing his story.'

'Why is he still alive to tell the tale?' Charles asked, and felt Anna stiffen further. She'd misunderstood his question.

So he continued, more for her sake than his father's. 'If it was a rogue, it wouldn't have let him leave after seeing him like that,' he clarified.

He hadn't had to kill a witness for a long time. Mostly they could rely on general disbelief in the supernatural and, in the Pacific Northwest anyway, Big Foot stories. One of the Oregon packs had made it a hobby to create Big Foot sightings ever since the damage one of their new wolves had done to a car had been attributed to Big Foot.

'The student said some crazy old man with a knife jumped out from nowhere and told him to run,' said Bran. 'So he did.'

Charles absorbed that for a minute. 'A crazy old man who *happened* to be there just as a werewolf decided to kill this kid? An old man wouldn't even slow a werewolf down.'

'I never claimed the story made sense.' His father's voice was dry. 'And we're not certain that the monster was a werewolf. I hadn't paid any attention to it until the hunter was killed in the same area only a month later.'

'What about that one? Are you sure the hunter was a werewolf victim?'

'My informant was Heather Morrell. She knows a grizzly kill from a werewolf.'

Heather was human, but she'd been raised in Aspen Creek.

'All right,' agreed Charles. 'You need me to go check it out? It'll be a few days before I'm up to it.' And he didn't want to leave Anna. 'Can you send someone else?' It would need to be someone dominant enough to control a rogue.

'I don't want to send anyone in to get killed.'

'Just me.' Charles could use a dry tone, too.

'Just you,' agreed Bran blandly. 'But I'm not sending you out hurt. Samuel's here for the funeral. He can go check this out.'

'You can't send Samuel.' His response was immediate.

The negative too strong to be just instinct. Sometimes his mother's spirits gave him a little help in planning for the future.

This time it was his father who waited. So he tried to figure out just why it was such a bad idea – and didn't like the answer he came up with.

'Since he came back from Texas, there's been something wrong with Samuel,' Charles said finally.

'He's suicidal.' Bran put it into words. 'I threw him at Mercy to see if she could shake him out of it. That's why I sent you to Chicago instead of Washington.'

Poor Mercy, poor Samuel. Charles ran a finger over Anna's arm. Thank God, thank all the spirits his father had never tried matchmaking for him. He looked down at Anna, and thought, thank goodness his father had sent him, and not Samuel, to Chicago.

The spirits responded to his impulsive prayer by interfering a bit further.

'Samuel's tough,' he said, picking through the warning images that were thrusting themselves at him. 'But he's a healer – and I don't think that's what this situation needs. I'll go. It'll have to wait a couple of days, but I'll go.' The unease that had held him since his father contacted him settled down. His decision felt right.

His father didn't think so. 'You took three silver bullets yesterday – or am I forgetting something? And lost control this morning.'

'Two bullets and a scratch,' Charles corrected. 'So I'll limp a little on the trail. My control is fine now.'

'You let Samuel take a look at you, then we'll talk.' His father hung up abruptly. But his voice continued in Charles's head, *I don't want to lose both of my children.*

Charles replaced the handset, and said to Anna, 'Ask.'

'Bran, the Marrok, is going to bring the werewolves out

to the public?' Her voice was hushed as if she could never imagine such a thing.

'He thinks that too many of the wrong people already know,' he told her. 'Science and computers have made it harder and harder for us to hide. Da hopes that he can control it better if he initiates the flow of information rather than waiting until our enemies or some innocent idiot decides to do it for us.'

She relaxed against him, thinking about it. 'That will make life interesting.'

He laughed, tucked her against him, and fell, blissfully, into sleep at last.

# 3

There was actually a town. Not much of a town, but it had a gas station, a hotel, and a two-story brick-and-stone building with a sign in front that proclaimed it the Aspen Creek School. Beyond the school, tucked back in the trees and barely visible from anywhere but the parking lot, was an old stone church. If not for Charles's directions, she might have missed it.

Anna eased his big green truck through the church parking lot into a spot designed for a much smaller rig. It was the only place left. She hadn't seen any houses, but there were a lot of trucks and other four-wheel-drive vehicles in the lot.

Charles's truck was older than she was, but looked as if it were brand-new. It had been driven less than fifty thousand miles, if she wanted to believe the odometer — about two thousand miles a year. Charles had told her he didn't like driving.

She turned off the engine and watched anxiously as Charles opened his door and slid to the ground. The drop didn't seem to bother him. The stain on his pink bandage had been no bigger this morning than it had been last night. But he still looked worn, and there was a flush under his skin that she worried about.

If they'd been in Chicago, attending a meeting with her old pack, she wouldn't have let him come. Too many of the wolves there would have taken advantage of his weakness. Or at least she'd have tried to stop him a lot harder than she'd tried this morning.

She had expressed her concern, eyes carefully trained on

the floor. In her experience, dominant wolves didn't like their prowess questioned and sometimes reacted badly. Not that she really thought he'd hurt her.

He'd merely said, 'No one would dare try me. My father would kill them if I didn't manage it first. I'm hardly helpless.'

She hadn't had the courage to question his judgment again. All she could do was hope that he was right.

She had to admit he looked anything but helpless, the folds of bandages hidden by the dark suit jacket he wore. The contrast between formal suit and his waist-length beaded-and-braided hair was oddly compelling. Of course his face, beautiful and exotic, and his big, tautly muscled body meant that he would be gorgeous in whatever he wore.

He looked a lot classier than she did. She'd had to wear jeans and a yellow button-up shirt because the only other thing she had was a couple of T-shirts. She hadn't expected she'd be going to a funeral when she'd packed.

She sighed and eased her door open so she wouldn't scratch the Subaru parked next to her. Charles waited for her in front of the truck and held out his arm in what was beginning to be a familiar gesture, however old-fashioned it might be. She tucked her arm into his and let him pick his own pace into the church.

In public he didn't limp, but she knew that sharp eyes would be watching the stiffness of his gait. She glanced up at him as they started up the steps, but she couldn't read anything in his face at all: he already had his public face on, expressionless.

Inside, the church sounded like a beehive, with a hundred voices intermingling so that she got a word here or there but nothing made any sense. She could smell the wolves, but there were humans here, too. The whole congregation bore the distinctive scent of sorrow, overlaid with anger and resentment.

When they walked into the chapel itself, every pew was tightly packed, and a few people even stood around the back. They turned when she and Charles walked in, all of them staring at her – an outsider, the only person in the whole freaking church wearing jeans. Or yellow.

She tightened her grip on Charles's arm. He glanced down at her face, then just looked around. In less time than it took to walk past three pews, everyone seemed to have found something urgent that pulled their attention elsewhere.

She clutched his forearm a little harder in gratitude and looked at the church itself. It reminded her a little of the Congregational church she'd grown up in with its dark woods, high ceiling, and cross-shaped interior. The pulpit was directly in front of the aisle they walked up, raised above the main floor by about two feet. Behind it were several rows of seats facing the congregation.

As they neared the front of the church, she realized she'd been wrong about its being completely packed. The first pew on the left was entirely empty except for Bran.

He sat looking for all the world as if he was waiting for a bus rather than a funeral, despite the designer charcoal suit he wore. His arms were spread to either side of him, elbows hanging over the back of the pew; his legs were stretched out and crossed at the ankle, eyes focused either on the railing in front of him, or on infinity. His face revealed no more than Charles's usual expression, which was wrong. She hadn't known him long, but the Marrok's face was a mobile one, not designed to be so still.

He looked isolated, and Anna remembered that the man the whole town had turned out to mourn had been killed by Bran. A friend, he'd said.

Beside her, Charles let out a low growl that caught his

father's attention. Bran looked over at them, and one eyebrow climbed up his face, robbing it of its blankness. He patted the bench beside him as he asked his son, 'What? You expected them to be happy with me?'

Charles turned on his heel, so Anna was abruptly face to chest with him. But he wasn't looking at her, he was looking at everyone else in the sanctuary – who once again looked away. As his power swept the church in a boiling rush, silence fell abruptly.

'Fools,' he said, loud enough that everyone in the church would hear him.

Bran laughed. 'Come sit down before you scare them all silly. I'm not a politician to worry about what they think of me, as long as they obey.'

After a moment, Charles complied, and Anna found herself sitting between them.

As soon as Charles was facing the front of the church, the whispering began, built up speed, and regained its previous level. There were undercurrents here, thick enough to choke on. Anna felt distinctly like an outsider.

'Where's Samuel?' Charles looked over her head at his father.

'He's coming in right now.' Bran said it without looking behind him, but Charles turned around so Anna did, too.

The man strolling up the aisle was almost as tall as Charles, his features a rougher version of Bran's. That roughness made them not so bland or young-looking as his father. She found him oddly compelling, though not handsome like Charles.

His ditch-water brown hair was cut carelessly, but somehow he managed to look neat and well dressed anyway. He held a battered violin case in one hand and a dark blue Western-cut jacket in the other.

When he was nearly at the front, he turned around once, taking in the people in a single glance. Then he looked over at Anna, and his face broke into a singularly sweet smile – a smile she'd seen an echo of on Charles's face. With that smile she could see past the superficial differences to the underlying similarities, a matter of bone and movement rather than feature-by-feature likeness.

He sat next to Charles and brought with him the crisp scent of snow over leather. His smile widened, and he started to say something, but stopped when a wave of silence swept through the crowd from the back to the front.

The minister, bedecked in old-fashioned clerical robes, walked slowly up the central aisle, an ancient-looking Bible resting in the crook of his left arm. By the time he reached the front, the room was silent.

His obvious age told her that he wasn't a werewolf, but he had a presence that made his 'Welcome and thank you for coming to pay your respects to our friend' sound cere-monial. He set the Bible on the podium with obvious care for graying leather. He gently opened the heavily embossed cover and set aside a bookmark.

He read from the fifteenth chapter of Paul's first letter to the Corinthians. And the last verse he spoke without looking down. '"O death, where is thy sting? O grave, where is thy victory?"'

He paused, letting his eyes trail over the room, much as Charles had, then said simply, 'Shortly after we moved back here, Carter Wallace came to my house at two in the morning to hold my wife's hand when our retriever had her first litter of puppies. He wouldn't charge me because he said if he charged for cuddling pretty women, he'd be a gigolo and not a vet.'

He stepped away from the pulpit and sat on the throne-like wooden chair on the right-hand side. There was the sound of shuffling and the creaking of wood, then an old woman stood up. A man with bright chestnut hair escorted her down the aisle, a hand under her elbow. As they walked by her pew, Anna could smell the wolf in him.

It took the old woman a few minutes to make it all the way to the top of the stairs to the pulpit. She was so small that she had to stand on a footstool, the werewolf behind her with his hands on her waist to steady her.

'Carter came to our store when he was eight years old,' she said in a breathy, frail voice. 'He gave me fifteen cents. When I asked him what it was for, he told me that a few days before, he and Hammond Markham had been in, and Hammond had stolen a candy bar. I asked him why it was he and not Hammond who was bringing the money. He told me that Hammond didn't know he was bringing me the money.' She laughed and wiped a tear from her eye. 'He assured me that it was Hammond's money, though, stolen from his piggy bank just that morning.'

The werewolf who had escorted her raised her hand to his mouth and kissed it. Then he lifted her into his arms, despite her protests, and carried her back to where they'd been sitting. Husband and wife, not the grandson and grandmother they appeared to be.

Anna shivered, suddenly fiercely glad that Charles was a wolf like her and not human.

Other people stood up and told more stories or read verses from the Bible. There were tears. The dead man, Carter Wallace – or rather Dr Carter Wallace, since he evidently was the town's vet – had been loved by these people.

Charles stretched his feet out in front of him and bowed his head. Beside him, Samuel played absently with the violin case, rubbing at a worn spot on the leather.

She wondered how many funerals they'd been to, how many friends and relatives they'd buried. She'd cursed her ageless, regenerative body before – when it had made it darned hard to commit suicide. But the tension in Charles's

shoulders, Samuel's fidgeting, and Bran's closed-down stillness told her that there were other things that made virtual
immortality a curse.

She wondered if Charles had had a wife before. A human
wife who aged as he did not. What would it be like when
people she'd known as children grew old and died while she
never got her first gray hair?

She glanced at Charles. He was two hundred years old,
he'd told her, his brother and father even older. They'd been
to a lot of funerals.

A rising nervousness in the congregation interrupted her
thoughts. She looked around to see a girl walking up the
aisle. There was nothing about her to suggest why she caused
such a stir. Though she was too far away to scent over this
many people, something about her shouted human.

The girl climbed the stairs, and tension sang in the air
as she paged through the Bible, watching the audience under
her lashes.

She put her finger on a page and read, '"For this is the
message that ye heard from the beginning, that we should
love one another. Not as Cain, who was of that wicked one
and slew his brother. And wherefore slew he him? Because
his own works were evil, and his brother's righteous."'

'Shawna, Carter's granddaughter,' Charles murmured to
her. 'This is going to get ugly.'

'She didn't study too hard,' said Samuel just as quietly
but with a faint touch of humor. 'There are sharper-tongued
writers than John in the Bible.'

She continued a few more verses, then looked straight at
the Marrok, who obliged her by meeting her eyes. Anna
didn't feel any of the Alpha's power, but the girl dropped
her gaze after no more than a half second.

'She's been away at school,' said Charles in that almost
silent voice. 'Anyone, werewolf or not, who was much farther

from him than Anna wouldn't have been able to hear it.
'She's young and full of herself – and has resented the hold
Da has on Aspen Creek long before our Doc Wallace made
the fatal decision to become a werewolf. But bringing that
to his funeral is inexcusable.'

Ah. Suddenly the tension and the anger made sense. Carter
Wallace had been Changed. He hadn't made the transition
well, and Bran had been forced to kill him.

Carter had been Bran's friend, he'd said. Somehow, she
thought as she glanced up at his shuttered face, she didn't
think he had many friends.

She reached up by her shoulder, where his hand dangled
oh-so-casually, and she took the Marrok's hand in hers. It
was an impulse thing; as soon as she realized what she had
done she froze. But by then, he had taken her hand in a
tight grip that belied his casual pose. It hurt, but she didn't
believe it was on purpose. After a moment, his grip gentled.

At the pulpit, Shawna began talking again, her bitterness
apparently unchecked by her inability to stare Bran down. 'My
grandfather was dying of bone cancer when the Marrok talked
him into the Change. Gramps never wanted to be a werewolf,
but, weakened and ill, he allowed himself to be persuaded.'
Her speech sounded memorized to Anna, like she'd practiced
it in front of a mirror.

'He listened to his *friend*.' She didn't look at Bran again,
but not even Anna, who hadn't known the dead man, was
uncertain whom she meant. 'So instead of dying from illness,
he died from a broken neck because Bran decided he didn't
make a good enough werewolf. Maybe Gramps would have
thought it a better death.' Her 'I don't' remained unsaid,
but it rang through the room after she left the pulpit.

Anna was prepared to hate her, but as the girl walked
past them with a defiant tilt to her chin, Anna noticed her
eyes were red and puffy.

There was a moment when she thought Charles was going to explode to his feet, she could feel that boiling rage building, but it was Samuel who rose. He left the violin case behind him as he walked up to take the podium.

As if blind to the atmosphere, he launched into a story about a very young Carter Wallace who evaded the keeping of his mother to go for a walk and ended up some three miles into the woods before his father finally found him not two feet from an irritated rattlesnake. Carter's werewolf father killed the snake – enraging his son. 'I never saw Carter that mad before or since.' Samuel grinned. 'He was sure that snake was his friend, and poor old Henry, Carter's da, was too shaken to argue the point.'

Samuel's smile died away, and he let the silence build before speaking again. 'Shawna was away when the debate took place, so I'll excuse her misinformation,' he said. 'My father did *not* think it was a good idea that Carter face the Change. He told all of us, Doc included, that Doc was too softhearted to thrive as a wolf.'

The pulpit creaked ominously under Samuel's hold, and he opened his hands deliberately. 'To my shame, I took his son Gerry's part, and between the two of us, his doctor and his son, we persuaded Carter to try it. My father, knowing that a man as ill as Doc was a poor risk, took the task of Changing him – and he managed it. But he was right. Carter could neither accept nor control the wolf inside. Had he been anyone else, he would have died in February with the others who failed the Change. But Gerry, whose task it most properly was, would not do it. And without his consent, my father felt he could not.'

He took a deep breath and looked at Carter's grand-daughter. 'He almost killed your mother, Shawna. I took care of her afterward, and I'll attest that it was luck, not any impulse on Carter's part, that spared her life – you can ask her yourself. How would a man whose life had always been devoted to the service of others have borne it if he had killed his own daughter? She asked the Marrok, in my hearing, if he would take care of the duty that her brother would not. By that time, the wolf in Carter was far enough gone he couldn't ask for it. So no, my da did not try to persuade Carter to Change – he was just the one who stepped up to the plate to handle the resultant mess.'

When Samuel finished speaking, he let his eyes drift slowly over the room as heads bowed in submission. He nodded once, then took his seat next to Charles again.

The next few people kept their eyes off the Marrok and his sons, but Anna thought it was embarrassment rather than the sullen anger that had been so prominent a quarter of an hour ago.

At last the minister stood up. 'I have here a letter that Carter gave me several weeks ago,' he said. 'To be opened in the event of his death – which he felt would be soon, one way or another.' He opened the letter and put on a pair of glasses.

'"My friends,"' he read. '"Do not mourn my passing, I will not. My life this past year has shown me that inter- fering with God's plans is seldom a good idea. I go to join my beloved wife with joy and relief. I do have one last request. Bran, you old bard you, sing something for me at my funeral."'

The church was very still. Charles felt a reluctant affection for the dead man. Bless Carter, who was as much a healer as Samuel. He had known what was coming, and how folks would take it, too – the Marrok included.

He stood up and held out his hand for his father's, as Bran, uncharacteristically, seemed to be taken totally by surprise. Bran didn't take it, but he released Anna and came to his feet. Anna pulled her hand to her lap and flexed it as if it hurt.

'Did you know that Doc was going to do that?' Charles whispered to Samuel, with a nod at the battered violin case as they followed Da to the front. If he'd known, he'd have brought something to play as well. As it was, he'd been relegated to the piano – which had three off-pitch keys to improvise around.

Samuel shook his head. 'I'd planned on playing something rather than talking.' Then a little louder as he opened the case and took out his violin, 'What are you singing, Da?'

Charles glanced at his father, but couldn't read his face. *Too many funerals, too many dead friends*, he thought.

'"Simple Gifts,"' Bran said after a moment.

Charles sat down at the piano while Samuel tuned the violin. When his brother nodded, Charles played the introduction to the Shaker tune. It was a good choice, he thought. Not sad, not overtly religious, and it fit Carter Wallace, who had been, mostly, a simple man – and it was a song that they all knew well.

> *'Tis the gift to be gentle, 'tis the gift to be fair,*
> *'Tis the gift to wake and breathe the morning air,*
> *To walk every day in the path that we choose,*
> *Is the gift that we pray we will never never lose.*

As his father's quiet voice finished the second verse, Charles realized that it fit his father, too. Though Bran was a subtle man, his needs and desires were very simple: to keep his people alive and safe. For those goals he was prepared to be infinitely ruthless.

He glanced over at Anna, where she sat alone on the bench. Her eyes were closed, and she mouthed the words with Bran. He wondered what she sounded like when she sang – and whether her voice would fit with his. He wasn't sure she sang at all though she'd told him she'd been working at a music store selling guitars when she met the wolf who attacked her and Changed her against her will.

She opened her eyes and met his. The impact was so strong he was amazed that his fingers continued playing without pause.

*His.*

If she knew how strongly he felt, she'd have run out the door. He wasn't used to being possessive, or to the savage joy she brought to his heart. It ate at his control, so he turned his attention back to the music. He understood music.

Anna had to make an effort not to hum along. Had the audience been purely human, she'd have done it. But there were too many people around her whose hearing was as good as her own.

One of the things that she'd hated about being a werewolf was she'd had to give up on so many of her favorite musicians. Her ears picked out the slightest waver in pitch or fuzz in the recording. But those few singers she could still listen to . . .

Bran's voice was clean and dead on pitch, but it was the rich timbre that made the hair on her neck stir in awed appreciation.

As he sang the last note, the man who was sitting on the bench behind her leaned forward until his mouth was almost against her neck.

'So Charles brought a toy home, eh? I wonder if he'll share.' The voice was lightly accented.

She slid forward on the bench as far as she could and stared fixedly at Charles, but he was closing the cover over the keys to the piano and had his back toward her.

'So he leaves you like a lamb among wolves,' the wolf

murmured. 'Someone so soft and tender would do better with another man. Someone who likes being touched.' He put his hands on her shoulders and tried to pull her back toward him.

Anna jerked out of his hold, forgetting the funeral and audience. She was done with letting just anyone touch her. She stumbled to her feet and whirled to face the werewolf, who leaned back on his bench and smiled at her. The people on either side of him slid away to give him as much room as they could – that was a better judgment of what he was than the easy curve of his lips.

Anna had to admit he was lovely. His face was refined and elegant, his skin, like Charles's, was teak and sunlight. His nose and black eyes said Middle East, though his accent had been pure Spanish – she had a good ear for accents.

He looked her age, twenty-three or -four, but for some reason she was absolutely certain he was very, very old. And there was a hint of wildness, of some sickness, about him that made her wary.

'Leave her alone, Asil,' Charles said, and his hands settled on her shoulders where the other man's had been. 'She'll gut you and leave you for the crows if you bother her.'

She leaned back against his warmth, more than a little surprised that he was right – or at least that her first reaction hadn't been fear, it had been anger.

The other wolf laughed, his shoulders jerking harshly. 'Good.' He said. 'Good. Someone should.' Then the odd humor left his face, and he rubbed it tiredly. 'Not long now.' He looked past Anna and Charles. 'I told you the dreams are back. I dream of her almost every night. You need to do it soon, before it's too late. Today.'

'All right, Asil.' Bran's voice sounded flat and tired. 'But not today. Not tomorrow. You can hold out a little longer.'

Asil turned to look at the congregation, who had been a

silent witness to it all, and spoke in a clear, ringing voice. 'A gift you have, someone who knows what needs to be done and will do it. You have a place to come home to, a safe place, because of him. I had to leave my Alpha to come here because he'd have let me rot in madness out of love.' He turned his head and symbolically spat over his left shoulder. 'A weak love that betrays. If you knew what I feel, what Carter Wallace felt, you'd know what a blessing you have in Bran Cornick, who will kill those who need killing.'

And that's when Anna realized that what the wolf had been asking Bran for was death.

Impulsively, Anna stepped away from Charles. She put a knee on the bench she'd been sitting on and reached over the back to close her hand on Asil's wrist, which was lying across the back of the pew.

He hissed in shock but didn't pull away. As she held him, the scent of wildness, of sickness, faded. He stared at her, the whites of his eyes showing brightly while his irises narrowed to small bands around his black pupil.

'Omega,' he whispered, his breath coming harshly.

Behind her, Charles stepped closer, but he didn't touch her as the cool flesh under her fingertips warmed. They all stood frozen in place. Anna knew that all she had to do to end this was to remove her hand, but she was strangely reluctant to do so.

The shock on Asil's face faded, and skin around his eyes and mouth softened into sorrow that grew and deepened before tucking itself away, where all private thoughts hid from too-keen observers. He reached out and touched her face lightly, ignoring Charles's warning growl.

'More gifts here than I'd believed.' He smiled tightly at Anna, eyes and mouth in concert. 'It's too late for me, *mì querida*. You waste your gifts on my old self. But for the respite, I thank you.' He looked at Bran. 'Today and tomorrow, and maybe the next day, too. To see Charles, the original lone wolf, caught with a foot in the trap of *amor* – this will amuse me for a while longer, I think.'

He freed himself with a twist of his wrist, captured her hand in his and, with a sly look at Charles, kissed her palm. Then he let her go and slipped out of the church. Not hurrying, but not dawdling, either.

'Be careful around that one,' Charles cautioned her, but he didn't sound displeased.

Someone cleared his throat, and Anna looked around to meet the eyes of the minister. He smiled at her, then looked at the church. The interruption of his service didn't seem to bother him in the slightest. Maybe he was used to were-wolves interrupting things. Anna felt a blush rise up her face and sank back down on the bench . . . wishing she could sink even farther. She'd just interrupted the funeral of a man she didn't even know.

'It is time to bring this to a close,' the minister said. 'Our mourning is done here, and when we leave, we must remember a life well lived and a heart open to all. If you would all bow your heads for a final prayer.'

# 4

Northwestern Montana, Cabinet Wilderness

Walter didn't know why he'd survived the beast's attack, any more than he understood how he'd survived three tours of 'Nam when so many of his friends, his comrades, had not. Maybe his survival both times was just luck – or maybe fate had other things in store for him.

Like another thirty years wandering alone in the woods.

If his survival after the beast's attack had been unlikely, the rest of it was just plain weird. The first thing he'd noticed was that the aching arthritis that had haunted his shoulders and knees, the throb of an old wound in his hip, had all disappeared. The cold no longer bothered him.

It took him a lot longer to realize that his hair and beard had regained the color of his youth – he didn't carry around a mirror.

That's when he began paying attention to the oddities. He was faster and stronger than he'd ever been. The only wounds that hadn't healed with the same remarkable speed as his belly were the ones on his battered soul.

He didn't really understand what had happened until the morning after the first full moon when he woke up with blood in his mouth, under his nails, and on his naked body: the memory of what he'd done, what he'd become, clear as diamonds. Only then did he know he had become the enemy, and he wept at the loss of the last of his humanity.

## Aspen Creek, Montana

With Charles's arm around her shoulder, Anna followed everyone to the frigid parking lot of the church. They stopped on the sidewalk and watched as the lot slowly emptied. A few of the people leaving the church glanced at Anna, but no one stopped.

When they stood mostly alone, Anna found herself under gray-eyed scrutiny that was wary, despite the friendly smile Samuel gave her.

'So you're the stray pup my brother decided to bring home? You're shorter than I expected.'

Impossible to take offense when clearly none was meant; at least he didn't call her a bitch.

'Yes,' she said, careful to resist the urge to squirm under his gaze or to babble endlessly as she sometimes did when she was nervous.

'Samuel, this is Anna. Anna, my brother, Samuel,' Charles said in introduction.

Apparently deciding Charles's brief introduction wasn't good enough, his brother reintroduced himself. 'Dr Samuel Cornick, elder brother and tormentor. Very nice to meet you, Anna—'

'Latham,' she told him, wishing she could come up with something clever.

He gave her a charming smile that, she noticed, did nothing to warm his eyes. 'Welcome to the family.' He patted her on the head, mostly, she thought, to irritate Charles.

Who said merely, 'Quit flirting with my mate.'

'Behave,' said Bran. 'Samuel, would you take Charles back to the clinic and look at his wounds? I have a job for him, but if he isn't going to recover soon, I'll have to find someone else to send. I don't think he's healing as well as he should be.'

Samuel shrugged. 'Sure. No problem.' He looked at Anna. 'It might take a while, though.'

She wasn't stupid. He wanted to talk to Charles without her there – or maybe it had been Bran, and Samuel was just helping out.

Charles picked up on it, too, because he said smoothly, 'Why don't you take the truck back to the house. Samuel or Da will give me a lift back.'

'Sure,' she told him with a quick smile – she had no reason to feel hurt, she told herself sternly. She turned and walked rapidly to the truck.

She could do with some time to herself. She had things she wanted to consider without Charles around to cloud her thinking.


Charles wanted to snarl at her relief at leaving him, implicit in her rapid retreat to the truck.

He fought down the irrational anger he felt toward Samuel, who had so charmingly sent her away, responding to the orders Bran had sent mind to mind. He could always tell when his father was talking to Samuel, something in Samuel's face gave it away.

Samuel waited until she'd gotten in the truck and driven out of the parking lot before he said, 'Did you kill the wolf who abused her?'

'He's dead.' For some reason, Charles couldn't keep his eyes off the truck. He hadn't liked sending her away. He knew that there was nothing to worry about, no one here would touch what was his – and the whole town knew what she was thanks to Asil's performance at the funeral.

Even the few people who weren't at the funeral, such as his father's mate – who had made quite a statement with her absence – would know of it before the hour was up. Still, he didn't like to send Anna off on her own. Not at all.

'Charles?' His brother's voice was quiet.

'That's why I asked you to have Anna leave,' Bran murmured. 'I wanted you to see the difference in him. He was like this yesterday, as soon as she left his sight. She's an Omega, and I think her effect on him is masking his symptoms. I think they didn't get all the silver out.'

'When was he shot?'

'The day before yesterday. Three times. One's a burn across his shoulder, one is through his chest and out the back, and a third through his calf. All silver.'

Charles watched the truck edge cautiously around the turn that would take her home.

'He's more sensitive to silver poison than – *Charles!*'

Hard hands grabbed his shoulders, and his father touched his face, capturing him with his gaze more effectively than his brother had captured his body.

'I have to go,' he told his Alpha, heart in his throat. He couldn't think, couldn't stay here. He had to protect her, battered though he was.

'Wait,' his father told him, and the command wrapped around his body like steel hawsers, freezing him where he stood when all he wanted to do was follow the truck. 'Samuel still needs a look at you. I'll send Sage to her, shall I?'

His father's touch, his voice, and something more helped him gather his thoughts. He was out of control.

He closed his eyes and drew on his father's touch to soothe the beast until he could think more clearly.

'I did it again, didn't I?' he asked, though he didn't really need Bran's affirmative. He took a deep breath and nodded. 'Sage would be good.'

He didn't like anyone in his house: his father and brother, yes, but other people only as necessary. Still, he didn't want Anna alone, either. Sage would do.

She wouldn't hurt his Anna and could protect her until

he was there. Keep the males away. Something restless inside settled down a little more firmly. But he watched as his father called Sage on his cell and listened to him ask her to go meet Anna. Then allowed himself to be towed off to the clinic in Samuel's car. His father followed in his Humvee.

'Da told me you had to kill Gerry,' he told his brother. Gerry had been Doc Wallace's son, responsible for hurting any number of people and killing several others in his quest to find a drug that could subdue Bran in a convoluted plot to force the good doctor to accept his dual nature. Gerry hadn't been concerned about collateral damage.

Samuel nodded, his face grim. 'He left me no choice.'

Even distracted by his need to protect his mate and the burn of the wounds that weren't healing right, Charles heard what his brother wasn't saying. So he gave it voice. 'You're wondering how many people we would kill to protect our da? How many we would torture and destroy?'

'That's it,' his brother whispered. 'We've killed people. Wolves and innocents for our father. How are we so different that we survive and Gerry deserved to die?'

If Bran had sent Samuel with Mercy to the Tri-Cities to cure his melancholy, it hadn't worked very well. Charles struggled to pull his attention from his mate and come up with something to help his brother. Without Bran touching him, it was more difficult than it should have been to collect his thoughts.

'Our father has kept the packs under his mantle safe and controlled. Without his leadership, we'd be as chaotic and scattered as the European wolves – and the human death toll would be a lot higher, too. What would the results be if Gerry's plan had succeeded?' Charles asked. Sage would take care of Anna for him. There was no reason for this unholy, driving need to be with her.

'Gerry thought his father would embrace the wolf in order to defeat the Marrok,' Samuel murmured. 'Who is to say that he wasn't right? Maybe he could have saved his father. Is it any more wrong, what he did, than when Da sends you out to kill?'

'And if Gerry was right? If all his plans had borne fruit, if all his father needed was a reason to accept his wolf, and if, with the help of Gerry's new drug, he killed our father and took over as Marrok – then what?' Charles asked. 'Doc was a good man, but how do you think he would be as the Marrok?'

Samuel thought, then sighed. 'He wasn't dominant enough to hold it. There'd have been chaos as the Alphas fought for supremacy, and Gerry tried to kill them off like a jackal in the shadows.' He parked in front of the clinic but made no move to get out. 'But wouldn't you kill for Da anyway? Even if it wasn't important for the wolves' survival in this country? Was Gerry so wrong?'

'He broke the laws,' Charles said. He knew that such things weren't so black and white for his brother. Samuel had never been forced to accept things as they were, not the way Charles had. So he picked through the facts for something that might help.

'Gerry killed innocents. Not for the survival of the pack, but for a thin chance of his father's survival.' He smiled a little as something, the right something, came to him. 'If either you or I kill an innocent to protect Da, and not for the survival of us all, he'd kill us himself.'

Tension left Samuel's shoulders. 'Yes, he would, wouldn't he?'

'Feel better being on the side of angels?' Charles asked, as their father pulled in next to them.

Samuel grinned tiredly. 'I'll tell Da you called him an angel.'

Charles got out and met his father's amused gaze over the hood of Samuel's car with a shrug.

\*   \*   \*

Samuel turned on the lights in the clinic and led the way to one of the examination rooms.

'Okay, old man,' he said. 'Let's see those bullet holes.' But his smile dropped away when Charles started to struggle with his suit jacket.

'Wait,' he said, and opened a drawer to grab a pair of scissors. When he saw Charles's face, he grinned. 'Hey, it's just a suit. I know you can afford to replace it.'

'Fittings,' snarled Charles. 'Four fittings and traveling to the city to be poked and prodded. No, thank you. Da, can you help me get this off and keep your son and his scissors out of reach?'

'Put the scissors down, Samuel,' Bran said. 'I expect that if he managed to get it on, we can get it off without cutting it. No need to growl, Charles.'

With help, sliding out of the jacket was possible, but it left Charles sweating and his father murmuring soothing words. They didn't even ask for his help unbuttoning the shirt when they took it off of him.

Samuel got a good look at the bright pink vet wrap and grinned. '*That* wasn't your idea.'

'Anna.'

'I think I like this little wolf of yours. She may scare a little easy all right, but she faced down Asil without breaking a sweat. And anyone who'd dare to wrap you in pink—'

Samuel was abruptly serious, though, when he cut through the silly pink stuff and saw the holes, fore and aft. He put his face next to the wound and sniffed before rewrapping Charles in something a little less spectacular.

Charles was amused to find he preferred the pink because *she* had put it on him.

'Almost lost you with that one, little brother. But it smells clean and looks like it's healing well enough. Drop the pants now, I want to look at that leg you've been trying not to favor.'

Charles didn't like to take off his clothes – too much Indian in him, he supposed. That and a little reluctance to bare his wounds. He didn't like other people knowing his weaknesses, even his brother and father. He reluctantly skimmed his slacks down.

Samuel was frowning even before he'd gotten the bright green wrap cut off. Once he did, he put his nose against it and jerked back. 'Who cleaned this out?'

'The Chicago pack has a doctor.' There weren't very many doctors who were werewolves. No one but Samuel as far as he'd known: the Chicago pack's doctor was one of the new ones Leo had been hiding from the Marrok. Being around all that blood and flesh made it pretty difficult for a were-wolf to keep his mind on healing – though he'd never noticed it bothering Samuel.

'He was a quack,' growled his brother. 'I can smell the silver from six inches out.'

'Poorly schooled in being a wolf,' corrected Charles. 'None of Leo's new wolves know what to do with their noses – including Anna. I doubt he thought to sniff for silver.'

'And I am under the impression that he was pretty fright-ened of you, too,' said his father from the corner he'd exiled himself to. 'You aren't exactly a good patient.'

'Up on the table,' Samuel told him. 'I'm going to have to do some digging. Da, you're going to have to help him while I do this.'

It hurt a lot worse than getting shot in the first place, but Charles stayed still while Samuel dug and probed. Sweat dripped off his forehead, and the urge to change and attack was held at bay, barely, by his father's hands on his.

He tried not to pay attention to what Samuel was doing, but it was impossible to ignore his running commentary completely. When Samuel shot saline solution through the wound, every muscle in his body tightened in protest, and he hissed.

But – 'Sorry, old man, there's some still in there.' And it was back to probe and cut. He wouldn't let himself cry out, but he couldn't stop the wolf-whine as Samuel flushed the wound with another round of saline – or the groan of relief when Samuel started bandaging, signaling the end of the torture.

While Charles was still down and out, trying to relearn how to breathe, Samuel said, 'I'm not staying here, Da.'

Charles quit worrying about his leg and watched Samuel's face. Samuel wasn't in any shape to be off on his own again. He assumed his father knew that – Bran was better with people than Charles was.

Bran didn't reply, just spun himself slowly, around and around on the little stool in the corner of the room.

Eventually, Samuel was driven to continue – doubtless just as Bran intended. 'I can't stay. Too many people who expect too much here. I don't want to be pack.'

Bran continued spinning himself around. 'So what are you going to do?'

Samuel smiled, a quick flash that made Charles's heart hurt with the lack of genuine feeling behind the expression. Whatever had happened to his brother in the years he'd gone off on his own had changed him, and Charles worried that the change was irrevocable. 'I thought I'd go tease Mercy for a while more.'

His voice and his face said casual, but his body was tense, giving away how much this mattered to him.

Maybe Da hadn't been crazy when he pushed Samuel and Mercy together – though in Charles's experience, romance was neither painless nor restful. Maybe painless and restful weren't what Samuel needed.

'What about Adam?' asked Charles reluctantly. Mercy

lived in the Tri-Cities of Washington state, and the Columbia Basin Pack Alpha wasn't dominant enough to hold his pack with Samuel in it – and Adam had been Alpha too long to adjust to another in that position.

'I already talked to him,' Samuel answered quickly.

'He's all right with you taking over?' Charles couldn't see it. Another wolf maybe, but not Adam.

Samuel relaxed against the counter and grinned. 'I'm not taking over his pack, old man. Just coming into his territory like any other lone wolf. He said he was all right with it.'

The Marrok's face was carefully neutral – and Charles knew what was bothering him. There had been nights that Samuel had to lean pretty hard on pack for stability the past two years, since he'd gotten back from Texas, and a lone wolf had no pack to lean on.

Samuel, like his father – and Asil – was old. Old was dangerous for werewolves. Age had never seemed to touch Samuel much – until he'd come back a few years ago after being gone on his own for over a decade.

'Of course,' continued Samuel, 'he doesn't know I'm moving in with Mercy.'

Adam had a thing for their little coyote, too, Charles suddenly remembered. 'So Mercedes decided to forgive you?'

'Mercy?' Samuel's eyes climbed to the top of his forehead, but for the first time in a long time the shadows left his eyes. '*Our* Mercy, who never gets mad when she can get even? Of course not.'

'So how did you get her to agree to you moving in?'

'She hasn't yet,' he said confidently. 'But she will.' Whatever scheme he had in mind brightened his eyes with their old joie de vivre. His father saw it, too. Charles could see him come to a sudden decision.

'All right,' said Bran abruptly. 'All right. Yes, go. I think it might be best.'

Whatever was wrong with Samuel, being back in Aspen Creek hadn't improved it any. Maybe Mercedes would have better luck. If she didn't kill Samuel – or his father, for that matter, for putting her in the line of fire.

Charles, tired of lying on his face in his underwear, sat up and fought the ringing in his ears that threatened to send him right back down.

'How's it feel?' Samuel asked, back in doctor mode.

Charles closed his eyes and took inventory. 'I don't feel like tearing down the door and leaving anymore, but that might just be because you've already done your worst.'

Samuel grinned. 'Nah. I could torture you for a while longer if I wanted to.'

Charles gave him a look. 'I am doing *much* better, thank you.' He hurt, but felt more himself than he had since he'd been shot. He wondered why the silver poisoning had made him so protective of Anna. He'd never felt anything like it.

'All right.' Samuel looked at Da. 'Not tomorrow or the next day. If he were anyone else, I'd tell you ten days at least, but he's not stupid and he's tough. With the silver gone, he'll heal almost as fast as usual. After Wednesday strangers won't be able to tell there's anything wrong, so he won't be in danger of being attacked because some idiot thinks he can take him. But if you're sending him out to take on a pack by himself, you'll need to send some muscle with him for a couple of weeks yet.'

Charles looked at his father and waited for his judgment. Running around the Cabinets in the middle of winter wasn't his favorite thing – those mountains didn't like travelers much. Still, he could do it better than anyone else his father could call upon here, wounded or not, especially if it wasn't just some rogue wolf but an attack on his father's territory.

Finally, Bran nodded. 'I need you more than I need speed. It'll keep a week.'

'What are you going to do about Asil?' asked Charles. 'Despite the best efforts of the Reverend Mitchell, Samuel, and Doc Wallace, himself – the pack is pretty ugly right now. If you have to kill him, there will be consequences with the pack.'

Bran smiled faintly. 'I know. Asil came to me a month ago complaining about his dreams and started asking me to put him out of his misery again. Not something I'd normally worry about, but this is the Moor.'

'Who is he dreaming of?' Samuel asked.

'His dead mate,' Bran said. 'She was tortured to death. He won't speak of it, though I know he feels guilty because he'd been traveling when it happened. He told me he'd quit dreaming of it when he joined our pack – but it started again last month. He wakes up disoriented and . . . sometimes not where he went to sleep.'

Dangerous, thought Charles, to have a wolf of the Moor's powers out and about under its own direction.

'You think his death can wait?' asked Samuel.

Bran smiled, a real smile. 'I think it can wait. We have an Omega to help him.' His father looked at Charles, and the smile broadened to a grin. 'She's not going to leave you for him, Charles, no matter what Asil says to tweak your tail.'

Charles's living room, though expensively decorated, was still warm and homey, Anna decided. It just wasn't *her* home. She wandered restlessly through the rooms before she finally settled in the bedroom, sitting in a corner on the floor with her legs pulled up, hugging herself. She refused to cry. She was just being stupid: she didn't even really know why she was so upset.

It had bothered her to be sent away – and at the same time she'd felt a rush of relief when she was alone in the truck.

Werewolves and violence, werewolves and death: they went together like bananas and peanut butter. It was better hidden here, perhaps, than it had been in Chicago, but they were all monsters.

It wasn't their fault, the wolves here; they were just trying to live as best they could with this curse that turned them into ravening beasts. Even Charles. Even the Marrok. Even her. There were rules to being a werewolf: sometimes a man had to kill his best friend for the good of all. Human mates grew old while the werewolves stayed young. Wolves like Asil tried to force others to attack them because they wanted to die . . . or to kill.

She drew in a shaky breath. If someone had killed Leo and his mate years ago, a lot of people would still be alive – and she'd be a senior at Northwestern with most of a degree in music theory instead of a . . . a what?

She needed to find a job, something to give her a purpose and a life outside of being a werewolf. Waitressing at Scorci's had saved her in more ways than just providing a paycheck. It's hard to wallow in self-pity while you were working your socks off eight to ten hours a day. Somehow, though, she doubted there was a job here for a waitress.

The doorbell rang.

She hopped up and rubbed her cheeks briskly – but her face was dry. The doorbell rang again, so she hurried out to answer the front door. Contrary, she told herself. She'd been so glad to get a few minutes alone, and now all she wanted was a distraction.

She glimpsed a gunmetal gray Lexus before her attention was captured by the woman who stood on the porch. Her expression was good-natured and friendly. She had dark blond hair neatly French braided and nearly as long as Charles's.

Werewolf, Anna's nose told her.

The woman smiled and held out her hand, 'I'm Leah,' she said. 'The Marrok's wife.'

Anna took her hand and released it quickly.

'Let's go in and chat, shall we?' said the woman pleasantly.

Anna knew Charles didn't like his stepmother – or airplanes, cars, or cell phones for that matter. Other than that, there was no reason for her unease. More to the point, there was no way to refuse her without giving offense.

'Come in,' she invited politely, stepping back.

The Marrok's wife walked briskly past her and into the living room. Once inside, she slowed down, giving the room her entire attention, as if she hadn't seen it before. Anna had the uncomfortable feeling that she was making a mistake, letting the woman in. Maybe Charles didn't let her into his house – she couldn't think of anything else that would account for Leah's fascination with Charles's furnishings.

Unless the whole examination was just a power play designed to make it clear that Anna wasn't nearly as interesting as the room. As Leah explored, Anna settled on the latter explanation – it wasn't a big enough room to demand so much time.

'You aren't what I expected,' Leah murmured finally. She had stopped in front of a handmade guitar that hung on the wall far enough from the fireplace so that the wood would take no damage from the heat. It might have been an ornament, except the fretboard was worn with playing.

Anna didn't say anything or move from her place near the door.

Leah turned to look at her, and there was nothing kind or friendly about her face now. 'He had to scrape the bottom of the barrel for you, didn't he? Had to go all the way to Chicago to find a baby, a woman who wouldn't present any kind of challenge at all. Tell me, do you sit and stay when he tells you?'

The nastiness of the attack made it more personal than just a desire to put a lesser wolf in her place. Leah, for all that she was the Marrok's mate, sounded jealous. Did she want Charles, too?

The door popped open, and a second woman came into the house with a wave of cold air and French perfume. She was tall and slender, like a runway model – she looked expensive. Her brown hair was streaked with gold highlights emphasized by gold glitter brushed across her cheekbones and, more heavily, over a pair of magnificent blue eyes.

Anna recognized her from the funeral – she was not only beautiful, but dramatic, as well, and the combination made her memorable. The other woman shut the door behind her and shed her ski jacket, tossing it casually on the nearest chair. She was still wearing the dark skirt and sweater she'd had on earlier.

'Oh, come now, Leah. "Sit and stay"? You can do better than that, darling.' Her voice was thick and purring with Southern charm. To Anna she said, 'Sorry just to barge in like this, but it sounded like you might need rescuing from our queen bitch.'

'Leave, Sage. This has nothing to do with you,' commanded Leah sharply, though she didn't seem inclined to take offense at the name-calling.

'Honey,' said the woman sweetly, 'I'd just love to do that, but I've got my orders from the boss – a step higher than you.' Bright blue eyes slid over Anna. 'You'd be Charles's Anna. I'm Sage Carhardt. Sorry about the rough welcome, but whatever makes our Charlie happy is sure to get her tail in a twist because our Alpha loves his sons.'

'Shut up,' Leah snapped, and power swept through the room, knocking Sage back two steps.

Funny, Anna would have sworn that Sage was the more dominant of the two . . . then she realized the energy tasted of the Marrok. *A woman takes her place from her mate,* she thought. She knew that, but hadn't understood that the power was real.

'You' – Leah had turned her attention to Anna – 'go sit on the couch. I'll deal with you in a minute.'

A prudent woman would have done it, Anna thought regretfully. The woman she had been a week ago would have cringed, sat, and waited for whatever hell would have followed. The Anna who was Charles's mate, who was Omega and outside of the pack order, lifted her chin, and said, 'No, thank you. I think you'd better leave and come back when my' – three years a werewolf but calling Charles her mate sounded wrong, and he wasn't her husband – 'when Charles is here.' The hesitation robbed her statement of much of its strength.

Sage smiled, her whole face lighting with delight. 'Yes, Leah, why don't you come back when Charles is here? I'd like to see that.'

But Leah wasn't paying attention to her. Her eyebrows lowered in puzzlement as she stared at Anna. 'Sit down,' she said, her voice low and rich with a power that once more slid over Anna and did not touch her.

Anna frowned back. 'No. Thank you.' She thought of something, and before she could stop herself, she said, 'I saw Sage at the funeral, but the Marrok was alone. Why weren't you beside him?'

'He had no business there,' Leah said passionately. 'He *killed* Carter. And now he pretends to *mourn* him? I couldn't keep him from going. He never listens to me anyway, does he? His sons are his advisors, all I am is a replacement for his lost love, the incomparably beautiful, self-sacrificing, Indian *bitch*. I can't stop him, but I won't support him, either.' By the time she was finished, a tear slid down her face. She wiped it off and looked at it and then at Anna with an expression of horror. 'Oh, *God*. Oh, my God. You're one of those. I should have known, should have known that Charles would bring something like *you* into *my* territory.'

She left in a rush of cold air and rattled power, leaving Anna trying not to show how bewildered she was.

'I'd have paid money to see that.' The smile was still spreading on Sage's face. 'Oh, honey,' she crooned, 'I am so glad Charles brought you home. First Asil, then Leah. Life is going to be so much more interesting around here.'

Anna wiped her sweaty hands on the sides of her jeans. There had been something odd about Leah's response, almost as if she'd been compelled to talk.

She swallowed and tried to look calm and welcoming. 'Would you like something to drink?'

'Sure,' Sage said. 'Though knowing Charles, he doesn't have anything good to drink. I'll have some tea and tell you about me. Then you can tell me about yourself.'

Charles had to let his father support him out to the Humvee.

'Yes, well,' said his da with a hint of a growl that told him just how worried Bran had been about him, 'that'll teach you to dodge a bit quicker next time.'

'Sorry,' he apologized meekly as he sat in the passenger seat.

'Good,' said Bran, shutting the door gently. 'Don't let it happen again.'

Charles belted in. He'd probably survive a wreck, but the way his da drove, the belt was useful in keeping him in his seat.

The burning heat that had kept his head from clearing was gone, but he wasn't well yet. Despite the soup Samuel had microwaved and made him eat, he felt as weak as a kitten. Brother Wolf was restless, wanting to find some dark and safe place to heal.

'You're really going to let Samuel be a lone wolf?' he asked once they were under way. The Marrok was possessive and territorial – it wasn't like him to allow someone who belonged to him to wander off. The last time Samuel had left, he hadn't asked permission, just disappeared. It had taken Charles a couple of years to track him down.

'I am so grateful to find something, *anything*, that Samuel wants to do, I'd do some blackmailing if I had to.'

'You haven't already?' He liked Adam, the Tri-Cities Alpha, but it surprised him that the Marrok hadn't had to force his agreement; not many Alphas would welcome a lone wolf as dominant as Samuel into their territory.

'Not yet—' said his da thoughtfully. 'Though I might have to help Samuel a little with Mercedes. She wasn't happy when I sent him back with her.'

'Samuel can get around Mercedes.'

'I hope so.' Bran tapped his fingers on the steering wheel. 'I like your Anna. She looks so delicate and shy, like a flower who would wilt at the first sharp word – and then she does something like facing down Asil.'

Charles pushed his shoulders back in the seat as they caromed around an icy corner and onto the back road to his house. 'You should see her with a rolling pin.' He didn't try hiding the satisfaction in his voice. He was feeling better all the time. His ears had quit ringing, and his control was back. A little food and sleep, and he'd be almost back to normal.

'Would you like to come in?' he asked more out of politeness than desire.

'No.' Da shook his head. 'Send Sage home, too. She'll want to talk, but you and Anna need some time. Anna was pretty upset by the end of the service.'

Charles looked up sharply. 'I thought that was just a reaction to the funeral. Too many people she didn't know.'

'No, there was something more.'

Charles ran through the last of the funeral service, but he couldn't see what his father had. 'I didn't notice anything.'

'Sure you did.' His da gave him a wry smile. 'Why do you think you were so frantic when she drove off?'

'Was it the business with Asil?' If Asil had upset her, maybe Charles would take care of him and his father wouldn't have to bother.

Bran shook his head and laughed. 'I keep telling you I can put thoughts in people's heads, but I can't take them out. I don't know what was bothering her. Ask her.'

Miraculously, they arrived at his door without mishap. Charles slid down out of the Vee and thought for a moment his knees were going to let him slide all the way to the ground.

His father watched him carefully, but didn't offer to help.

'Thanks.' He hated being weak, hated it more when people tried to baby him. At least he'd hated it until Anna.

'Get inside before you fall down,' was all his da said. 'That'll be thanks enough.'

Either moving helped, or the cold, but his knees quit wobbling, and he was walking almost normally again by the time he made it to the front door.

His father honked twice and drove off as soon as his hand hit the doorknob. Charles walked into the house to find Sage and Anna sitting across from each other in the dining room, a cup of tea in front of each of them. But his nose told him that Anna had had another visitor, too.

He'd felt silly when he'd had his father send Sage over. But Leah's scent made him glad of his paranoia. It hadn't taken Leah long to make her first move.

Sage broke off whatever she was going to say to Anna and

gave him a once-over instead. 'Charlie,' she said, 'you look like hell.' She jumped up, kissed him on the cheek, then went into the kitchen and dumped her cup in the sink.

'Thanks,' he said dryly.

She grinned. 'I'm going to go and leave you two honey-mooners to yourselves. Anna, don't you let him keep you here in his cave – give me a call and we'll do a girl's trip to Missoula for shopping or something.' She breezed by and patted Charles's shoulder lightly before exiting.

Anna sipped her tea and looked at him out of dark, un-fathomable eyes. She'd pulled her hair back with a band this morning, and he missed the whiskey-colored curls around her face.

'She called you "Charlie,"' she said.

He raised an eyebrow.

She smiled, a sudden expression that lit her face. 'It doesn't suit you.'

'Sage is the only one who gets away with it,' he admitted. 'Fortunately.'

She stood up. 'Can I get you some tea? Or something to eat?'

He'd been hungry on the way home, but suddenly all he wanted to do was sleep. He wasn't even too keen on walking down the hallway. 'No, I think I'll just go to bed.'

She took her cup into the kitchen and put both cups in the dishwasher. Despite his words, he followed her into the kitchen. 'What did your brother say?' she asked.

'There was still some silver in my calf. So he cleaned it out.'

She glanced sharply at his face. 'Not fun.'

He couldn't help smiling at her understatement. 'No.'

She tucked herself under his arm. 'Come on, you're swaying. Let's get you to bed before you fall down.'

He didn't mind her help at all. She could even have called

him Charlie, and he wouldn't have objected, as long as her side brushed his.

She helped him out of his clothes – he hadn't put his suit jacket back on, so it wasn't too painful. While he got in bed, she pulled down the blinds, shutting out the light. When she started to pull the covers up, he caught her hand.

'Stay with me?' he asked. He was too tired for talk, but he didn't want her alone with whatever his father had noticed was bothering her, either.

She froze, and the scent of her sudden terror tested the control he'd found since his brother had rid him of the last of the silver. There was nothing for him to kill except ghosts, so he controlled the surge of protective rage and waited to see what she would do. He could have released her hand, and he was ready to do so – but only if she pulled away.

He wasn't sure why it had scared her so badly when she'd slept with him last night, until she dropped her eyes to his hand on hers. Someone had grabbed her, he thought, maybe more than once. As rage began to rise in him, she turned her hand and closed it over his.

'All right,' she said a little hoarsely.

After half a second she pulled her hand out of his and sat on the bed to take off her tennis shoes. Still in her jeans and shirt, she lay next to him, her body stiff and unwilling.

He rolled over, giving her his back and hoping that would reassure her that he wasn't going to push her more. He was amused at himself to discover that it wasn't only for her sake that he'd asked her to stay. He felt better with her safe beside him. He fell asleep listening to her breathing.

He smelled good. As his body relaxed in sleep, she could feel the tension slide away from her own. She hadn't been wounded, but she was tired, too. Tired of being on display, tired of trying to figure out what she should be doing, tired of worrying that she had jumped out of one frying pan into a different one.

She had so many questions. She hadn't asked him about his stepmother's strange reaction to her, or about Asil, because he'd looked as if he'd fall asleep as soon as he quit moving – which was pretty much what had happened.

She looked at her wrist, but there were no new bruises there; he hadn't hurt her at all. She didn't know why the feel of his hand around her wrist had caused her to panic – most of the abuse she'd taken her wolf kept hidden from her. But her body retained the memory of a crushing grip and someone shouting at her while he hurt her . . . and she was trapped and couldn't get away from him.

Pulse pounding, she felt the change hovering as her wolf prepared to protect her again. She took in Charles's scent and let it flow over her, soothing the wolf; Charles would never hurt her, both she and her wolf were convinced of that.

After a moment, Anna gathered up her courage and slid under the covers. When he didn't wake up, she slid closer to him, stopping every few minutes as her body kept trying to remind her about how much stronger he was and how much he could hurt her.

Wolves, she knew from overheard conversations, usually craved touch. The men in the Chicago pack touched each other a lot more than was usual for a group of hetero-sexual males. But being close to another wolf had never brought her peace or comfort.

She could always call upon her wolf to help her as she had last night. Then she could tuck herself next to him and breathe in his scent with every breath of air she drew in. But with him asleep, she thought it was a good time to try to work out a few of her issues. The wolf could solve the immediate problem, but Anna wanted to be able to touch him without that.

It was the bed that was making it so difficult – it made her feel vulnerable, made it harder to force herself nearer. Asil had said that Charles didn't like to touch, either. She wondered why not. He didn't seem to mind when she touched him, quite the opposite.

She inched her hand forward until she could feel the sheets warm from his body heat. She rested her fingers on him and her body froze in panic. She was glad he was asleep, so he couldn't see her pull her hand back and tuck her knees over her vulnerable stomach. She tried not to shake because she didn't want him to see her like this: a coward.

She wondered that hope was so much harder than despair.

# 5

Anna methodically rummaged through the cupboards; Charles was going to wake up hungry. Happily, the man had his house stocked for a siege. She thought about Italian – she'd gotten rather good at cooking Italian food – but she didn't know if Charles liked it. Stew seemed a safer choice.

The chest freezer in the basement was full of meat wrapped in white freezer paper, neatly labeled. She brought up a package proclaiming itself to be elk stew meat to begin thawing on the counter. She'd never eaten elk before but assumed that stew meat was stew meat.

In the fridge she found carrots, onions, and celery. Now all she needed were potatoes. They weren't in the fridge or on the counters; they weren't on top of the fridge or under the sink.

Anyone as well stocked as Charles was bound to have potatoes *somewhere* – unless he hated potatoes. She was bent over with her head in a lower cupboard singing softly, 'Where oh where have my little potatoes gone,' when the sound of a cell phone made her jerk her head up and clunk it on the edge of the countertop.

The phone was in the bedroom, so she rubbed her head and waited for Charles to get it, but it just kept ringing.

Mentally shrugging, she tried scenting the potatoes; Charles had told her she didn't use her nose enough. But if there were any around, their scent was camouflaged by the spices and fruit Charles kept in his kitchen.

The phone on the wall began ringing. It was an old rotary phone, made half a century before caller ID. She stared in mounting frustration. This wasn't her home. After ten rings she finally picked it up.

'Hello?'

'Anna? Get Charles for me, please.' No mistaking his voice, it was Bran.

She glanced at the closed door to the bedroom and frowned. If all that noise hadn't woken him up, then he needed to sleep. 'He's asleep. Can I take a message?'

'I'm afraid that won't do. Please wake him up and tell him I need to talk to him.'

The 'please,' she thought, sounded like a courtesy only. It was an order.

So she set the handset down and went to wake Charles up. Before she got to the door, it opened. He'd pulled on a pair of jeans and a sweatshirt.

'Is it Da?' he asked.

When she nodded, he strode past her and picked up the phone. 'What did you need?'

'We have a problem,' Anna heard Bran say. 'I need you . . . and why don't you bring Anna, too. As soon as you can get here.'

Bran needed Charles. Charles was his enforcer, his assassin. He regularly put his life on the line for his father, and she was just going to have to get used to it.

Anna was pulling on her jacket by the time Charles hung up the phone. He retreated to the bedroom and came back with socks and boots in one hand.

'Can you help me with my boots?' he asked. 'Bending over is still a problem.'

She drove like someone who'd never driven over icy roads before. Maybe she hadn't. But she'd driven better this morning, and he didn't think the roads were any worse.

Evidently whatever had been bothering her was still at it.

He could smell her anxiety, but he didn't know what he could do about it.

If his ribs had been in better shape, he'd have taken over for her, but he contented himself with giving her directions. When she fishtailed the truck getting into his da's driveway and he tightened his grip on the door, she slowed down to a crawl. A chalky green SUV with government plates sat right next to the doorway: Forest Service. Whatever his father called about must have something to do with their rogue in the Cabinets, he thought. Maybe there had been another body.

Anna pulled in behind the SUV and parked.

'Do you smell that?' he asked Anna, as she came around the truck to where he waited.

She tilted her head and considered what she smelled. 'Is it blood?'

'Fresh,' he said. 'Does it bother you?'

'No. Should it?'

'If you were like any other wolf, Omega, you'd be getting hungry about now.'

She frowned up at him, and he answered her look. 'Yes, me, too. But I'm old enough it doesn't bother me much.'

He didn't bother knocking on the door; his father would have heard them drive up. He followed the scent of blood into the spare bedroom.

Samuel had been here. He recognized the neat wrapping of the bandages, even if he didn't recognize the middle-aged man who lay on the bed. The man was as human as Heather Morrell, who sat in the chair beside the bed holding his hand.

Heather looked up. He saw the flash of fear on her face but didn't do anything to mitigate it. Frightening people was part of what made him an efficient enforcer for his father. Besides, until he talked to his father and found out what was going on, there wasn't anything he could say to reassure her.

'Where's the Marrok?' he asked.

'He's waiting for you in his study,' she told him.

He took a step back and started to leave when she said his name softly.

He stopped.

'Jack's a good man,' she whispered.

He looked over his shoulder to find her staring at him intently. He could have asked her what she meant – but he needed to talk to his father first.

Anna didn't say anything at all, but he could tell from her rising tension that she had caught some of the undercurrents. Unless he missed his guess, Heather's friend Jack's continued existence was a matter of some doubt.

So he nodded and headed for the study, Anna trailing behind him.

The fire was lit – a bad sign, he knew. Da only lit the fire in here when he was worried. His father was sitting cross-legged on the floor in front of it, staring into the flames.

Charles stopped just inside the door, but Anna slipped by him and put her hands out to the flames. None of them spoke for a while.

Finally, Bran sighed and stood up. He walked slowly around Charles. 'How are you feeling?' he asked as he came around front.

His leg burned, and it was too weak to run on yet. He wouldn't lie to his father, but he didn't have to enumerate his aches and pains, either. 'Better. What do you need?'

Bran folded his arms across his chest. 'I've already killed someone I didn't want to this week, and I don't want to do it again.'

'Heather's Jack needs killing?' Did his father want him to do it? He glanced at Anna a little anxiously as she stepped nearer to the fire and hunched her shoulders, not looking at either of them. He didn't want to kill anyone else this week, either.

Bran shrugged. 'No. If it needs doing, I'll take care of it. I hope to avoid it. He's one of Heather's coworkers. They were out doing some work with Search and Rescue in the Cabinets, looking for another lost hunter, when they were attacked by a werewolf. No question about what it was. Heather saw it clearly. She shot it and drove it off – she's been carrying silver bullets since she identified what killed that other hunter. She told me her friend Jack made the connection between their attacker and the dead hunter while drifting in and out of consciousness on the way here.'

'She brought him here because he's been Changed?'

'She thought he might be, but Samuel says not. Not enough damage, not healing fast enough.' He made one of those gestures he was so good at; this one said, *I'm just an amateur, I'll leave it up to the experts.* 'His problem is apparently more blood loss than wound. And our Heather has been regretting bringing him here ever since Samuel made his pronouncement.'

'What are you considering?' He couldn't help but be aware of Anna listening to every word. Part of him wanted to hide this from her, to protect her from the nastier side of his life. But he refused to have a relationship with his mate based on half-truths and hidden things. Besides, she knew a lot about just how nasty things could be.

Bran leaned back in his chair and sighed. 'If a forest ranger comes out and claims he was attacked by a werewolf – an experienced, respected man like Heather's Jack – people are going to listen. And, before she clammed up, Heather told me that he's a forthright man. If he thinks that there's a danger to others, he's going to trumpet the news as loudly as he can no matter how crazy that truth sounds.'

Charles met his father's eyes. Another time, they might just have been able to let it go. If they killed the problem wolf and there were no more deaths, any fire that the ranger built would go out for lack of fuel. But his father believed that they were going to have to reveal themselves to the public soon – within months. They couldn't afford bad publicity.

To give himself time to see if there was a good way out of the dilemma, Charles asked, 'How did she manage to get him out?' He knew the Cabinets. This time of year a lot of the mountain range was snowshoe or four-footed travel only. Heather wasn't a werewolf, who could carry out a man who weighed more than she did.

'She called her uncle. Tag brought him out.'

Ah. So that was the reason Bran seemed merely reflective instead of closed down, the way he got when there was unpleasant business to take care of.

Charles gave his father a small, relieved smile. 'Drat the brat,' he said. Heather was forty-three, but he'd seen her born and she was still a child to him – and, more importantly, to her formidable uncle, Colin Taggart. 'So if you do as you should, and eliminate this apparently respectable, responsible innocent, you'll have an uprising on your hands?' Tag got pretty protective of those he considered his – and if he rescued this ranger, that was enough to make him Tag's. If Bran decided to eliminate Heather's ranger, he'd have to go through Tag to do it. Thank goodness.

Bran gave a put-upon sigh. 'I'd be happier about it if it didn't mean I had to send you out half-healed to go after some rogue wolf. I'm pretty sure if we eliminate the threat – and show Heather's Jack that his attacker was a criminal as well as a monster – Jack would be willing to hold his peace when we come out. But you'll have to do it soon.

I need that wolf dead before Jack is out of his bed and demanding to be let go.'

'There isn't anyone else you could send?' Anna asked in a low voice.

Bran shook his head. 'This needs to be handled quickly and quietly – and permanently. Charles is the only one I can trust to keep the human authorities in the dark if things get messy.' He smiled a little. 'I can also trust that he won't be joining the killer to go eat humans.'

Charles eyed his father narrowly; he could have put that in less . . . desperate terms. 'The wolf isn't likely to be more dominant than I am, so he can't outbluff me or recruit me,' he explained to Anna. 'And if things get "messy," I have a little bit of magic to cover up the evidence. I'm not as good as a real witch, but we're not likely to get high-level forensics out in the wilderness.'

'That and there isn't another wolf in Aspen Creek who could handle a hunt with a kill like this one without losing it.' Bran turned his gaze to Anna, who was still looking at the fire. 'Killing a sentient being is a bit more addictive than a hunt for rabbits under the full moon. Among other things, Aspen Creek is a sanctuary for wolves who have problems – or who are developing them. The kinds of wolves who could deal with hunting another werewolf are healthy enough to send out in the wide world. I don't usually keep them with me.'

'So all the wolves in your pack are psychotic?' she asked. Charles couldn't tell if she was joking or not. Maybe, he thought, giving the matter a little consideration, she wasn't far off.

Bran threw his head back and gave a shout of laughter. 'Not at all, my dear. But they aren't set up to deal with this. If I thought I was risking Charles's life, then I'd find someone else. He'll be uncomfortable, and it won't be easy – but there isn't a wolf in the country that knows the Cabinets as well as my son. And wounded or not, he can hold his own with any wolf you'd care to name.'

'You're sending him alone?'

Charles couldn't read her voice, but his father obviously saw something that intrigued him. 'Not necessarily.' He got that look on his face when he found a satisfactory solution to a problem that had been troubling him. Charles was just a little too slow to figure out what he'd meant in time to stop him. 'You could go with him.'

'No,' Charles said absolutely, but he had the sinking feeling that he was too late.

Bran didn't pay any attention to him at all. 'It won't be fun. Those are rugged mountains, and you're a city girl.'

'I'm a werewolf,' she said, her chin raised. 'I should be able to handle a little rough country, don't you think?'

'She doesn't have a warm coat, gloves, or boots,' growled Charles a little desperately. He could tell his father had already made up his mind, though he had no idea why Bran was so set upon it. 'This time of year we'll be using snowshoes — and she doesn't have any experience. She'll slow me down.'

His father had such a *look* when he wanted to use it. 'More than the hole in your leg will?' He folded his arms and rocked back on his heels. He must have read the obstinate refusal in Charles's face because he sighed and switched to Welsh. 'You need time to work things out between you. She doesn't trust any of us. Here there are too many people who would ruffle her feathers.' His father was a gentleman, he would never say a word against his mate, but they both knew he was talking about Leah. 'Your Anna needs to know you, and you don't reveal yourself easily to anyone. Take her out and spend a few days alone with her. It'll be good for her.'

'To see me kill the intruder?' Charles bit out in the same language his father used. She knew what he was, but he didn't want to rub her face in it. He'd gotten used to scaring everyone else, he didn't want to scare her, too. 'I'm sure that will just reassure her a whole lot.'

'Perhaps.' There was no give in his father once he'd decided on the proper course, and everyone who tried to stand in his way would be knocked aside as easily as bowling pins.

Charles disliked being a bowling pin. Mutely, he stared at his father.

The old bard smiled a little.

'Fine,' said Charles in English. 'Fine.'

She raised her chin. 'I'll try not to slow you down.'

And he felt as if she'd hit him in the stomach; he'd managed to make her feel unwanted, which hadn't been his intent at all. He had no gift for words, but he tried to mend things anyway.

'I am not worried that you'll slow me down,' he told her. 'Da's right. With this leg, I'm not going to be breaking any speed records. This isn't going to be fun, not in those mountains in winter.'

He didn't want her to see him kill again. Sometimes it was all right, and they fought him, like Leo had fought. But sometimes they cried and begged. And he still had to kill them.

'All right,' Anna said. The tightness in her voice told him that he hadn't undone the damage – but he couldn't lie and tell her that he wanted her with him. He didn't. And though he knew her ability to detect a lie was still pretty hit-and-miss, he wouldn't lie to his mate.

'I understand.' Anna continued looking at the floor. 'It won't be fun.'

'I'll call and have them open the general store,' said Bran. Impossible to see what he was thinking – except that he'd chosen not to help Charles. 'Get her equipped however you think best.'

Charles gave up and turned his attention to something he knew how to do.

'Tell them we'll be there in an hour,' he said. 'I'll need to talk to Heather and Tag first. We'll head out in the morning.'

'Take my Humvee,' Bran said, taking a key off his key ring. 'It'll get you farther in than your truck.'

*Aren't you just being so helpful, now?* thought Charles with frustrated bitterness. Bran couldn't read minds, but the small smile told Charles that he read his son's expressions just fine.

Charles wasn't surprised to see Heather waiting for them. She stood just outside the guest-room doorway, leaning against the wall with her gaze on her feet. She didn't look up as they approached, but said, 'I killed him by bringing him here, didn't I?'

'Did Tag go home?' asked Charles.

Heather looked up at him, examining his face. 'He said he'd had all the blood he could deal with for a while and went downstairs to watch a movie.'

'Your Jack will be fine,' Anna said, apparently impatient with Charles's neutrality. 'Charles and I are going to take care of the werewolf who attacked him – and hopefully that will be good enough that your friend won't freak out to the press.'

Heather stared at his Anna for a moment. 'Thank goodness for someone around here who doesn't act as if information were more precious than gold. You must be Charles's Chicago Omega.'

Anna smiled, but he could tell that she had to work at it. 'Wolves do tend to be secretive, don't they? If it helps, I think your bringing the other wolf – Tag, was it? – was the thing that tipped the balance.'

Heather glanced at Charles out of the corner of her eye,

and he knew she'd hoped for that when she called her uncle for help. Still, he read the truth in her voice when she said, 'He was the only one it occurred to me to call. I knew he'd come just because I asked him.'

Tag was like that.

'Is it possible that we could wake your Jack up?' asked Charles.

'He's been in and out,' she told him. 'He's just sleeping, not unconscious now.'

The human was a little older than Heather. His face was drawn and pale. As soon as Heather woke him up, the scent of his pain filled the room.

*Interesting*, thought Brother Wolf, seeing wounded prey. *An easy meal.*

Charles had never figured out if Brother Wolf was serious or being funny, since they both knew he'd never allow them to feed upon a human. He suspected, uncomfortably, it was somewhere in between. He pushed Brother Wolf back and waited until the human focused on him over Heather's shoulder.

'I am Charles,' he said. 'A werewolf. Heather, I'm not going to eat him.'

Heather backed out from between them though he could tell she wanted to stay there and protect her friend from him.

'Why did you attack us?' Jack whispered, working to get the words out.

'Not me,' Charles said. 'Ask Heather. She'll tell you. We just heard about the rogue a few days ago. I was wounded, and my father wanted to wait until I was healed before sending me after him. We thought that with the hunting season almost over, there was little danger in waiting a couple of weeks.'

'Wounded?'

Charles gritted his teeth to control the wolf – who was wildly disapproving – as he untucked his shirt and turned around. The burn across his shoulders was obvious, but he'd also been smelling his own blood since Anna had fishtailed, so he was pretty sure that the current bandage was blood-stained where it covered the hole in his back.

Neither Jack nor Heather was a threat – but Brother Wolf didn't care; displaying weaknesses for others was wrong. But it was important that Jack understood why they had waited. If they wanted him to keep quiet, Jack had to understand that they were capable of policing their own under normal circumstances.

'Bullet burn,' said Jack.

'And two more that hit,' Charles agreed, retucking his shirt.

'Jack used to be a policeman,' offered Heather. She'd kept her head averted, not looking at him, and Charles appreciated it.

'I had some problems in Chicago a few days ago,' Charles said.

'You'll need to heal,' Jack whispered.

Charles shook his head. 'Not if we have a werewolf out hunting people.' He looked at Heather. 'Was this unprovoked?'

She shrugged. 'I don't know for sure. He just broke cover and attacked. There are a lot of reasons the rogue could have done that – maybe he's set up territory or has something or someone he is guarding. But I barely tagged him, and he ran.'

'So he could be hunting,' Charles concluded. 'We can't afford to wait for him to find someone else to kill.'

Anna followed Charles down the stairs in a hunt for Heather's uncle Tag. The stairs ended in a narrow hall lined with steel doors, complete with thick iron bars ready to be set in the brackets on either side.

On one of the doors, the bar was in use. Whoever was in it had been making noise until they stepped out into the hall. Then he dropped into utter silence, and she could feel him listening to them as they walked by.

She might have asked Charles about it, but his face didn't invite questions. She couldn't tell if he was mad at her or just thinking. Either way, she didn't want to bother him. She had already annoyed him enough. She should have told him that she would stay behind.

But that would have meant he would go alone, wounded, to face some unknown rogue. His father seemed to think he could take care of himself, but he hadn't been there yesterday when Charles had been too hurt to move without help.

If Charles decided he didn't want her, what would she do?

There was a friendlier door at the end of the hall – no locks or bars. But as they approached it she heard the sound of an explosion.

'Hoo yah,' someone said with fierce appreciation.

Charles opened the door without knocking.

Anna had a quick impression of a huge TV screen connected to a variety of sleek black boxes and speakers by a rainbow spiderweb of cables. But what caught her eye and held it was a big man stretched over the back of a couch like a giant house cat. And 'giant' was the word.

Charles was a tall man, but she'd be willing to bet that Colin Taggart was taller by several inches and broader all the way around. Despite the cold, he wore Birkenstock sandals on his big feet, strapped over a pair of heavy wool socks, worn and frayed, but clean. Baggy khaki pants were topped by a tie-dyed T-shirt hanging down past his thighs. His hair was spectacularly orange-red and coarse like a pony's mane; it curled and matted in a hairstyle that might have been a deliberate attempt at dreadlocks or just lack of care. He'd pulled the whole mass away from his face with a substantial, ink-stained rubber band.

He hadn't been at the funeral, she thought. She'd have remembered him. Probably he'd been out getting his niece.

His skin was Celt-pale, with freckles dusted across his cheekbones. With his coloring and blade-sharp features he might as well have 'Irish' tattooed across his forehead. He smelled of some odd incense that overlaid a pleasant earthy tone that she couldn't quite place. He looked ten or fifteen years younger than his niece, and the only thing they had in common was the clear gray of their eyes.

After a quick glance at Charles when they entered the room, Tag turned his attention back to the TV and watched the last of the explosion, then aimed the remote in the TV's general direction and paused the movie.

'So,' he said in a surprisingly high voice. 'You don't smell like death.' It wasn't soprano, but a man that big should rumble like a bass drum. He sounded more like a clarinet. An American clarinet: his accent was pure TV announcer.

'If Heather's friend can keep his mouth shut, he'll be safe enough,' said Charles. 'We're going hunting bright and early in the morning. I'd appreciate if you could do a few things for me.'

The relaxed pose had been a ruse, Anna realized, as the other werewolf sat up and allowed himself to slide down onto the seat of the couch and used that momentum to come all the way to his feet. All with the controlled speed and grace of a *danseur noble*.

Standing, he took up more than his share of the small room. Anna took an involuntary step back that neither of the men appeared to notice.

He grinned, but his eyes were wary and he kept them on

Charles. 'All right then, as long as you're not going to kill my little friend, I'll be happy to oblige.'

'I need you and Heather to figure out exactly where they were when they were attacked – preferably on a map. See if she can pinpoint where the other werewolf victim was – and the grad student's attack, too.' Charles glanced back at Anna, giving her an impersonal once-over before turning his attention back to the other man. 'Then stop by Jenny's and see if she has some dirty clothes, something she's sweated in.'

The wolf's eyes narrowed. 'You're going to do that scent thing? Jenny's Harrison is about your size. You want me to grab something of his for you?'

'That would be good. Meet us back at my house in a couple of hours with the map and clothes.'

'Bran's really not going to execute Heather's man.' It was a statement, but there was a thread of uncertainty in Tag's voice.

Charles shrugged. 'Not right now, anyway. Not unless he decides to do something dumb.'

It didn't sound like reassurance to Anna, but Tag seemed to take it that way.

'Fine, then,' he said with a nod. 'See you in a couple of hours.'

Charles parked the Humvee in front of the house, probably because it wouldn't have fit in the garage. He was stiff and limping by that time, but when Anna tried to take the packages they'd amassed from the store, he just gave her a look. She raised both hands in surrender and let him take everything into the house himself.

He hadn't said anything personal to her since they'd left his father's study.

'Maybe you ought to take someone else,' she said, finally,

as she shut out the winter's cold. 'Another wolf might be more helpful.'

Charles turned and looked her in the face. He slowly took off his gloves while he stared at her, his eyes black in the dimmer light of the house. She met his gaze for a breath or two before dropping her own eyes.

'I don't like bringing reinforcements to a kill,' he told her after a moment. 'More wolves tend to muck things up.'

He took off his coat and set it deliberately across the back of the couch. 'This is a werewolf who is killing humans. It might be a plant, someone who intends to stop my father's plans to carefully unveil our presence to the humans. I've been considering that, though, and I don't think that's what is going on. It would take a desperate person to go into the Cabinets this time of year when Missoula or Kalispell are so much more convenient – and more sure to attract attention. Running around in the wilderness in the winter is too much trouble, I think, for a planned attack or a hardened killer. I think we're dealing with a rogue. Someone who doesn't know much and is trying to keep out of sight. Dangerous, as he has so ably demonstrated, but nothing I can't handle.'

'I'll do as you tell me,' she told the floor, feeling stupid for insisting on going and heartsick because he didn't want her with him. 'I'll try not to get in the way.'

'I would not have considered taking you without my father's insistence,' he said slowly. 'And I would have been wrong.'

His words took her totally by surprise. Half-suspecting that she'd mistaken him, she looked up to see his sheepish smile.

'I think,' he said, 'that even a werewolf deserves a chance, don't you? A rogue hiding out in the Cabinets is pretty desperate, and there's a good chance he's as much a victim as the dead hunter and Heather's Jack. But even if I knew for certain he was only moonstruck, out of control through no fault of his own – I'd still probably have to kill him if I went alone. But look at what you did with Asil this morning. If you come with me, we just might be able to give this wolf a chance.'

She weighed his words, but he seemed serious. 'You aren't angry? Don't wish I'd kept my mouth shut?'

He closed the distance between them and kissed her. When he pulled back, her heart was pounding – and not from fear. She could see his pulse beat in his throat, and he smelled of the crisp snow-covered outdoors.

'No,' he murmured. 'I don't want you to keep quiet.' He ran a light finger down her jaw. 'Tag will be here in a minute. Let me fix some food before he does.'

Though he was obviously still sore and claimed not to be much of a cook, he fixed the stew she'd been organizing when Bran had called. He did send her for the potatoes, which he kept hidden downstairs in a fifty-pound gunny-sack, but otherwise seemed perfectly content to do all the work himself.

She watched him cook, and the euphoria induced by his kiss faded. Here was a man used to being alone, used to depending upon himself. He didn't need her, but she was completely dependent on him.

While they waited for the stew to simmer, he turned on the small TV in the dining room, the only TV she'd seen in his house, and a cheery woman in bright lipstick told them it was going to be colder tomorrow. He sat down, and she took a chair on the opposite side of his oak dining table.

'As local as we get,' Charles told her as they watched the forecast. 'Missoula and Kalispell.'

She wasn't sure why she didn't just let the TV fill in the time.

'Your father told me I should ask you about contacting

my family,' Anna said, while the anchor woman introduced a story on local Christmas shopping over the weekend: retail sales down from last year, internet sales up.

'Is there some problem with them?'

'I don't know. I haven't talked to them since shortly after I Changed.'

'You haven't talked to your family for three years?' He frowned at her. Then a look of comprehension came to his face. 'He didn't let you.'

She looked at him a moment. 'Leo said that any human even suspected of knowing about us would be killed. And any prolonged contact with my family would be adequate cause to eliminate them. At his suggestion, I took offense at something my sister-in-law said, and haven't spoken to them since.'

'Idiot,' snapped Charles, then shook his head at her. 'Not you. Leo. Why should . . . I suppose he thought your family would object to the treatment you were receiving and cause a fuss – and I hope he was right. If you'd like to call them right now, go ahead. Or when we get back from this, we can fly to your family for a visit. Some things are best explained in person.'

Her throat closed up, and she tried to blink back sudden, stupid tears. 'I'm sorry,' she managed.

He leaned toward her, but before he could say anything, they both heard the unmistakable sound of a car driving up.

Without knocking, Tag blew in like a warm blizzard, a paper bag in one hand and a map in the other.

'Here you are.' He stopped and sniffed appreciatively. 'Tell me there's enough for a third. I've been out on your errands and haven't gotten a bite to eat.'

'Help yourself,' said Charles dryly since Tag had dumped his burdens and was already in the kitchen.

Anna heard him rattle around for a moment, then he was

striding into the dining room with three bowls of stew in his big hands. He set one in front of Anna, one in front of Charles, and one at a place next to Charles. Another visit and he had three glasses of milk and spoons. He handled the dishes with a professionalism that made Anna think that he'd spent some time as a waiter somewhere.

He kept an eye on Charles while he sat down, and Anna realized something that she'd been noticing subconsciously for a long time. Despite his casual demeanor, Tag was afraid of Charles, just as Sage had been, for all of her 'Charlie's.'

There was a reason, Anna thought, that Bran's mate Leah had come when Charles was occupied elsewhere, why she'd been unfamiliar with the house. Anna had recognized Heather's fear, but Heather was human. The others were all werewolves, and their reaction was in subtle body movements like Tag's watchfulness.

Tag took a couple of slurping spoonfuls that Anna's mother would have slapped his hand for, then told Charles, 'She needs feeding up. Leo never could take care of the gifts he was given.'

'He wasn't given Anna,' Charles said. 'He hunted her down.'

Tag's face stilled. 'He Changed an Omega by *force*?'

Shock, Anna thought, and disbelief.

'No,' Charles said. 'He hunted her, and when he found her, he set a mad-dog after her.'

'It'd take a crazy bastard to attack an Omega. You kill him?' The casualness of Tag's voice was a little too studied to be real.

'Yes.'

'Leo, too?'

'Yes.'

'Good.' Tag looked at her without meeting her eyes, then started in on his dinner again.

'I wasn't an Omega then,' Anna said. 'I was just a human.'

Charles gave her a small smile and started eating his stew. 'You were born an Omega, just as my father was dominant and dangerous from his first step, human or not. Being a werewolf just brings it out, and age puts a polish on it.'

'She doesn't know that?' Tag asked.

'Leo did his best to keep her ignorant and under his thumb,' Charles told him.

Tag raised a fuzzy red eyebrow at her. 'I never liked Leo, too damned underhanded by half. It's hard for a dominant wolf to hurt a submissive wolf if he's sane – our instincts tell us to protect them. Omega is one step beyond that. When you were human, you'd have been even more fragile than you are now – just ups those instincts. A human Omega is something that it takes a mad-dog – a wolf crazy with killing – to attack.'

Both men had started eating again before Anna decided to challenge his statement. 'None of the wolves in Leo's pack seemed to have trouble hurting me.'

Tag's eyes met Charles's, and she remembered that there was a wolf underneath the brash cheeriness.

'They should have had trouble,' said Charles harshly. 'If Leo hadn't pushed, they'd have let you be.'

'None of them stood up to him?' Tag asked.

'He'd weeded out the strong ones already,' said Charles. 'The others were under his thumb. They jumped when he told them.'

'You sure you killed him?' asked Tag.

'Yes.'

Tag's eyes skated across her again. 'Good.'

As soon as everyone finished eating, Tag got the map he'd brought and spread it over the table.

Anna collected the dirty dishes and cleaned up after dinner, while Charles and Tag mumbled over the map.

'All the attacks were within a few miles of Baree Lake,' Tag was saying when she came back to peer over Charles's shoulder. 'There's an old cabin in those woods, I've heard, but I've never seen it.'

'I know where it is. That's a good thought.' Charles tapped a finger on the map. 'It's about there, not too far from the attacks. I haven't been out to Baree Lake in the winter for ten or fifteen years. Is this still the best road?'

'That's the way I went in today. You'll want to take this little road here.' He pointed, but Anna didn't see a road.

'That's right,' Charles said. 'Then we'll hike over Silver Butte Pass.'

'Now the first attack was up this way.' He pointed slightly to the left of Baree Lake. 'Right on the trail you'd take in the summer, a couple of miles from the lake. The dead hunter was found here, about a half mile from the lake. He probably came up Silver Butte Pass, like you're going to. We had a lot of snow in late October; by hunting season the old forest service road would already have been impassable. Heather and Jack were attacked here, about four miles from their truck. I was able to drive another quarter of a mile closer – you'll be able to do a little better in the Humvee.'

Charles hummed, then said, 'It could be a lot worse; we could be trying to get to Vimy Ridge.'

Tag laughed shortly. 'Which is where you'd hole up. I wouldn't want to be the wolf hunting you in that place in high summer, let alone midwinter. Happily, Baree Lake is as close to a Sunday hike as you can find in the Cabinets.' He looked at Anna. 'Not that it's easy, mind you. But possible. The only way to get to Vimy Ridge in this weather is by chopper. The snowpack can get over fourteen feet deep in some of the high country – you'll see some of that up there in the ridges above Baree. You go with this old lobo, and you listen to him, or – werewolf or not – we'll likely be out searching for your dead body.'

'No need to frighten her,' Charles said.

Tag leaned back in his chair and smiled. 'She's not afraid. Are you, dovie?' And in that last phrase she heard a hint of an Irish lilt, or maybe Cockney. She might have a good ear, but she needed more than three words.

Tag looked at Charles. 'Heather had to hike to the high stuff to call me. Most of the Cabinets still don't get cell phone reception. I parked here' – he tapped the map – 'and walking around a little bit I found cell reception. I suggest you park near there and leave the cell phones in the car.'

Charles gave him a sharp look. 'In case this isn't a lone rogue?'

'You and Bran aren't the only ones who can add two and two,' Tag said. 'If this is an attack of some sort, you don't want to let the villains track you by that neat little locator cell phones carry nowadays.'

'I hadn't intended to,' agreed Charles. He leaned over the map again. 'Just from the attacks, it looks as though Baree is the center of his territory – but . . .'

'Once the snow falls, you aren't going to get a lot of people east or west of the lake,' Tag said decisively. 'Baree Lake could as easily be the edge of his territory as the center.'

Charles frowned. 'I don't think we'll find him to the east. If he was in that big valley on the other side of the ridge above Baree, the natural lay of land would set his territory through the valley and maybe up to Buck Lake or even Wanless, but not over the ridge. That climb out of the valley to Baree is next to impossible this time of year, even on four feet.'

'West then.'

Charles ran a finger from Baree to a couple of smaller lakes. 'I think we'll go to Baree and head west, over to the

Bear Lakes through Iron Meadows and back over this mountain to the Vee. If we haven't encountered him by then, I think it will be time to call out the whole pack.'

'You'll have to be careful, there's a lot of avalanche country up by the Bears,' Tag said, but Anna could hear the approval in his voice.

They spent some time planning a route that would take four days to hike. When they were finished, Tag touched his hand to his forehead as if tugging an invisible hat.

'Pleased to meet you, ma'am,' he told Anna. Then, without giving her time to say anything, he left as precipitously as he had come.

## 6

'He likes you,' Charles said, folding up the map.

'How do you know that?' she asked.

'People he doesn't like, he doesn't talk to.' He started to say something else but lifted his head and stared at the door with a frown instead. 'I wonder what he wants?'

Once he drew her attention to it, she heard the car drive up, too.

'Who?' she asked, but he didn't answer, just stalked out to the living room, leaving her to follow hesitantly.

Charles jerked open the door, revealing the wolf from the funeral. Asil. He had one hand raised to knock on the door. In the other he had a bouquet of flowers, mostly yellow roses, but there were a few purple daisy-looking things, too.

Asil adjusted to the reordering of his entrance smoothly, gifting Anna with a smile while avoiding Charles's gaze. It might have been the proper and right response to an obviously irritated wolf who was more dominant — except that his eyes were boldly locked on Anna's.

'I brought an apology,' he said. 'For the lady.' He was, Anna noticed, almost a foot shorter than Charles, just an inch or two taller than she was.

Standing next to Charles, she could see that their coloring was similar, dark skin and darker eyes and hair — black in artificial light. But the skin tone was different and Asil's features were sharper, Middle Eastern rather than Native American.

'For *my* lady,' said Charles, slowly, with a growl in his voice.

Asil smiled brilliantly, the wolf apparent in his face for an instant before it faded. 'For *your* lady, of course. Of course.' He handed the flowers to Charles, then said silkily, 'She doesn't carry your scent, Charles. Which is why I made the mistake.' He glanced up at Charles slyly, smiled again, then turned on his heel and all but ran back out to his car, which was still idling.

Anna hugged herself against the rage that she sensed sweeping through Charles, though she didn't understand why Asil's last words had made him so angry.

Charles shut the door and silently held out the flowers. But there was a savageness in the tension of his shoulders and body language that made Anna put her hands behind her and take a step back. She didn't want anything to do with Asil's flowers if they made Charles so angry.

He looked at her then, instead of through her, and something tightened further in the muscles of his face.

'I'm not Leo or Justin, Anna. These are yours. They're pretty, and they smell good, better than most flowers. Asil has a hothouse, and he seldom cuts the blooms from his plants. He was grateful for your help this morning, or he wouldn't have done it. That he could goad me when he gave them to you just made him a little happier. You should enjoy them.'

His words didn't match the fury she could smell – and even though Charles thought she didn't use her nose very effectively, she *had* learned to believe it over her ears.

She couldn't manage to meet his eyes, but she did take the flowers and walk into the kitchen, where she stopped. She had no idea where she could find a vase. She heard a noise behind her, and he set down on the counter one of the pottery jars from the living room.

'This should be about the right size,' he said. When she just stood there, he filled the jar with water himself. Slowly

– so not to spook her, she thought – he took the bouquet, trimmed the ends of the flowers, and arranged them with more expedience than art.

The sudden shock of fear, followed by shame for her cowardice, took her a while to work through. And she didn't want to compound matters by saying the wrong thing. Or doing the wrong thing.

'I'm sorry,' she said. Her stomach was so tight it was hard to breathe. 'I don't know why I get so stupid.'

He stopped fussing with the last flower, a purple one. Slowly, so she had plenty of time to back away, he put a finger under her chin and tilted it up. 'You've known me less than a week,' he told her. 'No matter how it sometimes feels. Not nearly enough time to learn to trust. It's all right, Anna. I am patient. And I won't hurt you if I can help it.'

She looked up, expecting black eyes and met golden instead. But his hand on her was still gentle, even with the wolf so close.

'It is I who am sorry,' he said. Apologizing, she thought, as much for the wolf as for his brief display of temper. 'This is new to me as well.' He grinned at her, a flash and gone. The oddly boyish expression managed to make him look sheepish despite a certain sharp edge. 'I'm not used to being jealous, or having so little control. It's not just the bullet wounds, though they don't help.'

They stood there for a while more, his hand under her chin. Anna was afraid to move for fear she would provoke the rage that kept his eyes wolf yellow or do something that might hurt him the way she'd hurt him with her flinch. She didn't know what Charles was waiting for.

He spoke first.

'My father told me that there was something bothering you when you left the church this morning. Was it Asil? Or was it something else?'

She took a step sideways. He let her go, but his hand slid from her face to her shoulder, and she couldn't make herself take another step and lose that touch. He was going to think she was a neurotic idiot if she didn't get a better grip on herself. 'Nothing was bothering me. I'm fine.'

He sighed. 'Six words and two lies. Anna, I'm going to have to teach you how to smell a lie, then you won't try them with me.' He pulled his hand back, and she could have cried out at the loss – even though part of her wanted nothing to do with him. 'You can just tell me you don't want to talk about it.'

Tired of herself, Anna rubbed her face, puffed out her cheeks, then blew like a winded horse. Finally, she lifted her gaze and met his again. 'I'm a mess,' she told him. 'Mostly I don't know what I'm feeling or why – and I don't want to talk about the rest yet.' Or ever. To anyone. She was a stupid coward and had gotten herself into a situation in which she was helpless. When they got back from the mountains, she would find a job. With money in the bank and something constructive to do, she could get her bearings.

He tilted his head. 'I can understand that. You've been uprooted from everything you know, dumped among strangers, and had all the rules you knew pulled out from under your feet. It's going to take some time to get used to. If you have questions about anything, just ask. If you don't want to talk to me, you can catch my father or . . . Sage? You liked Sage?'

'I liked Sage.' Did she have any questions? Her irritation at herself transferred to him just fine, even though she could tell he didn't mean to treat her like a child. He wasn't trying to be patronizing, only trying to help. It wasn't his fault that his soothing tone put her teeth on edge – especially when she could tell he was still angry about something. Did she like Sage? As if he had to go out and find friends for her.

She was tired of being afraid and uncertain. He wanted questions. She'd been taught not to ask – werewolves keep secrets as if they were gold in a vault. Fine.

'What was it that Asil said that pushed you from irritated to enraged?'

'He threatened to try to take you from me,' he told her.

She thought over the conversation, but didn't see it. 'When?'

'It takes more than this attraction between us to seal us together as a mated pair. When he told me that you didn't smell of me, he was telling me he knew we haven't completed the mating – and that he considered you fair game.'

She frowned at him.

'We haven't made love,' he told her. 'And there's a formal ceremony under the full moon that cements our bonds – a wedding. Without those, Asil can still make a play for you without retaliation.'

Yet another thing she'd never heard before. If she had been ten years younger, she'd have stamped her foot. 'Is there a book?' she demanded hotly. 'Something I can look up all this stuff in?'

'You could write one,' he suggested. If she hadn't been watching his mouth she'd never have seen the flash of humor. He thought she was funny.

'Maybe I will,' she said darkly, and turned on her heel – except there was nowhere to go. His bedroom?

She shut herself in the bathroom and turned on the shower to hide any sounds she made, a second barrier because the door she'd locked behind her wasn't enough.

She stared at herself in the mirror, which was beginning to fog. The blurring reflection only enhanced the illusion that she was looking at a stranger – someone she despised for cowardice and uncertainty, who was good for nothing except waiting tables. But that was nothing new; she'd hated herself ever since she'd been turned into this . . . this monster.

A pathetic monster at that.

Her eyes looked bruised, her cheeks pale. She remembered her panicked retreat from Charles's brief show of temper, how she'd helplessly apologized for forcing her company upon him in this expedition. And she despised herself even more. She didn't used to be like *this*.

It wasn't Charles's fault.

So why was she so *angry* with him?

Viciously, she stripped out of her clothes and stepped into the steaming shower, feeling some relief as the pain from too-hot water sliced through the stupid tangle of emotion she was wallowing in.

And in that moment of clarity she understood why she'd been so upset by the end of the funeral – and why she was so upset with Charles in particular.

She hadn't realized how much she wanted to be human again. She knew it was impossible, knew nothing could undo the magic that had been forced upon her. But that didn't mean she didn't want it.

For three years she'd lived with monsters, had been one of them. Then Charles had come. He was so different from them; he'd given her hope.

But that wasn't fair. It wasn't his fault part of her had decided that she wasn't just leaving her pack, she was leaving the monsters behind.

He'd never lied to her. He'd told her he was his father's enforcer, and she hadn't doubted it. She'd seen him fight, seen him kill. Even so, somehow she'd managed to convince herself that Montana would be different. That she could be normal, could be *human*, every day except for the full moon – and even that would be different here, where there was room to run without hurting anyone.

She should have known better. She *did* know better.

It wasn't Charles's fault that he was a monster, too.

It had been easy to lay the destruction of the Chicago pack's holding cell on the silver poisoning. But tonight, confronting Asil, he'd shown her that he wasn't any different than any other male werewolf: angry, possessive, and dangerous.

She'd allowed herself to believe that it was just the Chicago pack. That the mess Leo and his mate had created was the reason for the terrible thing the pack had been.

She'd wanted a knight in shining armor. A voice of reason in the madness, and Charles had provided it for her. Did he know that was what she'd been looking for? Had he done it deliberately?

As the water matted her hair and ran into her eyes and over her cheeks like tears, her last question clarified and answered her greatest fear: of course Charles hadn't set out to be her knight deliberately, that was just who he was.

He was a werewolf dominant enough to back down the Alpha of a pack without the resources an Alpha could draw on. He was his father's hit man, an assassin feared even by other members of his own pack. He could have been like Justin: ravening and cruel.

Instead, he knew the madness of what they were and managed, not just to overcome it, but to use it, to make something better. She had the sudden picture of his beautiful hands gently arranging *flowers* while his wolf craved violence in the worst way.

Charles was a monster. His father's assassin. She wouldn't allow herself to believe a lie again. If Bran had told him to, he would have killed Jack. Killed him knowing that the human was only a victim, that he was probably a good man. But it wouldn't have been casual. She'd seen the relief that had flowed over him when Bran had found an alternative to killing the human.

Her mate was a killer, but he didn't enjoy it. Looking at it clearly, she was a little awed at how he'd managed to be so civilized and still meet the demands of who and what he was required to be.

The water was cooling off.

She shampooed her hair, enjoying the way the soap rinsed away so easily; Chicago water was much softer. She conditioned her hair with something that smelled of herbs and mint, recognizing the scent from Charles's hair. By that time, the water was starting to become uncomfortably cold.

She took a long time combing out the tangles without looking at the mirror and concentrated on feeling nothing. She was good at that, having perfected it over the past three years. When she faced him again, she didn't want to be a whiney, scared-of-herself nitwit again. So she needed to control her fear.

She knew one way to do that. It was a cheat, but she gave herself permission, if only for tonight because she'd made such a fool of herself by hiding in the bathroom.

She stared at herself in the mirror and watched her brown eyes pale to silvery blue and back. So much and no more. The strength and fearlessness of the wolf wrapped around her and gave her calm acceptance. Whatever happened, she would survive. She had before.

If Charles was a monster, it was by necessity rather than choice.

She dressed in the yellow shirt and jeans, then opened the bathroom door slowly.

Charles was leaning, still golden-eyed, against the wall opposite the door. Other than his eyes, he was the epitome of relaxation – but she knew to believe the eyes.

She'd checked her own with a glance at the mirror before she'd opened the door.

'I've decided you need to know about Asil,' he told her as if there had been no break in their conversation.

'All right.' She stayed in the doorway, the steamy room warm at her back.

He spoke slowly and distinctly, as if he were pulling his words out from between his teeth. 'Asil's not really his name, though it's what most people call him. They also call him the Moor.'

She stiffened. Uneducated about her own kind she might be, but she'd heard of the Moor. Not a wolf to mess with.

He saw her reaction, and his eyes narrowed. 'If there is a wolf in this world older than my father, it might be Asil.'

He seemed to be waiting for her to comment, so she finally asked, 'You don't know how old Asil is?'

'I know how old he is. Asil was born just before Charles Martel, Charlemagne's grandfather, defeated the Moors at the Battle of Tours.'

She must have looked blank.

'Eighth century AD'

'That would make him . . .'

'About thirteen hundred years old.'

She leaned against the wall herself. She'd seen the weight of age on him, but she'd never have guessed how many years.

'So, the one you're not sure of is your father?' Thirteen hundred years was a long time.

He shrugged, the answer clearly didn't matter to him. 'Da's old.' He turned his amber eyes away from her face.

'Asil came here a while ago, fourteen – fifteen years, to ask my father to kill him. He settled for the promise of death instead – as soon as my father determines that he really is crazy.'

Charles gave her a small smile. 'Asil didn't have any problem with my father being his Alpha. But he had a problem with me being more dominant – which is why I think Da might be older than Asil. My relative youth is a thorn in his paw.'

Anna worked it out in her head. 'Didn't he talk about his Alpha in Europe? And I don't remember him being an Alpha in any of the stories about him.' There were a lot of stories about the Moor. He was almost a folk hero – or villain – among the wolves.

'Being an Alpha isn't easy,' Charles said. 'It's a lot of responsibility, a lot of work. Some of the older wolves get pretty good at concealing what they are from others – that's one of the reasons Alphas don't like old wolves moving into their packs. Asil's plenty dominant.' He smiled again, but this time it was more a baring of teeth. 'He'd been here a couple of months when I stepped between him and one of our nonwolf residents. He wasn't amused to find out that I really was more dominant than him.'

'He could submit to your father because he is older, to his other Alphas – because he wasn't really submitting. But, to have to obey you when you are so much younger and not even an Alpha . . .'

Charles nodded. 'So he digs at me, and I ignore him. Then he digs harder.'

'That's what tonight was?' Anna could see it. 'He was using me to dig at you.'

Charles tilted his head in a gesture that was more wolf than human. 'Not entirely. The Moor had a mate, but he lost her a couple of hundred years ago. She died before my time, so I never met her, but she was supposed to have been an Omega, like you.' He shrugged. 'He has never said so in my hearing, nor has my father. There are a lot of stories about the Moor, and until I saw his reaction to you at Doc's funeral, I'd put that one down to pure hype along with a lot of other legends connected to his name.'

The warmth from her shower was gone, and the coolness

of the water it left behind was chilly – or maybe it was recalling the way the old wolf had stared into her eyes in the church. 'Why did his reaction make you rethink it?'

She could tell from Charles's nod that she'd asked the right question. 'Because when he noticed what you are, he stopped bothering you to get to me – and became interested in you.' He took a deep breath. 'That's why he brought you flowers. That's why, when he threatened to try to woo you away from me, I had such a hard time controlling myself – because I knew he really meant it.'

She decided to think about that later and keep her attention on the conversation so she didn't push him inadvertently. 'Why are you telling me about Asil? Is this a warning?'

He looked away, his face back in its blank mask. 'No.' He hesitated, then said in a softer voice, 'I don't think so. Did you feel as if it was a warning?'

'No,' she said finally, as frustrated by the careful information that avoided something she could almost sense – the something that was keeping his wolf so close.

Before she could ask what was troubling him, he told her, face averted, as fast as he could get the words out. 'He wanted *you* to know that if, in the time before the first full moon, you decide not to have me – you could pick him instead.' Even with his head turned away, she could see the edge of his bitter smile. 'And he knew he could force me to tell you so.'

'Why did you tell me?' Her voice was soft.

He turned back to her. 'It is your right to know that although we are compatible, you can still refuse me.'

'Can you refuse me?'

'I don't know. I've never heard of a binding happening backwards like ours – Brother Wolf chose you, chose your wolf and left me to follow him. But it doesn't matter – I don't want to refuse you.'

The wolf gave her a clearer head in some things, but her wolf had chosen this man and made no bones about what she thought of choosing another. She was forced to push her back a little so she could get a clear sense of what he was trying to tell her.

'And I would do this *why*?'

Did he want her to refuse him?

Her throat was dry as dust. She, human and wolf both, craved him like a junkie just as she craved all the things he seemed to promise: safety, love, hope – a place to belong. She rubbed nervous hands on her thighs as if that would soothe her tension away.

He whispered, 'I hope you don't. But you need to be told of your options.' His hands were fisted on his thighs.

She smelled something sharp in his scent that she hadn't before. Damn Leo that he'd left her crippled by ignorance. She'd give her right hand to know what Charles was feeling, to know when he was telling the truth – and when he was just trying not to hurt her.

He was waiting for her answer, but she didn't know what to say.

'Options.' She tried for neutrality. What did he want of her?

Evidently not neutrality. His fists opened and closed twice. Nostrils flared wide, he looked at her with hot yellow eyes.

'Options,' he growled, his voice dropping so that she felt the rumble of it in her chest. 'Asil will spread the word, and you'll be buried in wolves who would be pleased to lay their lives down for the chance of being your mate.'

His whole body was shaking, and he leaned harder against the wall as if he were afraid he was going to try to tackle her.

She was failing him. He was losing control, and she wasn't helping, didn't know how to help.

She sucked in another deep breath and tried to let it wash away all of her insecurities. This was not a man who wanted to give up his mate. This was a man trying to do the honorable thing – and give her a choice, no matter how much it cost him. That was right, and the knowledge steadied her, and she let her wolf come back and give her the confidence she needed.

For her he shook like an alcoholic in need of his gin, because he felt she needed to know her options, no matter how his wolf felt about losing his mate. Her knight, indeed.

Her wolf didn't like seeing his unhappiness, wanted to bind him to her, *to them*, with chains and love until he could never think of leaving them again.

'Well then,' she said as briskly as she could manage under the weight of that revelation, a weight that made her feel warm and safe while her eyes burned with tears. Mostly her voice just sounded husky. 'It's a good thing there's something we can do to fix that little loophole right now.'

He stared at her, as if it was taking him a while to process what she had said. His pupils contracted, and his nostrils flared wide.

Then he launched himself off the wall and was on her, his big body pushing her with frightening intensity against the door frame. His mouth was nipping frantically on her neck. He hit a nerve that sent lightning down her spine, and her knees buckled.

As a rich musky scent rose from his skin, he lifted her into his arms in a jerky, uncoordinated move that banged one of her shoulders painfully against the door. She kept still as he stalked down the hallway with her; she'd seen a wolf in rut before and knew better than to do anything but meekly submit.

Except, she couldn't help touching his face to see if the

ruddy tinge on the edge of his cheekbones was warmer than the rest of him. And then her fingers had to linger on the corner of his mouth, where a small quirk so often betrayed the amusement he otherwise kept hidden.

He turned his head a little and closed his teeth on her thumb, hard enough she felt it, but not so hard that it hurt. Maybe, she thought, as he opened his mouth and released her thumb only to move his head and catch her ear in the same light nip that sent a wave of heat from her earlobe that scorched unexpected places, maybe she was in rut, too. She certainly had never felt like this before.

Even though there was no one else in the house, he closed the door with a foot, enclosing them in the dark warmth of his bedroom.

Their bedroom.

He didn't so much set her down on the bed as fall down with her, making urgent sounds that were more wolf than human while he did so. Or maybe it was her making the noise.

He ripped her jeans, getting them off, and she returned the favor. Feeling the heavy cloth part under her hands was satisfying. More satisfying was the warm silk of his skin under her fingers. His hands were callused, and though he was obviously doing his best to be gentle, they sometimes bit in as he struggled to move her where he wanted without lifting himself off of her.

With her wolf in ascendance, he didn't frighten her in the least. The wolf knew he would never hurt her.

She understood his passion because she felt the same way: as if nothing was more important than the touch of her skin to his, as if she'd die if he left her. The fear and her usual distaste of sex – even the wolf wasn't bestial enough to do more than endure what those others had done – was so far gone it wasn't even a memory.

'Yes,' he told her. 'Soon.'

'Now,' she ordered him sharply, though she wasn't sure exactly what she wanted him to do.

He laughed, and it rattled rustily in his chest. 'Patience.'

Her shirt ripped and her bra soon followed it, then it was her naked skin against his flannel shirt. Frantically, she tugged and pulled at it, popping buttons and half-choking him before she got it off. Her urgency seemed to inflame him, and his hands jerked her hips into position.

She hissed as he came into her carefully, and far too slowly. She bit him on the shoulder for the care he took. He growled something thickly that might have been words – or might not have. But only when he was satisfied that she was ready did he release the control he'd been holding on to by fingertips ever since Asil had left.

The first time was fast and hard, but not too fast for her. They'd barely finished when he began again. This time he set the pace and held her back when she would have forced him to speed up.

She'd never felt anything like it, or like the satisfied peace that followed her into sleep. She could get used to feeling like this.

She woke up in the middle of the night to the unfamiliar sound of the furnace turning on. Sometime in her sleep, she'd rolled away from him. He lay on the other side of the bed, his face relaxed. He was snoring lightly, almost a purr, and it made her smile.

She reached a hand toward him. Then stopped. What if she woke him up, and he was angry with her for disturbing his sleep?

She knew, *knew* he wouldn't care. But her wolf, who'd helped her through all they had done to her, who had let her enjoy his touch, was sleeping, too. Anna curled up on her side of the bed, finally rolling until her back was toward him. Her restlessness must have disturbed him, because suddenly he surrounded her, spooning in behind her. The sharp alarm she felt at the suddenness of his move woke the wolf.

He threw one arm over her waist. 'Go to sleep.'

With the wolf to protect her, she could give herself over to the way his body heat made her muscles and bones relax into the rightness of his presence. She gripped his wrist with one hand and held it over her belly before letting sleep grab her in return. Hers.

When he woke her up, it was still dark outside.

'Morning,' he said, his voice a rumble under her ear. It felt so good that she pretended to still be asleep.

He wrapped his arms around her and rolled over quickly twice. She managed a squawk as they rolled right off the bed. She landed on top of him, and her hip on his belly vibrated with his silent laughter.

'Like that, is it?' she muttered, and, before she remembered his wound, touched her fingers into the muscle just under his ribs.

'Quit that,' he mock growled, catching her hand so she couldn't tickle him again. He sounded amused, so she must not have hurt him. 'We have a job to do, woman, and you're slowing us down.'

'Hah,' she said, and wiggled her hip a little, making them both very aware that he'd probably agree to a delay in getting ready. Then she wiggled a little more determinedly and slipped free of his hold.

'Morning,' she told him. 'Time to go.' And she sauntered naked out of the room and down the hall to the bathroom.

\*　　\*　　\*

He watched her go with appreciation, aware of the spark of true happiness that lit his soul. She didn't look beaten at all this morning – and that little sashay of her hips told him that she was feeling pretty good.

He'd made her feel like that. How long had it been since he'd been the cause of someone else's happiness?

He lay back on the floor to enjoy it until his conscience kicked in. They had a job to do. The sooner they got out into the woods, the sooner they'd be back and free to play.

To that end, he tested out his wounds experimentally. They still hurt, and they'd slow him up a little – but as Samuel promised, he was feeling much better. And not just because of Anna.

He was dressed and collecting his winter gear from the closet – he'd have to find someplace else for all of it, so Anna could have half of the closet – when Anna came back in. She was wrapped in a bath sheet, having evidently lost some of her boldness while in the bathroom.

He decided to give her some space. 'I'll fix breakfast while you get dressed.'

Her eyes were on the floor as she skittered past him. If his ears hadn't been sharp, he wouldn't have heard her nervous 'Okay.'

But nothing would have kept the rank smell of fear from his nose. He froze where he stood and watched her keep her shoulders rounded in submission as she knelt on the floor by her box of clothes.

He tried to open the link between them . . . but it was no stronger than it had been yesterday or the day they'd first met.

He'd never been mated before, but he knew how it was supposed to work. Love and sex would bind human to human – then the wolf would choose, or not. Since their wolves had already clearly chosen, since he'd chosen, he'd been sure that their lovemaking would seal the bond.

He looked at her, the knobs of her spine and the sharp edges of her scapula showing clearly that she needed to gain some weight – a visible sign of the suffering that she'd endured in Leo's pack. The worst scars didn't show: werewolves seldom scar on the outside.

He opened his mouth to say something, but stopped. He needed to think some things through before he even knew what to ask. Or of whom to ask it.

He fed her breakfast, only a little closer to the answers he sought. But even distracted, it amused him how much satisfaction he got from watching her eat – even though she wouldn't look up at him.

'We're going to get a little later start than I expected,' he said abruptly as he rinsed his pans and stored them in the dishwasher. 'I've got a few things I'd like Heather to do – and I have another person I need to see.'

She was still in the dining room, but her silence spoke for her. She was still too intimidated by him or by last night to ask. For which he was grateful. He had no intention of lying to her – but he didn't want to tell her who he was going to talk to, either.

'I can finish the dishes then,' she offered.

'All right.' He dried his hands and stopped to kiss the top of her head – a quick, passionless kiss that shouldn't add to her tension, but still enough for Brother Wolf to feel satisfied that she knew who he belonged to. He was hers, whether she wanted him or not.

Heather was still at his father's, sleeping in the room next to her partner's. Bleary-eyed and tired, she made some

calls and some suggestions and arranged things to his satisfaction.

Which left him with only one more person to track down.
Fortunately, he'd found that most people were easy to locate
at five thirty in the morning.

## 7

Asil dreamed of a familiar house: small and well made, a house built for a warm climate with carefully tended orange trees by the door. He paused beside the bench positioned where it would catch the shade of the biggest orange tree when the sun was high in the sky. Running a finger over the clumsy jointing between two of the pieces that formed the back, he wished vainly that he'd had time to fix it.

Even knowing what was going to happen, he couldn't make himself stay by the bench, not when Sarai was in the house. He had no photographs of her, nor had any of the paintings he'd attempted ever done her justice. His artistic talent was plebeian at best. Only in his dreams did he see her.

He took only a step and found himself in the main room. Half shop, half kitchen, the room should have been utilitarian, but Sarai had hung baskets of plants and painted flowers on tiles set in the floor, making it feel welcoming. On the worktable set near the back of the room, his mate ground a cinnamon stick into fine powder with quick, competent hands.

He sucked in the air to savor her scent, flavored by the spice she worked with, as it often was. His favorite was Sarai and vanilla, but Sarai and cinnamon was almost as good.

She was so beautiful to him, even though he knew that others might not find her so. Her hands were callused and strong, with nails trimmed blunt. The short sleeves of her dress showed muscles gained both from her work and from running as a wolf in the wilds of the nearby hills. Her nose, which she despaired of, was long and strong, with a delightful little bump on the end.

He reached out, but he could not touch her. 'Sarai?'

When she didn't turn to him, he knew that it was going to be the bad dream. He fought to get free as hard as one of his wild-wolf cousins with a foot caught in an iron trap might have, but he couldn't chew off his leg or force the trap that held him here. So he had to watch, helpless, as it happened again.

Hooves rang on the cobbles he'd laid outside the door to keep the mud at bay. Sarai clicked her tongue lightly on the roof of her mouth in displeasure – she had always hated to be interrupted in the middle of mixing her medicines.

Still, she set her mortar and pestle aside and brushed off her apron. Irritated or not, he knew she would never turn up her nose at business. Money was not to be sneezed at, not in those days. And, for Sarai, there should have been nothing dangerous about a visitor.

A human soldier was no threat to a woman who was also a werewolf, and Napoleon's rise to power had interrupted that other, more dangerous, warfare. The few witchblood families left in Europe had quit killing each other at last, forced instead to protect themselves from the ravages of more mundane fighting. She had no reason to worry, and she couldn't hear Asil's frantic attempts to warn her.

The door opened, and for a moment, Asil saw what Sarai had.

The woman in the doorway was slight-boned and fragile-looking. Her dark hair, usually unruly and curly, had been tamed and rolled into a bun, but the severe style only made her look younger. She was sixteen years old. Like Sarai she was dark-haired and dark-eyed, but unlike her foster mother, her features were refined and aristocratic.

'Mariposa, child,' Sarai exclaimed. 'What are you doing

riding so far on your own? There are soldiers everywhere! If you wanted to visit, you should have told me and I'd have sent Hussan out for you to keep you safe.'

It had been two hundred years since anyone had called him by that name, and the sound of it hurt his heart.

Mariposa's mouth tightened a little. 'I didn't want to bother you. I'm safe enough.' Even in his dreams he knew that her voice sounded odd, unlike herself: cold. His Mariposa, his little butterfly, had been emotional above all, dancing from anger to sullenness to sunshine with scarcely a breath between.

Sarai frowned at her. 'No one is safe enough. Not in these times.' But even as she scolded her, she enfolded the girl she'd reared as her own in her arms. 'You've grown, child, let me look at you.' She took two steps back and shook her head. 'You don't look well. Are you all right? Linnea promised she'd take care of you . . . but these are dark times.'

'I'm fine, Sarai,' Mariposa told her, but the girl's voice was wrong, flat and confident – and she was lying.

Sarai frowned at her and put her hands on her hips. 'You know better than to try lying to me. Has someone hurt you?'

'No,' Mariposa replied in a low voice. Asil could feel her power amass around her, different now than it had been when they'd first sent her to her own kind for training. Her magic had been wild and hot, but this power was as dark and cold as her voice had been.

She smiled, and for a minute he could see the child she'd once been instead of the witch she had become. 'I've learned a lot from Linnea. She taught me how to make sure no one can ever hurt me again. But I need your help.'

The doorbell woke Asil up before he had to watch Sarai die again. He lay in his empty bed and smelled the sweat of terror and despair. His own.

\*   \*   \*

Charles made himself at home on the old wolf's porch swing and tried to lose himself in Indian time. It was a trick he'd never quite mastered – his grandfather had always grumbled that his father's spirit was too strong within him.

He knew Asil had heard the doorbell, he could hear the spit of the shower – and he'd never expect Asil to do him the courtesy of a quick appearance, especially when his visit had come at such an ungodly early hour in the morning. He and Anna would be getting a late start, but their prey wasn't a fish who was best caught in the dawn's light anyway. And this was more important to him than catching a rogue, even if that rogue was killing people.

He'd almost gone to his father instead of Asil after he'd talked to Heather at Bran's house. It was only the scent of his stepmother that kept him from knocking on Bran's bedroom door. This morning, Charles hadn't been up to the dance Leah would insist he perform. When she had driven him to being rude (and she would), his father would intervene; no one, not even one of his sons, was allowed to be disrespectful of the Marrok's mate. And then there would be no discussion anyway.

So he went to the only other person who might understand what had happened, why the bond between him and Anna wasn't complete: Asil, whose mate had been an Omega. Asil, who disliked him almost as much as Leah did, though for different reasons.

Brother Wolf thought that there might be a lot of amusement to be found in this morning's talk. Amusement or fighting – and the wolf relished them both.

Charles sighed and watched the fog of his breath disappear into the cold air. It might be that this was a wasted effort. Part of him wanted to give it more time. Just because the slow part of the mating process, when wolf accepted wolf, had been finished almost as soon as he first saw her, didn't mean that the other half would work so fast.

But something told him that there was more wrong than time alone could solve. And a man who had a werewolf for a father and a wisewoman for a mother knew when he ought to listen to his intuition.

Behind him, the door opened abruptly.

Charles continued to rock the porch swing gently back and forth. Encounters with Asil usually started with a power play of some sort.

After a few minutes, Asil walked past the porch swing to the railing that enclosed the porch. He hopped on it, one bare foot flat on the rail, leg bent. The other fell carelessly off to the side. He wore jeans and nothing else, and his wet hair, where it wasn't touching his skin, began to frost in the cold, matching the silver marks that decorated his back; Asil was one of the few werewolves Charles had seen who bore scars. The marks sliced into the back of his ribs where some other werewolf had damaged him – almost exactly, Charles realized, where his own wounds were. But Asil's scars had been inflicted by claws, not bullet holes.

He posed a lot, did Asil. Charles was never sure if it was deliberate or only an old habit.

Asil stared out at the woods beyond his house, still encased in the shadows of early morning before dawn, rather than looking at Charles. Despite the recent shower, Charles could smell fear and anguish. And he remembered what Asil had said at the funeral: that he'd been dreaming again.

'Sometimes my father can ward your sleep,' Charles murmured.

Asil let out a harsh laugh, bowed his head, and pinched his nose. 'Not from these. Not anymore. Now why are you waiting here for me this fine morning?' He made a grandiose gesture that took in the winter, the cold, and the time of day in one overblown movement of his arm.

'I want you to tell me about Omega wolves,' Charles said.

Asil's eyes widened with comically exaggerated surprise. 'Problems so soon, pup?'

Charles just nodded. 'Anna barely knows about being a werewolf. It would be helpful if at least one of us knew something about the Omega aspect.'

Asil stared at him for a moment, and the superficial amusement faded. 'This might be a long conversation,' he said at last. 'Why don't you come in and have a cup of tea?'

Charles sat at a small table and watched as Asil busied himself preparing tea as if he were a Japanese geisha, where every movement was important and exact. Whatever his dream had been, it had really thrown Asil from his usual game of playing the crazy werewolf. It was only seeing him like this that let Charles understand just how much of a performance most of Asil's histrionics were. This was what happened when Asil was truly disturbed: overly precise movements, fussing about nonsense and things that didn't matter.

It didn't make him any less crazy or any less dangerous, but he saw at last the reason his father had not put Asil out of everyone's misery, yet.

'Tea never tastes quite as good here,' the Moor said, setting a delicate china cup edged in gold in front of Charles. 'The altitude doesn't let the water get hot enough. The best tea is brewed at sea level.'

Charles lifted the cup and took a sip, waiting for Asil to settle down.

'So,' the other werewolf said, taking a seat opposite Charles, 'just what do you need to know about Omegas?'

'I'm not sure.' Charles ran a finger around the edge of the cup. Now that he was here, he was reluctant to expose the problem with Anna to a man who wanted to be his enemy.

He settled on, 'Why don't you start by telling me exactly how they differ from submissive wolves.'

Asil raised his brows. 'Well, if you still think that your mate is submissive, you're in for a real surprise.'

Charles couldn't help but smile at that. 'Yes. I deduced that right off.'

'We who are dominant tend to think of that aspect of being a werewolf as rank: who is obeyed, who is to obey. Dominant and submissive. But it is also who is to protect and who is to be protected. A submissive wolf is not incapable of protecting himself: he can fight, he can kill as readily as any other. But a submissive doesn't feel the need to fight – not the way a dominant does. They are a treasure in a pack. A source of purpose and of balance. Why does a dominant exist? To protect those beneath him, but protecting a submissive is far more rewarding because a submissive will never wait until you are wounded or your back is turned to see if you are truly dominant to him. Submissive wolves can be trusted. And they unite the pack with the goal of keeping them safe and cared for.'

He took a sip of tea and snorted. 'Discussing this in English sounds like I am talking about a sexual relationship – ridiculous.'

'If Spanish suits you better, feel free,' offered Charles.

Asil shrugged. 'It doesn't matter. You know about all of this. We have our submissive wolves here. You know their purpose.'

'When I met Anna, for the first time in my life, the wolf slept.'

All casualness erased, Asil lifted his eyes from his tea to look at Charles. 'Yes,' he whispered. 'That's it. They can let your wolf rest, let it be tranquil.'

'I don't always feel like that around her.'

Asil laughed, spitting tea in his cup, at which he gave a

rueful look, then set it aside. 'I should hope not, not if you are her mate. Why would you want to be around someone who emasculated you that way all the time? Turn you from a dominant to submissive by her very presence? No. She doesn't have to soothe you all the time.'

He wiped his mouth with a cloth napkin, which he tidied and set beside his cup. 'How long has she been a werewolf?'

'Three years.'

'Well then, I expect it's all just instinct right now. Which means that if you aren't feeling the effects all the time, either she feels very safe with you – or you've got her so unsettled she doesn't have any peace to share.' He grinned wolfishly. 'Which one of those do you think it is? How many people *aren't* afraid of you at some level?'

'Is that what bothers you?' asked Charles, honestly curious. 'You aren't afraid of me.'

Asil stilled. 'Of course I am.'

'You don't have the good sense to be afraid of me.' Charles shook his head and went back to his questions. 'Omegas serve much the same purpose in a pack as submissives, but more so, right?'

Asil laughed, a genuine laugh this time. 'So now do I defend myself by saying "of course I have enough sense to be afraid"?'

Charles, tired of the games, just sighed. 'There is a difference, between submissive and Omega. I can feel it, but I don't know what it means. Instead of following anyone's orders, she follows no one's. I get that.'

'An Omega has all the protective instincts of an Alpha and none of the violent tendencies,' Asil said, clearly grumpy at being pulled back to the point. 'Your Anna is going to lead you a merry chase, making sure that everyone in her pack is happy and sheltered from anything that might harm them.'

That was it. He could almost pull the strings together. Anna's wolf wasn't violent . . . just strong and protective. How had Anna's adjustment to being a werewolf – and to her systematic abuse – affected the wolf?

Thinking aloud, Charles said, 'Pain makes a dominant more violent while it does just the opposite to a submissive wolf. What happens to an Omega who is tortured?' If he'd been thinking of Asil rather than Anna, he would never have put it in those terms.

The Moor's face paled and his scent fluctuated wildly. He surged to his feet, knocking over his chair and sending the table spinning until it hit the far wall and crashed onto its side.

Charles rose slowly and set his teacup on the counter nearest him. 'My apologies, Asil. I did not mean to remind you of things best forgotten.'

Asil stood for a moment more, on the verge of attack, then all the taut muscles went lax, and he looked tired to the depths of his soul. Without a word he left the room.

Charles rinsed out his cup and turned it upside down in the sink. He was not usually so careless. Asil's mate had died, tortured to death by a witch who used her pain and death to gain power. For all that he found Asil irritating – especially his latest and most effective method of torment: Anna – he'd never deliberately use Asil's mate's death to torment him. But more apologies would accomplish nothing.

He muttered a soft plea for blessing upon the house, as his mother's brother had taught him, and left.

Anna was glad Charles drove this time. The icy roads gave him no apparent concern, though they slid around enough that she dug her nails into the handle conveniently located above the window of her door.

He hadn't said much to her this morning after he'd

returned from consulting with the forest ranger. His eyes were distant, as if the teasing, gentle man she'd woken up with was gone.

Her fault.

She hadn't expected to feel so much after she'd sent her wolf to sleep while she showered. They both needed the break after maintaining that fine balance, and she had just expected that the wolf would take that gut-wrenching *need* with her. Anna had never felt like that for any man – and it was both embarrassing and scary.

She'd showered for a long time, but it didn't go away. She might have been all right if it hadn't been for his playfulness this morning . . . but she doubted it. Feeling that strongly left you so very vulnerable, and she was afraid she couldn't keep it from her face.

When she had to leave the shower, she'd been so worried about not letting him know how she felt she hadn't noticed how her awkward shyness . . . and fear . . . had affected him. He'd come up with his own conclusions – all the wrong ones, she was afraid.

She glanced at his closed-off face. She had no idea how to fix this. The motion brought her face closer to her borrowed clothing. She lifted her arm and sniffed the sleeve of the shirt she wore and wrinkled her nose.

She didn't think he'd taken his eyes off the road, but he said, 'You don't stink.'

'It's just weird to smell human,' she told him. 'You don't think much about what you smell like until it changes.'

Before they'd left, he'd taken the clothes that Tag had brought over and had her put on the dirty T-shirt and donned a similarly dirty sweatshirt. Then he'd run his hands over her in a manner not quite impersonal, chanting in a language she'd never heard before, at once nasal and musical. When he was finished, she smelled like the human woman whose shirt she was borrowing, and he smelled like a human man.

He had a little magic, he'd told her, gifts inherited from his mother. She wondered what else he could do, but it felt impolite to ask. She'd never been around anyone who could actually work magic before, and it left her a little more in awe of him than she already was. The Chicago pack had stories about magic-using people, but she'd never paid much attention to them; she'd had more than enough to deal with just being a werewolf.

She fanned her fingers out on her thigh and stretched them.

'Quit worrying,' Charles told her, his voice gentle enough, but without the inflection that meant he was talking to her, not someone he'd just picked up off the street. She'd just realized this morning that he'd been talking to her differently – because he stopped.

The snow-covered mountains, taller than the Sears Tower, rose on either side of the road, as cold and solid as the man beside her. She wondered if it was his business face she was dealing with. Maybe he locked down everything in preparation for killing someone he didn't know in order to protect his pack – maybe it wasn't her fault.

She was uncomfortable and frightened – and trying to hide it. Asil had told him that everyone was frightened of him. He wished he knew what he could say to fix it. To fix something, anything.

After leaving Asil's, he'd turned the problem over in his head – problems, really, though he was starting to believe that they were two aspects of the same issue. The first was her fear of him this morning – or maybe fear of what they'd done with so much pleasure the night before. He had enough experience to ensure that she *had* enjoyed it. It hadn't seemed to bother her until she went to the shower. Since there were no monsters lurking in his house (besides him), he was pretty sure that it was something in Anna that had changed.

One of the danger signs they watched for in a new werewolf was a sudden change in personality or mood that seemed to have no obvious cause, an indication that the beast was gaining control of the human. If Anna hadn't been three years a werewolf and Omega besides, he'd have thought her beast was taking control.

Maybe the opposite was true. Omegas have all the protective instincts of an Alpha, Asil had said. Could her wolf have taken over last night?

His father taught the new wolves that the wolf was part of them, just a series of urges that needed to be controlled. It seemed to help most of them in the transition phase. Scaring them by telling them there were monsters living in their heads would certainly not help them gain the control necessary to be allowed out into the wide world.

It was a useful fiction that, as far as Charles could see, sometimes was true. His father, for instance, seemed to blend seamlessly from wolf to human and back. But most of the wolves who lasted eventually came to refer to their wolves as separate entities.

Charles couldn't remember *not* knowing that there were two souls that caused his single heart to beat. Brother Wolf and he lived together harmoniously for the most part, utilizing the specialized skills of either for the sake of their goals. It was Brother Wolf who hunted, for instance – but if their prey was human or werewolf, it was always Charles who made the kill.

He'd seen over the years that the werewolves whose human and wolf were almost entirely separate – like Doc Wallace – usually didn't survive long. Either they attacked someone older and stronger than they – or Charles had to kill them because they had no control over the wolf.

A werewolf who survived learned to integrate human and wolf and leave the human in the driver's seat for the most part; except for when the moon called, when they were very angry . . . or when they were hurt. Torture a dominant, and the wolf came to the forefront. Torture a submissive, and you were left with the human.

With all the protective instincts of an Alpha and none of the aggression . . . and three years of abuse, maybe Anna's wolf had discovered a way to protect her. That would explain why Leo had never succeeded in breaking her.

Maybe when his aggression last night had frightened her, her wolf had come out to play. And maybe that was why their human souls hadn't bonded the way their wolves had.

Except that couldn't be right, because he'd have noticed if the wolf was in ascendance. Even if he somehow had overlooked her eyes changing from brown to pale blue, he'd never have overlooked the change in her scent.

Charles was pretty sure it was something that Leo had done to her, or had someone else do to her, that was the root of his current troubles.

Getting angry wasn't going to help with Anna, that much he could be certain of. So he pulled his thoughts from various ways he might torture Leo, who was, after all, already dead, and tried to think his way to a solution.

Charles was better at frightening people than removing their fear. He wasn't sure how to discuss this morning, last night, and the way their mating had not been completed without making things worse.

If matters didn't improve, he'd go to his father for advice . . . or Heaven help them all, Asil, again. If he explained everything in plain words, Asil might laugh at him, but he was too much a gentleman to leave Anna in trouble.

That left him with one more task. She needed to know that the other males would still feel free to offer themselves, because that was dangerous to her and anyone around him when someone tried.

And because she had the right to know that she might be able to accept one of those other males – at least that seemed to be Asil's opinion. Charles thought that once their wolves had bonded it was permanent – but he didn't know anyone who'd had that happen *before* their human selves had bonded. Maybe Anna could find someone who didn't frighten her as he seemed to.


The Humvee was an artificial oasis, Anna thought. The heated leather seats and climate-controlled cabin seemed out of place in the endless expanse of still, frozen forest.

The dark, almost black, stands of evergreen trees stood out in stark contrast to the snow. Occasionally, roads, distinguishable more by the way they cut through the trees than by any vehicle track, branched off the highway they were traveling. As their road narrowed into a white scar between steep hills crowding in on both sides, she wondered if 'highway' was the right word for it.

'Our mating bond didn't become permanent last night,' he said out of the blue.

She stared at him, feeling the familiar flutter of panic. What did that mean? Had she done something wrong?

'You said that all we needed to do was . . .' She found she couldn't quite get the next few words out. In the cold light of day they sounded so crude.

'Apparently I was wrong,' he told her. 'I assumed since we'd gotten the most difficult part of being mated out of the way, all we needed was consummation.'

She didn't know what to say to that.

'It is probably better,' he said abruptly.

'Why?' She hadn't known if she'd be able to get out a word, but she sounded, to her ears, merely curious, none of the panicky feeling that had closed over her at his words evident in her voice.

But she didn't come anywhere near the disinterested neutrality he brought to his voice. 'The main reason I didn't want to bring you with me today was that I didn't want you to see me kill again, so soon. But I've been my father's assassin for a hundred and fifty years; I don't suppose that will change. It's only fair that you see me clearly, when the hunt is upon me, before you choose.'

The steering wheel creaked under the force of his grip, but his voice was still calm, almost detached. 'In my father's pack there are a number of wolves who would worship the ground you walk upon. Wolves who are not killers.' He sucked in a little air and tried to give her a reassuring smile – but it stopped somewhere short of effective since all it did was show strong white teeth. 'They are not *all* psychotic.'

He was trying to give her away again.

She looked at his white-knuckled hands – and suddenly she could breathe again. Telling her that she could look else-where was ticking him off, breaking that freaky calm he'd held since breakfast. She thought of his possessive rage last night and felt confidence steady her heart; he wanted her – no matter how stupid she'd been this morning. She could work with that. She couldn't stay embarrassed about how much she wanted him forever, right? A week or two, and she should be over it. And a year or so afterward, the strength of what she felt for him wouldn't scare her so badly, either.

Feeling better, Anna resettled herself in the Vee's roomy seat so she could get a good look at him. What had he been talking about before he offered to give her up?

Being a killer.

'I know about killers,' she told him. 'Leo's pack had Justin.

You remember him, right? He was a killer.' She tried to find a way to make the distinction clear. 'You are justice.' That wasn't the way – it sounded stupid.

'"A rose by any other name . . ."' he said, angling his face away from her.

She took a deep breath to see if her nose could help her read what he felt, but all she could smell were the two strangers who had donated their clothing. Maybe she just didn't know how to work her nose – or maybe he was better at controlling himself than most people were.

Charles was a careful man. Careful about what he said and careful of the people around him. One night in his bed, and she knew that. He *cared*. Cared about her, about his father, even about Heather's Jack. Her stomach settled as she gathered the hints and actions into a coherent picture. How hard, she thought, must it have been for a man who cared so deeply to learn to kill, no matter how necessary it was?

'No,' she said firmly. Ahead of them, and off to the right, a series of spectacular peaks thrust defiantly into the heavens. Their snowcapped summits, unfettered by trees or vegetation, gleamed in the sun so brightly that even through the tinted windows they dazzled her eyes and called to her wolf. This was a place a werewolf could *run*.

'A killer is just a murderer,' she told him. '*You* follow rules, carry out justice and – try not to hate yourself for being good at your job.'

Her assessment, following the debacle of last night, took Charles totally by surprise. He looked at her, but she'd shut her eyes and snuggled down for a nap – his Anna who had been terrified of him not five minutes ago. Sleeping was not the usual reaction people had when he pointed out that he killed people.

The road they were following had more tracks than usual

for this time of year – probably because of the Search and Rescue people. He hoped he and Anna wouldn't run into any of them.

The calls he'd had Heather make this morning should result in no more untrained volunteers and amateurs out in the woods, at least. He had wanted to limit the damage the rogue wolf might do as best they could.

Heather had, at his request, pointed out that the man they were looking for had been missing for too long. They were probably only looking for a body, so there was no sense in risking additional lives. She'd told them about Jack – though she'd blamed a cougar – and pointed out that a storm front was moving in.

The few searchers remaining were concentrating their efforts about twenty miles west of Jack's encounter with their rogue wolf – near where the missing man had left his truck, well away from any of the places the rogue werewolf had made his appearances. Charles and Anna shouldn't encounter the searchers at all.

They were climbing now. The Humvee's tires made a continuous crunching, moaning sound as they cut through the deepening snow. To the left, he occasionally caught a glimpse of the frozen creek, though mostly it was hidden by the thick brush choking the valley bottom. To the right, high-tension electrical wires ran between stark metal towers down a barren swath cut clear through the forest. Those wires, and the occasional need to maintain them, were the only reason for the lonely service road they followed.

Heat poured out of the Vee's defroster. The warmth of the vehicle's interior made the winter lands they drove through seem almost surreal, something separate from him. And as much as he usually hated that particular effect, he'd spent too much time in the snow and cold on horseback or on foot to dismiss the advantages of driving in as far as they could.

The climb got steeper, and he slowed the Vee to a crawl as it bounced and rolled over rocks and holes hidden by the snow. The wheels started to slip, so he slowed down and pushed the button to lock the axles. The resultant noise startled Anna awake.

Sometimes the extra width of the Humvee wasn't as useful as it might have been. He was forced to put his left tires up on the bank to keep his right on the road, such as it was. The resultant tilt of the vehicle made Anna take one glance out her window and close her eyes, shrinking in her seat.

'If we roll, it probably won't kill you,' he offered.

'Right,' she said in a snippy tone that delighted him for its lack of fear – at least fear of him. He wished he could tell how much of that was the wolf and how much Anna. 'I shouldn't worry about a few broken or crushed bones because I probably won't die.'

'Maybe I should have brought Tag's old Land Rover,' he told her. 'It's almost as good in the rough country, and it's a lot narrower. But it has a rougher ride, an unreliable heater, and doesn't quite get up to highway speed.'

'I thought we were going to a wilderness area,' she said, her eyes still tightly shut. 'Aren't motorized vehicles restricted?'

'That's right, but we're on a road, so it's okay.'

'This is a road?'

He laughed at her wry tone, and she made a rude gesture at him.

They topped the rise, and he managed to creep through the trees another couple of miles before it became too rough to continue. Someone had been out here in snowmobiles – probably the Search and Rescue – but most of the automobile tracks had disappeared a mile or more ago. The last set ended ten feet from where they sat – Tag's, he assumed.

*   *   *

'How long are we going to be out?' Anna, adjusting the pack, asked, as they left the truck.

'That depends upon our quarry,' he told her. 'I've packed for four days – we'll be walking in a loop that'll lead us back here. If he doesn't find us by then, we'll quit trying to be human and go hunting him.' He shrugged. 'This mountain range covers over two thousand square miles, so it might take us a while to find him if he's trying to hide. If he's guarding his territory and thinks we're human intruders, he'll hunt us and save us a lot of time and effort.'

Anna had been on a couple of camping trips with her family in Wisconsin while she was growing up, but nothing as isolated as this. The air froze her nostrils together when she breathed in too hard, and the tips of her ears got cold before Charles had pulled her hat down farther on her head.

She loved it.

'We need to keep our speed down,' Charles told her. 'So that we look as human as we smell.' But the pace he set seemed pretty brisk to her.

Walking with snowshoes wasn't as bad as she'd expected. When he'd tightened her straps to his satisfaction, he'd told her that the old beavertails or bearpaws had been almost as much trouble as help. The new snowshoes were one of the few inventions of modern life that he seemed to thoroughly approve of.

She had to scramble a bit to keep up with him. If this was slow, she wondered if he normally ran when he was in the woods, even in human form. None of his wounds seemed to be bothering him much, and there had been no fresh blood on his bandages this morning.

She pulled her thoughts away from why she'd had such a good look at the bandages this morning. Even so, she couldn't help but look at him and smile, if only a little to herself. Out in the snow and covered with layers of clothing and coats, she felt insulated from the terrors of intimacy and could better appreciate the good parts.

And Charles had a lot of good parts. Under his coat she knew exactly how broad his shoulders were and how his skin darkened just a little behind his ears. She knew that his scent made her heart beat faster, and how his weight anchored her rather than trapped her beneath him.

Traveling behind him, safe from that penetrating gaze that always saw more than she was comfortable with, she could look her fill.

He was graceful, even in the snowshoes. He stopped now and then and stared into the trees, looking, he told her, for any motion that was out of place. In the woods, the wolf was closer to the surface. She could see it in the way he used his nose, sometimes stopping with his eyes closed to take in a breath and hold it. And in the way he communicated with her more with gestures than words.

'We'll see more game down here than we will later, when we get higher,' he told her after pointing out a buck who was watching them warily from behind some heavy brush. 'Most of the bigger animals stay down here, where it's not as cold and there's more food and less snow.'

And that was all he said for a long time, even when he stopped and gave her a bit of this or that he expected her to eat, mutely holding out jerky or a small package of freeze-dried apples. When she refused a second handful of the latter, he'd tucked them in her pocket.

Though she was usually more comfortable with conversation than silence, she felt no impulse to break into the sounds of the forest with words. There was something here that demanded reverence – and it would have been hard to talk and pant at the same time anyway.

After a while, she began to find the atmosphere a little

spooky, which was pretty funny considering that she was a werewolf. She hadn't expected the trees to be so dark – and the shadow of the mountain made it seem much later than it really was.

Sometimes she felt a little déjà vu. It took her a while to pin it down, but then she realized it felt like walking down in the Chicago Loop. Though the mountains were taller than the skyscrapers, there was that same odd sense of claustrophobia as the mountains ate into the sky.

Charles's big, bright yellow backpack, selected for maximum visibility like her own neon pink one, was somehow reassuring. Not just the hint of civilization it carried with it, but that the man who carried it was as comfortable out here as she was in her apartment. The matte black rifle wasn't as friendly. She could handle a pistol – her father used to take her to the shooting range – but that rifle was as far from her father's .38 as a wolf was from a poodle.

The first time they climbed a steep section, it took her some time to figure out the best way to negotiate it in snowshoes. It was slower going and began to make her thighs burn with effort. Charles stayed beside her the whole way up. They climbed like that for over an hour, but it was worth it.

When they topped a ridge and briefly stood above the trees, Anna stopped dead, staring at the terrain below. The valley they'd been climbing, decked in white and bitter green, flowed away from them. It was spectacular . . . and lonely.

'Is this what it used to look like everywhere?' she asked in a hushed voice.

Charles, who was ahead of her because he'd only stopped after she did, glanced out over the wilderness. 'Not everywhere,' he said. 'The scrublands have always looked like scrublands. This spring I'll take you out into the Missions, and we'll do a little technical climbing. If you're enjoying this, you'll love that.' He'd been watching her, too, she thought, if he'd seen how much fun she was having.

'The Missions are even more spectacular than these – though they're pure hell if you are really trying to cross them. Straight up, straight down, and not much in between. Not that this is going to be easy, either. By the time they started setting aside wilderness areas, the only wild country left was pretty rugged.'

He put his hand in his pocket and pulled out a granola bar. 'Eat this.' And he watched until she pulled off a glove to rip the package open and gnaw on the carob-coated bar before starting on one for himself.

'You're a bit of a mother hen,' she told him, not sure whether to be irritated or not.

He grunted. 'If you were human, you'd be feeling this cold. It's only a little below freezing now, but don't underestimate the weather. You're burning a lot of fuel keeping warm, and you aren't up to fighting weight to start with. So you're stuck with me shoveling food down you as fast as I can for the duration of this trip – might as well get used to it.'

# 8

'We started later than I thought we would,' Charles told Anna. 'But we've made pretty good time anyway. Baree Lake is still a mile or so away, but we'll make camp here before it gets dark. The wind's blown most of the last snow off the trees, and the branches will shelter us from any snowfall tonight.'

Anna looked around doubtfully.

Her expression made him laugh. 'Trust me. You'll be comfortable tonight. It's getting up in the morning that takes some fortitude.'

She seemed to accept his assurance, which pleased him. 'When will we go by the place Heather and Jack were attacked?'

'We won't,' he told her. 'I don't want our scent anywhere near there. I want us to look like prey, not any kind of official investigators.'

'You think he cares one way or the other?'

Charles took off his backpack, set it on a rock that stuck out of the snow like a whale rising out of the ocean. 'If he's really a rogue defending his territory, no. If he's here to cause trouble for my father, he won't attack people who look like they might carry word of his work out to the world.'

She followed his lead and set her pack up out of the snow. He pulled a packet of raisins out of the pocket in his arm – the last packet he had handy, so he'd have to restock for the morning. She took it with a put-upon sigh, but opened it anyway and started munching.

With Anna occupied eating, he took a moment to examine

his chosen campsite. There was a better one near the lake; he'd intended to reach it sometime in the early afternoon and give Anna the chance to rest up. It wouldn't be the first day of hiking that got to her – he had some experience taking other greenhorns out into the mountains. It would be the third or fourth.

But the first rule of playing in the woods was to be flexible. They could have made it to his first pick before dark, but he thought that giving her some time to rest after the first hike was more important.

He'd slept here before, and the rock hadn't changed since he was a boy. The last time . . . he thought about it for a minute, but he couldn't pin it down. The bushes on the side of the rock hadn't been there, and he could see the stump of the old Douglas fir that had sheltered him from the east the last time he'd been here. He put his toe against the rotten stump and watched the wood crumble. Maybe fifty years ago, or seventy.

Charles laid down a ground cloth but didn't bother setting up the backpacker's tent. As long as the weather held out, he had no intention of making them that vulnerable to attack. He seldom used tents if he didn't have to – and never if he was out hunting something that might hunt him back. The tent blocked his vision, muffled sounds, and got in the way. He'd brought it for Anna, but only if necessary.

The old fir was too wet to be good fuel, but there were other downed trees. A half hour of hunting gave him a generous armful of dry wood coaxed from the corpses of a couple of old forest monarchs.

Anna was perched up on the big rock next to his backpack when he returned, her snowshoes leaning against the base of the rock. He took off his own and set about building a small fire, conscious of her eyes on him.

'I thought Indians built fires with friction,' she said when he took out a can of Sterno and a cigarette lighter.

'I can do that,' he said. 'But I'd like to eat sometime in the next day or so. Sterno and a Bic are much faster.' They were all right again, he thought. It had started when she fell asleep in the car, but throughout the whole hike up here, she'd been relaxing more around him. Until, during the last few miles, she'd grabbed his coat several times to point out this and that – the tracks of a wolverine, a raven that watched them from a safe perch in the top of a lodge-pole pine, and a rabbit in its winter white.

'What would you like to eat?' he asked her after he'd arranged the fire to his liking and put a pot of snow on to boil.

'No more jerky,' she said. 'My jaw is tired of chewing.'

'How about sweet-and-sour chicken?' he asked.

He stirred in the packet of olive oil and handed her the larger foil bag. She looked inside dubiously. 'It doesn't look like sweet-and-sour chicken,' she said.

'You need to pay more attention to your nose,' he admonished and took a bite of his own stew. It wasn't as good as dinner last night, but not too bad for something you poured water on and ate. 'And at least the sweet-and-sour chicken doesn't look like dog food.'

She leaned over and looked in his bag. 'Ewwe. Why did they do that?'

'They can only freeze-dry small pieces,' he said, pulling his bag back before she got her hair in it. 'Eat.'

'So,' she asked, back on her earlier perch, 'how long will our scent disguise last?'

He was pleased to notice that after she'd taken the first bite, she'd fallen on her food like a lumberjack.

'It won't matter,' he told her, as he made quick inroads

on his own meal, 'as long as we keep talking about what we're doing so that any wolf out there can hear us.'

She stopped eating and opened her mouth to apologize, then stopped midword to frown at him. He wondered if he should have smiled so she'd know he was teasing; but she got it, because she waved her spork at him. 'If there was a werewolf within hearing range, you'd know it. Answer the question.'

He seldom spoke of his magic to anyone, including his father – because Brother Wolf told him that the fewer people knew about it, the better weapon it was. But Brother Wolf had no objections to telling Anna anything she wanted to know.

So he ate a bite of beef and admitted, 'I don't know. As long as we need it to – unless we tick off the spirits and they decide to aid our enemies instead.'

She stopped eating a second time, this time to stare. 'You're not teasing this time?'

He shrugged. 'No. I'm not a witch to impose my will on the world. All I can do is ask, and if it suits their whims, the spirits allow it.'

She'd taken a mouthful of food and had to swallow hastily to ask, 'Are you a Christian? Or . . .'

He nodded. 'Like Balaam's ass, I am. Besides, as a werewolf, you know there are other things in the world – demons, vampires, ghouls, and the like. Once you know they're out there, you have to admit that God is present. That's the only possible explanation of why evil hasn't yet taken over the world and enslaved the human race. God makes sure that evil stays hidden and sly.' He finished off his food and put away his spork.

'Balaam's ass?' She muttered to herself, then caught her breath. 'Balaam's ass saw an angel. Do you mean you've seen an angel?'

He grinned. 'Just once, and it wasn't interested in me . . . but still, it sticks with you.' Gave him hope in the darkest night, in fact. 'Just because God is, doesn't mean there aren't spirits in these woods.'

'You worship spirits?'

'Why would I do that?' He wasn't crazy or stupid – and a man had to be one or the other to go out looking for spirits. 'All that would do is get me more work – and my father gives me more than enough work as it is.'

She frowned at him, so he decided to explain. 'Sometimes they help me out in this or that if I ask, but more often they have something they need done. And there aren't as many people who hear them as there used to be – which means more work for those of us who do. My father keeps me busy enough for three people. If I were seeking the spirits out in daily conversation, I wouldn't have time to tie my shoes. Samuel spends a lot of time trying to figure out where spirits fit into Christianity – I don't worry about it so much.'

He thought he was going to have to remind her to finish her food, but she stared at her bag for a bit, then took another bite. 'What do you do if they ask you to do something wrong?'

He shook his head. 'Most spirits are more friendly or unfriendly rather than good or evil.' And then, because the odd urge to tease her was still strong, he added, 'Except for the brain-sucking spirits who live around here waiting for silly hikers to camp under their trees. Don't worry, I'll keep them off of you.'

'Jerk,' she told her sweet-and-sour chicken, but not like she was bothered.

Somewhere out in the darkness a wolf howled. It was a long way off, a timber wolf, he thought. Twenty years ago there hadn't been any wolves to howl, but they'd been making steady progress back down into Montana from Canada for a decade or more. The sound made him smile. His father worried that there was no more room in this tame planet for predators, but he figured if humans had decided to allow the wolves back into their rightful place, they could adjust to werewolves given enough time.

Walter found the dead man, dressed in hunter orange, propped up against a tree. From the looks of him, he'd fallen from the rocks above where a game trail snaked along the edge of a short cliff. One leg had been broken, but he'd managed to drag himself a few yards. Probably he'd died of the cold a few days ago.

He must be the reason all the searchers had been hiking through the woods. He must have gotten turned around because no man with any sense would have gone hunting this far from a road without a pack animal of some sort. It was so far from where people had been looking that the chances of anyone finding the body were somewhere between slim and none. By spring there would be little left to find.

He thought about burying the body, but he'd have to dig through eight or ten feet of snow and another six of frozen ground. Besides, he didn't have a shovel with him. The dead man's feet were the same size as Walter's, so he took the boots as well as the gloves and parka – leaving behind the orange vest. Leaving the hunter's gun was a more difficult decision, but ammunition was hard to come by, and he had no desire to advertise his presence with gunfire.

He bowed his head and began a prayer. It wasn't a very good prayer because the only one he could remember was the prayer he'd said before bedtime as a kid. But he focused on it, because it was helping him ignore the beast inside him that saw the hunter as meat. It was hungry, and it didn't care where the meat came from.

He was just finishing the prayer when the demon howled.

He felt an answering growl rise from his belly, a challenge to his enemy. But he held the sound to himself. He knew about stalking evil . . . for a moment he was back in the war with Jimmy, sliding from shadow to shadow as they approached their commander's tent. The sobs of the village girl hid their approach.

For a moment he saw Jimmy's face as clearly as if he stood beside him again. Then he was back in the present standing over a dead man – a frozen corpse whose neck he'd sliced with his knife, just as he had the CO's all those years ago.

That little girl had never told anyone what had happened, though he and Jimmy had waited on pins and needles for several weeks. They could have killed her, too – but that would have made them as bad as the CO. Officially, he'd been killed by a sniper. He and Jimmy had snickered a little about that. Most snipers don't use knives.

He bent down and picked up the body. He couldn't let it be found with a knife wound. He'd take it somewhere a little more off the usual game trails.

He carried the corpse a mile or so and set it gently beneath a thicket of Oregon grape. He licked his lips and tasted blood. Startled, he glanced down at the body and noticed that the neck wound had been cleaned, the skin around it glistening just a little from saliva.

He grabbed a handful of snow and wiped off his mouth, torn between hunger and sickness – though he knew he couldn't have swallowed much because the corpse had been frozen through.

He walked away as quickly as he could manage without running.

'Anna?' Charles finished zipping together the sleeping bags.

She didn't answer him. She'd shed her coat and boots,

then climbed back on the rock. She stood barefoot, her wool socks in one hand.

If they'd been somewhere else, he'd have believed that she was enjoying the view, but they were tucked in the trees, where all she could see was more trees. She wasn't so much looking out as not looking at the sleeping bags and him. As soon as they'd finished eating, she'd started shutting down again.

The temperature had dropped ten degrees when the sun went down, and it was too bloody cold for her to be standing around barefoot and coatless. Werewolf she might be, but frostbite still hurt like sin.

But he wasn't going to get her into the bags without force or coaxing. He took his own boots off and stuck the socks into his pack. He took out two fresh pairs of socks and stuck them in the bottom of the sleeping bag, so they'd be warm tomorrow morning.

He'd packed an extra blanket, which he shook out and wrapped around his shoulders. Then he walked over and hopped up on the rock next to her. There wasn't a lot of room, but he managed to stand shoulder to shoulder with her.

'My cousins courted their women with blankets,' he told her without looking at her. She didn't say anything, just pulled her toes up and curled them together for warmth.

'It's called a snagging blanket,' he said. 'One of them would go up to the girl he was courting and slowly stretch an arm out—' He held on to the corner of the blanket and put his arm around her shoulders. 'And he wrapped the blanket over her. If she didn't duck away, he'd snag her close.' He tugged, and she took a step sideways until she was tucked under his arm with the blanket snug around them both.

'A snagging blanket?' There was amusement in her voice, but her body was still stiff.

Wolf, he thought, but not completely. If he hadn't been looking for it, he might not have smelled the distinctive scent of her wolf intermingled with the perfume that was Anna.

'My brother, Samuel, is even smoother with it than I am,' he told her, moving a little more until she stood in front of him, her cold feet on top of his.

She inhaled and let the air out in one long frosty breath, her body softening against him.

'Tell me about mating,' she said.

He tightened his arms around her. 'I'm kind of a novice at it myself.'

'You've never been mated before?'

'No.' He breathed in her scent and let it sink into him and warm his chest. 'I told you some of it. Mostly courting is just like it is with humans. Then they marry and eventually, usually, his wolf accepts her as his mate.'

'What if it never does?'

'Then it doesn't.' He was not nearly so sanguine as he sounded. 'I had all but given up finding a mate when I met you.' He couldn't help his smile as he thought of the bewildered joy of that first meeting. 'Brother Wolf chose you as my mate the moment he laid eyes on you, and I can only applaud his good sense.'

'What would have happened if you had hated me?'

He sighed against her hair. 'Then we'd not be here. I wouldn't want to end up like my father and Leah.'

'He hates her?'

He shrugged. 'No. Not really. I don't know.' How had they ended up on this subject? 'He'd never say anything one way or another, but matters are not right between them. He told me once, a long time ago, that his wolf decided that he needed a mate to replace my mother.'

'So what went wrong?' she asked, as her body softened into his.

He shook his head. 'I have no desire to ask the Marrok that question and suggest you don't, either.'

She thought of something else. 'You said something about a full-moon ceremony.'

'Right,' he said. 'There's a ceremony held under the moon to sanctify our bond – like a marriage ceremony, I suppose, though it is private. You'll also be brought fully into my father's pack then.' He felt her stiffen; the pack ceremony, which included the sharing of the Alpha's flesh and blood – literally – could be pretty frightening if you weren't ready for it. And why would Leo have done that right when he'd done so much else wrong? He decided it was something they could discuss when he wasn't trying to get her to relax and come crawl into sleeping bags with him. 'If you choose, we could do a separate marriage in the church if you'd like. Invite your family.'

She twisted so she could see his face. 'How can you tell that we aren't bonded?'

'It's almost like pack magic,' he told her. 'Some wolves can barely feel it. Pack magic is what allows an Alpha to draw on his wolves to give himself an edge in speed or quicker healing. It lets him control wolves under his power or find them if he needs to.'

Anna stilled. 'Or feed off their rage? I think Isabella did that; she liked it when the pack fought among themselves.'

'Yes,' Charles agreed. 'Though I've never seen my father do that. But you know what I mean?'

'Yes. Mating is like that?'

'On a smaller scale. It varies between couples. Sometimes it's just being able to tell where your mate is. My da says that's all he and Leah have. Sometimes it's more than that. One of the wolves in Oklahoma is mated to a blind woman. She can see now, as long as she's in the same room with him. More common are things like being able to share strength – or any of the other things an Alpha can get from his pack.'

He fell silent and waited for another question.

'My toes are cold,' he suggested after a bit.

'Sorry,' she said, and he rubbed her cheek with his thumb.

Touch was something he usually avoided. Touch allowed the others to get too close to him – a closeness he couldn't afford if he was to survive his job as his father's pet killer. It made Brother Wolf all the hungrier for it. With Anna, he let go of his usual rules. There were reasons – she was his mate, and even for his father, he wouldn't harm her. She was Omega and unlikely to go rogue. But the real reason, he admitted to himself, was that he could not resist the feel of her skin against his own.

'Rome wasn't built in a day,' he told her. 'Come sleep.' And then, when she stiffened against him, he said, 'It's too cold to do anything more interesting.'

She stilled. 'That was a lie, wasn't it?'

He buried his cold nose against her neck, startling a small laugh out of her. 'You're getting better. What if I said you're too tired, then?'

He stepped out of the blanket and wrapped it around her shoulders. Then he picked her up and jumped off the rock, bending his knees to make the landing gentler. He'd forgotten his wounds; as he carried her over to the sleeping bags, his injured calf ached fiercely. He ignored the sizzling pain. His chest wasn't happy with him, either, but when she settled into the sleeping bags with him, it would have taken a lot more than a couple of bullet holes to make him unhappy.

She was asleep long before he was.

They stopped by Baree Lake, but the only sign anyone had been nearby was a pair of snowmobile tracks across the frozen water. It was wilderness, but it was also Montana.

Snowmobiles didn't bother him as much as the dirt bikers because the snowmobiles didn't damage the land. He'd run into a couple dirt bikers here a couple of years ago, and had followed them to Wanless Lake, about twenty miles from the nearest road, where they had finally parked their bikes and gone swimming. He wondered how long it had taken them to get their machines back down without the spark plugs.

There was no easy way to get from Baree to the Bear Lakes in the winter. He and Tag had mapped out something that appeared to be a passable route – but if it got too rugged, he'd find a different way. All he wanted was for the rogue to see them and go hunting.

He thought about those snowmobile tracks though. Most of the Cabinets were too rough for snowmobiles. If you only wanted to go to Baree Lake and back, though – say to find a few victims and get some news coverage for a werewolf kill – they'd be fine.

An organized pack of renegades, determined to force Bran not to reveal the existence of werewolves to the real world, would require different treatment than a single rogue. He would keep the snowmobiles in mind and be ready to face multiple opponents if necessary.

Anna was a restful companion. She was clearly enjoying herself, despite being a little stiff this morning. She didn't complain as their trails grew rougher, requiring a lot more muscle. She was mostly quiet, which let him listen for other monsters in the woods. Since he tended to be quiet at times, he was glad that she didn't chatter. She'd woken up cheerful and relaxed and stayed that way – until they dropped into a small hanging valley.

He could measure her growing nervousness by the slow shrinking of the distance between them.

When she finally spoke, she was near enough that she

accidentally stepped on the back of his snowshoe with hers. 'Sorry.'

The resultant stumble hurt his wounded leg, but he'd never have told her that. 'No problem. Are you all right?'

He saw her consider a polite lie and discard it.

'It's kind of creepy here,' she said finally.

Charles agreed with her: there were a number of places in the Cabinets that felt like this. He couldn't be sure, but this felt worse than usual – it was certainly worse than the part of the mountains they'd crossed yesterday.

Her observation made him give a thorough look around them, in case she'd noticed something he hadn't. But there was nothing to be seen, nothing more threatening than the cliff face that rose above them and cast its shadow over the valley and the thick growth of green-black trees on all sides. But he didn't discount other forces at work.

The spirits of these mountains had never been welcoming, not like the Bitterroots or Pintlers. They resented intruders.

It might be that the spirits were just more active in this valley – or something could have happened. The more he thought about it, the more certain he was that it was more than just spirits making mischief. From last week or a hundred years ago, he couldn't tell, but something dark lingered beneath the snow.

'You're a werewolf,' he told her. 'Creepy shouldn't bother you.'

She snorted. 'I was never afraid of monsters until I became one. Now I'm afraid of my own shadow.'

He heard the self-directed derision and snorted right back at her. 'Baloney. I—' He caught a wild scent and stopped, turning his nose into the wind to catch it again.

Anna froze, watching him. He waited until the scent got a little stronger; their stalker was not worried that they would notice him.

'What do you smell?' he asked her softly.

She sucked in a deep breath and closed her eyes. 'Trees, and whoever you stole these clothes from and—' She stiffened as she caught what he had. 'Cat. Some kind of cat. Is it a panther?'

'Close,' he told her. 'Lynx, I think. Nasty-tempered but not a danger to us.'

'Cool,' she said. 'What a—' This time it was her turn to pause. 'What's that?'

'Dead rabbit,' he said, pleased. 'You're starting to pay attention to your nose.' He took another breath and reconsidered. 'It might be a mouse, but probably rabbit. That's why the lynx is still around; we've interrupted his dinner.' He was a little surprised that they'd run into a lynx here; cats usually stayed away from places that felt like this. Could it have been driven here by bigger predators?

She looked a little green. 'I really hate it that part of me is getting hungry smelling raw meat.'

It hadn't bothered her to smell Jack's blood. But he hadn't fed her in an hour, and she was hungry. Her body was burning up calories to stay warm. But hungry or not, it wasn't the time to feed her a real meal; he needed to get out of this little draw. So he handed her a bag of peanut butter crackers and got them going again. The peanut butter would make sure she started drinking out of her canteen; he wasn't sure she'd been drinking enough.

They hiked until the valley was behind them, and the dark feeling stayed behind, too, confirming his guess that it wasn't spirits.

'Lunchtime,' he said, handing her a granola bar and stick of jerky.

She took them, brushed most of the snow off of a downed tree, then hopped up on it. 'I was fine until we hit that valley. Now I'm bushed and frozen, and it's only one o'clock. How do humans do this?'

He sat beside her eating his own jerky – it tasted a lot better than pemmican, though it wasn't nearly as strengthening without all the fat. 'Most of 'em don't, not this time of year. I pushed us a little hard to get out of that valley, that's what you're feeling.' He frowned. 'You haven't been sweating, have you? Are your socks dry? I brought spares. Wet socks mean frostbite – you could lose a toe.'

She wiggled her snowshoes, which dangled a foot or so off the ground. 'I thought being a werewolf meant indestructible, short of death.'

Something in her face told him she was thinking about the beatings she'd been given to try to make her into something she was not.

'It might grow back,' Charles said, soothing Brother Wolf, who didn't like it when Anna was unhappy. 'But it wouldn't be fun.'

'Cool.' Then as an afterthought she told him, 'My socks are dry.'

'Let me know if that changes.'


The snowshoes were dragging at her feet. She gave Charles a mock-resentful glare – it was safe because she was glaring at his back. Bullet holes and all, he was obviously not having any trouble. He was barely limping as they scaled the side of another mountain. He'd slowed down, but that didn't help as much as she'd hoped. If he hadn't promised her an early camp at the top of the current climb, she probably would have just collapsed where she stood.

'Not far,' he said without looking around. Doubtless her panting told him all he needed to know about how tired she was.

'Part of it is the altitude,' he told her. 'You're used to more oxygen in the air and have to breathe harder to make up the difference.'

He was making excuses for her – and it stiffened her spine. She'd make this climb if it killed her. She dug the edge of her snowshoe into the snow in preparation for the next step, and a wild cry echoed through the trees, raising the hair on the back of her neck as it echoed in the mountains.

'What's that?' she asked.

Charles gave her a grim smile over his shoulder. 'Werewolf.'

'Can you tell where it came from?'

'East of here,' he said. 'The way sound carries out here, he's a few miles away.'

She shivered a little though she shouldn't be afraid. After all, she was a werewolf, too, right? And she'd seen Charles wipe the floor with her former Alpha despite having been shot several times.

'He won't hurt you,' Charles said.

She didn't say anything, but he was watching her face and his eyes softened. 'If you really don't like me using my nose to tell what you're feeling, you can try using perfume. It works a treat.'

She sniffed and smelled only the people who had loaned Charles their clothing. 'You don't use perfume.'

He grinned, his teeth white in his dark face. 'Too sissy for me. I had to learn to control my emotions instead.' Then he removed whatever starch she had left in her knees when he added, a little ruefully, 'Until I met you.'

He started up the mountainside again, leaving her scrambling behind him. Who was she that she could touch this man? Why her? Was it just that she was an Omega? Somehow she didn't think so. Not with that wry admission hanging in the air.

He was hers.

Just to be certain, she counted on her gloved fingers.

This time last week she'd been waiting tables at Scorci's, had never heard of Charles or walked a mile in snowshoes. Would never have dreamed of enjoying kissing a man ever again. Now she was tramping through the snow in below-zero weather with a silly smile on her face, hunting a werewolf. Or at least following Charles, who was hunting a werewolf.

Weird. And kinda nice. And there were fringe benefits to following Charles around – the view for one.

'Are you giggling?' Charles said in his Mr Spock voice.

He looked back at her, then executed one of those complicated turns that snowshoes required in order to reverse directions. He pulled off a glove and touched her nose, right where she knew freckles gathered. His fingers drifted down to trace the dimple in her left cheek.

'I like seeing you happy,' he said intently.

His perusal stopped her laughter, but not the warm fuzzy feeling in her stomach.

'Yeah?' she said archly. 'Then tell me that was really the last climb, and that this big flat spot we're standing on is where we're going to camp, and that I don't have to walk anymore today.'

She stood there looking like a cat in the cream, and he had not the foggiest notion why. He wasn't used to this. He was good at reading people, damn it. He had lots of practice, and Brother Wolf was all but empathic sometimes. And he still had no clue why she stood there looking at him with secret laughter still dancing in her eyes.

He bent until he could press his forehead against her wool hat and closed his eyes, breathing her in and letting the warmth of her spread over his heart. Her scent broke free of the bindings he'd set upon it and rushed over him like the smoke of a hookah.

No more human scent for them, but, absorbed in her, he couldn't make himself mind.

He still should have heard it. Smelled it. Something.

One moment he was standing next to Anna, the next he was facedown in the snow with something – werewolf, his tardy nose informed him – on his back and Anna underneath.

Teeth dug into the tough fabric of his jacket and ripped at his pack. He ignored the werewolf for Anna's sake and pushed himself (and the other werewolf) up to give her room to get out from under him, knowing it was probably a fatal decision.

Anna wriggled out from underneath him as fast as any sleight-of-hand magician's assistant could have. But she didn't listen to his order to run.

The attacking wolf didn't seem to notice her. It was so busy ripping up Charles's backpack it wasn't paying attention to anything else. Rogue, Charles thought – out of control if it was so far gone not to release its first hold for something more immediately fatal. Not that he was complaining.

Charles's human form was a little more fragile than the wolf, but it was almost as strong. Without Anna beneath him, it took him a bare instant to rip the bindings on his snowshoes apart to free his feet.

Silver foil packets dropped on both sides of him like confetti thrown at a wedding: freeze-dried meals. Doubtless Samuel would have come up with something funny about that – *Let's just see who ends up a frozen dinner.*

Grunting with the effort, Charles straightened his legs with as much speed and power as he could gather – and the move, combined with the werewolf's weight, ripped the fabric of Charles's coat and backpack. Holding on to the fabric and nothing else, the wolf was thrown off his back; a kick, and the wolf was ten feet away. Not far enough, and yet too far. He was between Charles and Anna – and he was closer to Anna.

Even as Charles frantically freed himself of the remnants of the pack – ruthlessly shredding anything that tried to stick – he realized how weird the attack was. Even an out-of-control rogue wouldn't have been entirely foiled by the pack. He'd have gotten a fang or claw in somewhere, but Charles was entirely unharmed.

The wolf had rolled to his feet but made no further move to attack. He was scared, that wolf. The scent of his fear flooded the air as he met Charles's eyes defiantly.

But he stayed where he was, between Charles and Anna. As if he were protecting her.

Charles narrowed his eyes and tried to place this wolf – he'd met so many. Gray on gray was not an uncommon coloring, though he was even thinner than Anna's wolf form, cadaverously thin. He didn't smell familiar – nor did he smell of a pack. He smelled as if he denned in Douglas fir, cedar, and granite – as if he'd never been touched by shampoo or soap or any of the accouterments of modern life.

'Who are you?' Charles asked.

'Who are you?' repeated Anna, and the wolf looked at her. Hell afire, so did Charles. When she used it, she could pull in any wolf she wanted almost as effectively as Bran, though he'd have done it by sheer force of personality. Anna made you want to curl up at her feet and bask in her peace.

Charles saw the moment when the wolf realized that there were no humans here to protect at all. He smelled the other wolf's anger and hatred as it flared, then vanished as it came up against his Anna. Leaving . . . bewilderment behind.

The wolf ran.

'Are you all right?' asked Charles, ridding himself of his clothes as rapidly as possible. He could have used magic to strip as he usually did, but he didn't want to risk using it here when he might need it for something more important later. The damned bandage around his ribs was tough, and it hurt when he shredded it with his fingernails as they lengthened. A bit of his snowshoe binding had tangled with a bootlace, so he broke the lace.

'I'm fine.'

'Stay here,' he ordered as he let Brother Wolf flow over him and rob him of speech. He shuddered as the shape brought with it the call of the hunt – and every minute the change took let the other get farther away.

'I'll be here,' she told him – and, as his wolf shape settled over him and solidified, more words flowed over him. 'Don't hurt him.'

He nodded before he disappeared into the woods. He wasn't going to have to kill anyone this trip. With Anna's help, he was going to bring that rogue in to safety.

As soon as he left, Anna found herself shivering as if someone had just removed her coat and left her bare to the ice and snow. She glanced around nervously, wondering why the shadows of the trees seemed suddenly deeper. The firs, which only moments ago had been just trees, now seemed to loom over her in silent menace.

'I'm a monster, damn it,' she said aloud.

As if in answer, the wind died and silence descended; a heavy, blanketing silence that seemed somehow alive, though nothing moved or made a noise. Even the little birds, chickadees and nuthatches, were quiet.

She glared at the trees, and that helped a little. But the feeling that something was watching her kept growing. Her nose told her there was nothing – but it hadn't told her about the wolf that had knocked her and Charles off their feet, either. Now that the wolf had skedaddled, her alarm system was in full swing.

How useful.

But thinking about the wolf reminded her of that odd feeling she'd had just a few moments ago, as if she could see through the strange werewolf's skin and into his soul, feel his torment, his need. She'd stretched out her hand and asked him who he was, part of her certain that he would come to her and answer.

When he'd run instead, it had torn her from the strange awareness. She couldn't put her finger on most of what she'd sensed from the wolf; she felt like a blind man seeing colors for the first time. But she would swear that he'd attacked to protect her – and that he'd done his best not to hurt Charles.

Something watched her. She sniffed, taking in the scent of the air, but smelled only the usual woodland scents.

She walked the perimeter of the clearing, but detected nothing with her eyes, ears, or nose. She walked it again anyway, with the same results. Looking a third time wasn't going to help matters. She needed to calm down, or she was going to go chasing after Charles in full panic. Yeah, that would impress him a whole lot.

Not that she'd ever done anything that might impress him.

She folded her arms over her stomach, which had started to ache with some emotion she couldn't name, wouldn't name. It might have been rage.

For three years she'd endured because, as bad as it was, she needed the pack. They were a visceral requirement her wolf could not do without. So she'd let them rob her of her pride, let Leo take control of her body and pass her around like a whore that he owned.

For a moment, she could smell Justin's breath in her face, feel his body holding hers down, the ache in her wrists and the pressure on her nose where he'd broken it with a carefully controlled, open-handed blow.

Blood dripped down her lip and down her new coat to splatter in the snow. Startled, she put her hand to her nose, but there was nothing wrong with it, though a moment ago she'd felt it swelling as it had the night Justin hit it.

But the blood was still there.

She bent down and took a handful of snow and pressed it against her nose until it burned uncomfortably. She put her hand to her nose and it came away clean this time, so it wasn't still bleeding. The question was, why had it started bleeding in the first place? And why had she suddenly started thinking about Justin?

Maybe the nosebleed had something to do with the altitude, she thought. Charles would know. She got clean snow and wiped her face with that, then a scrap of backpack that was nearby. She touched her nose, and her fingers came away clean. Whatever the cause, it had stopped. She scrubbed at the bloodstains on her jacket and succeeded only in smearing the blood around.

With a sigh, she looked for somewhere to put the bloody piece of fabric. She'd taken off her pack when she'd done her earlier reconnoitering. It sat in unharmed glory amidst foil-covered meals scattered in fanciful patterns with bits and pieces of Charles's backpack.

Typical man, she thought with experimental exasperation, leaving the woman to clean up the mess.

She gathered Charles's clothes and shook them free of snow. She stuffed them into her pack and then started putting the foil-clad meals on top. With a little organization, she was able to put most of the undamaged food in her backpack, but there was no way she would be able to stuff anything more into it. She gave the remains of Charles's backpack, sleeping bag, and snowshoes a frustrated look.

It wouldn't have bothered her so much, except this was a wilderness area and they weren't supposed to leave anything behind. She looked closely at Charles's backpack, but it had been ripped to shreds. The gun had taken damage, too. She didn't know much about rifles, but she suspected that they needed a straight barrel to work right.

She hit the jackpot, though, when one of the pieces of backpack turned out to be the ground cloth they'd slept on last night.

She smelled something as she knelt to spread the tough fabric out. She tried not to react to the scent, collecting all the leftover bits and throwing them in the center of the cloth. Everything except the gun. Even though it was bent, it was still reassuringly solid.

Whoever it was stayed very still, watching her – a human, not a werewolf.

Tied together, the cloth made a tidy bundle that they could carry out. As Anna moved the makeshift pack next to her backpack, she heard her watcher move out of the trees behind her.

'Looks like you had a mess on your hands,' said a friendly voice. 'Did you run into a bear?'

She sounded friendly enough. Anna turned to look at the woman who'd come out of the trees after watching her for too long to be entirely trustworthy.

Like Anna, she was wearing snowshoes, but she had ski poles in each of her hands. Deep brown eyes peered out from under her hat, but the rest of her face was covered in a woolen scarf. Underneath her gray hat, dark brown curls fell to her shoulders.

Anna took a deep breath, but all her nose told her was that the woman was human. Would a human's hearing be poor enough that all the noise of the fight might have been made by a bear rather than a pair of werewolves? Darned if she knew.

'A bear. Yes.' Anna gave her a smile she hoped would

cover up the amount of time it had taken her to reply. 'Sorry, I'm still a little off. I'm a city girl, and I'm not used to Mother Nature in all her glory. Yes, a bear. We scared it off, then discovered it had one of our—' What would they need so badly that a human man would have to go chasing after a bear? '—small packs. The one with the lighter in it.'

The other woman threw back her head and laughed. 'Isn't that the way it always works? I'm Mary Alvarado. What are you doing out here in the middle of winter if you're not used to the wild country?'

'I'm Anna . . . Cornick.' Somehow it seemed right to use Charles's name. Anna gave Mary Alvarado another wry smile. 'We haven't been married long. I'm not used to a new last name. You must be out looking for the hunter, too. We were told that no one else was going to be this far out. I may be green as grass, but my husband knows his way around.'

'Search and Rescue, that's me,' said Mary.

'Isn't everyone supposed to go by twos?' Anna asked. She wasn't sure about it, but it only seemed sensible. Heather and Jack had been hunting together.

Mary shrugged. 'I have a partner around here somewhere. We had an argument, and she took off in a huff. But she'll get over it soon and let me catch up.' She grinned conspiratorially. 'She's pretty hot-tempered.'

The woman took a step closer to Anna, but then stopped abruptly and looked around. Anna felt it, too, like a great wind of evil flowing through the trees.

Something growled.

# 9

In his hothouse, Asil trimmed dead blooms from his roses. They weren't as glorious as the ones he'd had in Spain, but they were a vast improvement over the commercially grown flowers he'd started with. His Spanish roses had been the result of centuries of careful breeding. It hadn't bothered him to leave them at the time, but now he regretted their loss fiercely.

Not as fiercely as he regretted losing Sarai.

He hoped that someone had taken them over, but the state he'd left his property in almost ensured his flowers had died before anyone figured out what to do with the estate. Still, he'd been exchanging cuttings and rootstock with other rose aficionados for several decades before he'd been forced to leave, so his work had not all been in vain. Somewhere in the world there were probably descendants of his roses. Maybe if Bran made him live a few more years, he'd go out looking for them.

Someone knocked briskly at the inner door, then opened it without waiting for a reply. He didn't even bother looking up. Sage had been invading his hothouse almost since he'd built it. He would have long ago reduced anyone else to shreds for interrupting his solitude. Slapping down Sage was as rewarding as beating a puppy: it accomplished nothing except to make him feel abusive.

'Hello, hello?' she called out, though her nose certainly told her exactly where he was.

It was her usual greeting – he thought that it was to make sure that he wasn't feeling homicidally reclusive that day.

He'd had a few of those right after he'd come to Aspen Creek. When she first started showing up, he'd wondered if the Marrok wasn't sending her to make sure he was still sane enough to leave alive. If so, it had been only prudent, and he'd long since quit caring one way or the other.

'I'm here,' he told her, not bothering to raise his voice. She'd hear him if he whispered, and he was finished pretending to be human.

He didn't look up from his work when she walked up behind him. His standards of beauty had broadened over the years, but even if they hadn't, Sage would have hit every chime he had.

Sarai had often thumped him soundly on the head for looking at other women, though she'd known he'd never stray. Now that she was gone, he seldom even looked. Flirting didn't make him feel disloyal to his dead mate, but he'd found he missed that thump too badly. Of course, given the opportunity to irritate the so-composed Charles, he had happily dealt with his memories.

'Hey, 'Sil. You're smiling – someone die?' She obviously didn't expect him to answer that, but continued, 'You have something I can do?'

'I'm deadheading,' he told her, though she could see that for herself.

Sometimes he was so impatient with all of it – meaning-less conversations that mimicked ones he'd had a thousand, thousand times. Just as he got tired of people who had to work out the same issues over and over.

He wondered how Bran kept his air of bemused interest at his people's petty problems. *Still*, thought Asil with a thread of self-directed, bitter amusement, *I must not be so tired of life, because I grabbed at the ring when Bran offered a chance at it, didn't I?*

Sage ignored his shortness with relentless cheer. It was

one of the things he liked about her, that he didn't have to constantly apologize for his volatile mood swings.

She took off her coat and settled in just to his right to start on the next row of bushes, so he knew she was in the mood for a good talk. Otherwise, she'd have started on the other side of the bushes, where she wouldn't get in the way of his work.

'So what do you think of Charlie's mate?' she asked.

He grunted. It had been wicked of him to tease Bran's boy, but he had been unable to resist; it wasn't often Charles was off balance. And Anna reminded him so much of his own Sarai, not in looks – Sarai had been almost as dark as he was – but they both had the same inner serenity.

'Well, I like her,' Sage said. 'She has more backbone than you'd think given the way her old Alpha abused her.'

That shocked him. 'Abuse an Omega?'

She nodded. 'For years. I guess Leo was a real piece of work – killed off half his pack or let his crazy mate do it. He even ordered one of his wolves to force the Change on Anna. What I don't understand is why Charles didn't slaughter the whole pack; none of them did anything to protect her. How hard is it to pick up the phone and call Bran?'

'If Leo ordered them not to, they wouldn't be able to call,' Asil said absently. He'd known Leo, the Chicago Alpha, and liked him, too. 'Not unless they were nearly as dominant as Leo – which is unlikely.'

Leo had been a strong Alpha, and, he would have sworn, an honorable man. Perhaps Sage was mistaken. Asil clipped a few brown-edged roses, then asked, 'Do you know why Leo did these things?'

She looked up from her own task. 'I guess his mate was going age-crazy. She killed all the females in the pack out of jealousy, then went out and turned a bunch of good-looking men, just for fun. Apparently Leo hoped that having an Omega like Anna in the pack would keep his mate stable. It worked, more or less. He had Anna brutalized, though, to keep her under his thumb.'

Asil paused, a cold chill running down his back. When speaking of an unmated female in a pack, 'brutalized' was a terrible word, much worse than 'abused.' This modern era's definition of 'abuse' was different than the one he'd grown up with. 'Brutalized' hadn't changed a bit.

'Brutalized how?' he asked hoarsely, suddenly remembering the rare rage he'd left Charles in when he'd brought Anna flowers. He had a brief image of a glimpse he'd had of Anna over Charles's shoulder. Had she been frightened?

Damn his penchant for causing trouble. What had he done?

Sage dug her fingers into the dirt, doubtless reliving her own brutal assault, which had resulted in her seeking sanctuary here in Aspen Creek a few years before he had come here. He should apologize for bringing that up, too. *Clumsy, clumsy, Asil*.

'What do you *think* they did to her?' she said finally, darkness clinging to her voice.

'*Allah*,' he said softly – he'd never managed to get Charles so worked up before. And he'd left that poor child to deal with the results, thinking that any Omega could soothe her mate. He hadn't realized she'd already been hurt before. Truly he should have forced Bran to kill him a long time ago.

'What's wrong?'

'I need to go talk to Charles,' he said, setting down his knife and getting to his feet. He was getting old and complacent, too ready to believe he was omniscient. He'd thought the boy had been waiting until his wounds were healed before consummating their attachment – instead he'd almost certainly been trying to give the girl time.

That Charles had come this morning to ask about Omegas might mean that something had gone wrong . . . and on the heels of that thought, he realized that Charles hadn't been asking about Sarai when he asked what happened if an Omega was tortured. He'd been asking about Anna.

'Talking with Charles is going to be difficult,' Sage said dryly. 'He took Anna and went after some rogue over in the Cabinets. There's no cell phone reception out there.'

'The Cabinets?' He frowned at her, remembering the limp Charles had been hiding in church yesterday. He'd been doing a better job this morning, but Asil could still see he was stiff. 'He was wounded.'

'Umm.' She nodded. 'I heard he got shot in Chicago, silver bullets. But there's some rogue werewolf running around attacking people. Killed one and wounded another in less than a week – Heather Morrell's partner was the one wounded. If we're going to keep it out of the news, the rogue has to be taken out as soon as possible, so he doesn't hurt anyone else. And who else does Bran have to send after him? Samuel's not suitable, even if he hadn't just headed back to Washington this morning. Word is that Bran's worried it might be a ploy on the part of the European wolves, to see if they can cause enough trouble that Bran reconsiders going public. So he needs a dominant wolf.'

How Sage knew so much about everything that went on in the Marrok's pack had ceased to astound Asil a long time ago.

'He could have sent me,' said Asil, not really paying attention to his own words. It was good news if Anna had gone with Charles, wasn't it? Surely it meant he hadn't done any permanent harm to her with his teasing.

Sage looked at him. 'Send you? Could he, really? I saw you at church yesterday morning.'

'He could have sent me,' Asil repeated. Sage, he knew,

was beginning to suspect that his madness was feigned. Bran probably thought so, too, since he hadn't just killed him, though Asil had requested it of him repeatedly – fifteen years of 'not yet.' It was too bad that both Sage and Bran were wrong. His madness was a more subtle thing, and it might kill them all in the end.

Asil was a danger to everyone around him, and if he weren't such a coward he'd have made Bran take care of the problem when he'd first arrived here, or any day since then.

He could have at least taken out the lone rogue wolf; he owed Bran that much.

'I don't think Charles was hurt too badly,' she said in conciliatory tones.

So Charles had been successful at hiding his wounds from Sage, but he knew better. It would take a lot to make *that* old lobo move so badly at the funeral, where so many could see.

Asil took a deep breath. Charles was tough, and he knew the Cabinets better than anyone. Even wounded, a single rogue wolf would be no match for him. It was all right. He'd just make sure and apologize to both of them when he saw them next – and hope he hadn't caused any irreparable damage with his goading. He'd just been so jealous. The peace that Anna brought him had made him remember . . .

*Ah, Sarai, you'd be so disappointed in me.*

'Are you all right?'

He knelt again and picked up his shears. 'I am fine.'

But why would the Europeans send only one wolf? Maybe they hadn't. Maybe Charles would need backup.

He sighed. He owed the boy an apology that shouldn't wait. If he knew where they had started, he could track Charles down and make sure he hadn't done any real damage to the bond between him and his mate.

'I need to talk to Bran,' he said. He threw down the shears

again and strode out the door, closing the greenhouse door behind him.

When he exited the air lock, the cold fell over him like the cloak of the ice queen. The contrast between it and the artificially warm and moist air of his greenhouse was so great he gasped once before his lungs made the adjustment. Sage followed him, pulling on her coat, but he didn't wait for her.

'I don't *know* that it is the Europeans,' Bran told him calmly after Asil expressed his opinion of the wisdom of sending Charles out wounded after an unknown foe, in words that were less than diplomatic. 'More likely it is simply a rogue. The Cabinets are remote and might appeal to someone trying to run from what he has become. Even if it were the Europeans, there was only one wolf. If there were two wolves, Heather wouldn't have been able to drive off the one who attacked them.'

He paused, but Asil just crossed his arms over his chest and let him know by body language that he still thought Bran had been stupid.

Bran smiled and put his feet up on his desk. 'I didn't send Charles alone. Even if there are two or three werewolves, Charles and Anna between them should manage. More than two or three I would have sensed when they came so close to Aspen Creek.'

That made sense. So why was dread growing in his soul? Why was every instinct he had telling him that sending Charles out after this rogue was such a stupid thing? And when had he stopped worrying about Charles and started worrying about what they chased? About the werewolf they chased.

'What did the wolf look like?' He rocked slowly from one foot to the other but didn't bother controlling himself. He was too busy thinking.

'Like a German shepherd,' Bran said. 'Tan with dark points and the saddle, with a bit of white around his front feet. Both the grad student who escaped it and Heather described it the same way.'

The door to Bran's study opened, and Sage burst in. 'Did . . . I see he made it here. What's wrong?'

'Nothing,' said Bran gently. 'Asil, go home. I want you to rest today at home. I'll let you know as soon as I hear something.'

Asil stumbled by Sage, no longer worried about Charles at all. That coloration might be common in Alsatians – German shepherds – but it was not seen much in werewolves.

Sarai had looked like that, tan and dark brown with a saddle-shaped dark patch of fur on her back. Her left front paw had been white.

Too upset to be careful of his strength, he broke the door handle of his car and had to slide in from the passenger side. He didn't remember the drive to his home, just a need to go hide that was even more powerful than the necessity of obeying his Alpha.

He didn't bother garaging his car; for tonight it could face the elements, just as he must. He went to his bedroom and opened his closet. He took her favorite shirt, frayed by age and handling, from the hanger. Even to his nose it no longer smelled like Sarai, but it had touched her flesh and that was all he had. He put it on his pillow and slid onto the bed, rubbing his cheek against her shirt.

It had happened at last, he thought. He was crazy.

It could not possibly be his Sarai. First, she would never kill anyone without cause. Second, she was dead. He'd found her himself, days after she'd died. He'd taken her poor body and washed it clean. Had burned it with salt and holy water. Knowing who had killed her, he wanted there to be no way to raise her from the dead, though neither Mariposa's family nor the witch they'd sent her to for training were of the family of witches who played with the dead.

No. It wasn't Sarai.

His stomach hurt, his throat hurt, and his eyes burned with tears – and with the old rage that curdled his blood. He should have killed the witch but had been forced to run instead. Run, while his wife's killer lived, because he was afraid of what Mariposa had become. Afraid of the witch who hunted him as she'd hunted his Sarai.

Only, when he could stand running no longer, when it was apparent that time was not going to kill her as it ought, he'd come here – to die and join his beloved at last. But he let the Marrok . . . and, later, his roses persuade him to wait.

And she hadn't found him here. Maybe she'd quit looking at last, having grown more powerful with each year until she didn't need him. Maybe the Marrok's power protected him, as it protected the rest of the pack.

As he lay panting on his bed, the conviction grew that the time had come for his death. He folded the shirt lovingly where it was and strode back to his front door. He would persuade Bran this time.

But he couldn't open the door, couldn't force his hand to touch the doorknob. He roared his anger, but that changed nothing. He could not disobey Bran. He'd been so distressed that he hadn't noticed that Bran had given him a true order: until tomorrow he would have to stay here, in this house where he'd lived for all these years alone, hiding from his mate's murderer.

Tomorrow, then. He calmed himself with the thought. But first he'd repair what he had damaged. Tomorrow he'd help Charles with the rogue, give him anything he could think of that might be useful to him for dealing with an Omega for a mate – and then it would be over. As relief rushed through him, he found it in himself to smile. If Bran wouldn't kill him, after yesterday, he was certain that Charles would be happy to oblige.

He was calm as he climbed back into his bed, the weight of years lightened by the closeness of their ending. He touched the shirt with his hand and pretended that she was there next to him.

Gradually, the pain eased, cushioned by his knowledge that it would soon be gone forever and be replaced by peace and darkness. But for now there was only emptiness. He might have slept then, but curiosity, his besetting sin, made him consider the wolf who was killing others so near the Marrok's own territory.

Asil sucked in his breath and sat up.

So near the Marrok's territory. It killed, looking so much like his dear love. So near the Marrok's territory, or so near to Asil?

And then there were his dreams . . . his dreams always got stronger when the witch got too close.

Sarai hunting humans? He rubbed his eyes. Sarai barely hunted on the full-moon nights. Besides, Sarai was dead.

Despite the horror of imagining the witch so close, he discovered there was hope in his heart. But he knew that Sarai was dead, just as he knew that Mariposa had somehow stolen the bond between him and his mate.

That should have been beyond her, beyond any witch. The wolves kept their magics secret from others. Surely, if one of the families had discovered how to steal the bond between werewolves, they would have done it more than this once, and he would have heard of it by now. It had probably been an accident, a side effect of something else – but in all the years he'd been running, he'd never figured out what, unless it was the immortality Mariposa seemed to have gained upon Sarai's death.

Though he kept it closed as tightly as he could, he still felt the pull of the bond sometimes. As if Mariposa was trying to use it as she had that first day, before he realized what was wrong.

He'd thought it was Sarai. He knew that something was wrong, but the distance between them kept him from understanding exactly what. Then he'd woken in the middle of the night, tears falling from his eyes, though he didn't remember what he was dreaming. He'd reached for his Sarai . . . and touched alien madness.

He'd run all the rest of the way home, two full days, his bond locked down tight so he wouldn't touch that . . . ugliness again. And when he found Sarai dead and the house smelling of magic and Mariposa, he knew what had happened.

Two months later, the witch started to hunt him; he never had figured out exactly what she wanted. He, who had run from nothing, ran from a child not yet into her second decade of life. Because if she took Sarai, he could not guarantee that she could not take him. He was too old, too powerful to be a tool in the hands of a witch, dead or alive.

And his Sarai was dead. He squashed any faint hope lingering in his heart. She was dead, but maybe Mariposa had discovered some way to use the shape of her wolf, an illusion maybe.

That sounded right. Three attacks, and twice the victim had escaped. Humans don't often escape from werewolf attacks.

He was not unfamiliar with black magic. His mate had been a herbalist – it had been she who first taught him how to grow plants indoors. She had sold her herbs to witches until the vendettas between the witch families made it too dangerous. Illusions were among the very basic tenets of witchcraft. Making an illusion that could hurt or kill someone . . . he'd never heard of that. But his suspicion that Mariposa was behind the attacks settled into conviction; all

the more reason he find Charles and tell him what he might
be facing.

Besides, it wasn't in him to allow another person to fight
his battles – and if this was Mariposa's mischief, then she
was after him.

He closed his eyes but opened them almost immediately.

He was making a mountain of a molehill. Bran referred
to the werewolf as 'he.' It was just a rogue. He was letting
his own fears color the facts.

*But it hadn't been a werewolf who sighted the rogue*, a small
voice argued. *Would a pair of humans have noticed if the wolf
was female?* Female werewolves were not nearly as common;
Bran could be assuming it was a male.

He hadn't seen the witch for almost half a century, hadn't
caught a scent of her since he'd come to this continent. He'd
covered his tracks and asked Bran to keep his presence here
quiet.

And if she were here and wanted him, why hadn't she
just come and gotten him?

It wasn't her . . . he waited for relief to flood him. It was
*probably* not her.

Sarai was lost to him. She was two centuries dead; he'd
buried her himself. He'd never heard of an illusion that could
harm people.

Maybe the illusion had been the body he'd burned . . .

*Rest,* Bran had told him, and he felt his body growing
sluggish despite the frantic roiling of his mind. He set his
seldom-used alarm for 12:01 A.M. Bran might have ordered
him to stay here until morning, but Asil could interpret
'morning' as he chose. And in the morning, he'd go out and
find his answers.

Anna found herself moving before she had time to think.
Mary put out her hand and ended up with a handful of

Anna's hair when she tore herself loose – to put herself between the human and whatever was in the trees. It sounded to her like a werewolf, but the wind would not cooperate and bring its scent to her. Had the wolf Charles was chasing doubled back?

But the monster that emerged from the shadows of the underbrush was bigger than the one Charles was following. It looked almost like a German shepherd, except that it weighed a hundred pounds more, had longer teeth, and moved more like a cat than a dog.

There were two werewolves.

What if there were more of them? What if Charles had gone off to hunt one wolf and found himself surrounded?

The werewolf ignored the other woman, focusing completely on Anna. As it leaped forward, Anna ran, too. The snowshoes didn't help, but she didn't have to go far – and she was a werewolf, too.

Three strides and she snatched Charles's broken rifle off the ground by the barrel. Planting both feet, she swung it at the attacking monster with the experience of four summers of softball and the strength of a werewolf.

It was clear the other wolf hadn't expected Anna's strength. It hadn't bothered to dodge her strike at all. No one was ever going to fire the rifle again, but Anna hit the wolf full on the shoulder with a crack that told her she'd broken bone. It rolled with the blow, but let out a yip of pain as it came back to all four feet.

Something sizzled past Anna, and the wolf yelped again as blood blossomed on one hip. A small rock fell to the ground. The wolf looked over Anna's shoulder, then, with a last growl, it took off through the trees. Anna didn't try to follow it, but she kept her eyes on the woods where the shepherd-colored wolf had disappeared.

'Are you all right, honey?'

The sound of Charles's cautious voice made her head spin with sheer relief. She'd hoped that it had been him who'd thrown the rock, but it might have been Mary's missing partner, too. She dropped the remains of the rifle on the ground and ran to him.

'Hey,' he said, wrapping his arms around her. 'It was only a dog – a damned big dog. But you're fine now.' Though he was clearly playing to the human, his arms were fiercely protective as he pulled her against his coat – which was a dark red that suited him better than the brightly colored coat the wolf had ripped up.

It was a good thing, she thought, that he could clothe himself when he changed. Otherwise, they'd have something of a problem explaining why he'd been running after a bear in his birthday suit.

'That was some stone throwing,' she murmured to him, stifling an inappropriate giggle.

She'd done it, she thought. She'd defended herself against a monster and won. Safe in Charles's arms, exhilaration rapidly eclipsed everything else she'd been feeling. She had not only kept it from hurting her, but she'd defended someone else, too.

'Old skills,' he told her. 'My uncles taught me when I was growing up. I can do better with a slingshot. Any distance weapon is better than trying to drive off a ravening beast with a broken rifle. Who's your friend?'

She took a last sniffly breath, and then stepped away from his warmth. The woman was crouched, wide-eyed, with her back against a tree. 'Mary, this is my husband, Charles. Charles, this is Mary . . .'

'Alvarado,' said the woman in a shaken voice. '*Madre de Dios*, what was that?'

Anna obviously believed the woman was nothing more than a fellow hiker. Anna's blood stained her jacket – but it looked like it had only been a nosebleed, probably caused by the altitude. Charles brushed Anna's face with his hand and let what Samuel called his 'Good Ol' Injun' expression take over.

Samuel always said it was scary seeing the jovial expression and knowing what lurked behind it – but most people weren't as perceptive as his brother.

'Pleased to meet you.' Charles let his grin reach his eyes until they lit up as he looked at the woman.

She was bundled up against the cold, so he couldn't get a good look at her – but that didn't matter. His memory for scent was better than faces, and his nose told him he'd never seen her before.

He kept in mind that there were two werewolves somewhere nearby, but he'd deal with the monster at hand first.

He let go of his mate and took two long strides forward, two strides that not so incidentally put him between Anna and the woman. 'I'm sorry I was out chasing that—' He could have cursed his distraction – he didn't want to admit to chasing after a werewolf at this juncture. Not that the woman wouldn't know what it was that he and Anna had driven off, but if she didn't already know that he and Anna were werewolves, too, he didn't want her to figure it out. And if she did, well, then he didn't want her to know that he knew that she was something preternatural – one that used magic. He'd give her as little information as he could manage. So he stopped midword, but before the pause was very long Anna finished his sentence for him.

'—that *stupid* bear.' Anna gave him a chiding glance as if she thought he paused because he had almost sworn. He hadn't expected that she'd be so quick. 'Did you find the pack with our lighter?'

Was that what he was supposed to be doing? He shook his head. 'You know what they say about not being about to outrun a bear? They're right. Especially since it tore up my snowshoes, and I had to wade through the snow.'

That wolf had been as clever a prey as he'd ever chased. He hadn't heard it or seen it before it attacked, and it had disappeared as thoroughly as if it had never been. He might be persuaded that Anna had distracted him so he hadn't heard it approach – though nothing like that had ever happened to him before. But there had definitely been something uncanny about the way the wolf disappeared.

As soon as he realized he'd lost the trail, Charles hadn't wasted time trying to pick it up again. He headed back, not wanting to chance the wolf swinging back to attack Anna. So he'd given up for the moment and returned – just in time, as it turned out.

Mary Alvarado straightened, then stumbled forward, as if she'd lost her balance. The move left her just in front of him, resting a hand on his chest. He felt the weave of her spell as it slid off his protections.

The scent of Anna's fury all but lit up the forest – was she *jealous*? This was far too dangerous a situation to let himself get distracted . . . but, didn't Anna know he wasn't interested in anyone but her?

'There shouldn't be bear up here this late in the year,' said the woman, sounding shaken. He couldn't decide if she knew what he was or not.

'Bears don't sleep straight through the winter, ma'am,' Charles said, looking down at her as if he didn't mind her hand on his chest, which he did. Would have minded even if she didn't make his skin crawl. Not fae, he decided. Not a spirit or ghoul – both of those he'd met up here a time or two. Something human. Not a sorcerer, either, though his wolf reacted to her that way; something evil then. 'They don't go into a true hibernation. They'll get up now and then. It isn't usual, but you'll see 'em sometimes even in the dead of winter. Our bad luck we ran into one. But that dog that attacked you two was really strange.'

Black magic, that's what he smelled on her. A witch, then, a black witch. Damn it. He'd rather face a dozen ghouls than a black witch.

'Aren't there wild dogs?' Anna asked tightly. 'I thought that sometimes they form packs just like wolves.'

'This is pretty remote for that,' Charles told her, without looking away from the witch. 'Sometimes you'll see a dog loose – but most domestic animals can't survive a Montana winter without help.'

Something stirred behind the woman, and he let his eyes go unfocused to make seeing the spirit clearer. The shadow of a wolf showed him its teeth, then dashed away – as if he needed more warning than his nose to see that there was something dangerous about this woman.

Perhaps it was time to bring some things out into the open – before Anna decided to be hurt instead of just jealous.

He let his mask slide away and smiled gently at Mary. She wasn't observant enough to see Brother Wolf peeking out – either that or she liked a little danger, because she leaned into her hand while she looked up at him.

'But knowing that a domestic animal would not have survived this winter doesn't matter, does it, Mary Alvarado? Because you know quite well it was a werewolf.'

A blank look fell over the other woman's face. If he hadn't known what she was, he might have mistaken it for bewilderment. 'A what? There's no such thing as a were-wolf.'

Her act fell apart when she tried to meet his eyes – she'd been avoiding that. But a woman who was used to batting her eyes at men sometimes forgot not to do it to a were-wolf. She didn't take a step back, but she wanted to; he saw it in her face.

'No? Then there is no such thing as a witch, either.' Charles's voice was even softer.

She let her hand drop away. 'Who are you?'

'No.' He shook his head. 'I think you get to answer the questions first. Who are you?'

'I'm looking for the missing hunter,' she said.

That was truth as far as it went. He frowned at her a moment, trying to find some way to make that a half-truth. 'To get him to safety?' he murmured. Or to use him for her magic?

She gave him a sad smile. 'I doubt that there is a need for that by now. He's been lost in the woods with a rogue werewolf. How likely do you think it is that he is still alive?'

'So you knew about the werewolf?'

She raised her chin. 'The werewolf is why I am here.' Truth. 'Who are you? And what do you know about witches and werewolves?'

It was possible she was exactly who she represented herself as. He knew that there were witches who regularly worked for the various law-enforcement agencies. He also knew that just because she was a black witch didn't mean that she wasn't actually out looking for the missing man. Witches often hired themselves out – and sometimes, even if only by chance, a black witch could find herself on the side of the angels.

She'd been careful in her answers, though, and he did not discount what the spirits told him. She was no ally of his. The spirit-wolf was usually his guide – though he'd always thought it would have been more ironic if it had been a deer or rabbit. That show of fangs might not mean she was an enemy, but it did indicate that she wasn't friendly.

'You can leave the werewolf to us, now,' he told her. 'It's not your business.'

'It is,' she said calmly.

Truth. The full truth this time. How very interesting that a witch would believe a werewolf to be her business.

'You don't want to get in my way,' she told him softly, her breath caressing his face in a sweet flow.

'No,' he said, taking a step back from her and shaking his head – but he couldn't remember what he was objecting to.

'Now it is my turn for questioning.'

If he'd been capable of it, he would have cursed his own arrogance, which had kept him from grabbing Anna and running as soon as he realized what she was. All he could do was wait for the witch's questions.

Witch, he'd called her – and she hadn't denied it. Doubtless that meant something, but Anna had no idea what. Had the witch been following them? Or the werewolves?

Whatever she was, if she didn't get her hands off Charles pretty damn soon, Anna would do it for her, using a method involving pain and maybe blood.

The violent urge caught her by surprise, and she hesitated just long enough for Charles to stagger away from the witch. Something had happened, some balance had shifted. The air smelled faintly of ozone, as if, despite the time of year, lightning was ready to strike.

The hair on the back of Anna's neck rose helpfully – as if she *needed* any further evidence that something was wrong. Too bad the hair on the back of her neck didn't tell her what it was and what she could do about it.

'I'm looking for a man,' said Mary, her voice still incongruously sounding like a cheerleader's. 'His name is Hussan, though he also goes by Asil or the Moor.'

'I know him,' responded Charles, his voice sounding thick and reluctant.

'Ah,' she smiled. 'You are a werewolf. Are you one of the Marrok's? Is Asil in Aspen Creek, too? Is he one of the Marrok's wolves?'

Anna frowned at Charles, but he didn't seem to object

to the witch's questions – or the amount of knowledge she had.

He just nodded stiffly, and said, 'Yes' as if the word was dragged out of him.

Something was very wrong. Anna took a step sideways, and the remains of the rifle clicked on the aluminum edge of her snowshoe.

The witch muttered a word and flung it at Anna with a flick of her fingers, leaving Anna unable to move.

Charles growled.

'Hush, I haven't hurt her,' the witch told him. 'I have no wish to face the Marrok yet by hurting one of his wolves. She's a werewolf, too, I assume. That would explain why she was able to damage my guardian so badly. Tell me. What do you think would be the best way to get Asil to come here?'

'Asil doesn't leave Aspen Creek,' he told her, his voice rough with rage.

Anna stole his anger for herself; it was better than the panic that was her alternative. Her wolf stirred as she seldom did unless called – being held against her will was something she disliked as much as Anna.

Anna knew nothing about magic, not even the magic she knew was part of every pack's existence. Leo had told her she didn't need to know, and she hadn't been brave enough to ask again. She didn't know what Charles could do, or couldn't – but she was fairly certain that they wouldn't be standing there with Charles answering the witch's questions if he could have done something about it. She was afraid her ignorance and stupidity were going to cost them both.

When her wolf asked to take over, Anna allowed it. If she could do nothing about it with her human half in charge, maybe the wolf could do better.

Though she didn't start shifting, her perception of the

world changed, shadows faded back. She could see farther and more clearly, but the beauty and intensity of the colors grew dull. It wasn't as silent as she'd thought. There were birds in the trees – she could hear the soft sound as they shuffled their feet on the bark of the tree branches.

But more interestingly, she saw a web of light encasing Charles in sickly strings of yellow and green. Unable to drop her head, she couldn't see the web that held her. But her skin's sensitivity allowed her to feel the fine strands like a net of dental floss.

If it had been only her in danger, Anna was pretty sure that she'd have been standing in that one spot until spring thaw. Her wolf had submitted meekly to all the beatings, the forced sex – giving her only the strength to endure and something to hide behind when life became unbearable. But her mate was in trouble. A roar of anger hid itself under her diaphragm, making breathing difficult – but caution told her she needed to wait for the right opportunity.

'If you died, who would the Marrok send?' the witch asked.

The implied threat brought a roaring in Anna's ears that muffled Charles's reply, rage burning painfully through the spell holding her motionless.

'He would come himself.'

The witch pursed her mouth as if trying to decide whether that was something she wanted or not.

Anna couldn't move her feet, but with the wolf in charge she could move her hand through the agony caused by the witch's spell. She grabbed the cablelike end of the net that held her as if she were a villain in a Spider-Man comic. She wound it around and around her palm, then brought it to her other hand.

She couldn't look for long at the multiple strands she held together or they dazzled her eyes and made her head ache, but she didn't have to; the witch's cable of magic cut into her hands so she knew where it was.

She set her free hand on the cable just before it widened into the net that held her and pulled with both hands. She expected it to break or hold, as if it were really cable. Instead, it pulled like taffy, thinning gradually as she shifted her grip to pull it again and again.

If the witch had looked at her, she might have seen what Anna was doing. But the witch was only paying attention to Charles now.

Dominant, Anna thought gratefully, was more than just a rank in the pack. Charles's presence was such that when he walked into a room, everyone looked at him. Add to that effect Anna's own fragile appearance and utter lack of dominance, and it would require an effort on the witch's part to focus on Anna as long as Charles was there. An effort Mary Alvarado wasn't making.

Anna lost track of the question-and-reluctant-answer session. All of her being was focused on her task. Even taffy thins to nothing and breaks at some point.

Anna froze as the cable dissolved into nothingness, but the witch didn't appear to notice that her hold on Anna was gone.

What now?

She focused on the net that held Charles.

She would have to be fast.

Werewolves are very fast.

She darted between them, grabbing the cables of magic in both hands. The spell the witch used on Charles was a lot stronger, and it hurt to touch the strands. Pain radiated from her skin into her bones, settling into her jaw with a sharp, throbbing ache. She could smell burning flesh, but there was no time to assess the damage – a violent pull, and the spell shattered.

And Anna kept going. She grabbed the broken rifle from the snow and threw it as hard as she could. It hit the witch in the face with an audible snap.

She gathered herself for attack, but Charles grabbed her by the arm and tossed her ahead of him. 'Run,' he snarled. 'Get out of her line of sight.'

# 10

It didn't take Anna any time at all to discover that running in snowshoes sucked. They caught in the rocks, they caught in the brush, they brought her to her knees twice, and only Charles's hand on her elbow kept her from falling all the way down the mountainside. Jumping downed trees was . . . interestingly difficult. However, Charles, without snowshoes, was sinking up to his knees and deeper with each step – so she was properly grateful for hers.

That's not to say they were slow. It amazed Anna what terror could do for her speed. After the first, terrifying sprint-slide down the steep slope they'd spent hours climbing, she lost track of time and direction. She kept her eyes on Charles's red coat and stayed with him. When Charles slowed down at last, they were all alone in the forest.

Still they didn't stop. He kept her going at a fast jog for an hour or more, but he chose their path more carefully, staying up where the snow was shallower and his lack of snowshoes didn't hamper them.

He hadn't said a word after his command to run – but she thought it might be because he couldn't; and it wasn't any witch's spell.

His eyes were brilliant yellow, and his teeth were bared. He must have a good reason for staying in human form, but it was costing him. Her own wolf had slid back to sleep after the initial panic of their flight was over, but Charles's was right on the edge of taking over.

She had a whole slew of questions to ask. Some were immediate concerns like: Could the witch match their speed when a human couldn't? Could Mary use her magic to find them? Others were just matters of interest. How did you figure out she was a witch? Why could she only see the magic after her wolf was in control? Was there an easier way to break a witch's spell? Even an hour later her hands burned and ached.

'I think—' said Charles finally as his smooth rapid strides slowed to a halting limp. Her tired legs were grateful that he sounded winded, too. '—that Asil has some questions to answer.'

'You think he knows her? Why is she after him?' Anna asked. She had spent a long time assuming that the were-wolves (other than herself) were on the top of the food chain, but Charles's defeat at the hands of the witch shook her worldview. She was willing to believe that *anyone* would run from that witch.

'I don't know if Asil knows her. I haven't seen her in Aspen Creek, and she'd have been about ten when he incarcerated himself there. But if she's looking for him, he probably knows why.' All of this was said in rapid three-word bursts as he struggled to slow his breathing.

She walked next to him and hoped that some of the quietness she was supposed to be able to bestow would help him. His breath slowed long before hers lost the ragged edge of their run, but she was back to normal before he said anything more.

'She shouldn't have been able to do *that*. She made me fawn at her feet like a puppy.' His voice darkened to a growl.

'She shouldn't be able to control you with her magic?' asked Anna. 'I thought that witches could do that kind of thing.'

'To a human, maybe. The only person who should have that kind of control over wolves is their Alpha.' He snarled, fisted his hands, then said in a rough voice unlike his own,

'And even my *father* can't get a reaction like that from me. He can stop me in my tracks, but he can't make *me* do something I don't want to.'

He sucked in a slow breath. 'Maybe it's not her, maybe it's me. I didn't hear the first werewolf at all. I've been thinking about it, and I don't think it was downwind of us. I should have heard him, or smelled him – and he shouldn't have been able to lose me so easily.'

Her first reaction was to reassure him somehow, but she bit that back. He knew more than she did about magic and about tracking. Instead, she tried to look for reasons. Tentatively, she ventured, 'You were shot only a couple of days ago.'

He shook his head. 'That's not it. I've been wounded before. It's never stopped me from doing what I needed to do – and usually if I'm hurt it makes me more aware, not less.'

'Are the werewolves we're after connected to the witch, somehow?' Anna asked. 'I mean, if she controlled you, maybe she can control them, too. Maybe she did something so that you wouldn't sense them.'

He shrugged, but she could tell it bothered him. And he was hurting. Watching him closely, she thought that it was more than his leg that was bothering him. All the running he'd been doing had to be hard on his chest wound, too.

'Do you need new bandages?' she asked.

'Maybe,' he said. 'I'd have you check, but we don't have anything to remedy the situation with us. There's a good first-aid kit back in Da's car, and that's where we're heading now.'

She was about two steps behind him, so he didn't see her surprise, which was good, she thought. Dominant wolves didn't back down much. 'You aren't going after her?'

'She caught me once,' he said. 'And I don't know how.

Usually my personal magic would have allowed me to shed her imprisoning spell. That's a pretty basic one, evidently – I've had three different witches try it before this. Without knowing how she did it, it's not worth trying to fight her and risk her defeating us without warning Da. The wolves, both of them, are not as worrisome as she is. Da needs to know what's going on – and maybe Asil can shed some light on who she is and what she wants.'

There was something bothering her, but it took a dozen yards of progress before she thought of what it was. 'Why here? I mean, I know she was looking for Asil – and it sounds like she got some sort of information indicating he was in Aspen Creek. Did you catch her excitement when you told her he was here? She wasn't sure. So what is she doing here and not in Aspen Creek?'

'Baiting a trap,' he said grimly. 'My father was right about that, but not about who or why. All she had to do was kill a few people and make it look like a werewolf, and the Marrok would be sure to send someone after it. Then she could take him and question him. Much safer than driving into Aspen Creek and facing off with my father.'

'Do you think both the wolves are hers?' She'd asked him that before . . . but it was bothering her. She'd made a connection of some kind with the first wolf, the one Charles had run after. She didn't want him to be in league with a witch.

As he had the first time she'd asked him, Charles shrugged, winced when it hurt him, then half growled, 'I don't know any more than you do.' He trudged on a few steps. 'It seems likely. The wolf that attacked you almost certainly was. Since you are an Omega, a normal wolf would have gone after her first.'

He stopped suddenly. Just stood still. 'We ran out of the clearing the same way as the wolf who attacked you.'

She had to think about it, but he was right. 'There was a path through the brush there.'

'Did you see any tracks? Any blood? You cut her shoulder open with the rifle, and she was bleeding pretty good.'

'I—' Would she have noticed? She thought carefully about their escape, Charles pushing her ahead of him. 'There was blood on the snow where I hit her, and it followed her path into the trees. But we were going through unmarked powder as soon as we were out of the clearing. She must have gone by a different route.'

Charles turned so he faced her. The corners of his mouth were tight with pain, and from the grayish undertone of his skin, she was pretty sure he was in a lot worse shape than he wanted her to know.

'She?' he said softly.

'She. I got an up-close and personal. Trust me.'

'She.' He repeated. 'That makes life more interesting. Her coloring was unusual.'

'No.' Anna frowned at him. 'She looked like a German shepherd.'

'It's not unusual for a German shepherd,' he agreed. 'But I've never seen a werewolf who looked like that. I've heard of one, though.'

'Who?'

'Asil's mate.'

'Asil's mate is supposed to be dead, right?' said Anna. 'So you think she's really alive and working with a witch? Is that why they're looking for Asil?'

'Asil told my father she was dead, and that he burned her body and buried the ashes himself.' Almost as an afterthought, he said, 'No one lies to my father. Not even Asil. But that makes the absence of tracks pretty interesting.'

'What are you saying? She wasn't a ghost. The butt of

the rifle hit *something*. If Asil's mate is dead, then her resemblance has to be coincidental.'

He shook his head. 'I don't know what she was. But I don't believe in coincidences.' He started off again.

'I thought most witches were human,' she said after mulling the whole thing over for a while.

'Yes.'

'Then they aren't immortal. You told me Asil's mate died a few centuries ago. And this witch isn't much older than I am. Do you think maybe the wolf is in charge?'

'I don't know,' he said, holding back a tree branch so it didn't swing back and hit her. 'That's a good question.'

He fell silent again as he led her up another ripple of land. Mountains looked so simple from a distance, just one long walk up and another down the other side. The reality was a series of climbs and descents that seemed to cover a lot of ground and still went nowhere.

They must have been running longer than she'd realized because it was starting to get dark. She shivered.

'Charles?'

'Mmm?'

'I think my socks must have gotten wet. I can't feel my toes.' He didn't say anything, and she worried that he might think she was complaining. 'It's all right. I can still go on for a while yet. How much longer until we get to the car?'

'Not tonight,' he said. 'Not if your toes are numb. Let me find somewhere that will give us a little shelter – there's a storm coming through tonight.'

Anna shivered a little harder at the thought. At the tail end of a particularly long shiver, her teeth started chattering.

Charles put his hand under her arm. 'A storm will be good. I heard bone go when you hit that wolf. If it isn't a phantasm of some sort, it'll take it a while to repair. A heavy snow and a good wind will keep it from picking up our trail.'

He caught sight of something uphill, and it seemed to Anna that they climbed forever until they reached a small bench of land littered with downed trees.

'Microburst last spring, maybe,' he told her. 'It happens sometimes.'

She was too tired to do anything but nod, while he waded through the trees until he found something he liked – a huge tree propped up by another, both of them leaning against a hump of land, creating a cave with an uninviting floor of snow.

'No food,' Charles said grimly. 'And you need food to combat the cold.'

'I could go hunting,' offered Anna. Charles couldn't. He had been limping badly for a long time. She was so tired she could have fallen asleep standing up, and she was cold. But she was still in better shape than he was.

Charles shook his head. 'I'll be damned if I'll send you off on your own in this country with a storm waiting to unleash – not to mention a witch and two werewolves lurking about.'

He lifted his head and sampled the air. 'Speak of the devil,' he said softly. Anna sniffed the air, too, but she didn't smell anything. Just trees and winter and wolf. She tried again.

'You might as well come out,' Charles growled, looking out into the darkness below their bench. 'I know you're there.'

Anna turned around, but she didn't see anything out of place. Then she heard the sound of boots in the snow and looked again. A man stepped out of the woods about ten yards down the mountain. If he hadn't been moving, she probably wouldn't have seen him.

The first thing she noticed was hair. He didn't wear a hat, and his hair was an odd shade between red and gold; it hung in ragged, ungroomed tangles down his back and blended into a beard that would have done credit to Hill or Gibbons of ZZ Top.

He wore an odd combination of animal skins, rags, and new boots and gloves. In one hand he held the bundle she'd made of the things that had been in Charles's backpack, and her own bright pink backpack was slung over one shoulder.

He tossed them both toward Charles, and the packs landed halfway between them.

'Your stuff,' he said, his voice at once hoarse and mumbly, with a healthy dose of Tennessee or Kentucky. 'I saw her set the beast on you – which makes you her enemy. And along the lines of "the enemy of my enemy is my friend," I thought I'd bring your stuff to you. Then maybe we could talk.'

It hadn't been the man's scent that had clued Charles in that they were being shadowed, but a host of smaller things: a bird taking flight, the hint of a sound, and a feeling that they were being watched.

Once the stranger stepped out of the trees, Charles could smell him as he should have been able to for some time because the wind was favoring Anna and him. Werewolf.

Though he brought a peace offering and said he wanted to talk, his body language told Charles the other wolf was ready to take flight.

Careful not to look straight at him or move in any way that might spook him, Charles left Anna where she was and walked down to pick up Anna's pack and their ground tarp filled, he supposed, with everything that had been in his backpack. Without saying anything, he turned his back to the stranger and started back up the mountain.

It wasn't as foolish as all that because Charles kept his

eyes on Anna and watched her face for any sign of attack. Then he deliberately cleaned the snow off the top of a log and sat on it. The man, he saw, had followed him until he stood where the packs had first landed, but he came no farther.

'I think it would be a good idea to talk,' Charles said. 'Would you join us for a meal?' He met the man's eyes, letting him feel the weight of the invitation that was just short of an order.

The man shifted his weight from one foot to the other, as if ready to run. 'You smell like that demon wolf,' he rasped. Then he shot Anna a shy glance. 'That thing's been killin' and killin' up here. Deer, and elk, people, even a griz.'

He sounded like it was the bear that troubled him the most.

'I know,' Charles said. 'I was sent here to take care of the wolf.'

The man dropped his eyes as if he couldn't bear to look Charles in the eye anymore. 'Thing is . . . thing is . . . it got me, too. Infected me with its evil.' He took a step back, wary as an old stag.

'How long have you been a werewolf?' Anna asked. 'It's been three years for me.'

The man tilted his head at the sound of Anna's voice, as if he was listening to music. And for a moment his agitation slowed down.

'Two months,' ventured Charles, when it became obvious that the other man was too caught up in Anna's spell to speak. He understood that feeling. The sudden peace as Brother Wolf settled down was as startling as it was addictive. If he'd never felt it before, he doubted he'd be talking, either. 'You stepped between the werewolf and the grad student this fall. Just like you stepped between Anna and me when you thought I might hurt her.'

It fit, Charles thought, though it added complications to just what the other werewolf was. Only another werewolf could infect a human. But he was certain that the beast's tracks stopped as soon as it would have been out of sight.

The sound of Charles's voice was enough to make the man jerk his gaze away from Anna. He knew who the dangerous one was here.

'I was going to let him die. The student, I mean,' the other man said, confirming Charles's theory about who he was. 'There was a storm coming, and it'd probably have killed him if he'd been in the wild when it hit. The mountains here demand respect, or they'll have you for lunch.' He paused. 'There's a storm coming soon.'

'So why didn't you let the werewolf kill him?' Anna asked.

'Well, ma'am,' said the man, staring at his feet rather than looking at Anna. 'Dying by the storm, or from a bear attack, those things just happen.' He stopped, evidently having trouble putting the difference into words.

'But the werewolf didn't belong here,' said Charles, with a sudden inkling about why this wolf was so hard to sense and why he'd received no warning of his attack. From the clothes he wore, he looked as though he'd been living here a very long time.

'It is evil. And it turned me into a monster, too, just like it is,' the man whispered.

If Charles had been a split second faster, he could have kept Anna back. But he was tired, and he'd focused on the other wolf. Before he knew it, Anna was slipping and sliding down the mountainside. She was in a hurry and about four paces from their new acquaintance her snowshoes did an excellent job of acting like skis.

Charles forced himself to stillness as the other man caught his mate by an elbow and saved her from sliding down the mountainside. He was almost certain this man was no threat to her. Charles managed to convince Brother Wolf to stand down and give Anna a chance to work her magic and tame the rogue; this was why his father had sent her, after all.

'Oh, *you* aren't evil,' Anna said.

The man froze, one hand still on her sleeve. Then the words poured out of him as if he couldn't stop them. 'I know about evil. I fought with it and against it until blood ran like the rain. I still see their faces and hear their screams as if it were happening now, and not nearly forty years ago.' But the tightness in his voice lightened as he spoke.

He released his hold on Anna, and asked, 'Who are you?' He fell to his knees beside her, as if his legs could no longer hold him up. 'Who are you?'

He'd moved too fast, though, and Brother Wolf had had enough. As quick as thought, with complete disregard to his injuries, Charles was beside Anna, managing to keep his hands off the rogue only because as soon as he got near her, Anna's Omega effect spread over him, too.

'She is a wolf-tamer,' Charles told the other man. Even Anna couldn't keep the possessive anger completely out of his voice. 'Peace-bringer.'

'Anna Cornick,' Anna said. He liked the way it tripped off her tongue and smelled like God's own truth. She knew she was his – and as easily as that, Brother Wolf settled down contentedly. So he didn't grab her hand when she touched the stranger on the shoulder, and said, 'This is my mate, Charles. Who are you?'

'Walter. Walter Rice.' Ignoring Charles as if he was no threat at all, Walter closed his eyes and swayed a little on his knees in the snow. 'I haven't felt like this since . . . since before the war, I think. I could *sleep*. I think I could sleep forever without dreaming.'

Charles held out his hand. 'Why don't you come eat with us first.'

Walter hesitated and took another good long look at Anna before taking Charles's gloved hand with his own and coming to his feet.

The man who introduced himself as Walter ate as if he were half-starved – maybe he was. Every once in a while, though, he'd stop eating to look at Anna with awe.

Sitting between them, Charles repressed a smile – which was something he was doing more often than he ever remembered since he'd found his Anna. Watching her squirm under Walter's worshipping regard was pretty funny. He hoped he didn't look at her like that – at least not in public.

'It's not as if it's anything I'm doing,' she muttered into her stew with carrots. 'I didn't *ask* to be an Omega. It's like having brown hair.'

She was wrong, but he thought she was embarrassed enough right now without him arguing with her over something he wasn't entirely sure he was supposed to have heard. Or at least she was mostly wrong. Like dominance, being an Omega was mostly personality. And, as his father liked to say, identity was partly heritage, partly upbringing, but mostly the choices you make in life.

Anna brought peace and serenity with her wherever she went – at least when she wasn't scared, hurt, or upset. Some of her power depended upon her being a werewolf, which magnified the effect of her magic. But a larger part of it was the steel backbone that made the best of whatever circumstances she happened to be in, the compassion she'd shown to Asil when he'd tried to scare her, and the way she hadn't been able to leave poor Walter out in the cold. Those were conscious decisions.

A man made himself Alpha, it wasn't just an accident of birth. The same was true of Omegas.

'Once,' said Walter quietly, pausing in his eating, 'just

after a very bad week, I spent an afternoon camped up in a tree in the jungle, watching a village. I can't remember now if we were supposed to be protecting them or spying on them. This girl came out to hang her wash right under my tree. She was eighteen or nineteen, I suppose, and she was too thin.' His eyes traveled from Anna to Charles and back to his food.

*Yes*, thought Charles, *I know she's still thin, but I've had less than a week to feed her up.*

'Anyway,' the old vet continued, 'watching her, it was like watching magic. Out of the basket the clothes would come, all in a wad, she'd snap 'em once, and, like that, they'd fall straight and hang just so. Her wrists were narrow, but so strong, and her fingers quick. Those shirts wouldn't dare disobey. When she left, I almost knocked on her door to thank her. She reminded me that there was a world of daily chores, where clothes were cleaned and everything was in order.'

He glanced at Anna again. 'She likely would have been terrified by a dirty American soldier showing up at her door – and like as not wouldn't have a clue what I was thanking her for, even if she understood what I was saying. She was just doing as she always did.' He paused. 'But I should have thanked her anyway. Got me through a bad time and several bad times since.'

They were all quiet after that. Charles didn't know if Anna understood his story, but he did. Anna was like that woman. She reminded him of winters spent in front of a fire while his da played a fiddle. Times when he knew that everyone was full and happy, when the world was safe and ordered. It wasn't like that often, but it was important to remember it could be.

'So,' said Charles, as Walter ate the last of his third freeze-dried dinner. 'You've lived here in the mountains for a long time.'

Walter's spork stilled for a moment, and he looked at Charles suspiciously. Then he snorted and shook his head. 'It's not like it's important anymore, is it? Old news.'

He ate another bite, swallowed, and said. 'When I got back from the war, everything was okay for a while. I had a short fuse, sure, but not enough to bother about. Until it got worse.' He started to say something but ate another bite instead. 'That part matters even less, now, I suppose. Anyway, I started reliving the war – like it was still going on. I could hear it, taste it, smell it – but it would turn out that it was only a car backfiring – or the neighbor chopping wood. Stuff like that. I moved out before I hurt my family more than I already had. Then one day an enemy soldier came up behind me. It was the uniform, you know? I hurt him, maybe killed him . . .'

That last sentence the man had choked out was a lie.

Walter looked at his feet, snorted, turned his head to meet Charles's eyes. And when he spoke again, his voice was cool and controlled, the voice of a man who had done a lot of bad things – just like Charles. 'I killed him. When he was dead I realized he wasn't one of the Viet Cong, he was a mailman. That's when I figured no one was safe around me. I thought I'd turn myself in, but the police station . . . well, policemen wear uniforms, too, don't they? The bus depot was right next to the station, and I ended up on a bus for Montana. I'd come here camping with my father a time or two, so I knew I could get away from people up here. There wasn't anyone to hurt up here.'

'You stayed in the mountains for all those years?' Anna put her chin on her hand, and Charles noticed that two of her nails were broken to the quick – and looked around until he saw her gloves sitting beside her.

Walter nodded. 'God knows I knew how to hunt. Didn't have a gun – but hell, half the time your gun didn't work in the jungle, either.'

He pulled a knife nearly as long as his forearm out from somewhere and contemplated it. Charles tried to figure out where it had come from. There weren't actually all that many people who could move that fast, werewolf or not.

Walter looked sideways at Anna, then back to the knife, but Charles knew he'd seen the sympathy on Anna's face, because he tried to downplay his survival. 'It wasn't that bad, really, ma'am. Winters can get rough, but there's an old cabin I stay in now and then if conditions get too bad.'

Walter wasn't the only one who escaped to the mountains, Charles thought. There had been a few places, twenty years ago, where whole communities of broken men had holed up in the wilds. Most of the old soldiers had healed and moved on years ago – or died.

Before this trip he wouldn't have believed there was anyone here; the Cabinets had little gentleness to share with the hearts of men. Charles had never come here that he hadn't felt the old places pushing him out on his way. They weren't meant for man – even one who had a Brother Wolf. Even in the old days, the trappers and hunters had avoided this area for somewhere with a gentler nature.

A man who lived here over thirty years, though, might not be an intruder anymore. He might be accepted as part of the mountain.

Charles looked into the night-dark sky and thought that a man who stayed here that long might become beloved of those spirits. Spirits who could hide someone even from Charles's own keen senses.

Walter wiped the spork in the snow and handed it back to Charles. 'Thank you. I haven't eaten like that in . . . a long time.'

Then, as if his words had just run out, he closed his eyes and leaned against the nearest tree.

'What do you know about the werewolf that attacked you?' Charles asked.

Walter shrugged without opening his eyes. 'They came in the fall on a four-wheeler and took over my cabin. After it Changed me . . . I did a little hunting of my own. Wish I'd seen it before it confronted that boy. If I'd been a little faster that day, I might have killed it – if I'd been a little slower, it'd have killed me. Good thing silver's bad for werewolves.' Walter heaved a loud sigh, opened his eyes, and pulled the long blade out of a forearm sheath again. This time Charles saw him do it – though, come to think of it, he hadn't seen him put it away.

'This old knife of mine burns my hand now when I clean it.' He looked at his hands, or maybe the knife. 'I figured I was dead. I hurt that demon bad with this old blade – it's got silver etched into it, see? But the monster opened my gut before it fled.'

'If a werewolf attack almost kills you, you become one,' Anna said in a low voice.

Did she still regret that? Charles was overcome with the wild desire to kill them all again, Leo and his mate, the whole Chicago pack – but at the same time he was pathetically grateful that his mate was a werewolf who wouldn't fade and die the way Samuel's wives all had.

Brother Wolf stirred and settled down, just like Walter had.

'The wolf who attacked you didn't come back to you, then, after you Changed?' Charles asked.

Usually when a wolf Changed someone, it was drawn back to the new werewolf for a while. Mostly, Samuel had theorized to him once, some genetic imperative to make sure that an untaught, uncontrolled werewolf wasn't going to draw too much unwanted attention.

Walter shook his head. 'Like I said, I tracked her down

myself, after the first full moon – she and that woman. What is she anyway? She sure as hell ain't human – sorry, ma'am – not with the things I seen her do. She tried to call me to her the first time I Changed. I didn't know what she was, only that she smelled bad – like the beast. I thought for a while that she and the beast were the same creature, but then I saw them together.'

It had begun snowing gently an hour ago, but now big, fat flakes fell with more intensity, sticking to eyelashes and hair. A little more of his tension fell away; snow would hide them.

'Have you ever seen the wolf in her human form?' Charles didn't know what Asil's mate looked like in her human form, but a description might be useful.

Walter shook his head. 'Nope. Maybe she doesn't have one.'

'Maybe not.' Charles didn't know why he was so sure that the other werewolf wasn't what she seemed. They'd been running, it was possible he'd missed her tracks. But he tended to believe his instincts when they were whispering this strongly.

He turned his attention to Walter. Two months, and he'd had the control this afternoon to stop his attack as soon as he'd realized that Anna was a werewolf and not a victim. That was more control than most new wolves had.

'Your control is very good for someone who has only just been Changed – especially someone who didn't have help,' Charles observed.

Walter gave him a grim look, then shrugged. 'Been controlling a beast inside me ever since the war. Except that now I grow fangs and claws, it ain't that much different. I have to be careful – like when I went after you. When I'm the wolf, I like the taste of blood. If I'd broken skin instead of ripping up your pack . . . well, then my control ain't so good.' He glanced at Anna again, as if worried about what that would make her think of him.

Anna gave Charles an anxious look. Was she worried about Walter?

The thought that she might try to protect another male from him brought a snarl from his chest that never made it to his face. He waited until Brother Wolf quieted, then said, 'For someone who's been a wolf for only a couple of moons with no one to help him that is *extraordinarily* good.'

He looked directly at Walter, and the other wolf dropped his eyes. He was dominant, Charles judged, but not enough to think of challenging Charles – most wolves weren't. 'You thought Anna was in danger, didn't you?' he said softly.

The rawboned man shrugged, making his crudely stitched-together cape of furs rustle. 'Didn't know she was a werewolf, too. Not until I was right between you.'

'But you knew I was.'

The man nodded his head. 'Yes. It's that smell, it calls to me.' He shrugged. 'I've lived alone for all these years, but it's harder now.'

'Wolves need packs,' Charles told him. It had never bothered him to need other wolves, but there were some wolves who never adjusted to it.

'If you'd like,' he told Walter, 'you can come home with us.'

The man stilled, his eyes still on his feet, but every other part of him focused on Charles. 'I'm not good around people, around noise,' he said. 'I still . . . here it doesn't matter if sometimes I forget it's forest and not the jungle.'

'Oh, you'll fit right in,' said Anna dryly.

Walter jerked his gaze to her face, and she smiled warmly at him, so Charles got to watch the man's ears turn red.

'Charles's father's pack has a lot of people who don't quite fit in,' she told him.

'My father's pack is safe,' said Charles. 'He makes it so. But Anna is right, he has more than a few wolves who would not be able to live elsewhere. If you want to move to another pack after a while, he'll find somewhere that you feel welcomed. If you can't handle it, you can come back here as a lone wolf – after we take care of the witch and her pet werewolf.'

Walter glanced up and away. 'Witch?'

'Welcome to our world.' Anna sighed. 'Witches, were-wolves, and things that go bump in the night.'

'So what are you going to do with her?'

'The witch told us she was looking for Asil, who is a very old wolf who belongs to my father. So we thought we'd get out of these mountains, then we'll have a long talk with Asil,' Charles told him.

'And in the meantime?' Walter rubbed his fingers over his forearm, where his knife once more lay sheathed under his clothing.

'You need to come and meet with my father,' Charles told him. 'If you don't, he'll send me out to take you in, will-ingly or no.'

'You think you can force me to come with you to your father's pack?' The man's voice was low and deadly.

'Oh, that was well done,' Anna snapped, obviously upset with him, though Charles didn't know what he'd done wrong. His father would not tolerate a rogue so close to his pack, and he wouldn't agree to name Walter a lone wolf unless he met him for himself.

But Anna had already turned her attention to Walter. 'What do you want to do? Stay up here all alone? Or come down with us when we go to get a little help – and come back here again to deal with the rogue and her witch?'

Charles raised an eyebrow at her, and she raised hers back. 'That wolf harmed him. We're here on pack business – for

Walter this is personal.' She looked back at the other man. 'Isn't it?'

'Evil must be destroyed,' he said. 'Or it takes over everything it touches.'

She nodded, as if he made perfect sense. 'Exactly.'

They were going to sleep as wolves tonight, Charles declared. Anna didn't object, even though her stomach tightened at the thought.

She'd been growing used to sleeping with Charles, but another wolf made her nervous, no matter how deferentially he treated her. But as soon as the sun went down, the temperature dropped another ten degrees. With only one sleeping bag, she knew that Charles was right, and there was no choice.

She changed a hundred yards from the males, shivering barefooted in the snow – where she'd moved after first trying the bare ground under a big fir tree – whoever called them needles knew what they were talking about.

The cold made the pain of change worse and stars dance in her vision. She tried to gasp quietly, tears leaking down her cheeks as her joints and bones rearranged themselves and restretched her flesh over them, and her skin split to become fur.

It took a long, long time.

Afterward, she lay panting and miserable on the ice-crystal-covered snow, too tired to move. Even cold, she discovered, had a smell.

Gradually, as her misery faded, she realized that for the first time since last night, when Charles had curled around her and surrounded her with his warmth, she felt toasty-warm. As the initial agony faded to aches and pains, she stretched, making her claws expand and lengthen like a big cat's. Her back popped and crackled all the way down her spine.

She didn't want to go back and curl up with a strange male only feet away. The wolf wasn't afraid of the male. She knew he wasn't likely to behave like the Others. But she didn't much like the idea of touching anyone other than Charles, either.

Near but out of sight, a wolf, Charles, made a quiet sound, not quite a bark or a whine. Wobbly as a newborn foal, she staggered to her feet. She paused to shake the snow off her pelt and give herself a moment to get used to four paws before starting back, her clothes in her mouth. Charles trotted up to her, then grabbed her glove-stuffed boots and escorted her to their bed for the night.

Walter waited for them just outside their chosen shelter. As soon as she could see him, she knew that she wasn't the only one who wasn't excited about sleeping nose to tail with a stranger. Walter looked miserable, hunched over with his tail carried low.

Charles directed Walter with a flick of his ear to lie down in the shelter he'd found for them. Walter burrowed in, and it was Anna's turn. Charles pushed her after Walter, set her boots where they wouldn't fill with snow, then lay in front of them both where he could protect them. There wasn't a lot of room, even though Walter had tucked himself as close to the trees at their back as he could.

As Anna settled against him, Walter shook with stress. Poor thing, she thought. To have been alone for so long, and then be expected to adjust instantly to pack behavior. His suffering had an odd effect on her own discomfort. Concerned for him, she stretched out and buried her nose in Charles's ruff. She made herself relax, hoping that would help Walter do the same.

*This* was pack, she thought, as warmth rolled over her from both of the other wolves. Trusting Charles to watch for harm with his better-trained senses. Knowing that both wolves had proven themselves ready to put themselves between her and harm, and it was safe to sleep. This was better, much better than her first pack.

It was a long time before Walter quit imitating a stone statue and relaxed against her more comfortably. But not until he put his nose on her hip with a sigh did she allow herself to drift off to sleep.

## 11

Pain kept Charles awake while his mate and the rogue slept. His leg and chest were making it quite clear that he'd been pushing too hard. If he wasn't careful, he wasn't going to make it down the mountains. But it was the thought of the witch that kept him alert as the snowstorm wailed around them.

He'd never felt anything like that, obedience wrapping him in impossible layers until he could do nothing but respond as she asked. He was too dominant for even his father to do that — but he'd heard it described. The descriptions had fallen short by a long shot. If he hadn't already been convinced of the correctness of his father's careful screening of the dominants under his rule before he allowed them to become Alphas, that would have done it. How terrifying it was for someone to have that kind of power over you, even if you trusted him. His respect for the bravery of the submissives in his father's pack had gone up another couple of notches.

If Anna hadn't distracted the witch and broken the spell . . . He drew in a harsh breath, and Anna made a little noise in her throat, comforting him, even in her sleep.

Panic long since over — or mostly over — he'd had time to think about the way that spell had worked. And he still had no idea how the witch had been able to use his . . . *his father's* pack bonds the way she had.

His father needed to know that she could do that, that a *witch* could break into the pack's magic. As far as he knew, nothing like that had ever happened before. Only his pain, and the understanding that he was going to have to pay attention to the limits of his body, kept him where he was, instead of running to the car. He had to warn his father.

If Anna hadn't been there . . . and how had she known what to do?

Outside of pack magic, most wolves had very little magic – and he'd have sworn that Anna was no exception. He knew her scent very well, and she did not smell of magic. If their mating had been completed, then she might have drawn on his . . .

He lifted his head and smiled toothily. *Anna* wasn't mated yet, but her wolf was. He'd felt her call on her wolf when the witch bespelled her, but he hadn't thought it would do any good. Fat lot he knew. The wolf had used his magic to break the witch's spell. And Anna hadn't been accepted into the Marrok's pack yet, so the witch's infiltration of the pack bonds hadn't allowed her to get to Anna the way she'd controlled him.

A soft sound amidst the howl of the wind broke his train of thought; something was walking in the trees. Even though it was a safe distance from where they slept, he listened and waited for the fickle wind to shift and carry scent to him. If it was the witch, he would gather his chicks and run, aching chest and leg be damned.

But it was someone else who stepped out of the trees and stopped so he could get a good clear look at him. Asil. Slowly Charles crawled out from under the tree. Anna sighed and resettled – exhaustion making it hard for her to wake up. He held very still until he heard her breathing even out again.

Then he started toward their intruder.

Since Asil had joined the Marrok, Charles had never seen him outside Aspen Creek; he didn't like it that the first time was here and now. It told him that whatever Asil knew, it wasn't going to make his life easier. He also didn't like his inability to cover up his limp.

Charles seldom bothered showing off, but he did this time. He called the magic to him and let it rip through his body, changing as he walked. It hurt, but he knew it didn't show on his face or make his limp any worse. If he'd been healthier and the spirits willing, he might even have been able to conjure up a new pair of snowshoes instead of having to wade. At least the snow on the bench, regularly scoured by the wind, was only a foot or so deep most places – half of that had fallen tonight.

Asil smiled a little, as if he recognized Charles's power play for what it was, but he dropped his eyes. Though Charles knew better than to trust the submission in the other's body language, it was enough for now.

Charles kept his voice low. 'How did you find us?'

It was an important question. They were nowhere near the place they'd have been camping if he and Anna had followed the trip as he'd outlined it with Tag. Had he done something stupid that would let the witch find them, too? The oddities of the past twenty-four hours had badly shaken his confidence – and that, and his half-crippled body, was making him crankier than usual.

Asil kept his shoulders relaxed under the thick coat he wore. 'As we age, we all gain abilities, yes? Your father can talk to his wolves in their heads, no matter how far away they are. Me, I can always track my pack mates. If you hadn't taken off like scared rabbits, I'd have come upon you hours ago.'

'Why are you here?' Charles gritted out. He wasn't irritated about the 'scared rabbit' comment. He wasn't.

Getting angry around Asil never was a good idea. The self-absorbed, arrogant Moor would feed you your anger back with a healthy dose of humiliation. Charles had never fallen victim, for all of Asil's baiting, but he'd seen many who had. You don't survive as long as Asil had without being a cunning predator.

'I came to apologize,' Asil said, raising his eyes so that Charles could read the sincerity in them. 'Sage told me something of what Anna endured. If I had known what you were dealing with, I would not have made trouble between you and your mate.'

'You didn't make trouble between us,' said Charles. Impossible, though, to doubt that Asil meant what he said.

'Good. And whatever assistance I can offer to help you and your mate is yours.' He looked toward the log where Anna and Walter were hidden. 'In my fit of remorse, it occurred to me that I might be of some assistance with your rogue. But, it looks as though you have everything under control.'

Charles felt his eyebrows rise. *Under control* was not exactly how he'd have described the last day. 'Appearances are deceiving, then. Do you know why a witch would be looking for you?'

Asil's face went blank, his body utterly still. 'Witch?'

'She was asking about you, specifically.' He rubbed his forehead because he'd be damned if he'd rub his aching chest while Asil could see him. 'Or how she could tap into my father's pack bonds to take tighter control of me than my father has ever managed?'

'A witch,' Asil said. 'Here?'

Charles nodded curtly. 'If you don't know anything about her, how about a female werewolf who seems to be connected with her somehow? One whose coloring matches your mate's—'

His voice trailed off because Asil, his face still oddly blank, dropped to his knees; not like he was kneeling before Charles, but more as if the joints had quit working right. It reminded

Charles of the way Walter had done the same thing earlier, but it wasn't wonder or the unexpected grace of Anna's presence that caused this.

The scent of Asil's violent emotions washed over him, impossible to sort out anything specific from the storm except that pain and horror were both in the forefront.

'It is her, then,' Asil whispered. 'I had hoped that she would die and be gone forever. Even when I heard what the rogue looked like, I hoped it was someone else.'

That was why Charles didn't believe in coincidences. 'You know the witch?'

The Moor looked at his black-gloved hands, then buried them in the snow. He closed his eyes and shuddered. When he opened them, they sparkled with gold highlights. 'It's her. She stole it, and she can no more hide from me if I look, than I can hide from her here.'

Charles took a deep breath and counseled himself to patience. 'What did she steal – and who is she?'

'You know,' Asil said. 'She's the one who killed my Sarai.' He took his snow-covered hands and scrubbed them on his forehead. Then he added the unbearable part. 'She stole my mate bond when she did.'

Charles knew – as did anyone who had heard the stories of the Moor – that Asil and his wife's mate bond had brought with it an unusual gift, empathy.

He didn't do anything dumb, like ask Asil if he was certain – though he'd never in his life heard of such a thing. And to be tied to a witch, a black witch, with empathy was possibly the worst thing he'd ever heard of. No wonder Asil had asked his father to kill him.

'This witch looks to be barely out of her teens. Sarai died two centuries ago.'

Asil bowed his head and murmured, 'I swear to you, I did not expect her to find me. Your father's safeguards held for all this time – if they hadn't, I'd have forced him to kill me the very first day I came to Aspen Creek.' He swallowed. 'I should not have allowed him to make me one of the pack, though. If she reached through the pack bonds, the only access she could possibly have is through me, though our mate bond.'

Chilled, Charles stared at the Moor and wondered if he could possibly be as mad as he'd always claimed. Because if he wasn't, this witch was even more of a problem than Charles thought.

Crystalline wolf eyes gazed up at him, looking out of Asil's dark face while snow coated both of them. 'Tell me about the wolf who looked like my Sarai.' Desperation and despair colored the old wolf's voice.

'I never met your mate,' Charles's voice softened. 'But the wolf with the witch is large, even for a werewolf. She's colored like a German shepherd, fawn with black points and back. There's some white on her left front foot, I think.'

'First two toes,' Asil spat, coming to his feet in a rage that was undeniably real, for all that it had come upon him instantaneously. 'How dare she use Sarai's form for her illusions?'

Charles folded his arms. He was going to have to sit down soon, the pain was making him light-headed. 'It's not an illusion, Asil. Not unless an illusion can pass on lycanthropy. The rogue we found here is her first victim. She attacked him, and he drove her off – then Changed at the next new moon.'

Asil stilled. 'What?'

Charles nodded. 'There's something strange about that wolf. She's only solid sometimes. Anna hurt her, and she fled, but as soon as she was out of sight, her tracks and blood just stopped.'

Asil's breath caught.

'You know something?'

'They were all dead,' he whispered.

'Who?'

'All the witches who knew . . . but then we all under-estimated Mariposa.'

'*Mariposa?* As in butterfly?'

Asil's eyes were black in the night. 'I am not a witch.'

Which seemed like an odd answer to his question. Charles considered him. 'But you've been alive a long, long time,' Charles suggested. 'And Sarai was a herbalist, a healer, wasn't she? You know some things about witchcraft. You know what this wolf is.'

'Mariposa is the witch. We raised her, Sarai and I,' said Asil starkly. 'She came from a family of witches that we knew – my mate was a herbalist. She knew most of the witches in that part of Spain, kept them supplied with what they needed. One day a tinker came to our door with Mari; she was eight or nine years old. From what we gleaned later, Mariposa's mother had only just enough power to protect her youngest daughter from the attack of another clan of witches. Her parents, grandparents, brothers, sisters, and all were dead – and her mother, too. The tinker found the little girl wandering by the burnt remnants of her house and thought my wife would take her in, as he knew that my wife had done considerable trade with that family.'

He sighed and turned away, looking out over the narrow, dark valley below them. 'That was a bad time for all of us in Europe. The Inquisition had taken a terrible toll just a couple of centuries before – and when it was over, the witches started fighting for power. Only Napoleon kept them from exterminating each other entirely.'

'I know the story,' Charles told him. The only Western European witch bloodline to survive the power struggle was the Torvalis line, which was interbred with the Gypsies. Witches still were born here and there into mundane families, but seldom had a tenth of the power of the old families. The Eastern European and Oriental witches had never established the kind of dynasties the Western European witches had.

'They guarded their spells from each other,' Asil told him. 'So each family tended to specialize. Mariposa's family was one of the greatest of the witch families.' He hesitated. 'But she was only a *child*, and this was their greatest spell. I can hardly believe they entrusted her with it.'

'What was it?'

'Her family was said to have guardians on their grounds, great beasts who patrolled and killed for them – but never needed food or drink. It was rumored that they made them from living creatures – they had a menagerie.' He sighed. 'Such powerful spells, as you well know, are never made without blood and death.'

'You think your butterfly used such a spell on your mate?'

Asil shrugged. 'I don't know anything. All I can do is speculate.' He sucked in a breath. 'She told me, before we sent her to another witch for teaching, she told me that the only place she really felt safe was with Sarai and me.'

He paused, then said bleakly, 'I was in Romania when it happened. I dreamed Sarai was being tortured and consumed. Her heart had ceased beating, her lungs could not draw in air, but she lived and burned with pain and power. I dreamed Mariposa consumed my love until she was no more. It took her a long time to die, but not as long as my journey from Romania back to Spain. When I crossed our threshold, Sarai had been dead for a while.'

He looked out to the forest, but his eyes were blind, seeing something that had happened a long time ago. 'I burned her corpse and buried the ashes. I slept in our bed, and when I awoke, Mariposa was waiting for me – in my head where only Sarai belonged.'

He sighed, scooped up a handful of snow, and threw it off to the side. 'I wasn't Sarai, to be blinded by the child she had been. Besides, I could feel her madness. I knew when Mariposa decided she wanted me, so I escaped. I ran to Africa, and the distance helped thin the link. By that time I figured out that if I was too close, she could make me do whatever she wanted.' He opened his mouth and panted several times as if he were in wolf form and distressed.

'For years I waited, sure that she would die. But she never did.' Asil hugged himself, then turned and faced Charles once more. 'I think it must be some side effect of what she did to Sarai, that she stole Sarai's immortality as she stole our bond. I could not for the life of me understand why she'd do either − but if her intent was to create such a creature as her family was known for . . . it all makes sense. She watched her whole family murdered, watched her mother die protecting her from the spell designed to kill everyone in her home.'

Charles heard the sympathy in the other man's voice and countered it with truth. 'So she killed your wife, who had taken her in, protected her, and watched over her. She tortured her to death to provide herself with something that could protect her.' Black witch, his instincts had said − and black witches were a nasty bunch, one and all. 'And now she wants you − probably for the same thing.'

'Yes,' whispered Asil. 'I've been running for a long time.'

Charles rubbed his forehead again, but this time because he felt a headache coming his way. 'And now you decided to come here and present yourself to her, gift-wrapped.'

Asil gave a choked laugh. 'I suppose that's how it seems. Until you told me she was here, I was still convinced that my suspicions were unfounded.' His face lost the touch of amusement, and he said, 'I am glad I am here. If she has some part of my Sarai, I have to stop her.'

'I was considering calling Bran here,' Charles told Asil. 'But I'm starting to believe that might not be the smartest move.'

Asil frowned.

'Who is more dominant?' Charles asked him. 'You or me.'

Asil's eyes had been darkening during their conversation, but at Charles's question they brightened fiercely. 'You. You know this.'

'So,' said Charles, staring him down until the other's amber eyes turned away in defeat, 'how did the witch, using your mate bond and your ties to the pack, control *me*?'

As soon as Charles went out to talk to Asil, Anna had begun her change. She needed to deal with that wolf with her tongue rather than fang and claw. He was too good at riling her mate – and Charles was still volatile from his encounter with the witch.

She didn't give any thought to Walter until she was naked and panting in the cold night air. She might have had three years to get used to being nude in front of people she didn't know well, but he hadn't.

She glanced at him, but he had his head turned away from her and was staring intently at a nearby tree trunk, the perfect gentleman.

She quit worrying about him and scrambled into her chilly clothes and boots because she could sense Charles's rising rage at Asil; Asil had put the Marrok and his pack at risk. But more than that, she was worried that neither Charles nor Asil realized how close Charles was to his breaking point. She found it curious that she did.

Boots on, coat on, Anna rolled out of their sleeping place and onto her feet. She didn't bother with the snowshoes – it was still early night. She glanced at the waxing moon; only a few more days until full moon. For the first time that didn't make her sick with anxiety. With Walter in wolf form at her heel she trekked across the bench where Charles and Asil waited.

It was a bad sign, she thought, that neither Charles nor Asil seemed to hear her approach.

'Could she be tapping the Marrok for power, like Leah does?' Anna asked.

Both men turned to stare at Walter and her, Charles clearly unhappy that he hadn't noticed their approach. Asil, the legs of his jeans soaking wet, seemed more concerned with Walter, who had his ears pinned back and was showing his teeth.

Anna put her hand on Walter's neck as she performed the introductions. 'Asil, this is Walter. Walter, this is Asil – the wolf we told you about.'

Asil frowned at the black wolf, who stared right back and lifted his lips to display his fangs.

'Stop that,' she told Walter, hoping he would listen to her. What they didn't need right now was a dominance fight. It always took a while for a new wolf to establish his place in the pack. Interesting that Walter didn't immediately assume Asil was higher-ranked. 'We need everyone in fighting shape.'

'Walter rescued someone from the witch's wolf and ended up Changed,' Charles said. 'He's agreed to help us.'

He could have phrased that a lot differently, Anna thought. Her hand touched the top of Walter's head protectively. Instead of dismissing the new wolf, Charles had made it clear that the wolf was under his protection and was a valuable participant in their attempt to foil the witch.

Pleased as she was, she didn't want Charles and Asil to fight, so she said again, 'Could Mary . . . Mariposa be drawing on the Marrok's power through the pack bond?'

Charles quit frowning at Asil, and said, 'It certainly felt like my father's power. But my father cannot hold me like that.'

Asil looked grim. 'A strong enough witch can control any werewolf who doesn't have a pack to protect him. It is forbidden by witch law, but it is possible. One of the problems Sarai and I had with Mariposa was that she was making people do things – like kill family pets. And she has had time to grow even more powerful. I think that because she is, through me, a de facto member of the pack – she might have managed to combine your father's powers with her own.'

Anna wasn't certain of the implications, but Charles was obviously very unhappy.

'Are we still going down to talk to the Marrok?' Anna asked. 'Even if he can't come here, shouldn't we warn him?'

Charles went very still.

'What do you think your father would do if we told him the whole of it?' Asil asked.

Charles didn't answer.

'Yes,' Asil agreed. 'That's what I think, too. He'd be out here – after he forced all of us to go home. No matter that it would be an incredibly stupid thing to do. He protects his own and has as much confidence in his reputation of invulnerability as everyone else does. Killing Doc Wallace left him hurting – and he won't risk losing anyone else for a long time. Certainly not his son.'

'No witch could control my father,' Charles said. But Anna could hear the doubt in his voice. Maybe he did, too, because he turned his head, and said, more softly, 'We'll have to go after them ourselves.'

Asil suddenly raised his face to the wind and closed his eyes. Then he became very still.

Charles whirled toward their campsite – Anna turned to look as well, but she didn't see anything. Not at first.

She seemed to coalesce from the wind and snow. Her fur glistened silver, gold, and shadow. They all froze, staring at her as she stared at Asil. After a few seconds, the wolf hopped off the log and walked slowly forward, whining. Her tail wagged, just a little.

Asil started to move toward the wolf, but Charles grabbed him, holding him back.

'Sarai?' Asil said hoarsely, limp in Charles's grip.

The wolf lowered her head and dropped her tail in a classic submissive pose. She whined again. Beside Anna, Walter growled and placed himself between her and the other wolf. But the witch's werewolf had eyes only for Asil.

The wolf made a pleading, grieving sound. Then she turned and ran. Anna was watching her, so she didn't see what Asil did, only that he was suddenly free from Charles's hold and running after the wolf who wore his mate's semblance.

Charles didn't give chase. He just watched as the pair of them disappeared into the darkness.

'That's not good, is it?' Anna murmured.

'No.' Charles's voice was grim.

'So what are we going to do? Should we track them?'

'No.' Charles looked at Walter. 'But I don't think we need to, do we? The witch is still staying at that old forest-service cabin.'

Walter yipped a soft agreement.

'We're not going to tell the Marrok?' The wind picked up again, and Anna shivered. 'Are you sure that's wise? Does your father have a witch in his pay who could help? My old pack shared one with the other Chicago pack.'

'Asil's witch has found a way to control a werewolf who has the protection of a pack,' Charles said. 'I've never heard of anything like that – so I don't think she's been spreading the word. Thankfully, witches are so jealous of each other. But if she's the only witch who knows how – we need to keep it that way. We can't bring a witch into this.'

He was still watching the place where the witch's pet had disappeared into the darkness.

'What about your father?'

'Asil is right. He'd want to handle the witch on his own.'

'Could he?'

Charles started to shrug but stopped halfway, as if it hurt. 'She didn't have any trouble with me. That doesn't mean that my father couldn't fight her off – but if not . . . my father controls all the werewolves in North America, Anna. All of them. If she took him, she could have them all.'

'Is that what she wants?'

Charles was swaying a little, she saw. 'I don't know. She's been looking for Asil for a long time – but my father is quite a prize.'

Anna took a step closer to Charles and wrapped an arm around his waist to steady him. 'Are we safe here for the rest of the night? Or will she come for us?'

He looked down at her and sighed. 'Safe as anywhere, I expect. She has Asil to occupy her. Poor old Moor. If I were in any kind of shape, I'd have gone after them. But he's on his own tonight.' A humorless smile came and went on his face. 'We don't have any choice but to spend the rest of the night here,' he told her. 'I need food and rest before I'm good for another mile of travel.'

She parked him on one of the downed trees, in a place that was somewhat sheltered from the wind, and rebuilt the campfire. Walter blocked the wind as she used a glob of Sterno and the lighter to force a fire out of the driest chunks of wood she could find. While the water heated, Anna rebandaged Charles's ribs with strips of a clean shirt. Docile as a child, he let her do it.

She fed him two of the freeze-dried meals, gave one to Walter, and ate another. When they were finished, she kicked piles of snow onto the struggling fire until it was out completely, then urged Charles back into their original shelter. She was too tired to try changing again, and Charles was in worse shape. Walter curled up in front of them both, effectively blocking the wind and snow that tried to reach them.

Anna opened her eyes in the darkness, certain that something had wakened her again. She raised her head from Charles's warm, sweet-smelling skin and looked around. Walter was nowhere to be seen, and sometime in the night, she and Charles had reversed positions, so he lay between her and danger.

The wind and snow had ceased, leaving the forest silent and waiting.

'*Me transmitte sursum, Caledoni,*' she murmured. Too bad Scotty wasn't around to beam them to safety. There was something about the heavy atmosphere that was frightening.

She listened hard but heard nothing. The weighted silence pounded on her ears and made the beat of her heart even louder in the stillness of the winter night.

Her heartbeat, her breath was the only thing she could hear.

'Charles?' she whispered, touching his shoulder tentatively. When he didn't respond, she shook him.

His body fell away from her. He'd been lying on his side, but he rolled limply out from under their barely adequate shelter and onto the snow. The moonlight illuminated him almost as well as daylight could have.

Her breath stopped in her chest, followed by a rush of pain that made her eyes water; blood had drenched his back all the way through his coat. Black glistened on her fingers: blood, his blood.

'No,' she sat up, hitting her head on the dead tree they

were sleeping under, but she ignored the pain and reached out to him. 'Charles!'

Bran sat bolt upright in his bed, heart pounding and breathing rapidly. The cool air of his bedroom brushed over his sweating body. *Witch.*

'What's wrong?' Leah rolled over and propped her chin on her hands, her body relaxed and sated.

'I don't know.' He took a deep breath, but there had been no strangers in his room. Though his head cleared quickly, the memory of his dream eluded him. Everything except that one word: *witch.*

His cell phone rang.

'What's wrong, Da?' Samuel's voice was wide-awake. 'Why did you *call* me?'

It took Bran a moment to understand Samuel wasn't talking about a phone call. He rubbed his face and tried to remember. *Witch.* For some reason the word sent cold chills down his spine.

Maybe he'd been dreaming of the past. He didn't do it often anymore. And when he did, it wasn't about the witch – it was about all the people who died beneath his fangs after the witch was dead.

No, it didn't feel like a dream of memories. It felt like a warning. As soon as he thought that, he felt again the urgency that had woken him up. Something was wrong.

'What did I say?' His voice obeyed him, sounding only calm and curious.

'Wake up,' Samuel said dryly.

'Not very helpful.' Bran ran his fingers through his hair. 'I'm sorry for disturbing you, I was asleep.'

Samuel's voice softened, 'Was it a nightmare, Da?'

As if in response to his question, Bran saw an image – *part of his dream* – 'Charles is in trouble.'

'From a rogue?' Samuel spoke with polite incredulity. 'I've never seen a rogue that could make Charles break a sweat.'

*Witch.*

But not his witch, not the witch who had turned him into a monster so long ago. Dead, but never forgotten. A different witch.

'Da?'

'Wait, let me think.'

After a moment he said, 'Charles and Anna went out after the rogue two days ago.' Sometimes just speaking things aloud helped him jog loose whatever he'd been dreaming about. Dream warnings sucked – he eventually remembered what they were about, but sometimes only *after* everything was over.

'Asil came by that evening. He was angry with me for sending Charles out so soon after he'd been wounded,' Bran said.

'*Asil* was worried about Charles?' Samuel sounded skeptical.

'Exactly my thought. Astounding. Though he wasn't too upset until—'

'What?'

Bran rubbed his forehead. 'I'm too old. I forgot. What a stupid thing . . . Well, that's explained.'

'Father?'

He laughed. 'Sorry. Asil took off yesterday morning, presumably after Charles, but I just figured out why. The rogue's description matches Sarai's wolf – Asil's mate.'

'She's been dead a long time.'

'Two hundred years. Asil told me he'd burned her body and buried the ashes himself. And old as he is, he still cannot lie to me. She's dead.'

Leah rolled off of her side of the bed and gathered up her clothing. Without looking at him, she stalked out of his bedroom to her own. He heard her shut her door behind her and knew he'd hurt her by having this conversation with Samuel, instead of his mate.

But he had no time to apologize – he'd just got an odd insight.

*Witch.*

'Samuel,' he said, feeling his way. 'Why would you burn a body?'

'To hide its identity. Because it's too cold to bury a body. Because their religion requires it. To prevent the spread of disease. Because there are too many bodies, and no one has a bulldozer handy. Am I getting warm?'

He was too worried to be amused. 'Why would Asil have burned Sarai's body in Spain during the Napoleonic wars?'

'Witch.'

*Witch.*

'I dreamed of a witch,' Bran said, sure now that it was true.

'The Moor's mate was tortured to death over days,' Samuel said reflectively. 'I always assumed it was a vampire. A witch would never have been capable of holding a werewolf for days – kill her, yes. But not torture.'

'I know of one who could.'

'Grandmother's been dead for a long time, Da,' Samuel said cautiously.

'Killed and eaten,' Bran said impatiently. 'I merely pointed out that we know of one exception. Where there is one, there may be others.'

'Sarai was the *Moor's* mate, and they were part of a pack. It wasn't like it was with us. And Sarai was killed two hundred years ago. Witches live a human life span.'

'Asil told me he'd been dreaming lately. Of *her*. I assumed he meant Sarai.'

There was only silence on the other end of the phone. Samuel knew about those dreams, too.

'I don't know *anything*,' said Bran. 'Maybe Sarai was killed by a vampire, and the wolf having her coloring is just coincidence. Maybe Asil burned Sarai's body because he couldn't stand to think of her rotting in the grave. Maybe my dream was just that, and Charles is coming back with our rogue right now.'

'You know,' said Samuel reflectively, 'you just proved your point better by arguing against it than you did arguing for it. I wonder if that says anything about how your mind works.'

'Or yours,' said Bran, smiling despite himself. 'I'm going out to check on Charles.'

'Good,' said Samuel. 'Do you want me to come back?'

'No. Are you staying with Adam or Mercy?'

'I am your son,' he said smugly despite the underlying worry in his tone. 'At Mercy's, of course.'

Bran smiled as he hung up the phone. Then he got out of bed and dressed for a drive.

He paused outside of Leah's closed door, but what was wrong between them could not be changed. He didn't even want it to change, only regretted that she was so often hurt. In the end he let her be.

He didn't leave a note; she wouldn't care where he was going or why.

Anna's throat hurt from crying as she lay over Charles's cooling body. Her face was wet with tears and blood that froze in the bitter cold. The ends of her fingers burned from the snow.

He was dead, and it was her fault. She should have realized the bleeding was worse than he'd let on. She'd only had him a few days.

She levered herself off him and sat cross-legged on the cold ground, studying his exotic and handsome face. He'd lived two hundred years or more, and she knew so little of that time. She wanted all the stories. What had it been like growing up a werewolf? What mischief had he gotten up to? She didn't even know his favorite color. Was it green, like his bedroom?

'Red. It's red.' His voice whispered in her ear, startling her.

But that was impossible, wasn't it?

She reached out to touch Charles's body, but she just blinked once and was lying flat on her back underneath a Charles who was very much alive, though the left side of his face looked as if some beast had clawed him.

She was panting, and her hands hurt as they slowly changed back to human. *Was she the one who'd hurt him?* Her heart felt as though it had been stopped in her chest and only now started beating.

'Charles?' she managed.

His face didn't move very much, but she saw his relief anyway, and felt it in the relaxing of his hold.

Briefly he put his face down against her neck and breathed against her ear. When he pulled back, he rolled off of her, and said, 'All you had to do was ask.'

She sat up, feeling weak and disoriented. 'Ask?'

'What my favorite color was.'

She stared at him. Was he making a joke of it? 'You were dead,' she told him. 'I woke up and there was all of this blood and you weren't breathing. You were dead.'

A growl from behind startled her; she'd completely forgotten about Walter.

'I smell it, too, wolf,' Charles said, the gouges on the side of his face rapidly fading. 'Witchcrafting. Did the witch take anything of you, Anna? Skin, blood, or hair?'

When the wolf had appeared, Mary had grabbed at her hair.

'Hair.' Her voice was so hoarse she almost didn't recognize it.

'When there are witches about, it's good to keep them at a distance,' he said. 'Your hair allowed her to get into your dreams. If you had died there, you'd have died for real.'

She knew that would be important in a minute, but not right now. A little frantically she unzipped his coat. He caught her hands, and said, 'What is it you want? Can I help?'

His hands were so warm, but he'd been warm before. 'I need to see your back.'

He released her, stripped out of his coat, and, still kneeling, turned so she could see that the strips of shirt she'd wrapped around his torso were free of blood. She put her head against his shoulder and breathed in his scent. Underneath, she could smell old blood and the tang of a healing wound.

She grabbed his shirt in both hands and tried to collect herself.

'It was just a nightmare?' she said, afraid to believe. Afraid that had been the truth and this was the dream.

'No,' he said. 'It was the sum of the worst of your fears.' He turned in her grip and wrapped both arms around her, surrounding her cold body with his heat. He whispered in her ear, 'We've been trying to wake you up for about fifteen minutes.' He paused, then said, 'You weren't the only one who was frightened. Your heart stopped. For almost a minute I couldn't get you to breathe . . . I . . . I imagine you'll have bruises. CPR is one of those things I find pretty difficult; the line is so thin between forcing air out and breaking ribs.'

He tightened his hold, and whispered, 'One of the problems with having a brother who is a doctor is that I know how few of the people who need CPR survive.'

Anna found herself patting him on the back – up on his shoulder, well away from his wound. 'Yeah, well, I bet most of them aren't werewolves.'

He pulled back after a moment, and said briskly, 'You're cold. I think it's time for more food. We've still got a couple of hours before daylight.'

'How are you?'

He smiled. 'Better. A lot of food, a little rest, and I'm almost as good as new.'

She watched him closely as he pulled a few packets of food out of the pack – things that didn't need hot water. More freeze-dried fruit and jerky.

She ripped a piece of jerky loose with her teeth and chewed. 'You know, I used to like this stuff.' Eating the bits she fed him, Walter spread himself out over her feet. Big as he was, he soon had her frozen toes toasty warm.

They lay down again, Anna sandwiched between the males, Charles at her back once more.

'I'm afraid to go back to sleep,' she said. And it wasn't because he'd told her the witch could have killed her, either. She couldn't face seeing Charles's dead body again.

Charles tightened his hold on her and began singing softly. His song was Native American – she recognized the nasal tone and odd scale.

Walter sighed and moved into a more comfortable position as they all waited for morning.

# 12

The darkness bothered Bran not at all as he followed Tag's directions to the place he and Charles had thought would be the best starting point. He passed Asil's Subaru and hesitated – if Asil had been going after Charles, he'd have known the fastest way there.

But Charles would be headed back to his car if something had gone wrong. So Bran kept driving.

Other things he might do ran through his head. There were witches in the pay of the wolves. Not his pack – he didn't deal with black witches, and most white witches weren't powerful enough to be useful. But there were witches available to him.

If he had a two-hundred-year-old witch capable of holding and torturing a werewolf for two days – he had no intention of advertising the fact and encouraging other witches to imitate this one. Especially since she, like Bran's mother, might have gotten her ability through some kind of binding to a werewolf.

No. Best keep the witches out of it.

He could call Charles back.

That was a harder thing. Telepathy was how his mother had gotten her nasty little chains upon him in the first place. She was why he could no longer read the thoughts of others.

After he'd killed the witch who was his mother, the backlash had taken that talent from him – one of the many blessings of her death. Slowly he'd regained the ability to talk mind to mind, but never to listen in.

The only reason his mother had been able to catch him

through his talent was that it was one she shared. A rare thing, even among witch born. He'd be surprised if there was another witch with that ability in North America. But he was still too cowardly to try until he knew for certain that his son was free of Asil's witch.

Of all the magic users in this old world, Bran despised and feared witches above everything. Probably because, had matters been different, he would have been one himself.

He turned off the highway and drove up Silver Butte. Tracks of a wider-than-normal vehicle preceded him. Charles had followed the plans that far, anyway.

Getting Charles's truck up the path the Vee had taken was a little tricky, driving all his other worries out of his mind. He was starting to think he should have parked beside Asil's car when he drove around a blind curve and almost hit the Vee, which was nose to bark with a tree.

He stopped with no more than six inches between Charles's truck and the Vee. He shut off the engine and parked the truck right there because the trees were too thick to go around, and he didn't trust that smooth white snow not to hide a ditch.

There had been no safe place to turn around anywhere in the last quarter of a mile; he wondered if he was going to have to drive the whole trek backward on the way out. He smiled sourly to himself; that wouldn't matter so much if they didn't make it out.

Asil had had time to meet up with Charles. Asil knew about witches. Surely his son and the Moor could handle anything they found. If Charles stuck to his route, Bran hoped to find the lot of them before nightfall and get them out of there.

He left the key in the ignition. No one was likely to come up here and steal the truck – and if anyone did . . . well, he could deal with Charles.

He hadn't bothered to wear a coat since he intended to go wolf anyway. He stripped in the warm cab, steeled himself, and jumped out of the truck before completing the change. Opening car doors while in wolf form was possible – but usually it left some damage behind. And despite his son's frequent mutterings about how much he hated cars, Charles was fond of his truck.

Bran settled into a steady lope, something that he could maintain all day. It had been a long time since he'd run in these mountains. They had never been a favorite hunting ground, though he couldn't put a finger on why not. Charles maintained that the Cabinets didn't welcome intruders, and he supposed that was as good an explanation as any.

Following Charles's intended route backward seemed to be the best manner to begin. Their whole loop wasn't more than thirty miles, and he could run the whole thing and be back to the cars just after nightfall.

Except for the small porch with old green paint peeling off, the cabin hadn't changed substantially since the last time Charles had seen it, maybe fifty years earlier. It wasn't much to look at, a small log cabin like a hundred other such places in the wilds of Montana, most of them built during the Depression by CCC crews.

The logs were grayed by years of sun, rain, and snow. A battered four-wheeler with new cat tracks sat unobtrusively between the back of the cabin and the forest that crowded in behind.

Charles stopped Anna about thirty yards downwind, where the trees still hid them adequately. As soon as he stopped her, Walter flattened himself on the ground at her feet, just as if he were her devoted pet dog . . . who weighed about the same as the average black bear and was capable of considerably more destruction.

Walter's devotion was so obviously nonsexual that Charles couldn't find it in himself to object. He kept remembering Walter's impassioned, 'I think I could sleep.' He knew about being haunted by memories of death and murder. If she managed to give Walter some peace, he was welcome to it.

Charles stared fiercely at the cabin and wished he wasn't frightened. It had been a long time since he'd been afraid like this. He was used to being worried about Samuel, his father, and, more recently, Anna, but not about himself. The memory of how Asil's witch had held him obedient to her as if she were his Alpha cut through his self-confidence with a large dollop of reality.

He rubbed Anna's shoulder lightly. He *knew* she wasn't as fragile as she looked, no werewolf was that fragile. And the old soldier was a survivor; Charles took some comfort from that.

'I won't be able to help directly,' Charles told her. 'If I get in her line of sight, she'll have me again. With a pack Alpha, distance counts, and so does eye or body-to-body contact.'

Neither Walter nor Anna was a member of his father's pack, so they had no connection to Asil. Except for Anna's wolf's bond to Charles, that left them as vulnerable as any lone wolf. But he knew it usually took witches a while to gain a hold on a lone wolf – long enough that he could offer himself up instead.

Her control of him had been instantaneous.

He hated witches. Other magic users' abilities didn't bother him so much. Druids influenced the natural world: weather, plants, and some animals. Wizards played with nonliving things. But witches used the mind and body. Anyone's mind and body. They toyed with things that were alive – or had been alive. White witches weren't so bad, though maybe that was only because most of them had less magic than he did. Black witches gained power by killing or torturing things: from flies to humans.

'All right,' his Anna said, as if she'd faced witches every day of her life. 'If they are here, you'll take on her wolf . . . and probably Asil. That should keep even you pretty busy.'

The few hours of rest he'd had, a lot of food, and a slow, easy pace this morning had done much to restore Charles to himself. It gave him a chance at taking down the witch's pets.

Anna shivered a little under his hand, a combination of eagerness and nerves, he thought. She had reacted to that dream as if it had been an attack on him rather than on her, though she was the one who had stopped breathing.

Walter raised his eyes to Charles, and he saw in the other's gaze a determination to protect her by any means necessary. It bothered Brother Wolf to see that in another male's eyes, but under the circumstances, Walter was in a better position to save her than Charles was.

'I'm going to do a little recon. For this part, I'd like you to wait here, all right?'

'I'll wait,' Anna said.

'Don't get impatient, this might take a while.'

The cabin was backed up to the forest, with twenty feet cleared around the front and one side. It was not where he would have chosen to hide from werewolves . . . but then, he didn't think that she was afraid of him at all. He certainly hadn't given her any reason to fear him.

To his surprise, Walter followed him, disappearing into the shadows until the only way Charles knew the other wolf was there was from his scent. The spirits of this forest had indeed taken Walter as their own to lend him their protection. His grandfather had been able to disappear like that.

A stone's throw from the cabin, Charles became convinced it was empty. When Walter appeared a few yards ahead of him, tail wagging a slow message, he knew he was right. But he still waited until he'd circled the little structure and opened the door before he sent Walter back for Anna.

Inside, there was barely room for the narrow cot and small table that were the only furnishings, unless he wanted to count the narrow ledge of a mantelpiece above the fireplace. The cot was brand-new and still had sales tags on it. The table looked like it was older than the cabin.

The hearth showed signs of a recent fire. The dead animal on the floor in front of it advertised who was living here: witches and dead things went together. There were witches who didn't kill, but they were far less powerful than their darker sisters.

The plank floor had shiny new nails and crowbar marks where she had pried it up and nailed it back in again. When he stepped near the cot, he knew exactly why; he'd felt power circles before. Some witches used them to set guard spells to keep things they valued safe, and others used them to store power for drawing upon later. Since the cabin hadn't kept him out and he didn't feel the need to leave, he could only assume that the circle was the latter kind – which meant that there were more dead things under the floor. He took a deep breath, but the dead animal he'd already seen might account for the scent of death – and nothing was rotting. Either the animal she'd killed to draw her circle hadn't been dead long – it had frozen in the cold – or she had a spell to disguise it to keep away scavengers. Changing what the senses of others perceived was one of the major powers of the witch.

His father said that Charles might have been a witch if he'd chosen to study. Bran hadn't urged him to do so, but he also didn't discourage it, either; a witch in his pack would have given him even more power. But the subtler magics of his mother's people suited Charles, and he'd never regretted the path he'd chosen less than he did right now, standing in the middle of this poor cabin stained with evil.

The scent on the sleeping bag on the cot was fresh enough that he decided the witch had slept there the night before. The table held the remnants of a fat black candle smelling of blood more than wax, and a mortar with some ashes in the bottom – the remnants of Anna's hair, he thought. Something personal to allow her into Anna's dreams.

'What is that?' Anna said in a little voice from the doorway. He felt immediately better for her presence, as if she somehow lessened the evil that had seeped into the wood and brick.

Someday he'd tell her that, just to see the bewildered disbelief in her eyes; he was beginning to know her well enough to predict her reaction. It gave him some satisfaction.

He followed her gaze to the eviscerated and skinned body laid out in front of the fireplace. 'Raccoon, I think. At least that's what it smells like.' It also smelled of pain and had left claw marks on the floor, probably after it had been nailed down. He saw no reason to tell Anna it probably hadn't been dead when the witch mutilated it.

'What was she trying to do?' She stayed in the doorway, and Walter settled in behind her. Neither of them made any attempt to come inside.

He shrugged. 'I have no idea. Maybe it was to power the spell she worked on you last night. A dark witch gains power from others' pain and suffering.'

Anna looked sick. 'There are worse monsters to be than a werewolf, aren't there?'

'Yes,' he agreed. 'Not all witches use things like this, but it's hard to be a good witch.'

There was a scrying bowl, still filled with water, on the floor next to the raccoon. The interior temperature of the cabin wasn't much warmer than outside; if it had been there long, it would have been ice. They hadn't missed the witch by much.

He didn't want to, but he touched the dead animal to see how long ago she'd worked her misery on it. Its flesh was still . . .

It moved weakly, and he had his knife out and its neck severed as quickly as he could manage, nauseated by the knowledge that it had still been alive. Nothing should have been able to live through the torture it had undergone. He gave a more thoughtful look to the floorboards. Maybe the reason there was no smell of rot was because what she had down there, anchoring her power circle, wasn't dead, either.

Walter growled, and Charles echoed the sentiment.

'She left it alive,' Anna whispered.

'Yes. And likely she'll know we killed it.' Charles cleaned his knife on the sleeping bag, then put it back in its sheath.

'So what do we do now?'

'Burn the cabin,' Charles said. 'Most of witchcraft is potions and spells. Burning her place of power will cripple her a bit.' And release whatever poor thing or things she had trapped underneath the cabin, too. He wasn't going to tell Anna about that unless he had to.

Anna found a half-full five-gallon can of gasoline tied onto the four-wheeler, and Charles doused the cot and then the bonfire he'd built in the middle of the floor with the witch's firewood. He sent Anna and Walter away from the building before lighting the tinder with a match. The gasoline burned his nose as the fire flared hotly to life. He waited until he was sure it was hot enough to burn the cabin before he left.

He trotted toward Anna and Walter, who'd stopped some distance away. When he reached them, he caught Anna's hand and tugged her farther, urged on by the itch between his shoulder blades. Which was why they were fifty yards away when the cabin exploded, knocking them all to the ground.

Anna raised her face out of the snow and spat some dirt out of her mouth. 'What happened? Did she have some dynamite or something?'

Charles rolled over and sat up, fighting not to show how much falling with a chest wound had hurt. 'I don't know. But magic and fire have an odd, synergistic effect sometimes.' He looked at where the cabin had been and whistled soundlessly. There was almost nothing left of it, just a few rows of stone on the ground where the base of the fireplace had been. Pieces of four-wheeler and cabin were scattered almost to their feet, and the trees nearest the cabin had been splintered like toothpicks.

'Wow,' Anna said. 'Are you all right, Walter?'

The wolf came to his feet and shook himself, looking into Anna's face with adoring eyes.

'She knew we'd be hunting her,' said Charles. 'She tried to hide this from us. I didn't smell any trace of her when Walter and I circled the cabin. Did you, Walter?'

The big wolf had not.

'So what do we do?'

'Despite all our fears, I think it's time to call my father.' He smiled at Anna. 'We're not too far from the car, and he knows something's wrong anyway. He woke me up last night – that's how I knew you were in trouble. He's not stupid, and he knows a few other witches we can call upon.'

Bran had been running for several hours or so when he heard them.

'I told you he was most likely to send Tag if Charles needed help,' said Asil. 'I told you he wouldn't be such a fool as to come himself.'

Bran planted all four feet and slid to a stop. Asil hadn't

spoken loudly, but he'd known Bran would hear him. Which meant it was already too late to escape.

Witches could hide in plain sight if they had some sort of hold on you. And Asil was clearly not speaking to Charles, so he belonged to the witch. And he belonged to Bran. That was enough of a connection for hide-me spells to work on Bran.

He turned to face Asil and found him standing on a boulder the size of a small elephant. Next to Asil, a smallish woman bundled against the cold held on to Asil as if she thought the wind might blow her off the rock.

'Why he'd think that Tag would do any better than I, I don't know,' continued Asil coolly. There was hell in his eyes, but the rest of his face and his body language matched the voice.

'Come here, *señor*,' the woman purred – and she facilitated their meeting by climbing down the boulder with unusual grace.

She spoke with an American accent except when she spoke pure Castilian Spanish – aristo Spanish. Part of him was interested in the fact that she'd been here long enough to pick up an American accent. His ear was too good to be fooled about which one was her native tongue – even if he hadn't known that he was hunting for a witch who had killed Asil's mate in Spain. Part of him was interested in the wolflike dexterity she'd displayed as she hopped down the boulder after Asil. No human could move that well, witch or not. But when Bran's mother had enslaved him, she could move like that, too.

He'd have been horrified, except that worse happened: he came to her call like the well-trained pet he'd once been – a long, long time ago.

'Tag,' the witch purred as she walked around him. 'Colin Taggart. A little on the small side . . . for a werewolf.'

He was aware, though she was apparently not, of the tension that held Asil as he waited for her to discover how he'd misinformed her, without ever lying. 'I told you he'd send Tag' was not 'Look, there's Tag.' Asil was trying, and Bran gave him credit for it, knowing how difficult to balance upon was the line he was treading.

From the fear radiating off of him, Asil knew what the consequences of a witch trying to make Bran a pet might be. There weren't many people left who would remember what had happened when Bran had broken free of his mother at last: Samuel, Asil . . . He couldn't think of a third, it had been a long time ago. Likely the witches themselves didn't know why it was forbidden to try to take a werewolf for a pet or familiar – not that most of them had the power to do it.

Bran would hold out for a while. First, the witch could make a mistake – especially if she didn't know whom she held. Second, he was afraid that this time no one would be able to kill him. It had been Samuel who brought him out of it before . . . and Samuel wasn't as certain of himself as he used to be.

The control the witch asserted over him had to be won by blood and flesh, and the only flesh and blood bonding he'd done was to his own pack. She must have used Asil to insert herself into his pack – but how?

While she looked him over, he searched his link to Asil for something that touched a witch. He paid very little attention to the witch as she talked at him. With the dexterity of a very long lifetime, Bran slid through Asil and found a dead woman – it could only be Asil's mate. It was an impossibility.

No one could link to a dead woman; he knew that because when Blue Jay Woman, Charles's mother, died, he'd tried to hold on to her.

But, impossibilities become possible when you added a witch into the mix.

He couldn't go exploring further; the woman was dead, and her link was through Asil – but the only way the witch's control of him made sense was if she was tied closely to Asil's dead mate. Then she could run her own magic through that link and take control of any of Bran's wolves.

He took the time to give Asil a cold look. Asil would have known that the bond to his dead mate was still in place – and he should have told Bran. He had the feeling that there were more things he should have known.

The witch had somehow kept the mating bond alive while she killed Sarai.

He hated witches.

'Colin Taggart,' she purred. 'You are mine now. Your will is mine.'

He felt the magic she poured at him. Some of it slid off him like honey on warm toast: lingering a bit, here and there. But then it attached and solidified as she paced around him whispering the words of her spelling. It didn't hurt precisely, but it made him feel claustrophobic, and when he tried to move, he couldn't.

Panic flared, and something stirred where he had long ago buried it. He took a deep shuddering breath and tried to shut the witch out of his awareness. Panic was very, very dangerous – far more dangerous than this witch.

So he turned his attention to other things.

First, he tried to cut Asil off from the pack. If he broke the tie between him and Asil, he might stand a chance of freeing himself from the witch. He should have been able to do it, but the oddities in Asil's mate bond and the way the witch had twisted it fouled the pack magic until he wasn't certain that he could cut Asil free of anyone: Sarai, the witch, the pack, or Bran, even with a full blood-and-flesh banishment ceremony.

The beat of the witch's chant changed, and he felt her control tighten around him until he couldn't breathe . . . No.

He tuned the witch out entirely and set about minimizing the damage as best he could.

He constricted the connections he had to his pack until he could barely feel them. If he'd had a normal pack, he might have chanced dropping the reins entirely – but there were too many who could not stand on their own for long. Constricting them would help hide them from a witch's magic – and make it difficult for her to use them if she tried.

Through Asil she had him, but if he could help it, she wouldn't access any more of his pack. If Asil managed to keep her thinking he was Tag, she wouldn't even know where to look.

There were a few old ones whose control had become delicate; those he gave to Samuel, cutting them from him entirely. It would be a jolt to Samuel, but the wolves knew his son and wouldn't protest. Samuel could handle them for a while.

He didn't know if a witch who so obviously had some of the attributes of a werewolf would know enough about wolves to untangle what he did, but he would make it as difficult as he could. At the very least he would slow her down.

But the real reason for his urgency was so that when . . . *if* he went mad, he wouldn't take the whole pack with him immediately. Someone – Charles was his best hope, though Asil might manage it – would have a chance to kill him.

He finished his work before the witch finished hers. It had been centuries since he was so alone in his own head. Under different circumstances, he might almost have enjoyed it.

He didn't fight the witch when she snapped her fingers and told him to heel. He walked at her left side while Asil, in human form, escorted her from the right.

Somehow he didn't think that she perceived the shadow-creature that almost paced beside Asil. He wouldn't have noticed himself if he hadn't seen the snow dent ever so slightly under wolf paws he couldn't see – but he could smell her and the magic on her.

Guardians, they once called such things. A charismatic name for such abominations, he'd always thought. He had been pleased when he'd heard that the family with that spell had at last been eliminated. Obviously his information hadn't been completely accurate. Even at the peak of their power, though, he'd never heard of them making a guardian from a werewolf.

Bran looked at Asil, but he couldn't tell if the Moor knew part of his mate accompanied them – as if she'd been called into being so often she almost had a presence outside of her creator's call. Guardians, he recalled, were destroyed every seven years to prevent just such an occurrence. Sarai's wolf had been around for two hundred years – he wondered how much autonomy she had.

'Tell me, Asil,' the witch commanded, her arm tucked into the Moor's as if he were some long-ago gentleman and she a lady strolling through a ballroom rather than two-foot-deep snow. 'How did you feel when Sarai chose to protect me rather than stay true to you?'

There was truth in her words; she believed that Sarai had made a choice. From the hesitation in Asil's steady footfall, he heard it, too.

'Was that what she did?' he asked.

'She loved me better than she loved you,' the witch said. 'I am her little butterfly, and she takes care of me.'

Asil was silent for a moment, then he said, 'I don't think you've been anyone's Mariposa for a long time.'

The witch stopped and switched abruptly to Spanish. 'Liar. *Liar*. You don't know anything. She loved me. Me! She stayed with me when you went off on your journeys. She only sent me away because of you.'

'She *loved* you,' he agreed. 'Once. Now she is no more. She cannot love anyone.'

Looking out of the corner of his eye at the faint paw prints that were set into the snow so close to Asil's hip, Bran wasn't so sure.

'You were always stupid,' the witch said. 'You made her send me away. She would have kept me home where I belonged.'

'You were a witch, and you had no control of your powers,' Asil said. 'You needed to be trained.'

'You didn't send me to be trained,' she shouted, tears glistening in her eyes as she jerked her arm free and backed away. 'You sent me to *prison*. And you *knew*, I read the letters you wrote to her. You knew what kind of training that witch provided. Linnea wasn't a teacher, she was a prison guard.'

Asil looked down at the witch, blank-faced. 'It was send you to Linnea or kill you. Linnea had a reputation for rehabilitation.'

'Rehabilitation? I did *nothing* wrong!' She stamped her foot as if she were still a child rather than a witch fully a hundred years older than she should have ever been.

'Nothing?' Asil's tone was cool. 'You tried to poison Sarai, twice. Villagers inexplicably lost pets. And you tried to pretend you were Sarai and came to my bed. I think Sarai would have forgiven you everything except that.'

The witch screamed, a wordless, almost inhuman scream of rage – and in the distance there was an explosion.

The witch froze in her tracks, then bowed her head, grabbing her temples. Bran felt her control loosen. In that moment he attacked. Not physically. She still had control of his body.

He used the bonds as she had, throwing his rage through the link to Asil and to Sarai and beyond. If he'd had five minutes, or maybe even three, he'd have broken free. He did something to the link she held to Sarai, but it wasn't enough.

The witch recovered too soon – but he cost her. She pushed him out of the link and spelled the bindings to prevent him doing it again. When it was over he was still her wolf – but she had blood trickling out of her nose.

'You told me this was a lesser wolf,' she spat, and if she hadn't been so hurt, Bran thought she might have killed Asil then and there. 'And I believed you – just as I believed you were sending me away for my own good. I should know better. He is smarter than that. When you failed, you and that other wolf – Bran would send only the best. You lie and lie as if it were the truth.'

'You don't want to believe me,' Asil said. 'But you can taste truth – your link to Sarai is strong enough. You were a danger to yourself and us. We did it for your own good. It was that or kill you.'

She flicked a trembling finger at him. 'Shut up.'

Asil's face lost its cool composure, and he grimaced. As he continued, his voice was breathless with pain. 'What you have done is an abomination. This thing you have turned Sarai into doesn't love you, she serves as a slave serves, without the ability to choose, just as I do. Bran is more than you can handle. He will kill you – and it is your own fault.'

'I won't die,' she shouted at him. 'I didn't die when Linnea tried to kill me – she didn't know how powerful I was or how much my mother had taught me. I killed her and her pet students and studied the books she left behind – for months I wrote to you and signed the letters from her while I studied. But I knew that I would die without protection. Even my mother died. So I took Sarai as my guardian, and she gave me her long life so that she would never live without me.

You can't do that to someone against her nature. You can't. She had to love me for it to work.'

Not true for the guardian spell, thought Bran, but perhaps for the binding that allowed Asil's witch to share in a werewolf's immortality. Maybe that was why his mother had used him, rather than the pet she used to Change him and Samuel.

'Did *you* love *her*?' Asil asked.

'Of course I loved her!'

He grimaced, and whispered, 'I would have given my life for hers – and you stole it for yours. You don't know what love is.'

Suddenly she was calm. With a queenly lift of her chin, she said, 'I'll live longer than you. Come along, I have business to attend to.' She looked down at Bran. 'You, too, Colin Taggart. We have things to attend to.'

He sent a question to Asil, not knowing if the witch's magic would allow it. *How important is it that she not know who I am?* His mother had made certain that the only one he could talk to mind to mind was her. But this witch was not of his mother's family, so it should work.

The witch reached out an imperialistic hand, and Asil gave her his arm. 'Now, how long do you suppose it will be before Bran comes himself – and how many wolves will he bring with him?'

Asil glanced back at Bran, and as soon as the witch couldn't see his face, he shot his eyes up to the sky answering Bran's question. It was very important that she not know who he was.

'Soon,' Asil told the witch. 'And I don't think that he'd bring any wolves at all. Once you take him, you'll have all of his pack.'

That last sentence had been meant for him. Well, then, he'd protected his pack as best he could for now.

'Good,' the witch said. 'Let's go deal with his son and

that interfering bitch, shall we? Maybe I'll prepare a present of him for Bran – a welcoming gift. What do you think he'd like best? A wolf pelt or human skin. The pelt is soft and warm, but human skin is so much more horrifying – and more useful afterward. Take me to Charles.'

*It* stirred in him, the berserker making itself felt. He soothed it and himself, with the knowledge that Charles was a wily old wolf, an experienced hunter. If she hadn't taken him yet, if that explosion had been him, then Charles knew what he faced. She wouldn't take *him* by surprise.

*Watch out, my son. The witch is after you. Run.*


Charles half expected the witch to come hurrying back, but he caught no sign of her all the way back to the Humvee. Which was where things quit going their way.

'Isn't that your truck?' Anna asked him.

'Yes,' he said grimly. He opened the door and let his nose tell him what he already knew. His father had driven it here. The cab was cold. He'd come hours ago.

As Tag had promised, it took only a little wandering around to find a place he could call.

The phone call to Bran's cell turned up the phone in his father's pants pocket, neatly folded on the truck's seat. A call to his father's mate only established what he'd already known – his father had left in the middle of the night, and Leah didn't like Bran's younger son any the better for it. Samuel was more helpful, though Charles didn't like what he had to say.

Charles ended the call after a few unsatisfactory minutes. 'You heard all that?'

'Your father knows that we might be hunting the witch who killed Asil's mate. He knows that Asil came here looking for us.' She touched his shoulder.

On the off chance it might help him figure out what his

father was up to, Charles gathered such magic as belonged to him as his mother's son and reached out to the pack.

'Charles?'

He was astounded to find himself still on his feet. His head felt as if someone had clubbed him, and he had to blink a couple of times to see. All he could think was that the unimaginable had happened – Bran was dead.

'Charles, what's wrong?'

He held up a hand as he focused his attention on the blankness that had always been his link to his father, and through him, the rest of the pack. What he found let him breathe again.

'Da's shut down the pack bonds.' He gave Anna a smile as bleak as he felt inside. 'He's not dead; they're not gone completely.'

'Why would he do that? What does it mean?'

'I don't know.' He looked down at Anna. 'I want you to take Walter and drive to Kennewick, Washington, where my brother is.'

She folded her arms and gave him her stubborn look. 'No. And don't try that again. I felt that *push*. You can be as dominant as you want, but remember it doesn't work on me. If she's using the pack bonds, Walter and I might be your ace in the hole. I'm not going to leave you here, and you might as well stop trying to make me.'

He frowned at her fiercely – a look that had cowed older, more powerful people – and she tapped her finger on his breastbone. 'Won't work. If you leave me here, I'll just follow you.'

He wasn't going to tie her up – and he had the sinking feeling that was the only way he'd be able to leave her behind. Resigned to his fate, he organized them for another trek into the wilds. They'd travel light. He repacked Anna's pack with food, fire-starting equipment, and their pot for heating water.

He found the pair of snowshoes that lived behind the seat of his truck in the winter. Everything else he left in the truck.

'Do you think he's found her already?' Anna asked, as they trudged back into the mountains, following his father's tracks.

'I don't know,' he told her, though he was afraid he did. Unless Bran really could read minds, the only way Charles could see Bran knowing the witch was using their pack magic against them was if he'd seen it for himself.

He wished he knew if following his father was smarter than getting in the car and driving to southern Mexico. Part of him wanted to believe in the myth of the invulnerable Marrok, but the smarter part, the part that had stood meekly answering the witch's questions, was all too aware that his father was a real person, however old and powerful: he wasn't invulnerable.

Charles drew in a breath. He was bone-deep tired, and his chest hurt, and his leg. Worse than they had earlier this morning. He was not so stupid that he did not know why. His father had been feeding him strength from the pack.

Even with his spare snowshoes walking was hard. If she had Bran, Charles was no longer sure they had even a chance of saving themselves.

He didn't tell Anna. Not because he thought it would frighten her – but because by voicing his fears, he might make them real. She knew anyway; he saw it in her eyes.

*Watch out, my son. The witch is after you. Run.*

'Now that was useful, Da,' he said out loud. 'Why don't you tell me where you are, or where you're going?'

'Charles?'

'My father can talk in people's heads,' he told her. 'But he claims not to receive. Which means when he tells you something, you can't argue or ask him for what you need.'

'What did he tell you?'

'The witch has him, and she's coming after us. She has Asil – she can find us. He didn't give me any useful information, like where they are or anything like that.'

'He told you to leave.'

'He told me to run.' Charles glowered at her. With the pack bonds constricted so far, his father's order had been more like a suggestion. 'Damned if I'm going to leave him to her.'

'Of course not,' Anna said. 'But we're going the wrong direction.'

'What do you mean?'

'I think they'll be headed to the cabin we blew up.'

Charles stopped and looked at her. 'Why?'

'If she asks Asil to find us, that's where he'll go – to give us a chance to escape.' She gave him a tired grin. 'Asil is practiced at hedging orders – I've heard the stories.'

It sounded like something the old bastard would do at that. If he hadn't been so tired, he might have thought of it himself. At any rate, it was better than wandering in his father's footsteps.

Charles looked down at Walter. 'You know the fastest way to the cabin from here?'

Even as they turned around and followed Walter, Charles knew they were making a mistake. His father was right, they should run. Every instinct told him so. But as long as there was a chance to save Bran, Charles couldn't leave him to his fate. Listening to your instincts, his father liked to say, was not the same thing as being blindly obedient to them.

Anna understood the impulse that had driven Charles to try to send her and Walter to his brother and out of danger. She felt the same way.

Charles was slowing down. Some of it was walking through snow that was two inches thick one place and hip high in others; even with them both in snowshoes, it was hard going. Most of it, she was pretty sure, was from his wounds.

Walter, still in wolf form, had taken to walking next to Charles and steadying him unobtrusively with a well-placed shoulder.

When she saw Charles shiver, she stopped.

'Change.' She knew it wouldn't help much, but the wolf had four legs to bear his weight instead of two. The wolf would generate heat better than the human, and his fur coat would retain it. She knew from her own extensive experience that the wolf could function better wounded than her human form.

It was a measure of Charles's exhaustion that he didn't bother arguing but simply stripped. He stored his snow-shoes, bandages, boots, and clothes tidily in some brush.

When he was naked, she could see all of his wounds clearly. They looked horrible, gaping desecrations of the smooth perfection of muscle and bone.

He crouched down so he didn't have as far to fall if he lost his balance when he changed. The new view of the hole in his back wasn't as bad as the last time she'd seen it. Despite everything, he was healing.

His change took almost as long as most wolves would have. The bullet hole looked odd on wolf-shaped ribs; the entry and exit wounds no longer lined up, the larger exit wound above the smaller hole.

'We'll need to rest and eat before we get there,' she told him. 'We won't do your father any good if we are exhausted.'

He didn't answer her, just put his head down and followed Walter.

Walter's shortcut was the roughest ground so far, leaving Anna cursing her snowshoes and the brush that caught at her bindings and hair. They were scrambling up a steep bit when both the wolves stopped and dropped to the ground.

Anna followed suit and tried to see what had alarmed them.

## 13

She hadn't told him *how* to find Charles, so Asil started them back toward her cabin. He'd carefully explained to Mariposa that he'd felt Charles there, that Charles might have decided to wait where he thought they would come.

It was possible that Charles had done just that – so he wasn't lying to her, precisely. Bran had somehow shut down the pack links, so Asil couldn't check, but he was pretty sure Charles was nowhere near the cabin. The boy was cautious, and he had his fragile new mate with him. He'd have taken off to contact Bran before the last sliver from the cabin's explosion had fallen. The witch and Sarai's wolf was one thing – but the boy would know he stood not a chance against Asil as well.

Charles should be well on his way to the cars by now. Asil didn't know the mountains here that well, but he had a good head for distances. He'd have to track him after they got to the cabin – or what was left of it – but if Charles was smart enough to drive away, the witch's search would be fruitless.

Of course, if Charles found out his father was out here, too, the damn fool would probably head right back into the maw of danger; he was that kind of heroic idiot.

Still, it would be a while before they reached the cabin, so Asil had bought Charles that much of a head start. He didn't know what to do that might help more than that.

Besides, he wanted to see Mariposa's face when she saw the wreckage. Destroying the cabin had been smart, smarter than he thought Charles was. Maybe he hadn't been giving Bran's pet assassin a fair shake.

He hoped that Charles had killed the poor coyote trapped so near death but held alive by Mariposa's will and magic. He never wanted to spend another night listening to some poor tortured creature breathe in ragged gasps in the space beneath the floor he lay upon. It had taken him most of the miserably long night to figure out what it was. For the longest time he'd had the terrible suspicion that it had been the lost hunter everyone had been making such a fuss over.

He never wanted to watch someone cut up a live animal again, either. Never wanted to see Sarai's beloved person filled with some stranger who watched the witch as if she were her goddess and did her bidding. His Sarai would never have fetched an animal for Mariposa to hurt. Would never have fetched Asil. She'd done it without orders, too. Mariposa hadn't expected him.

Guardians were supposed to be obedient, incapable of thinking for themselves. He thought there was more to the wolf than Mariposa's mindless guardian. It was the same stupid hope that had led him into this mess.

If only Charles's Anna hadn't been an Omega, he thought, his rage would have rendered the lure of Sarai's form useless. He felt that rage now – helpless tearing sorrow that his Sarai's wolf had been stolen and turned into . . . a thing.

If he'd stayed with Charles, helped him figure out what to do about Mariposa, maybe they'd have had a chance. But Anna's presence had dulled his pain and left only the knowledge that whatever the witch had done to Sarai, she hadn't broken his bond with her. When the wolf who looked like his Sarai left, he'd had to follow.

No, he was too old to be blaming other people for his mistakes. It had never been Anna's fault, it was his own. He was too old to believe in happy endings. The best thing he could do for Sarai was make certain that her wolf died this time.

When Mariposa had scried with water this morning and discovered a new wolf was coming, he'd known who it was. Had known what a disaster it would be if she got her hands on Bran. So when she'd asked him what other wolf Bran would send after Charles, he'd lied. And he'd lied with the truth. The next wolf Bran would have *sent* was Tag.

Asil didn't look at Bran, pacing beside them with all the ferocity of a golden retriever. Bran was always a deceptive bastard, gentle and mild right up until he ripped your throat out. He had many other fine qualities as well.

Asil'd been sure that, even with the weakness he, himself, had left in Bran's defenses, the old one would somehow wiggle out. Maybe if he'd been able to give him more warning? If he'd told Bran everything when he'd first come to Aspen Creek years ago?

Too late, too late.

Asil wasn't troubled by modesty. He knew his own strengths, which were many – and *he'd* fallen victim to her. He didn't know why he'd managed to convince himself that Bran would be able to resist her when he hadn't been able to.

At least she didn't know who Bran was. Yet.

He wished it had been Samuel in the woods instead of Charles. Charles was a thug, a killer. He didn't say much, just lurked silently behind his father to inspire the terror that Bran should have been able to cause by himself if he weren't so concerned with looking like a harmless boy.

Asil'd seen Charles in action a time or two – and he was impressive, Asil had to give that to him. Charles might be strong and swift, but what they needed here was subtlety, not brawn. Samuel was old and canny. Educated. Charles was a killer who'd be half-distracted by his new mate, a helpless and fragile mate. She wasn't much like his Sarai, who had been a warrior in her own right.

Something brushed his hip.

He glanced down, but didn't see anything, even when it touched him again. Unobtrusively, so as not to attract the witch's attention, he dropped his hand and it landed on a furry back – that wasn't there to any of his other senses. Even so, he knew what he touched. Foolishly, hope grew in his heart as his fingers closed on a silky coat he'd once been very familiar with.

*Can the witch change shape?*

Bran again, dragging him back to reality. Unfortunately Mariposa noticed his hesitation.

'Is there something wrong?' she asked.

'A lot of things,' Asil told her. She'd been right, he was happy to mislead her with the truth as much as he could. She hadn't yet acquired the ability of all good Alphas to ask specific questions. Bran was a lot harder to deceive.

'My Sarai is dead, and I am not.' He unobtrusively sampled the air and relaxed as the wilderness gave him a better answer for her. 'And there is something in the trees – a large predator that is not a bear. I have heard that there are wolverines in this place.'

She shrugged off the predator and quit paying attention to him. He wondered if she knew she was humming Sarai's favorite song. Did she do it to torment him with the memory of what was lost, or because she derived comfort from it?

Bran waited until Mariposa was occupied with her own thoughts before he talked to Asil again.

*The witch has the immortality, the strength, and the speed of a werewolf. Can she change shape, too? Is she really a werewolf? Disguising her scent somehow, so she smells human and witch, but not werewolf? Or is she just borrowing from her creation?*

Asil shrugged. He'd never seen her change. He looked down at the hand still buried in invisible fur. Maybe there was a chance to learn more about Mariposa.

For almost two centuries, as soon as he realized that the mating bond gave Mariposa access to him, he'd blocked the connection as best he could. But the worst had happened, so what was the danger in it anymore?

He dropped his shields and only iron control allowed him to keep walking as if nothing had happened as Sarai's love flooded him like an ocean wave. For a while all he could do was put one foot in front of another.

Some few mated pairs could talk to each other mind to mind, but with Sarai it had always been emotion. Over the years, practice had allowed it to develop into something not so much different from telepathy.

She was so happy he'd finally let her in so she could drink of his energies, create herself from him, rather than Mariposa. He opened himself to her so that she could do as she wished. If it had been the witch behind it, it would have been fatal, but he was confident that this was his Sarai. She sipped only a little from him as he learned from her.

Sarai was dead, he'd never have her back. He understood it, because it was something this half-living shadow of his mate understood. If he succeeded in killing Mariposa, even this shadow of his mate would be gone forever – if not, she'd be trapped in this half-life that was a living hell. He understood, but part of him couldn't be bothered with future mourning while he absorbed the joy that something of her remained to him.

*What?*

He could feel Bran's frustration and wondered how much he sensed of what he and Sarai were doing. Did he need Bran to know? Sarai thought so, so he tried to tell him.

'I know now that your guardian isn't her, but she feels like Sarai. I sometimes think about what it would be like to speak to her. Just once more,' he said, and was rewarded when Mariposa's nails sank into the sleeve of his white coat.

'She is here; she is Sarai. But she is *mine*,' Mariposa said. 'You don't need to talk to her. She doesn't want you.'

But Bran had understood; Asil could see in the thoughtful gaze his Alpha turned on him. He could stop there. But Mariposa was laying claim to someone who was *his*.

'She still loves me,' Asil replied, knowing it was just going to antagonize her. 'Part of her does. I could see it in her eyes when she came to get me.' And what he'd seen *had* been real, he knew that now. Fiercely, he held the thought to him. 'She came to me – you didn't send her.'

'She belongs to me.' The witch sounded agitated. 'Just as you do.' She stopped as she spun the thought around and found something that pleased her. She turned to him and gave him a seductive smile. 'You love me, too.' He felt her reach out to him through the bond he shared with Sarai's wolf and felt her quiet panic that the witch would see what they were doing. She was so afraid – and he couldn't bear it.

So he set out to distract Mariposa. It wasn't as if it was difficult.

He bent down and took her mouth in a carnal assault. After a bare moment's surprise, she welcomed it. He had known, all these years, what the real basis for her obsession with Sarai was. He'd tried to tell Sarai when he'd first understood, but she wanted to see only the good in people. She thought he was too suspicious – and vain, which was true enough. She thought that obscured his judgment, which was not true.

She hadn't believed him when he told her that Mariposa had fixated on him, until that night, the second time Mariposa had poisoned Sarai. The girl had tried to disguise herself as his mate. It had been useless, of course. She might have been able to change what she looked like, but she smelled nothing like his mate. If Sarai had been only human, she would have been dead from the poison; instead she'd been sick for three days. Mariposa had meant her to die.

Only then had Sarai agreed there was something wrong with the girl that she couldn't fix. Only then had she agreed to send Mariposa away.

He kissed Mariposa until she was breathless and panting, until the scent of her arousal rose in heated waves. Then he released her, wiped his mouth with the back of his hand, and told her the absolute truth. 'I don't love you. I never loved you.'

She heard it in his voice, felt it in his unaroused body. For a moment her face was blank with shock, and he might almost have felt sorry for her. Almost. If he didn't think about Sarai, about the poor coyote under the cabin floor and the raccoon she'd carved to pieces and kept alive – not because she needed it alive for her spell but because it pleased her to do so.

The next moment her shock was over. She gave him a cynical smile, a whore's smile. 'Maybe not, but you wanted me. I saw it in your eyes. I see it now. I am young and beautiful, and she was old and big like a cow. You wanted me, and she knew it. She was jealous and sent me away.'

He raised an eyebrow at her. 'You're mixing up your stories. I thought it was *I* who was jealous of the great love Sarai bore you. I thought I was the one who sent you away because Sarai loved you. Isn't that what you said?'

'*¡Cabrón!*' She stomped her foot. '*Hijo de puta.*'

Hard to believe that she was two centuries old and not the young girl she looked and acted. Like Peter Pan, she'd never grown up.

'She loved *me*. She chose me in the end. That's why she is with me and not with you. But' – she held up a finger – '*you* wanted me. That's why she made me go away. You wanted me, and it made her angry. I was young and helpless, a child in your care, and you wanted me.'

'Why would I want you?' he asked her coldly. 'I had Sarai, who was more woman than you could ever be. I wanted Sarai; for Sarai I lived and died. You were never more to me than a stray pet Sarai wanted to take care of.'

He let his truth ring in her ears, and when her hands came up, full of magic, he made no move to defend himself. He was confident that she wouldn't kill him – not before she convinced him that she was right. Or until he drove her into a real rage.

Honor demanded that he fight to live as long as he could, to try to stop this threat he'd brought to the Marrok. Anything short of death, Asil could handle. And while she was concentrating on him, she wasn't paying any attention to what he and Sarai were doing – and, more importantly, she wasn't paying any attention to Bran.

But Sarai's wolf wasn't so sanguine. In the instant before the witch's power hit him, she flashed him pictures of things that she'd seen the witch do to people. Things that might have made him question his earlier assessment that as long as he didn't die, he'd be fine.

If he'd needed proof that he was only dealing with a shadow of his mate, he'd have known it then. Sarai would have known that scaring him in advance wasn't helpful. But it did remind him that if he didn't block her out, she'd feel his pain, too. And even if she was only a shadow, he didn't want her hurt. He pulled up his shields to block Sarai out just before the witch hit him with more fury than finesse.

He screamed because he wasn't braced, because it hurt worse than he'd thought possible, and because his wolf decided that it wasn't going to let him just lie down and take it.

Changing at that moment was as imperative as it was stupid. Pain quadrupled and sizzled down nerve endings he wished he didn't have. Time changed for him, seconds became hours until he existed only in a limbo of agony. Then it stopped. His whole body went numb as he completed the change. It was only a moment, a space of freedom that Sarai bought him as she took his pain for him. Leaving him in wolf form, standing two feet from Mariposa and in full control of his body.

For the first time, Mariposa looked frightened, and he ate that fear as if it were fresh, dripping meat. He paused to savor it before he launched himself upon her. But that gave her one instant too many because she had time to scream his mate's name.

'Sarai!'

And his open jaws met with fur instead of skin, with Sarai's blood and not Mariposa's. As his fangs sank deep, the pain of Mariposa's magic ripped through him again, only to stop when Bran made his move.

'This stuff isn't vile,' Anna told Charles. 'If I were, say, five and still enjoyed sticky-creamy sweet things, I might actually like it.'

Anna barely whispered while she munched on freeze-dried ice cream. He'd apparently convinced her that consuming calories was important. It was too bad that she fed it to Walter and him, too. Though Walter seemed to appreciate it.

Charles grunted as he stared down the valley at the small figures who walked across the meadow. The wind blew the occasional word their way, but it was coming from the wrong direction to alert the others that they were being watched.

'I wonder why he's doing that,' Anna said, as Asil changed to his wolf.

It didn't look deliberate to Charles – maybe it was some sort of bizarre punishment. But if so, it backfired. Asil staggered to his feet – and in the middle of it, his movements were suddenly graceful and directed as he launched himself at the witch.

All three of them – Charles, Anna, and Walter – stood up. They were too far away to affect the outcome, but . . .

The thing that looked like Asil's mate's wolf just appeared out of nowhere to intercept him. And that's when his father made his move. The witch, distracted by the fight between the two wolves, almost missed it.

Almost.

And Charles was too far away to change what happened.

Asil felt her frustration, but Sarai couldn't ignore the prime directive of her creation, guarding Mariposa. Not yet. He hadn't given her enough. So they fought because she couldn't stop until he was dead or the witch stopped her.

Normally, it would have been no contest. Warrior she might have been, but Asil had taught her all that she knew, and in this form he outweighed her by fifty pounds of muscle. He was faster and stronger, but she was fighting to kill him. He was fighting to stay alive without hurting her.

If she killed him, she would have forever to grieve, and he couldn't bear it. He felt the witch's leash fall away from him, saw Sarai hesitate as it fell from her as well.

And then that moment of freedom was over.

'Asil, sit,' Mariposa said, her voice hoarse, but the whip of her power settled over him and forced him to do as she said, leashed and held as tightly as ever.

'Sarai, stop.' She hadn't noticed that Sarai had made no move to continue her attack. Because she wasn't looking at Sarai; she was still looking at Bran.

Asil followed her gaze.

At first he thought Bran was dead. But Mariposa staggered over to the still figure and kicked it. 'Up. Get up.'

Stiffly, it rose to its feet. The body was still Bran's, a gray wolf with a silly splash of white on the end of his tail. But when it looked up at the witch, there was nobody home.

Asil had seen zombies with more personality. And if he hadn't been a wolf, he'd have used the sign his mother had taught him to ward off evil, which would have been useless. It wouldn't work unless it was made by a witchblood – and if Mariposa didn't know it, he didn't want to be the one to teach her.

Even the guardian, shadow of his mate that she was, had more inside than whatever animated the Marrok.

Satisfied Bran was obeying her again, she looked at Asil. 'Hussan, change back to human.'

Ah Allah, it hurt. Too many changes in too few hours, but her orders were pitiless. He staggered to his feet and felt the sharp kiss of the ice crystals in the snow. Cold didn't usually bother him – less even than most werewolves. But he felt it now.

'Put on your clothes,' she snapped.

They were torn and bloody, but better than standing naked in the winter winds. His hands shook, making it hard to unlace his boots. He could only find one sock, and it was so wet he didn't put it on; blisters were the last of his worries.

Asil was afraid, terrified. No witch he'd ever seen, and he'd known a lot of them over the years, had been able to do something like that to a wolf with no more than the magic she had at hand. To a human, yes – to a dead human. He'd been making a mistake, he realized. Thinking of her as the child, however powerful, she had been, but she'd had two hundred years to acquire knowledge and power.

Cautiously, he felt down the pack ties toward his Alpha and felt . . . nothing. Had she really done to Bran what she'd done to his Sarai? Two centuries was a long time to study and learn. Maybe she'd found a way to make another guardian for her protection, a way that took minutes instead of four days of torture.

Then he realized that Bran himself was shutting him out, that the pack bindings were still in place. The understanding gave him hope; he looked at the Marrok again, but still saw only a dim intelligence that bore no resemblance to the man Bran had been . . . *was*.

Just to be certain, Asil examined the pack ties again, but *someone* was actively shutting them tight. And the only person he knew who could be doing it was Bran.

But they weren't shut down entirely.

Something eased out from Bran and touched him with black cold fingers, oozing slowly into his soul. Sarai whined softly as she realized what it meant before he did, but then she'd always been better at this sort of thing than he was – he'd always thought of anger as something hot and quick. This was worse.

*Berserker.*

He had been in North Africa at the time, not even a century old. But even there he'd heard the stories. *Deathbringer.* Whole villages killed, from old woman to day-old infant. There were songs and stories, most of them lost now to time.

A witch had forced the Change on her son and her grandson – so she could play with them. For years she held them as pets, to do her bidding. It made her the most dangerous witch in the British Isles. And then her son broke free.

He killed his mother and ate her. Then he killed every living thing within miles. He found a home in the dark heart of the great Welsh forests – and for years nothing lived within a day's walk of his den.

Great hunters of a generation, human, werewolf, or other, sought to win their honor or prove their courage – and they died. Some came to visit vengeance for lost loved ones.

They died. Even the fools who didn't understand, who were unlucky enough to venture too close to the monster, they died, too.

Then one day, or so he'd heard, Bran had walked out of the wilderness, his son at his side. No more berserker, only a harper, a teller of tales, and lone wolf.

Given enough time, even the most horrific story drifts to legend, then nothing. Asil was pretty sure that he was the only one, except for Samuel, of course, who knew enough to understand just what it was that the witch had done.

She thought she had the Marrok under her control. But then, Mariposa had always rewritten reality to suit her.

'. . . *him of eagum stod ligge gelicost leoht unfaeger*,' Asil quoted softly.

'What did you say?' Mariposa was white and visibly exhausted, but her leash was strong and unbreakable.

'*Beowulf*,' he told her. 'Roughly translated it is, I believe . . . "from his eyes shone a flaming, baleful light." I'm not a poet to do the translation in verse.'

She looked suspiciously at Bran, but saw only eyes so dull they were more brown than amber. Asil knew it, because he kept looking himself.

*From his eyes shone a flaming, baleful light.* Grendel owed something to Bran's time as a berserker, as he did to other stories handed down over the centuries. But the lack of intelligence in his Alpha's eyes and the cold black rage flowing slowly from Bran into every werewolf tied to him was far more frightening than Grendel or Grendel's mother, those fierce monsters of the epic poem, could ever have been. He hoped that it was only infecting the immediate pack, but he was very much afraid it might spread to all of them.

Death would flow through the world as it had not since the Black Plague, when a third of Europe had died.

And there would be no peace for a werewolf in this world ever again.

'You are afraid,' she told him. 'As you should be. For now I allow you to be yourself – but if you continue to trouble me, I will make you my pet, as I have made him. Pets are less useful than Sarai, incapable of responding to anything except direct orders – I had planned on making you a guardian, like Sarai. You'd best be careful I don't change my mind.'

She thought he was afraid of her. And he had been, until the monster she had created surpassed her. She had no idea.

She took two steps toward Asil, then slapped him hard. He made no move to defend himself. She was hampered somewhat by her size, but she hit him at full strength, Sarai's strength. Reflexively, he licked the blood from his lip.

'That is for lying to me about who this werewolf was. It is the Marrok, not some stupid lesser wolf. You knew, you *knew* – and you let me believe him to be someone else. He might have hurt me. And you are supposed to keep me safe, have you forgotten? I was given into your keeping so you could make me safe.'

Eventually, old wolves lost touch with reality. The first crisis was when all the people they had known died, and there was no one left who had known them when they were human. The second came at different times to different wolves, when the change in the world left them no place where they could feel at home.

And Mariposa had never been stable, even before she killed Sarai. However, if she thought he wanted to keep her *safe* . . . truly she was mad.

'But your betrayal didn't really matter,' she told him with a girlish toss of her head. 'I can keep myself safe, too.

This one is mine.' She glanced at Bran. 'Change. I want to see your face. I've never been able to find a photo of you, Bran Cornick.'

Asil found himself holding his breath as his Alpha obeyed. Would the pain of the change be the straw that allowed the monster to break free of her chains?

They waited in the cold, Asil, his shadow-mate, and the witch as the change happened. Their breath rose like steam, reminding him for some silly reason of the time, years ago, that Bran took the Marrok pack, all the wolves who belonged only to him, in a hired bus to stay at the big hotel in Yellowstone Park in the dead of winter. He'd rented all the rooms so they could run and howl all night in the snow-covered geyser basin with no one to see them but a few buffalo and elk.

'You can't hide in your hothouse all the time,' he'd told Asil, when Asil politely requested not to go. 'You have to make new memories sometimes.'

Asil closed his eyes and prayed for the first time since Sarai had been taken from him – though he'd once been a truly devout man. He prayed that Allah would not allow Bran to become such a monster that he destroyed his careful creation of a home, a haven for his wolves.

When Asil opened his eyes at last, Bran stood naked in the snow. He wasn't shivering, though it was only a few degrees above zero, well below freezing. His skin was pale and thin, showing the blue veins that carried blood back to his heart. There were a few scars, one that ran across his ribs and one just under his right arm.

'Pretty enough body,' said Mariposa. 'But you all have those, you wolves. A little more delicate than I like my men.' She pursed her lips and shook her head. 'I was expecting something . . . a little more impressive. A Marrok should be . . .' She looked at Asil. 'More like Hussan. A man other people turn their heads to watch. A man who makes other men walk wary. Not one who needs his son to impress visitors and do his killing. You see, I've done my research. When I heard that, I knew that you were too weak to hold all those packs on your own.'

She was trying to goad Bran, Asil thought incredulously. Testing her hold to make sure there was no more independence in her slave. Hyperventilating wasn't going to help matters, Asil told himself a little desperately. Couldn't she see the monster inside the still exterior?

The only thing that kept him from panic was the knowledge that her assessment of him was more likely to amuse Bran than enrage him. Of course, Bran was not exactly himself anymore.

'Can you change back?' she asked Bran when he made no response to her judgment. 'I don't have shoes for you, and I'd prefer not to have to cut off your feet because of frostbite.'

'Yes.' Bran slurred the word, dragging out the last sound, almost as if he were drunk.

She waited for him to start, but finally gave an impatient sound, and said, 'Do so.'

Before he had completed the change she motioned Sarai to her and climbed on her back as if her guardian were a donkey. Asil bit back his anger, anger that was too large for the small attack on Sarai-who-was-not-Sarai's dignity. He glanced nervously at Bran and tried very hard to be calm.

'When he is finished changing, the two of you catch up with us.'

Sarai brushed against him, leaving behind a flood of affection and worry. As soon as she was out of sight, he felt that insidious anger ramp up – as if Sarai's presence had helped calm Bran, as if she were still the Omega she had once been . . . and why not?

He dropped to one knee and bowed his head, hoping against hope that when the other werewolf arose, he would still be bound, by the witch or his own will.

Though he dare not do it with the proper motion, and it had been a long time since he'd been a good Muslim, he could not stop the impulse to pray. '*Allaahu Akbar*—'

The witch flung out her hands, and even as far away as Charles was, he could feel the stain of her magic – corrupt and festering magic, but powerful. Very powerful.

Charles saw his father fall – and then Bran was gone.

He froze. Breathless with the suddenness of it. The cool presence that had been there for as long as he could remember left a huge, empty silence. His lungs didn't want to move, but suddenly he could get air in and all Brother Wolf wanted was to howl to the heavens.

Charles fought and fought to keep Brother Wolf quiet, but there was an odd undercurrent of savage rage that he'd never felt before, deeper and darker than the usual violent urges; and he understood, or hoped he did.

Bran wasn't gone. He was Changed.

His father mostly talked of the present or near present. Ten years, twenty, but not a hundred or more. It was something Charles had grown to appreciate as he himself grew older.

But Samuel could sometimes be persuaded to tell stories to his younger brother. And Bran as berserker had been one of his favorite stories until he'd grown old enough to understand that it wasn't just a story. If it weren't for that story, he might have been tempted to overlook the darkness seeping into him, he might have thought that Bran had truly been broken.

He used his hope to soothe Brother Wolf, and together they ran down the pack magic that cradled them in the

Alpha's care. Searching, searching, they found it, changed, shut down almost entirely, until only a little of the poison rage seeped through. Bran still lived.

But as what?

# 14

Though Charles wanted to pelt down the hill as soon as the witch was gone, he led the way in a slow, controlled jog that Anna could easily keep up with in her snowshoes.

As they got closer, the trees and underbrush obscured the place where Asil and his father waited. Cautiously, Charles slowed and stopped.

He looked at her and then at Walter. She nodded silently and crouched where she was. Walter settled in like the old soldier he was. If it weren't for him, Charles would have stayed right where he was. He would not chance Anna's life on a hunch. But Walter would take care of her if something happened, so Charles was free to take a risk.

When Charles walked out into the open, Asil had finished his prayer, but just knelt where he was, with his head bowed – as if he were trying very hard not to give offense to the Marrok.

'Slowly,' murmured Asil without looking up. Asil's ears had always been keen – or maybe he'd picked up Charles's scent. 'We are bound to her, your father and I. I must do what the witch has commanded, as if she were my Alpha.' He turned his head finally and met Charles's eyes with despair. 'Your father she has bound tighter. She figured out who he was and took his free will from him like a puppet master attaching strings to his marionette.

'I'm hoping,' Asil explained, still in that soft, soft voice, 'that when he comes out of this change he is still sane.' Tiredly he rubbed his jaw. 'I have to wait and see, but you do not. You need to take your mate and leave here, gather up the pack in Aspen Creek and run to the ends of the earth. If she holds him, every wolf who owes him allegiance will be hers.

'She's quite mad – she wasn't exactly stable before – but she's tied herself to Sarai's dead wolf. The living and the dead do not good bedfellows make.'

Charles waited.

Asil gave him a slight smile. 'I think that she overestimates her strength. If she does not hold him . . .' He looked at Bran. 'Well, then, *perdito*, I think then it is better to be far, far away.'

Bran staggered to his feet and stood like a newborn foal, with his legs spread out so he wouldn't fall. There was nothing in his eyes. Nothing at all.

If not for the lump of icy wrath that was gathering in his stomach, a gift from his father, Charles would have believed him wholly taken over.

One more shift, Charles thought, and maybe he could do one more after that, but he was going to have a hell of a hangover if he did. Not for the first time he wished he'd inherited his father's ability to speak inside other people's heads. It would save a lot of energy.

He changed, hoping Asil could wait until he was able to talk. It took a little longer than he was used to – and he was afraid he might be stuck as a human longer than he'd calculated.

But finally he was through – and naked as a jaybird. He didn't have the energy to pander to his modesty.

'It is too late, she is already coming,' he told Asil. 'When a witch has such a hold, she can see through their eyes.' His brother had told him that. 'They are living golems for her.'

Asil closed his eyes. 'We are undone.'

'You despair too easily,' Charles said. He couldn't say much about Anna or Walter without the chance that it would be immediately carried to the witch. 'Our pack has an Omega to call upon. Maybe it will be enough.'

'Do you know what he was?' Asil asked.

'Yes.'

Asil looked at the Marrok. 'Kill him now, if you can. If you love him, if you care about the pack.'

Charles looked at his father, who looked as frail as a were-wolf could look. Not a wolf to inspire fear in the hearts of those who beheld him – more fool them.

He laughed harshly. 'If you think I could kill him, you are a fool. He is the Marrok – and not nearly as weak as he looks. Never believe what you see with my father.'

That was true, and Charles was hurt. Even breathing hurt.

He should leave, thought Charles, as his father's empty eyes ran over him. He'd already proven that the witch could take him when she pleased. All he could be was a liability.

*Stay. I need you.*

'For what?' he asked. He looked, but even with his father's voice in his head, he could only see a dumb beast in the Marrok's eyes.

*Because you are the only one I know I won't kill.*

Anna listened to them talk and wrapped her arms tightly over her stomach. She knew that Charles was counting on her – on her and Walter to be his ace in the hole.

The problem was, she wasn't much of an ace. A deuce maybe, or a joker, but not an ace. Walter had been a soldier, he was a better bet.

'Do you know this place? Can we move somewhere we can see them and still stay hidden?' she whispered to Walter.

He started off at a right angle to where Charles was talking to Asil. Anna followed him as quietly as she could. He moved through the woods like Charles did, as if he were a part of it.

He took her closer than she'd thought possible, to an old

tree whose branches were dense and brushed the ground only a dozen yards from where the Marrok stood on four feet and stared at his son.

The werewolf wiggled under the branches, and Anna followed him on her hands and knees and found herself in a dry dark cave covered with a thick pad of old tree needles that poked into whatever patch of bare skin got near them but cushioned her knees. She crawled over them and lay flat on her belly so she could see out from under the branches and look out beyond the tree.

They were a little uphill from Charles, and, she was afraid, upwind. She ought to change; as a wolf she was stronger, and she had claws and fangs instead of the fingernails that were her only weapon. When she tried though, she knew it was too soon and she wasn't going to make the change. Even the effort left her weary and trembling.

Walter settled next to her, and the warmth of his big body let her know just how cold she was. She pulled off one of her gloves and buried her hand in Walter's fur to warm it up.

'He's talking to you?'

Charles held up a hand to keep Asil quiet. He needed to think. His father had a plan, that much was clear. But he didn't seem inclined to share it . . . if he could.

'What does the witch want with me?' asked Charles.

'I don't—' A funny look came over Asil's face. 'Sarai thinks she will kill you, to break your father and regain power she lost when you destroyed the cabin. I think she's done this before, taken over a pack, I mean. Sarai sounds as if this is a pattern.' He paused. 'If I'm understanding this right, though, the others she took eventually died. Not quite. Faded until there was nothing left of them.' He put his hands to his temples as if he had a headache.

Ah, thought Charles as his adrenaline rose. The ties of

love are very strong. Maybe the witch was going to lose Sarai to Asil.

He set that aside for later consideration and thought about what Asil had said. 'She might get a surprise if she tries to take over my father's pack,' he said. 'Anna thinks we're a bunch of psychotics.'

Asil smiled a little. 'She's right, you know.'

Charles held out a hand and pulled Asil to his feet, staggering a little drunkenly as he did so. 'You look a little rough. Are you hurt?'

Asil dusted the melting snow off his torn pant leg, though it was already soaked through. 'No. Just a few scrapes. Mostly torn cloth.' He gave Charles a thorough look. 'At least I have clothes.'

Charles was too tired to play that stupid one-upmanship game. 'So the witch will kill me,' he said, looking at his father and trying to figure out what the old wolf was up to.

'Maybe.' Asil dusted the snow off his other pant leg. 'Or she'll have him do it – or maybe Sarai or me. Your pain, your death, matters. Who brings it to you does not. As long as she's there to collect. But I bet she'll order your father to do it. She always liked to hurt people.'

If he hadn't just been thinking about the way Asil's presence allowed Sarai to break the witch's control, he might not have understood the significance of that.

The cunning old wolf. Charles slanted an admiring glance at his father. 'So that's it. What did your mother do all those years ago? Order you to kill Samuel?'

Asil frowned at him, but before he could say anything a wolf burst through the trees, carrying the witch. Charles felt the familiar coldness settle over him, as Brother Wolf settled in for a fight. His father might be an expert manipulator, but he wasn't in top form and there were too many factors out of anyone's control.

Sarai stopped well out of easy reach and kept herself between the witch and Charles as the witch slid off her back. Her protectiveness seemed to be instinctive – like a mother caring for her young.

The witch – Mary, she'd called herself, and Asil called her Mariposa, Butterfly – was smaller than he remembered, or maybe she just looked small next to Asil's mate. There was no scarf to hide her features this time. She looked young, as if the ugliness of the world had never touched her.

'Charles,' she said. 'Where is your woman?'

He waited, but the impulse to answer didn't sweep over him. He remembered the strangled pack bonds and a sudden, fervent hope sprang up – his father might have solved one of his problems.

'She is about,' he said.

She smiled, but her eyes were cool. 'Where, exactly?'

He tilted his head. 'Not where I left them.' Brother Wolf was sure, though he didn't know how the wolf knew.

She stilled, narrowing her eyes at him. 'How many wolves are in your father's pack?'

'Including you and your creature?'

Her eyes opened a little. 'My, my, Asil certainly wasted no time telling you our business. Yes. By all means include us.'

'Thirty-two . . . maybe thirty-three.' There was no harm giving her information that would do her no good here and now. He just wasn't sure if he should count Samuel or not.

'Tell me why I should let you live,' she said. 'What can you do for me that your father cannot?'

Sarai's attention was on Asil. She, at least, was convinced that the witch had Charles under control. He wasn't going to get another, better opportunity.

One benefit of experience was that he didn't give himself away with surges of adrenaline or emotion. 'You should let me live because that might be the only thing that keeps you alive.'

'What do you mean?' An eyebrow raised, and she cocked her head in a way that was almost wolflike.

Did he trust his father's calculations? His father was gambling that he could break the witch's hold if she ordered Bran to kill him.

There were other things Charles could try. Maybe there would be a time when he could attack her without risking so much. All he would need was a half second when he was within touching distance and the others were not.

But he could fight now – in a day of the witch's tender care that might not be the case.

Charles looked down as if ceding authority to her, and he whispered the next words slowly; unconsciously she took a step forward, listening. 'My fath—' And in the middle of the second word he launched himself at her with every ounce of speed he had left in him.

'Sarai!' The witch screamed in utter terror. If he'd been in top form it wouldn't have been enough. But he was slowed down by exhaustion and by his wounds. The wolf who had been Sarai hit him like a freight train and knocked him away from the witch before he could touch her.

He'd hoped surprise would allow him to kill the witch outright, but he was realistic. So he'd planned on the hit and let the force of the contact power his roll away from Sarai, rather than break his ribs.

Now that the fight was on, his old wounds bothered him only distantly – and mostly as a drag; one of his legs was slower, and his punches wouldn't be as effective.

Wounded and in human form, most people would be forgiven for thinking that the other wolf would have the advantage. They would be wrong.

If she'd really been Asil's mate, he would have been in a quandary. But she wasn't. Charles knew it, even if poor Asil was caught by his mating bond, confused by the ability of this poor imitation to ape a living creature. The spirits of the mountains knew she was dead, and they sang it to him as they gave him back some of his strength.

She caught him with a claw along one side, but she was, in the end, a simulacrum of an Omega wolf, while Charles had spent most of his life hunting down other werewolves and killing them. Even wounded, he was faster than she was, moving out of her way as water moves around a rock. Thirty years of various martial arts gave him an advantage her age could not, by itself, overcome.

He drew the fight out as long as he dared, but he was tired, and the worse fight was still ahead.

Anna fumbled at the bindings of the snowshoes to get them off. The snowpack on the ground between them and Charles was broken up and no more than six inches deep anywhere she could see. She'd be faster without them. If only she could figure out when she would be of use.

If she'd had the damned, clunky snowshoes off earlier, she'd have run out when the female wolf attacked Charles. But as Anna ripped and tore at the snow-crusted catches, it soon became apparent that Charles had that fight well in hand. He stood relaxed and at ease while the battered female wolf circled him, looking for an opening. A little calmer, Anna ripped off the second snowshoe. She wouldn't be wearing them again, no one would, but she could move now if she had to.

Unfortunately, she wasn't the only one who saw who was in charge of the fight.

'Asil,' said Mary. 'Help her.'

The Moor looked at the witch for a moment, then pulled off his shirt and dropped it on the ground. He stalked to the battle with the ease of a warrior who understood death and welcomed it. If Anna hadn't been so worried about

Charles, if she'd been watching a movie, she'd have sat back, eaten popcorn, and enjoyed the view. But the blood was real.

She leaned forward and realized she had a death grip on the back of Walter's neck. She loosened her hand and rubbed his fur in apology.

One minute Asil was walking toward the fight, the next he was at full speed. He passed Charles at an oblique angle and hit Sarai with an elbow strike on the side of the neck. She went limp and he snatched her up over his shoulders and ran.

'Asil!' But the witch gave no command, and Asil jumped off a rise and hit the steep side of the mountain on the edge of his feet. At the speed he was going, he might as well have had skis on.

Help, Anna realized, could have a lot of meanings. From the shelter of the tree, Anna couldn't see Asil, but she could hear the sound of something moving very fast down the side of the mountain, away from any further orders he might be given.

The whole thing had taken maybe twenty seconds. If Anna had been distracted, Charles was not. He ran at the witch, but she threw something at him that brought him down into the rucked-up snow. The force of his attack kept his body moving toward the witch in an awkward tumble.

'No!' the witch shrieked hysterically as she rapidly backed away from him. Anna had to remind herself that this witch was old. As old as Charles for all that she looked fifteen or sixteen. 'I *have* to be safe. Sarai! Sarai!'

Anna braced herself to intervene, but Charles put his hands on the ground and levered himself up. Whatever she'd done to him had hurt, but she couldn't see it in his face, just in the slowness of his movement. Surely if he needed her, he'd find some way to signal?

She glanced at the werewolf beside her, but though he

was alert and focused, he didn't seem worried. Of course, he didn't know anything more of witches than she did – and he'd only known Charles for a day.

Anna wasn't the only one who had noticed how slowly Charles was moving. The witch put both of her hands to her face.

'I forgot,' she gasped, half-laughing, and then she pointed a finger at him and said something that didn't sound like Spanish to Anna. Charles flinched, then clutched his chest. 'I forgot. I can defend myself.'

But Anna wasn't listening to her, she was watching Charles's face. He wasn't breathing. Whatever the witch had done to him would be fatal if allowed to continue. She didn't know much about witchcraft, and doubtless most of it was wrong. But the witch had released Charles once, with sufficient distraction. Maybe it would work one more time.

Anna was through waiting for a signal.

She erupted from the shelter of the tree and reached full speed within two strides; her old track coach would have been proud of her. She ignored the nagging ache of her overused thighs and the bite of cold in her chest, focused only on the witch, only dimly aware of the wolf running at her side.

She saw the witch drop her hands and focus on Anna. Saw her smile and heard her say, 'Bran, Marrok, Alpha of the Marrok, slay me your son, Charles.'

Then she raised a finger and flicked it at Anna. Anna had no time to prepare when something hit her from the side and knocked her to the ground, out of the pathway of the spell.

It came at last, Charles thought. The witch's command rang in his ears – which were well and truly ringing anyway with whatever she had done to him. It came at the worst possible time because he was half-blind and stumbling, and he had no idea how long it would take his father to break her command over him.

If he broke it.

But he could not burden his father with his death, so he gathered his wits and figured out from where the wolf was attacking with his nose and the sense that told him when something hostile was watching, because nothing else was working properly.

He reached out, grabbed fur as tightly as he could, and let the force of his father's nearly silent charge push him over on his back, then used his feet to make sure Bran continued over and past him.

It wasn't that neat of course. His father was quicker than Sarai had been. Quicker, stronger, and a damn sight better with his claws. Still, his da's most formidable weapon – his mind – was fogged by the witch's hold, and Charles was able to throw him without taking too much damage. The leftover momentum was sufficient for him to roll to his feet and await his father's next attack.


Walter was a deadweight on Anna, and she rolled him aside as gently as she could. If she hurt him, he didn't show it. His body was limp and moved without resistance, and she could only hope that she wasn't damaging him further. He'd knocked her out of the way and taken the witch's spell himself.

She came to her feet and scrambled toward the witch. She couldn't afford to stop and make sure Walter was all right until she'd done something, anything, to keep the witch from doing more harm.

'You don't want to hurt me,' the witch said, widening her chocolate eyes. 'You want to stop.'

Anna's run slowed until she stood motionless, so close to

the witch that she could smell the mint of her toothpaste. For a moment she had no idea what she was doing or why.

'Stay there.' The witch unzipped her coat and reached inside, pulling out a gun.

Omega, Anna remembered, meant she didn't have to take orders – and as easily as that she could move again. With a precision that she'd learned from a brother who'd boxed in high school, and the speed and power she owed her were-wolf nature, she punched the witch in the jaw. She heard the pop as the witch's jawbone broke and she fell face-first on the ground, unconscious.

She took a deep breath and looked at the battle raging between Charles and his father. For a moment they were moving too swiftly for her eye to follow, then Charles stood motionless, except for the rapid rise and fall of his breath, just out of reach of his father, his body both ready and relaxed. Blood oozed from slices on his shoulder and thigh. A single rip, running from under his left arm across his abdomen to his right hip, looked to be more serious. The Marrok stood to one side shaking his head very slowly, shifting his weight from side to side.

She should kill the witch and free the Marrok.

She turned back and looked down at the limp body. The girl looked so innocent, so young to have caused such harm.

Anna had killed someone before, but that had been almost an accident. Killing in cold blood was different.

Walter knew how to kill. Instinctively, she looked for him, but he hadn't moved . . . except his eyes. Surely they had been closed when she'd left him. Now they were open, and a whitish film coated them.

Anna found herself kneeling beside him without really knowing how she had gotten there. No heartbeat, no breath. This man had survived a war and over thirty years of self-imposed isolation, and he'd died for her. She fisted her hands – one gloved, one not – in his fur.

Then she walked over to the unconscious witch, grabbed her chin and the top of her head and twisted with more than human strength. It was easy, just like in the movies. One crack, and the witch was as dead as Walter.

She released the witch, stood up, and took one step back, breathing far too hard. It was so quiet in the forest, as if the whole world had taken a deep breath and not let it out. As if she were the only living creature in the whole world.

Numbly, she turned on her frozen feet to see the Marrok standing over Charles's body.

She'd been too late.

As the sun slowly set, setting the sky aflame behind the dark mountains, Asil held Sarai, still unconscious, in his arms. He buried his nose against her neck, breathing in the familiar scent he'd never thought to smell again. She was so beautiful.

They weren't so far that he couldn't hear the fight, but out of the witch's sight, she'd have a harder time controlling him.

Asil waited. He'd done all he could to take them both out of the battle since they'd only be on the wrong side if they fought. It was the best he could do.

So he held Sarai on his lap and tried to forget that it was the last time.

If Mariposa succeeded, she would kill him. He'd taken Sarai away from her again, and she wouldn't stand for it. If Charles or Bran succeeded in killing Mariposa, his Sarai would be gone for good. A witch's creations did not survive their maker.

So he held her and breathed in her scent and pretended that this moment would never end. Pretended it was Sarai he held . . . almost he caught a hint of cinnamon.

As her scent faded into fir and pine, snow and dreary winter, he wondered if he had been able to see the future that long ago day when a frightened and bruised child had been brought to his home, would he have had the fortitude to kill her? He put his head down on his knee in bleak despair, holding tight to a small, battered scrap of buff fur.

He didn't have it in him to be glad that Mariposa was dead and Sarai's wolf freed at last.

Which would have been a premature celebration at any rate, because madness swept through him like a fire in a forest in August. He was too tired, but the rage didn't care, just gathered him in an implacable grip and demanded that he change. A wild howl echoed down the mountainside, and Asil called out in return.

The Beast had awakened. Asil opened his hand and let the wind take the last part of Sarai from him before he answered his master's call.

Anna didn't think about running until she was halfway to Charles and sprinting.

He couldn't be dead. She could have killed that blasted witch two or three minutes earlier. It couldn't be her fault he was dead – that his father had killed him.

She brushed by the Marrok, and his power roared over her as she dashed through it and fell, sliding in the snow. She crawled the last two feet to Charles. His eyes were closed, and he was covered with blood. She reached out, but she was afraid to touch him.

She was so sure he was dead that when his eyes opened, it took a moment for it to register.

'Don't move,' he whispered, his eyes focused beyond her. 'Don't breathe if you can help it.'

Charles watched the wolf who was no longer his father stalk forward, madness mated to cunning in an unholy combination.

Bran had miscalculated. Maybe if the witch hadn't died and broken the control unexpectedly. Maybe if Charles had just given his father his throat at the beginning of the fight, trusting that his father couldn't kill him, even under compulsion. Maybe if it had been Samuel here, instead of him.

Or maybe it was something that would have happened no matter what anyone had done, once the witch had subjugated his father entirely – the way Bran's mother had subjugated him so many centuries ago.

'Why' didn't matter anymore, because his clever, chameleon-like da was gone. In his place was the most dangerous creature who had ever set foot on this mountain.

Charles had thought he was done in. His chest burned, and he was having real trouble breathing. One of those sharp claws had pierced a lung – he'd had that happen often enough he knew what it felt like. He was on the point of giving up, when Anna suddenly appeared – taking no more notice of his da than if he'd been a poodle.

With Anna in danger, Charles found himself much more alert – though his attention was split in his frantic need to know that she was all right.

She looked terrible. Her hair was sweat-dampened and deformed by her absent hat. Windburns reddened her face that he wouldn't have noticed was dirty, too, except for the tear tracks that ran from her eyes to her jaw in ragged lines. He whispered a warning to her, but she smiled (as if she hadn't heard a word he'd said or the danger he'd implied) – and terrified as he was, he was momentarily dumbstruck.

'Charles,' she said. 'I thought you were dead, too. No. Don't move—' And she put her hand on his shoulder to make sure he didn't. 'I . . .'

Asil growled hungrily, and Anna turned to look.

Asil was not a small wolf. He wasn't as big as Samuel or Charles, but he was big enough. His fur was so dark a brown as to be mistaken for black in the growing shadows. His ears were pinned, and there was saliva dripping from his jaws.

But Anna wasn't stupid – her attention, like most of Charles's, focused on the Marrok. Bran was watching them as a cat waits for a mouse to do something interesting – like run.

Her breath caught, and the scent of her fear forced him to sit up – which was a dumb move – but his da was watching Anna now and ignored Charles.

Caught in Bran's mad gaze, Anna reached out instinctively and grabbed Charles's hand.

And it happened.

Unexpected, unheralded, the mating bond settled over him like a well-worn shirt – and for a moment he didn't hurt, wasn't tired, sore, beat-up, cold, naked, and terrified. For a moment his father's rage, eating him up from the shadows, was as nothing to the joy of the moment.

Anna took a deep breath and gave him an astonished look that clearly said, *You told me we needed sex for this to happen. You're supposed to be the expert.*

And then reality settled in.

He gave her a jerk that skidded her back so he was mostly between her and the two mad wolves, who were watching her with utter intentness.

She freed her hand gently, and he was glad of it – he told himself – he needed both hands to defend them. If he could manage to get to his feet.

He could feel her scooting farther behind him, which he appreciated – though he'd half expected her to fight him. Then two cold hands settled on his bloody shoulders and she leaned against his back, one of her breasts pressed on his old wound.

She drew in a breath and began to sing. And the song

she chose was the Shaker song that his father had chosen to sing for Doc Wallace's funeral, 'Simple Gifts.'

Peace swept over him like a tropical wind, as it hadn't since the first couple of hours after he'd met her. She had to be tranquil, Asil had said, or something of the sort. She couldn't give calm that she didn't have. So she sang and drew the peace of the song into her – and gave it to the wolves.

On the third line Charles joined in with a descant that complemented her rich alto. They sang it through twice, and when they were finished, Asil heaved a sigh and settled on the snow as if he were too exhausted to move.

Charles let Anna pick the songs. The next one was the Irish song 'The Black Velvet Band.' To his weary amusement, she picked up a little bit of an Irish lilt as she sang it. He was pretty sure from the phrasing, she'd learned the song from listening to the Irish Rovers. In the middle of 'The Wreck of the Edmund Fitzgerald,' his father walked tiredly over to Anna and put his head in her lap with a sigh.

The next time he saw Samuel, he'd have to tell his brother that his Anna defeated the Marrok at his worst with a couple of songs instead of the years it had taken Samuel.

Anna kept singing as Charles heaved himself to his feet – not a pleasant experience, but his father's claws and fangs weren't silver, and even the worst of the new wounds were healing. It was dark but the moon was bright, not yet full, but waxing strong.

He stepped over Asil, who was sleeping so deeply he didn't even twitch, and walked to the bodies. The witch's neck was broken, but he'd feel better when they burned her body to ash and gone. Walter was dead, too.

Anna finished her song, and said, 'It was for me.'

He looked over at her.

'The witch threw some spell at me, and Walter got between us.'

Anna was pale, and there was a bruise forming along her cheek. Despite the food she'd been eating, he thought she'd lost some weight the last few days. Her fingernails were torn, and her right hand, which was gently petting his father's muzzle, was cut on the knuckles where she'd punched someone – presumably Mariposa.

She was shivering a little, and he couldn't tell if it was the cold or shock, or both. Even as he thought about it, Bran curled around her, sharing his warmth.

Walter had been right: Charles hadn't been taking very good care of her.

'Then Walter died as he lived,' he told his mate. 'A hero, a soldier, and a survivor who chose to protect what was precious to him. I don't think, if you could ask him, that he would have any regrets.'

# 15

In the end it was the cold that drove Anna. She couldn't stay any longer staring at the bodies: the man who had died for her and the woman she'd killed. But it was the cold, leaching the heat from her body that gave her the impetus to move.

Wearily, she got to her feet, disturbing the wolves who were piled around her in the futile effort to keep her warm. She looked apologetically at Charles. 'I know the cars are only a couple of hours away – can you show me how to get there?' She looked at the corpses and then back to Charles. 'I can't stay here anymore.'

With a groan, Charles stood up. Bran steadied him a little when he staggered. Asil rose with the others. Only Bran looked fit for travel.

'I'm sorry,' she said, 'but I can't eat enough to stay warm. And I can't manage to change to the wolf.' As soon as night had fallen, the temperature had started to drop, and it was only getting colder.

Charles bumped her with his head and started off, limping badly. Bran stayed by her side just like Walter had. She clenched her fingers in the ruff on the back of his neck, forgetting that he was the Marrok in her need for tactile comfort.

In the dark, the forest should have been eerie, but either she'd gotten used to them, or Charles's woodland spirits were being helpful at last. Weariness dogged her steps, and her jaw chattered unmercifully. She took an incautious step and her foot broke through the crust on the top of the snow and she found herself waist deep in snow, too tired to pull herself out.

The pack on her back rattled, and then Asil pushed a candy bar under her hand. Unenthusiastic, she tore the package open with her teeth and started chewing. It tasted like cardboard, and she wanted to put her face down in the snow and sleep. But Asil growled at her – subsiding unrepentantly when Bran growled back. Charles didn't make any noise, just stared at Asil with yellow eyes. It was the threat of violence more than anything that made her swallow and swallow until the sticky stuff was gone.

She struggled out of the snow and tried to stay away from places where the white stuff spread out in smooth sheets. Not that she didn't fall into drifts again. The wolves had trouble, too, but not as much as she did.

When she first saw the vehicles, she thought she was hallucinating.

The truck was behind the Humvee, so she went to it. She fumbled with the door until she got it open. There wasn't really room for three werewolves and her, but they managed somehow. She shut the door, turned the key, and waited with numb patience until warmth started filling the cab.

It was only then that she realized that the wolf sitting on the bench seat next to her was Bran. Charles took shotgun, and Asil settled on the passenger floor and closed his eyes. Bran curled up against her and put his muzzle on her thigh. He was shivering now and again – and she didn't think it was the cold that was bothering him.

When the truck was blowing hot air, she pulled off her gloves and held her fingers against the heater vent until she could feel them – and then untied her boots and took them and her wet socks off, too. There were puddles of water under her feet, but the melted snow had warmed, so she didn't mind it too much. She stuffed all of her discards behind the seat.

Backing the truck down the narrow road was miserable. The road rose and fell, so half the time she couldn't see it out her rear window and had to depend upon the side mirrors. By the time she was driving forward down the road, her hands were shaking with stress, sweat ran down her back – but the truck was still in one piece.

The cab smelled like warm, wet fur; the clock on the dash said it was three in the morning, and her toes ached and throbbed as they warmed up at last.

She'd driven for about a half hour when a gray Suburban, coming up the opposite way, flashed its lights at her and stopped. Even though they were on the highway, she stopped beside it and rolled her window down. She hadn't seen another car all night, so she decided not to worry about traffic.

The windows of the other SUV were dark, so the only person she could see was Tag in the driver's seat. He frowned at her, 'Bran told me to gather a few of the pack for a cleanup. Everyone okay?'

It took her a moment to realize how Bran had told him. She glanced around at her comrades, none of whom looked okay to her. 'What did Bran tell you?' Her voice was tired and slurred.

Tag's frown deepened, but he answered her. 'That there are two dead bodies up there, a witch and a wolf. We're to gather up everything and do a general cleanup.'

Anna nodded. 'The Humvee is at the top of the road. We left the keys in it. I suppose Asil has a vehicle somewhere, but I don't know where it is.'

Tag's face went still for a moment as if he were listening to something she couldn't hear. He gave her a little smile and tapped his temple a couple of times. 'Bran does. We'll bring them back. Are you all right to drive back?'

It was a good question, and she wasn't sure if she was lying when she told him, 'Yes.'

'All right.' The sound of his motor changed as he shifted it into gear, but he didn't drive off or roll up the window. Instead, he said hesitantly, 'Something happened . . . I felt such . . .'

'Witch,' said Anna firmly – and truthfully as far as it went.

If Bran wanted everyone to know about what Asil's witch had done to him, he could tell them himself. She rolled up her window and started down the road again.

She'd been worried she wouldn't be able to find Charles's house, but she made it just fine. It looked snug and safe covered with a new fall of snow.

She let them all into the house and staggered off to the bathroom, then the bedroom. She stripped off her filthy and wet clothes, then crawled under the covers in her underwear. She fell asleep while the three wolves were sorting out how they were going to fit on the bed with her.

'Is she all right?' his father asked.

Charles closed his eyes and *listened*. All he could tell was that the bond between him and his mate was strong and solid. He couldn't tell yet what their bond would mean, what gifts it would bring. His ears, though, told him she was singing.

'She'll do,' he said.

Asil raised his cup of tea in salute. Like his father, Asil was freshly showered and dressed in an extra pair of sweats.

A car drove up his road and parked in front of the house.

'My car,' said Asil, not bothering to get up.

Sage opened the door without knocking and peered cautiously through the opening. When she saw Bran, she stomped snow off her feet and came inside. 'Someone needs to shovel,' she told Charles. "Sil, I brought your car, and you can have it back if you'll drop me off at my place.'

'Cleanup finished?' Bran asked mildly.

Sage nodded. 'Tag says it is. He took Charles's truck to the crematorium to take care of the bodies. He told me to let you know the wolf will be scattered the usual place, and he's got four pounds of salt to mix with the witch's ashes. He'll bring the results to your house for disposal.'

'Very good,' Bran said. 'Thank you.'

While Sage had been speaking, Asil had gathered his dishes and taken them to the kitchen. 'I'll head out with Sage.' He took a deep breath, then bowed formally to Bran. 'About the things I did not tell you – I'll expect your visit in the next few days.'

Sage drew in a sharp breath, but Bran let out a sigh. 'You're a little old for a spanking. I don't have anything to tell you that you don't already know' – he raised an eyebrow – 'unless you have another witch or something worse after you that might endanger the pack? No? Then go home and get some rest, old friend.' He took a sip of tea, and then said, 'I hope this means you'll quit asking me to kill you. It gives me indigestion.'

Asil smiled. 'I expect I'll continue to give you indigestion – but probably not for that reason. At least not for a while yet.' He turned to Charles and gave him the same formal bow. 'Thank you for your help.'

Charles tipped his head behind him toward the bathroom where the shower was still running. 'Anna killed the witch.'

Asil's smile grew sly. 'I'll have to thank her properly, then.'

Charles gazed coolly into his eyes. 'You just do that.'

Asil threw back his head and laughed. He took Sage by the shoulder and walked her out, stepping barefoot into the snow without a wince.

After the car drove off, Bran said, 'You'll still have trouble with that one – but he won't mean it anymore. I think I'll head home, too. Leah will be concerned.'

Charles shrugged off Asil – he was more worried about other matters. 'Are you sure? You are welcome to stay here for a while more.' He'd never forget that Other, the berserker who lurked underneath his father's easygoing facade.

His da smiled, but it only emphasized the haunted look in his eyes. 'I'm fine. Take care of your mate – and let me know when you'd like to make things official. I'd like to get her formally linked with the pack as soon as possible. This week is the full moon.'

'This moon is good.' Charles crossed his arms over his chest and tilted his head. 'But you must be tired if you think you can lie to me like that.'

Bran, who had been halfway to the door, turned back. This time the smile lit his eyes. 'You worry too much. How about – I *will* be fine. Is that better?'

That was truth.

'If you run into trouble, call me, and I'll bring Anna right over.'

Bran nodded once and left, leaving Charles to worry. Only when Anna, warm and damp from her shower, came into the room whistling a familiar tune did his concern for Bran subside.

'*Crep, strep, venefica est mortua,*' she told him.

'What is dead?' he asked her, then he thought about the tune and smiled.

'Ding, dong, the witch is dead,' she clarified, taking the seat next to him. 'And so is a good man. Do we celebrate or mourn?'

'That's always the question,' he told her.

She stretched her fingers out on the table. 'He was a good man, you know? He deserved a happy ending.'

He covered her fingers with his own, searching for the right words, but they didn't come.

After a moment, she leaned her forehead against his shoulder. 'You could have died.'

'Yes.'

'Me, too.'

'Yes.'

'I think I'll take the happy ending he gave us and make it matter.' She wrapped both arms around him fiercely. 'I love you.'

He turned and pulled her onto his lap. His arms were shaking, and he was very careful not to hold her so hard he might hurt her. 'I love you, too.'

After a long while she looked up. 'Are you hungry, too?'

Bran felt the monster stir uneasily as he left his son's house. He'd thought he'd had it caged at last – unpleasant to discover that the cage he'd devised was flawed. Very nearly more than unpleasant.

The last time he'd felt that way was when Blue Jay Woman died. He'd held on to the Beast by the finest of threads – and it had scared him. He couldn't afford to love someone like that ever again.

It was still dark when he parked in the garage. They'd slept the clock around at Charles's house, and it was a couple of hours still before dawn came. He entered his house quietly and eased up the stairs.

Leah wasn't in her room.

He knew, before he got to his door, that she was sleeping in his bed. Silently, he let himself in and shut the door behind him.

Curled up on his side of the bed, she hugged a pillow. Tenderness welled up in him; asleep she looked soft and vulnerable.

He pushed the tenderness away in that there was too much danger. He knew his sons had never understood his marriage, his mating. It had taken him a few years after Blue Jay Woman's death to find Leah, a woman so selfish and stupid he was certain he could never really love her. But love wasn't necessary for the mating bond – acceptance was, trust was – and love was a bonus he couldn't afford.

With Blue Jay Woman he'd found that the mating bond was the answer to the Beast – spreading out the cost of control. He needed the mating bond to hold the monster he could become at bay. But he could not afford to lose anyone else he loved the way he had loved Blue Jay Woman. So he'd found an acceptable compromise in Leah.

He stripped off his clothes, making noise now. Leah woke when the sweatshirt hit the floor.

She sat up and rubbed the sleep from her face, but when his pants followed the shirt, she pouted at him, and said, 'If you think that you're—'

He closed her mouth with his, and fed the Beast with her skin, her scent, and the noises she made as he pleasured her. She stopped resisting after the first kiss. When he finished with her, she cuddled close, trembling a little with aftershocks.

And the Beast slept.

The pack ran through the cold-silenced forest like the Wild Hunt of the old stories, fatal to any creature unfortunate enough to cross its path.

Anna was just as glad that nothing did. She didn't mind a good hunt, at least the wolf in her didn't, but she could still taste Bran's flesh and blood, given to her to cement her place in his pack. The flavor was sweet and rich – and that bothered Anna a lot more than it did her wolf – and she would rather decide how she felt about it before she replaced it with the flesh and blood of something else.

Charles had been dropping steadily back, and she stayed with him, following when he broke free of the pack. In front of the other wolves, he'd behaved with solemn dignity. When they were alone, he dodged suddenly sideways, knocking her off her feet before she could brace herself – and the game was on. She and Charles played until she noticed he was favoring his bad leg, and then they rested.

They'd been married that afternoon in the little church in town. Sage had whisked her away for an emergency trip to Missoula the day before, so she'd even had a proper gown. Asil had supplied the bouquet and decorated the chapel with his roses.

She hadn't known that Charles had contacted her family until she'd stepped into the chapel and her father had been waiting in the aisle to escort her in instead of Bran. Her brother had been standing with the groomsmen, next to Samuel.

So she'd been married with tears streaming down her face. The minister had stopped the ceremony and handed her a tissue to wipe her nose, which had made her laugh.

Her favorite moment, though, was after the ceremony, when her father, thin and tall and stooped, had shook his finger at Charles and threatened him with death and dismemberment if he didn't take care of her. All the wolves who'd heard – which meant all the wolves in the room – had watched with amused awe as Charles had meekly bowed his head as if her father had been the Marrok.

Anna settled against Charles as they rested in the woods, his fur soft and thick against her own. He'd taken them in a circle, she saw, because they were above Bran's house and she could see the lights inside, where her father and brother were still up – probably talking about her. She hoped they were happy for her. Judging from the past few days, this new life of hers wasn't going to be easy, but, she thought, she would like it just fine.

Somewhere in the wilds surrounding them, a timber wolf called to his mate. Anna jumped to her feet, nipped Charles's nose playfully, and took off with him in hot pursuit.

# ABOUT THE AUTHOR

**Patricia Briggs** lived a fairly normal life until she learned to read. After that she spent lazy afternoons flying dragon-back and looking for magic swords when she wasn't horseback riding in the Rocky Mountains. Once she graduated from Montana State University with degrees in history and German, she spent her time substitute teaching and writing. She and her family live in the Pacific Northwest, and you can visit her website at www.patriciabriggs.com

Find out more about Patricia Briggs and other Orbit authors by registering for the free monthly newsletter at www.orbitbooks.net